Blood Harvest

www.**rbooks**.co.uk

Also by S. J. Bolton

Sacrifice
Awakening

For more information on S. J. Bolton and her books, see her website at
www.sjbolton.com

Blood Harvest

S. J. Bolton

BANTAM PRESS

LONDON · TORONTO · SYDNEY · AUCKLAND · JOHANNESBURG

TRANSWORLD PUBLISHERS
61–63 Uxbridge Road, London W5 5SA
A Random House Group Company
www.rbooks.co.uk

First published in Great Britain
in 2010 by Bantam Press
an imprint of Transworld Publishers

A CIP catalogue record for this book
is available from the British Library.

ISBNs 9780593064115 (hb)
9780593064122 (tpb)

Addresses for Random House Group Ltd companies outside the UK
can be found at: www.randomhouse.co.uk
The Random House Group Ltd Reg. No. 954009

The Random House Group Limited supports The Forest Stewardship
Council (FSC), the leading international forest-certification organization. All our
titles that are printed on Greenpeace-approved FSC-certified paper carry the FSC logo.
Our paper procurement policy can be found at
www.rbooks.co.uk/environment

Typeset in 11.5/14pt ACaslon by
Falcon Oast Graphic Art Ltd.
Printed and bound in Great Britain by
CPI Mackays, Chatham, ME5 8TD.

2 4 6 8 10 9 7 5 3 1

Mixed Sources
Product group from well-managed
forests and other controlled sources
www.fsc.org Cert no. TT-COC-2139
© 1996 Forest Stewardship Council
FSC

For the Coopers, who built their big, shiny new house
on the crest of a moor . . .

'Battle not with monsters, lest ye become a monster, and if you gaze into the abyss, the abyss gazes also into you.'

Friedrich Nietzsche, German philosopher (1844–1900)

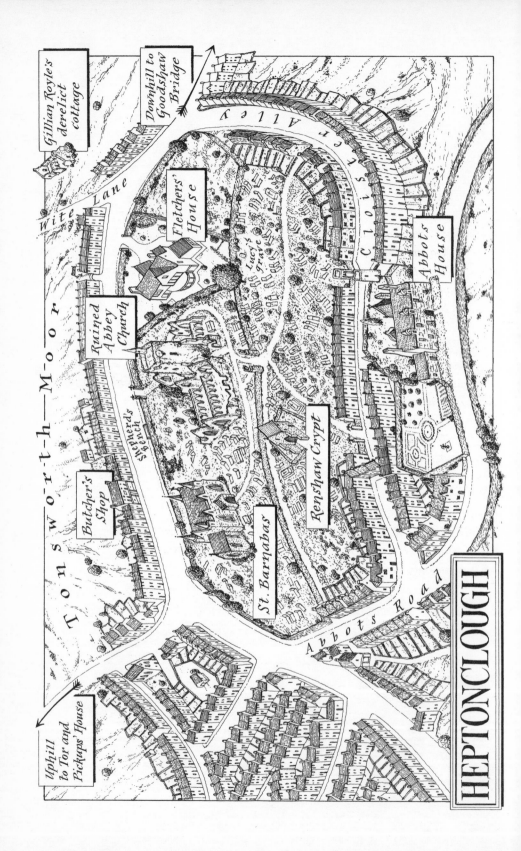

Gillian Royle's derelict cottage

Downhill to Goodshaw Bridge

Cloister Alley

Fletchers' House

Lucy's Grave

Abbots House

W i t e L a n e

Ruined Abbey Church

T o n s w o r t h — M o o r

Shepherd's Bench

Renshaw Crypt

Butcher's Shop

St. Barnabas

Abbots Road

Uphill to Tor and Pickups' House

HEPTONCLOUGH

'She's been watching us for a while now.'

'Go on, Tom.'

'Sometimes it's like she's always there, behind a pile of stones, in the shadow at the bottom of the tower, under one of the old graves. She's good at hiding.'

'She must be.'

'Sometimes she gets very close, before you have any idea. You'll be thinking about something else when one of her voices jumps out at you and, for a second, she catches you out. She really makes you think it's your brother, or your mum, hiding round the corner.'

'Then you realize it's not?'

'No, it's not. It's her. The girl with the voices. But the minute you turn your head, she's gone. If you're really quick you might catch a glimpse of her. Usually, though, there's nothing there, everything's just as it was, except . . .'

'Except what?'

'Except now, it's like the world's keeping a secret. And there's that feeling in the pit of your stomach, the one that says, she's here again. She's watching.'

Prologue

3 November

ITHAD HAPPENED, THEN; WHAT ONLY HINDSIGHT COULD HAVE told him he'd been dreading. It was almost a relief, in a way, knowing the worst was over, that he didn't have to pretend any more. Maybe now he could stop acting like this was an ordinary town, that these were normal people. Harry took a deep breath, and learned that death smells of drains, of damp soil and of heavy-duty plastic.

The skull, less than six feet away, looked tiny. As though if he held it in his palm, his fingers might almost close around it. Almost worse than the skull was the hand. It lay half hidden in the mud, its bones barely held together by connective tissue, as though trying to crawl out of the ground. The strong artificial light flickered like a strobe and, for a second, the hand seemed to be moving.

On the plastic sheet above Harry's head the rain sounded like gunfire. The wind so high on the moors was close to gale force and the makeshift walls of the police tent couldn't hope to hold it back completely. When he'd parked his car, not three minutes earlier, it had been 3.17 a.m. Night didn't get any darker than this. Harry realized he'd closed his eyes.

Detective Chief Superintendent Rushton's hand was still on his arm, although the two of them had reached the edge of the inner cordon. They wouldn't be allowed any further. Six other people were

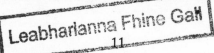

in the tent with them, all wearing the same white, hooded overalls and wellington boots that Harry and Rushton had just put on.

Harry could feel himself shaking. His eyes still closed, he could hear the steady, insistent drumbeat of rain on the roof of the tent. He could still see that hand. Feeling himself sway, he opened his eyes and almost overbalanced.

'Back a bit, Harry,' said Rushton. 'Stay on the mat, please.' Harry did what he was told. His body seemed to have grown too big for itself; the borrowed boots were impossibly tight, his clothes were clinging, the bones in his head felt too thin. The sound of the wind and the rain went on, like the soundtrack of a cheap movie. Too much light, too much noise, for the middle of the night.

The skull had rolled away from its torso. Harry could see a ribcage, so small, still wearing clothes, tiny buttons gleaming under the lights. 'Where are the others?' he asked.

DCS Rushton inclined his head and then guided him across the aluminium chequer plating that had been laid like stepping-stones over the mud. They were following the line of the church wall. 'Mind where you go, lad,' Rushton said. 'Whole area's a bloody mess. There, can you see?'

They stopped at the far edge of the inner cordon. The second corpse was still intact, but looked no bigger than the first. It lay face-down in the mud. One tiny wellington boot covered its left foot.

'The third one's by the wall,' said Rushton. 'Hard to see, half-hidden by the stones.'

'Another child?' asked Harry. Loose PVC flaps on the tent were banging in the wind and he had to half-shout to make himself heard.

'Looks like it,' agreed Rushton. His glasses were speckled with rain. He hadn't wiped them since entering the tent. Maybe he was grateful not to see too clearly. 'You can see where the wall came down?' he went on.

Harry nodded. A length of about ten feet of the stone wall that formed the boundary between the Fletcher property and the churchyard had collapsed and the earth it had been holding back had tumbled like a small landslide into the garden. An old yew tree had fallen with the wall. In the harsh artificial light it reminded him of a woman's trailing hair.

'When it collapsed, the graves on the churchyard side were disturbed,' Rushton was saying. 'One in particular, a child's grave. A lass called Lucy Pickup. Our problem is, the plans we have suggest the child was alone in the grave. It was freshly dug for her ten years ago.'

'I'm aware of it,' said Harry. 'But then . . .' He turned back to the scene in front of him.

'Well, now you see our problem,' said Rushton. 'If little Lucy was buried alone, who are the other two?'

'Can I have a moment with them?' Harry asked.

Rushton's eyes narrowed. He looked from the tiny figures to Harry and back again.

'This is sacred ground,' said Harry, almost to himself.

Rushton stepped away from him. 'Ladies and gentlemen,' he called. 'A minute's silence, please, for the vicar.' The officers around the site looked up. One opened his mouth to argue but stopped at the look on Brian Rushton's face. Muttering thanks, Harry stepped forward, closer to the cordoned area, until a hand on his arm told him he had to stop. The skull of the corpse closest to him had been very badly damaged. Almost a third of it seemed to be missing. He remembered hearing about how Lucy Pickup had died. He took a deep breath, aware that everyone around him was motionless. Several were watching him, others had bowed their heads. He raised his right hand and began to make the sign of the cross. Up, down, to his left. He stopped. Closer to the scene, more directly under the lights, he had a better view of the third corpse. The tiny form was wearing something with an embroidered pattern around the neck: a tiny hedgehog, a rabbit, a duck in a bonnet. Characters from the Beatrix Potter stories.

He started to speak, hardly knowing what he was saying. A short prayer for the souls of the dead, it could have been anything. He must have finished, the crime-scene people were resuming their work. Rushton patted his arm and led him out of the tent. Harry went without arguing, knowing he was in shock.

Three tiny corpses, tumbled from a grave that should only have contained one. Two unknown children had shared Lucy Pickup's final resting place. Except one of them wasn't unknown, not to him anyway. The child in the Beatrix Potter pyjamas. He knew who she was.

Part One
Waning Moon

1

4 September (nine weeks earlier)

THE FLETCHER FAMILY BUILT THEIR BIG, SHINY NEW HOUSE on the crest of the moor, in a town that time seemed to have left to mind its own business. They built on a modest-sized plot that the diocese, desperate for cash, needed to get rid of. They built so close to the two churches – one old, the other very old – that they could almost lean out from the bedroom windows and touch the shell of the ancient tower. And on three sides of their garden they had the quietest neighbours they could hope for, which was ten-year-old Tom Fletcher's favourite joke in those days; because the Fletchers built their new house in the midst of a graveyard. They should have known better, really.

But Tom and his younger brother Joe were so excited in the beginning. Inside their new home they had huge great bedrooms, still smelling of fresh paint. Outside they had the bramble-snared, crumble-stone church grounds, where story-book adventures seemed to be just waiting for them. Inside they had a living room that gleamed with endless shades of yellow, depending on where the sun was in the sky. Outside they had ancient archways that soared to the heavens, dens within ivy that was old and stiff enough to stand up by itself, and grass so long six-year-old Joe seemed drowned by it. Indoors, the house began to absorb the characters of the boys' parents, as fresh colours, wall-paintings and carved

17

animals appeared in every room. Outdoors, Tom and Joe made the churchyard their own.

On the last day of the summer holidays, Tom was lying on the grave of Jackson Reynolds (1875–1945), soaking up the warmth of the old stone. The sky was the colour of his mother's favourite cornflower-blue paint and the sun had been out doing its stuff since early morning. It was a *shiny day*, as Joe liked to say.

Tom wouldn't have been able to say what changed. How he went from perfectly fine, warm and happy, thinking about how old you had to be to try out for Blackburn Rovers to . . . well . . . to not fine. But suddenly, in a second, football didn't seem quite so important. There was nothing wrong, exactly, he just wanted to sit up. See what was nearby. If anyone . . .

Stupid. But he was sitting up all the same, looking round, wondering how Joe had managed to disappear again. Further down the hill, the graveyard stretched the length of a football field, getting steeper as it dropped lower. Below it were a few rows of terraced houses and then more fields. Beyond them, at the bottom of the valley, was the neighbouring town of Goodshaw Bridge where he and Joe were due to resume school on Monday morning. Across the valley and behind, on just about every side, were the moors. Lots and lots of moors.

Tom's dad was fond of saying how much he loved the moors, the wildness, grandeur and sheer unpredictability of the north of England. Tom agreed with his dad, of course he did, he was only ten, but privately he sometimes wondered if countryside that was predictable (he'd looked the word up, he knew what it meant) wouldn't be a bad thing. It seemed to Tom sometimes, though he never liked to say it, that the moors around his new home were a little bit too unpredictable.

He was an idiot, of course, it went without saying.

But somehow, Tom always seemed to be spotting a new lump of rock, a tiny valley that hadn't been there before, a bank of heather or copse of trees that appeared overnight. Sometimes, when clouds were moving fast in the sky and their shadows were racing across the ground, it seemed to Tom that the moors were rippling, the way water does when there's something beneath the surface; or stirring, like a sleeping monster about to wake up. And just occasionally, when the sun went down across the valley and the darkness was coming, Tom couldn't help thinking that the moors around them had moved closer.

'Tom!' yelled Joe from the other side of the graveyard, and for once Tom really wasn't sorry to hear from him. The stone beneath him had grown cold and there were more clouds overhead.

'Tom!' called Joe again, right in Tom's ear. Jeez, Joe, that was fast. Tom jumped up and turned round. Joe wasn't there.

Around the edge of the churchyard, trees started to shudder. The wind was getting up again and when the wind on the moor really meant business, it could get everywhere, even the sheltered places. In the bushes closest to Tom something moved.

'Joe,' he said, more quietly than he meant to, because he really didn't like the idea that someone, even Joe, was hiding in those bushes, watching him. He sat, staring at the big, shiny-green leaves, waiting for them to move again. They were laurels, tall, old and thick. The wind was definitely getting up, he could hear it now in the tree-tops. The laurels in front of him were still.

It had probably just been a strange echo that had made him think Joe was close. But Tom had that feeling, the ticklish feeling he'd get when someone spotted him doing something he shouldn't. And besides, hadn't he just felt Joe's breath on the back of his neck?

'Joe?' he tried again.

'Joe?' came his own voice back at him. Tom took two steps back, coming up sharp against a headstone. Glancing all round, double-checking no one was close, he crouched to the ground.

At this level, the foliage on the laurel bushes was thinner. Tom could see several bare branches of the shrub amongst nettles. He could see something else as well, a shape he could barely make out, expect he knew it wasn't vegetation. It looked a little like – if it moved he might get a better look – a large and very dirty human foot.

'Tom, Tom, come and look at this!' called his brother, this time sounding as if he was miles away. Tom didn't wait to be called again, he jumped to his feet and ran in the direction of his brother's voice.

Joe was crouched near the foot of the wall that separated the churchyard from the family's garden. He was looking at a grave that seemed newer than many of those surrounding it. At its foot, facing the headstone, was a stone statue.

'Look, Tom,' Joe was saying, even before his older brother had stopped running. 'It's a little girl. With a dolly.'

Tom bent down. The statue was about a foot high and was of a tiny, chubby girl with curly hair, wearing a party dress. Tom reached out and scratched away some of the moss that was growing over it. The sculptor had given her perfectly carved shoes and, cradled in her arms, a small doll.

'Little girls,' said Joe. 'It's a grave for little girls.'

Tom looked up to find that Joe was right – almost. A single word was carved on the headstone. *Lucy.* There could have been more, but any carving below it had been covered in ivy. 'Just one little girl,' he said. 'Lucy.'

Tom reached up and pulled away the ivy that grew over the headstone until he could see dates. Lucy had died ten years ago. She'd been just two years old. *Beloved child of Jennifer and Michael Pickup*, the inscription said. There was nothing else.

'Just Lucy,' Tom repeated. 'Come on, let's go.'

Tom set off back, making his way carefully through long grass, avoiding nettles, pushing aside brambles. Behind him, he could hear the rustling of grass being disturbed and knew Joe was following. As he climbed the hill, the walls of the abbey ruin came into view.

'Tom,' said Joe, in a voice that just didn't sound right.

Tom stopped walking. He could hear grass moving directly behind him but he didn't turn round. He just stayed there, staring at the ruined church tower but not really seeing it, wondering instead why he was suddenly so scared of turning round to face his brother.

He turned. He was surrounded by tall stones. Nothing else. Tom discovered his fists were clenched tight. This really wasn't funny. Then the bushes a few yards away started moving again and there was Joe, jogging through the grass, red in the face and panting, as if he'd been struggling to keep up. He came closer, reached his brother and stopped.

'What?' Joe said.

'I think someone's following us,' whispered Tom.

Joe didn't ask who, or where, or how Tom knew, he just stared back at him. Tom reached out and took his brother's arm. They were going home and they were doing it now.

Except, no, perhaps they weren't. On the wall that separated the older part of the church grounds from the graveyard that stretched down the hill, six boys were standing in a line like skittles, watching. Tom could feel his heartbeat starting to speed up. Six boys on the wall; and possibly another one very close by.

The biggest boy was holding a thick, forked twig. Tom didn't see the missile that came hurtling towards him but he felt the air whistle past his face. Another boy, wearing a distinctive claret and blue football shirt, was taking aim. With quicker reflexes than his older brother, Joe threw himself behind a large headstone. Tom followed just as the second shot went wide.

'Who are they?' whispered Joe as another stone went flying overhead.

'They're boys from school,' Tom replied. 'Two of them are in my class.'

'What do they want?' Joe's pale face had gone whiter than normal.

'I don't know,' said Tom, although he did. One of them wanted to get his own back. The others were just helping out. A rock hit the edge of the headstone and Tom saw dust fly off it. 'The one in the Burnley shirt is Jake Knowles,' he admitted.

'The one you had that fight with?' said Joe. 'When you got sent to the headmaster's office? The one whose dad wanted to get you kicked out of school?'

Tom crouched and leaned forward, hoping the long grass would hide his head as he looked out. Another boy from Tom's class, Billy Aspin, was pointing at a clump of brambles near the little girl's grave that Joe had just found. Tom turned back to Joe. 'They're not looking,' he said. 'We have to move quick. Follow me.'

Joe was right behind as Tom shot forward, heading for a great, upright tomb, one of the largest on the hill. They made it. Stones came whistling through the air but Tom and Joe were safe behind the huge stone structure, which had iron railings around the outside. There was an iron gate too and, beyond it, a wooden door that led inside. A family mausoleum, their father had said, probably quite large inside, tunnelled into the hillside, with lots of ledges for generations of coffins to be placed on.

'They've split up,' came a shout from the wall. 'You two, come with me!'

Tom and Joe looked at each other. If they'd split up, why were they still close enough for Tom to feel Joe's breath on his face?

'They're knob-heads,' said Joe.

Tom leaned out from behind the crypt. Three of the boys were walking along the wall towards Lucy Pickup's grave. The other three were still staring in their direction.

'What's that noise?' said Joe.

'Wind?' suggested Tom, without bothering to listen. It was a pretty safe guess.

'It's not wind. It's music.'

Joe was right. Definitely music, low, with a steady rhythm, a man's deep voice singing. The knob-heads had heard it too. One of them jumped down and ran towards the road. Then the rest followed. The music was getting louder and Tom could hear a car engine.

It was John Lee Hooker. His dad had several of his CDs and played them – very loud – when their mother was out. Someone was driving up the hill, playing John Lee Hooker on his car stereo, and this was the time to move. Tom stepped sideways, away from the shelter of the mausoleum.

Only Jake Knowles was still in sight. He looked round and saw Tom, who didn't hide this time. Both boys knew the game was up. Except . . .

'He's got your baseball bat,' said Joe, who'd followed Tom into the open. 'What's he doing?'

Jake had got Tom's bat and his ball too, a large, very heavy red ball that Tom had been warned on pain of a prolonged and tortuous death (which was how his mum talked when she was serious) not to play with anywhere near buildings, especially buildings with windows and was she making herself clear? Tom and Joe had been practising catches earlier by the church. They'd left both bat and ball near the wall and now Knowles had them.

'He's nicking them,' said Joe. 'We can call the police.'

'I don't think so,' said Tom, as Jake turned away and faced the church. Tom watched Jake toss the ball gently into the air. Then he swung the bat hard. The ball sailed into the air and through the huge stained-glass window at the side of the church. A blue pane shattered as the car engine switched off, the music died and Jake fled after his friends.

'Why did he do that?' said Joe. 'He broke a window. He'll get murdered.'

'No, he won't,' said Tom. 'We will.'

Joe stared at his brother for a second, then he got it. He may have been only six and annoying as hell, but he was no knob-head.

'That's not fair.' Joe's little face had screwed up in outrage. 'We'll tell.'

'They won't believe us,' said Tom. Six weeks in his new school: three detentions, two trips to the headmaster's office, any number of serious bollockings from his class teacher and no one ever believed him. Why would they, when Jake Knowles had half the class on his side, jumping up and down in their seats they were so eager to back him up. Even the ones who didn't seem to be Jake's mates were too scared of him and his gang to say anything. Six weeks of getting the blame for everything Jake Knowles started. Maybe he was the knob-head.

He took hold of Joe's hand and the boys ran as fast as they could through the long grass. Tom climbed the wall, looked all round the churchyard, and then bent down to pull up Joe. Jake and the other boys were nowhere in sight but there were a hundred hiding places around the ruins of the old church.

An old sports car was parked just by the church gate, pale blue with lots of silver trim. The soft roof had been folded back over the boot. A man was leaning across the passenger seat and fumbling in the glove compartment. He found what he was looking for and straightened up. He looked about Tom's dad's age, around thirty-four or thirty-five, taller than Tom's dad, but thinner.

Beckoning Joe to follow, Tom picked up the baseball bat (no point leaving evidence in plain sight) and ran until they could scramble into their favourite hiding place. They'd discovered it shortly after moving in: a huge rectangular stone table of a grave, supported on four stone pillars. The grass around it grew long, and once the boys had crawled underneath they were completely hidden from view.

The sports-car driver opened the car door and climbed out. As he turned towards the church, the boys could see that his hair was the same colour as their mother's (strawberry blonde, not ginger), and curly like their mum's, but his was cut short. He was wearing knee-length shorts, a white T-shirt and red Crocs. He walked across the road and into the churchyard. Once inside, he stopped on the path and looked behind him, then span slowly on the spot, taking in the cobbled streets, the terraced houses, both churches, the moors behind and beyond.

'He's not been here before,' whispered Joe.

Tom nodded. The stranger walked past the boys and reached the main door of the church. He took a key from his pocket. A second later the door swung open and he walked inside. Just as Jake Knowles appeared at the entrance to the churchyard. Tom stood up and looked round. Billy Aspin was behind them. As they watched, the other members of the gang appeared from behind gravestones, clambering over the wall. The brothers were surrounded.

2

'IT HAD BEEN BURNING FOR THREE HOURS BEFORE THEY
managed to put it out. And they said the temperatures inside,
at the point of – I can't remember what they said . . .'

'Origin?' suggested Evi.

The girl sitting opposite nodded. 'Yes, that's it,' she said. 'The
point of origin. They said it would have been like a furnace. And her
bedroom was right above it. They couldn't get anywhere near the
house, let alone upstairs, and then the ceiling collapsed. By the time
they managed to get it cooled down enough, they couldn't find her.'

'No trace at all?'

Gillian shook her head. 'No, nothing,' she said. 'She was so tiny,
you see. Such tiny soft bones.'

Gillian's breathing was speeding up again. 'I read somewhere that
it's unusual, but not unheard of,' she went on, 'for people to . . . to
disappear completely. The fire just burns them up.' The girl was
beginning to gulp at the air around her.

Evi pushed herself upright in her chair and the pain in her left leg
responded immediately. 'Gillian, it's OK,' she said. 'Get your breath
back. Just take it steady.'

Gillian put her hands on her knees and dropped her head as Evi
concentrated on getting her own breathing under control, on
focusing on something other than the pain in her leg. The wall
clock told her they were fifteen minutes into the consultation.

Her new patient, Gillian Royle, was unemployed, divorced and alcoholic. She was just twenty-six. The GP's referral letter had talked about 'prolonged and abnormal grief' following the death, three years earlier, of her twenty-seven-month-old daughter in a house fire. According to the GP, Gillian had severe depression, suicidal thoughts and a history of self-harm. He'd have referred her sooner, he'd explained, but had only just been made aware of her case by a local social worker. This was her first appointment with Evi.

Gillian's hair trailed almost to the floor. It had been highlighted once, but now, above the old blond streaks, it was an unwashed mouse-brown. Gradually, the rise and fall of the girl's shoulders began to slow down. After a moment she reached up to push her hair back. Her face reappeared. 'I'm sorry,' she began, like a child who'd been caught misbehaving.

Evi shook her head. 'You mustn't be,' she said. 'What you're feeling is very normal. Do you often have difficulty breathing?'

Gillian nodded.

'It's completely normal,' Evi repeated. 'People who are suffering immense grief often experience breathlessness. They suddenly start to feel anxious, even afraid, for no apparent reason and then they struggle to get their breath. Does that sound familiar at all?'

Gillian nodded again. She was still panting, as if she'd just run a race and had narrowly lost.

'Do you have any mementoes of your daughter?' asked Evi.

Gillian reached to the small table at her side and pulled another tissue from the box. She hadn't cried yet but had been continually pressing them against her face and twisting them round in her scrawny fingers. Tiny twists of thin paper littered the carpet.

'The firemen found a toy,' she said. 'A pink rabbit. It should have been in her cot but it had fallen down behind the sofa. I suppose I should be glad it did, but I can't help thinking that she had to go through all that and she didn't even have Pink Rabbit wi—' Gillian's head fell forward again and her body started to shudder. Both hands, still clasping flimsy peach-coloured paper, were pressed hard against her mouth.

'Did it make it harder for you?' asked Evi. 'That they didn't find Hayley's body?'

Gillian raised her head and Evi could see a darker gleam in her eyes, a harder edge around the lines of her face. There was a lot of anger in there as well, struggling with grief to get the upper hand. 'Pete said it was a good thing,' she said, 'that they couldn't find her.'

'What do you think?' asked Evi.

'I think it would have been better to have found her,' Gillian shot back. 'Because then I'd have known for sure. I would have had to accept it.'

'Accept that it was real?' asked Evi.

'Yes,' agreed Gillian. 'Because I couldn't. I just couldn't take it in, couldn't believe she was really dead. Do you know what I did?'

Evi allowed her head to shake gently from side to side. 'No,' she said, 'tell me what you did.'

'I went out looking for her, on the moors,' replied Gillian. 'I thought, because they hadn't found her, that there must be some mistake. That she'd got out somehow. I thought maybe Barry, the babysitter, had managed to get her out and put her in the garden before the smoke got too much for him, and that she'd just wandered off.'

Gillian's eyes were pleading with Evi, begging her to agree, to say yes, that was quite likely, perhaps she's still out there, wandering around, living off berries, Gillian just had to keep looking.

'She would have been terrified of the fire,' Gillian was saying, 'so she'd have tried to get away. She could have got out of the gate somehow and wandered up the lane. So we went out looking, Pete and me, and a couple of others too. We spent the night walking the moors, calling out to her. I was so sure, you see, that she couldn't really be dead.'

'That's completely normal too,' said Evi. 'It's called denial. When people suffer a great loss, they often can't take it in at first. Some doctors believe it's the body's way of protecting us from too much pain. Even though people know, in their head, that their loved one is gone, their heart is telling them something different. It's not uncommon for bereaved people to even see the one they've lost, to hear their voice.'

She paused for a second. Gillian had pushed herself upright in the chair again. 'People do that?' she asked, leaning towards Evi. 'They see and hear the dead person?'

'Yes,' said Evi, 'it's very common. Has it happened to you? Did you – do you see Hayley?'

Slowly Gillian shook her head. 'I never see her,' she said. For a second she stared back at Evi. And then her face deflated, collapsing in on itself like the air slowly trickling out of a balloon. 'I never see her,' she repeated. She reached for the tissues again. The box fell to the floor but she'd managed to keep hold of a handful. She pressed them to her face. Still no tears. Maybe they were all used up.

'Take your time,' said Evi. 'You need to cry. Take as much time as you like.'

Gillian didn't cry, not really, but she held the handful of tissues to her face and allowed her dried-up body to sob. Evi watched the second hand make its way round the clock three times.

'Gillian,' she said, when she judged she'd given the girl enough time. 'Dr Warrington tells me you still spend several hours a day walking the moors. Are you still looking for Hayley?'

Gillian shook her head without looking up. 'I don't know why I do it,' she mumbled into the tissues. 'I just get this feeling in my head and then I can't stay indoors. I have to go out. I have to look.' Gillian raised her head and her pale-grey eyes stared back at Evi. 'Can you help me?' she asked, suddenly looking so much younger than her twenty-six years.

'Yes, of course,' said Evi quickly. 'I'm going to prescribe some medication for you. Some anti-depressants to make you feel better, and also something to help you sleep at night. These are a temporary measure, to help you break the cycle of feeling so bad. Do you understand?'

Gillian was staring back at her, like a child relieved that a grown-up had finally taken charge.

'You see, the pain you've been feeling has made your body sick,' continued Evi. 'For three years you've not been sleeping or eating properly. You're drinking too much and you're wearing yourself out on these long walks over the moors.'

Gillian blinked twice. Her eyes looked red and sore.

'When you're feeling a little better in the daytime and you're sleeping properly at night, then you'll be able to do something about the drinking,' continued Evi. 'I can refer you to a support group. They'll help you get through the first few weeks. Does that sound like a good idea?'

Gillian was nodding.

'I'm going to see you every week for as long as it takes,' said Evi. 'When you're starting to feel better in yourself, when you feel you have the pain under control, then we have to work on helping you adjust to your life as it is now.'

Gillian's eyes had dulled. She raised her eyebrows.

'Before all this happened,' explained Evi, 'you were a wife and mother. Now your situation is very different. I know that sounds harsh, but it's a reality we have to face together. Hayley will always be a part of your life. But at the moment she – the loss of her – is your whole life. You need to rebuild your life and, at the same time, find a place for her.'

Silence. The tissues had fallen to the floor and Gillian's arms were crossed tightly in front of her. It wasn't quite the reaction Evi had been hoping for.

'Gillian?'

'You're going to hate me for saying this,' said Gillian, who was starting to shake her head. 'But sometimes, I wish . . .'

'What do you wish?' asked Evi, realizing that for the first time since she'd met Gillian, she really didn't know what the girl's answer was going to be.

'That she'd just leave me in peace.'

3

*T*HE SLEEPING CHILD HAD SOFT PALE HAIR, THE COLOUR OF *spun sugar. She lay in her buggy, fast asleep in the sunshine. A fine-mesh net was stretched tight across the buggy, from top to bottom, protecting her from insects and from anything else that might be scurrying about the garden. A damp curl clung to her plump cheek. Her fist was pressed against her mouth, the thumb sticking out at right angles, as though she'd fallen asleep sucking her thumb before a thought in a dream made her spit it out. Her tummy rose and fell, rose and fell.*

Somewhere around two years old. Legs still plump enough to toddle, lips just beginning to form words. Her eyes, when open, would have the trusting innocence of the freshly made person. She hadn't learned yet that people could hurt.

A bubble of saliva formed in the gap between her tiny pink lips. It disappeared then formed itself again. The child sighed and the bubble broke on the air. And the sound seemed to travel through the still September morning.

'Ah, da da da,' muttered the girl, in her sleep.

She was just beautiful. Exactly like the others.

4

JOE JUMPED UP AND RAN. WITHOUT THINKING, TOM FOLLOWED and the two boys sped up the steps and through the open church door. Tom caught a glimpse of the fair-haired man ahead, getting closer to the altar, and then Joe dived behind the back pew. Tom did the same.

The flags on the floor were dusty. Beneath the pews Tom could see cobwebs, some complete and perfect, others torn up and festooned with the corpses of long-dead flies. The tapestry prayer-cushions were hanging neatly from hooks.

'He's saying his prayers,' whispered Joe, who was peering over the top of the pew. Tom pushed himself up. The man in shorts was kneeling at the altar steps, his elbows resting on the rail, looking up at the large stained-glass window on the front wall of the church. He did look like he was praying.

A sudden noise outside made Tom look round. The church door was open and he caught a glimpse of a figure running past outside. Jake and his gang were still out there, waiting. A sudden tug pulled him down below the rim of the pew.

'He's heard something,' whispered Joe.

The boys hadn't made any noise that Tom had been aware of, but he felt a stab of alarm. If the man found them, he might order them outside, where Jake and the others were waiting. Joe had risked raising his head again. Tom did the same. Shorts Man hadn't moved but he wasn't praying any more, that much was clear. His head was

31

upright and his body had stiffened. He was listening. Then he stood up and turned round. Joe and Tom ducked so quickly they banged their heads together. Now they were for it. They were in church without permission and, to all intents and purposes, they'd broken a window.

'Who's there?' called the man, sounding puzzled but not cross. 'Hello,' he called. His voice carried easily to the back of the church.

Tom tried to stand up. 'No!' hissed his brother, clinging to him. 'He doesn't mean us.'

'Of course he means us,' Tom hissed back. 'There's no one else here.'

Joe didn't answer, just gingerly lifted his head, like a soldier peering out over a parapet. He glanced down and nodded at Tom to do the same. Shorts Man was walking slowly towards a door to the right of the altar. He reached for the handle and pulled it open. Then he stood in the doorway, looking into the room.

'I know you're in there,' he called, like a parent playing hide and seek. He was northern, but not from Lancashire, or Yorkshire just over the border. Further north, Tom guessed, maybe Newcastle.

Tom raised his hands and did his 'What?' face at Joe. There were three people in this church and they were two of them.

'Are you going to come out and say hello?' said the man, in a voice that Tom knew was supposed to sound as though he didn't care one way or another but didn't quite manage it. He was nervous. 'I'm going to have to lock up in a minute,' he went on, 'and I really can't do that while you're hiding.' Then he spun round on his heels to face the other side of the building. 'Getting beyond a joke now, folks,' he muttered, as he walked quickly to the other side of the church and disappeared behind the organ. This was the boys' chance. Tom tugged on Joe's arm. They stepped into the aisle just as Billy Aspin appeared at the main doorway, grinning at them. Tom grabbed Joe and dragged him back behind the pew again.

'Hello,' said a Geordie voice above their heads. Shorts Man was in the pew in front, looking down at them.

'Hi,' replied Joe. 'Did you find her?'

Shorts Man frowned. 'How did you two get from the vestry, to behind the organ, to back here without me seeing you?' he asked.

'We've been here all the time,' said Tom.

'We saw you saying your prayers,' added Joe, in the sort of voice he might use if he'd seen someone having a wee behind the altar.

'Did you now?' asked Shorts Man. 'Where do you two live?'

Tom wondered for a second whether there was any chance they'd get away with not telling him. The man was standing between the boys and the door, but if Tom dodged one way—

'Next door,' said Joe. 'The new house,' he went on, as if he hadn't already made it clear.

The man was nodding. 'I have to lock this building up,' he said, stepping into the aisle. 'Come on.'

'How come you have a key?' asked Joe, who'd moved too far away for Tom to prod him. 'Only the vicar's allowed to have a key. Did he give it to you?'

'The archdeacon gave it to me. Right, before I lock up, are there any more of you in here?'

'There can't be,' said Tom. 'We came straight in behind you. We were, er, playing hide and seek with some boys outside. No one followed us in.'

Shorts Man nodded. 'OK,' he said. 'Out we go.'

He waved his hand towards the door, meaning that Tom and Joe should go first. Tom set off. So far, so good. Jake and the others wouldn't dare try anything if he and Joe appeared with an adult. And the man hadn't noticed the broken—

'Tom, your ball,' called Joe as he darted off to one side. Tom closed his eyes and had his own private conversation with God about whether little brothers were strictly necessary.

When he opened his eyes again, Joe had retrieved the ball from among the broken glass and Shorts Man's eyebrows had disappeared into his hair. He held out his hand for the ball. Tom opened his mouth and shut it again. What was the point?

'Who's the boy with the shaved head?' asked Shorts Man. 'The one who was standing on the wall as I drove up?'

'Jake Knowles,' said Joe. 'He's in Tom's class. He keeps getting him into trouble. They were throwing stones at us with cater-bolts and then he nicked Tom's bat.'

'Did he now?'

'They're waiting for us outside.'

'Oh aye?'

'They're going to duff us up when we go out. They're knob-heads.'

'What's your name?' asked Shorts Man, and Tom didn't even bother trying to signal to Joe that it really wasn't a good—

'Joe Fletcher,' said Joe. 'And he's Tom. I'm six and he's ten, and Millie's two and my dad's thirty-six and my mum's—'

'Steady on, pal.' Shorts Man looked as though he found Joe highly amusing. He should try living with him. 'Come on, let's get locked up.'

5

EVI STOOD AT THE WINDOW OF HER ROOM, BREATHING deeply, waiting for the combination of paracetamol and ibuprofen to kick in. Her consulting room was three floors up and looked directly out over the hospital's accident and emergency department. As she watched, an ambulance pulled up into the parking bay and a paramedic jumped out, followed by the ambulance driver. They opened the rear doors and began moving the wheelchair lifting gear into position.

Breathe in and out. The medication would work, it always did. It just seemed to take a little longer some days. Across the road from the hospital was a retail park. The supermarket car park was already busy. Friday morning. People were stocking up for the weekend. Evi closed her eyes for a second and then raised her head, looking out over rooftops, office blocks, away into the distance. The large northern town where she worked most days had been built along a wide valley. Moors stretched up on either side. A bird taking off from her window ledge could fly directly to the nearest peak, some four or five miles away. From there, it could look down on the moor, where Gillian Royle still spent the greater part of her days. Evi turned back to her desk. She had fifteen minutes before her next patient.

She'd already written up notes on the consultation with Gillian before taking the painkillers. Every day, she tried to stretch the time in between taking them by another five minutes. Back at her desk, she Googled the website of the *Lancashire Telegraph*. It didn't take long to find the article she was looking for.

> The town of Heptonclough is in shock following the fire three nights ago at a cottage in Wite Lane. Local man Stanley Hargreaves said he'd never seen a fire burn as fiercely. 'None of us could get near it,' he told *Telegraph* reporters. 'We'd have saved the young lass if we could have.'

The story explained that the attending fire-and-rescue team were still reviewing evidence but believed the blaze could have been caused by a ring left burning on the gas hob. Bottles of oil around the cooker would have acted as accelerants. The stone cottage, one of the older buildings in Heptonclough, was some distance from the main part of the community and no one had spotted the blaze until it was far too late to contain the fire. The *Telegraph* article concluded:

> Barry Robinson, fourteen, who was babysitting for the family, is currently recovering in Burnley General Hospital after being found unconscious in the garden by firefighters. Although suffering from the effects of smoke-inhalation, doctors expect him to make a full recovery. His parents tell us he has no recollection of discovering the fire or leaving the house.

Evi's phone was ringing. Her next patient had arrived.

6

'WHERE HAVE YOU TWO BEEN? MILLIE AND I HAVE been shouting for you for ten minutes now.'

The woman on the doorstep wasn't much taller than her eldest son and, even in a loose shirt and jeans, looked as though she didn't weigh much more either. She had strawberry-blonde hair that curled to her shoulders, and large turquoise eyes. As the eyes travelled up from her sons to Harry, they opened a bit wider in surprise.

'Hello,' she said.

'Lo,' said the chubby little girl who was sitting on her mother's hip, rubbing her eyes as though she'd not long woken from a nap. Her hair was the exact warm blonde shade as her mother's, whereas the older boy, Tom, had very fair hair and his brother's was a dark, glossy red. All four of them, though, had the same pale-skinned, freckled faces.

'Hi,' said Harry, giving the toddler a wink before turning back to the mother. 'Good morning,' he went on. 'Sorry to bother you, but I found these two hiding in the church. They seem to have been having some trouble with a group of older boys. I thought I'd better see them safely home.'

The woman was frowning now, looking from one boy to the other. 'Are you both OK?' she asked.

'They were throwing stones at us with cater-bolts and then they ran away when they heard Harry. This is Harry,' said

Joe. 'He was saying his prayers in the church. We saw him.'

'Well, that's what it's for, I suppose,' said the woman. 'Pleased to meet you, Harry, and thank you. I'm Alice Fletcher, by the way. Would you . . . like a cup of coffee? I take it you're not a psychopath? Because if you are, I should probably make you drink your coffee on the doorstep.'

'I'm a vicar,' said Harry, who could feel his face glowing, the way it usually did when faced with a pretty woman. 'We tend not to be psychopaths,' he added. 'The archbishop doesn't really encourage it.'

'A vicar?' said Alice. 'Our vicar, you mean? The new one?'

'That's me.'

'You can't be a vicar,' said Joe.

'Why not?'

'Vicars don't wear shorts,' Joe told him. 'And they're really old. Like grandads.'

Harry grinned. 'Well, the shorts I can probably work on,' he said. 'The rest I'll have to leave to time. Do vicars have to drink their coffee on the doorstep?'

Alice too had been staring at Harry, as though she couldn't quite believe it either, but was a bit more polite than her younger son. Then she stepped back so Harry and the boys could come inside. She closed the door behind them as Joe and Tom led the way along the hallway, kicking off trainers as they went.

'What's a psychopath?' Harry heard Joe whisper as the boys pushed open the door at the end of the hall.

'Jake Knowles when he's grown up,' replied Tom, lifting his brother into the air.

Alice and Harry followed the boys into the kitchen and Millie started wriggling to be free. Once on her feet, she tottered over to the boys. Joe, in Tom's arms, had his hands around a large biscuit tin.

'Bic bic,' said Millie, looking surprisingly sly for one so young.

Alice gestured to Harry that he should sit down at the table, before crossing to the kettle, giving it a little bounce to see if there was any water inside and switching it on. The table still carried the remains of breakfast whilst a stack of plates and cutlery was piled up beside the sink.

'You're not from these parts,' she said, as she spooned coffee grains into the filter.

'Look who's talking,' replied Harry. Her accent was making him think of mint juleps and fragrant air, of heat so intense it seemed solid. 'Let me guess. Texas?'

Movement behind made him glance back at the children. Millie was chewing a ginger nut and eyeing up a chocolate finger in Joe's hand.

'You're a few states out. I'm from Memphis, Tennessee,' said Alice, gesturing at the sugar bowl. Harry shook his head. On his right, Joe had put one end of the chocolate finger between his lips before bending down and offering the rest of it to Millie. She fastened her teeth on it and started munching just as Joe did the same. They ended up kissing each other and bursting into giggles.

'That's enough now, you three. It's not long till lunch,' said Alice, without turning round. Harry saw the two boys exchange a glance before Joe stuffed three chocolate fingers and a ginger nut into his pocket and made a hasty retreat from the room. Millie, entrusted with a custard cream, stuffed it down the neck of her dress and toddled out as her eldest brother watched with a smile of pride on his face. Tom pushed a handful of biscuits into his own pockets, then realized Harry had been watching. His face turned a shade pinker as he looked from the visitor to his mother.

'We're just going into the lounge,' he announced.

'OK, but I'll have those biscuits back first,' said Alice, holding out one hand. Tom gave one last glance at Harry – who shrugged in sympathy – before handing over the booty and slinking out.

For a second all was quiet. The room seemed too empty without the children. Alice put mugs, sugar bowl, spoons and a milk bottle on the table.

'Have you lived here long?' Harry asked, knowing they couldn't have. The house was unmistakably new.

'Three months,' said Alice. She turned from Harry and started putting dirty plates and bowls into the dishwasher.

'Settling in well?' Harry asked.

The dishwasher loaded, Alice bent to a cupboard under the sink and took out a cloth and some spray disinfectant. She rinsed the cloth under the tap and began wiping down the counter top. Harry wondered if his presence might be unwelcome, in spite of the offered coffee.

'These things take time, I suppose,' replied Alice after a moment, bringing the coffee to the table and sitting down. 'Will you be living here in town?'

Harry shook his head. 'No, the vicarage is a few miles down the hill. In Goodshaw Bridge,' he said. 'I have three parishes to take care of. This one is the smallest. And probably the most challenging, given that there's been no organized worship here for several years. What do you think, will the natives be friendly?'

Another pause. Definitely awkward this time. Alice poured the coffee and pushed the milk in Harry's direction.

'So the church is opening up again,' she said, when he had helped himself. 'That'll be good for the town, I guess. We're not great churchgoers, but I guess we should make the effort, what with living so close. When are you open for business?'

'Couple of weeks yet,' replied Harry. 'I'm being officially installed into the benefice next Thursday down at St Mary's in Goodshaw Bridge. It would be great to see you and the family.'

Alice nodded her head vaguely and then silence fell again. Harry was starting to feel decidedly uncomfortable when Alice seemed to make a decision. 'There was a lot of local opposition to our moving here,' she said, leaning away from the table. 'This house was the first new building in the town in over twenty years. Most of the land and a lot of the houses are owned by the Renshaw family and they seem to control who moves in and who doesn't.'

From elsewhere in the house came the sound of raised voices and a high-pitched squeal from Millie.

'My churchwarden here is a man called Renshaw,' said Harry. 'He was on my interview panel.'

Alice nodded. 'That will be Sinclair,' she said. 'He lives in the big house on the other side of the church grounds with his oldest daughter and his father. Old Mr Tobias came round the other day and stayed for coffee. Seemed quite taken with the children. Jenny, the younger daughter, introduced herself in the post office a couple of weeks ago and said she'd call round. As I said, these things take time.'

More giggling from the other room.

'Is that your husband?' asked Harry, indicating a photograph on the window ledge behind her. It showed a good-looking man in his thirties, cowboy hat pushed back over dark hair. He wore a blue polo shirt the same colour as his eyes.

She nodded. 'This has been his dream for years,' she said. 'Building our own house in a place like this, keeping chickens, having a vegetable plot. Of course, he's not here most of the—'

She was interrupted by a sharp knocking on the front door. Muttering an apology, she left the room. Harry looked at his watch. He heard the pad pad pad of tiny footsteps and, a second later, Millie reappeared in the kitchen, pulling a shiny red duck on a stick. She began to circle the table as he heard Alice open the front door. He took a last glug of coffee and stood up. He really had to go.

'Alice, hi. I've been meaning to call for ages. Is this a good time?' The woman's voice was light and clear, with no trace of accent. He knew she'd be young, privately educated and probably rather beautiful, maybe just a tiny bit horsy, even before he reached the door of the kitchen and could see down the hall. She was standing just inside the front door. Right on all counts.

'Are you and Gareth free next Friday, by any chance?' she was asking Alice. 'We're having some people round for dinner.'

Her blonde hair had too many tones and lights in it to be anything other than natural. It fell to her shoulders and was held back by expensive sunglasses. She had the face of an alabaster statue, and she made the tiny, pretty Alice look like a doll.

'It'd be great if you could join us,' she said, putting a pleading expression on her face, but it was obvious she didn't expect a negative response.

As Harry walked down the hallway, ready to make his excuses and leave, the boys appeared from a room to one side.

The newcomer was wearing jeans and a cream linen shirt. She managed to look casual and expensive at the same time. Before Alice could respond, she spotted Harry and her mouth twisted in amusement. 'Hi,' she said, as Harry felt his face colour.

'Jenny, this is Harry. Our new vicar,' said Alice. 'Joe has already had a word with him about the expected clerical dress-code in these parts. Harry, this is Jenny Pickup. She and her husband have a farm a couple of miles out of town.'

'Reverend Laycock?' she said, holding out her hand. 'How great. We'd just about given you up. Dad's been waiting in for you for the past hour.'

Harry took her hand. 'Dad?' he repeated.

'Sinclair Renshaw,' she replied, letting go of his hand and tucking her own into her pockets. 'Your churchwarden. We knew you were arriving this morning. We thought you'd come to the house.'

Harry glanced at his watch. Had he had a firm arrangement with his churchwarden? He didn't think so. He'd just left a message that he'd be arriving late morning and would visit the church.

'Whoa, speak of the devil,' she went on, looking out of the open front door. 'Here he is, Dad. I've found him.'

Harry, six feet and a fraction himself, had to look up to meet the other man's eyes as he stepped over the threshold. Sinclair Renshaw was in his late sixties. His thick white hair fell over his forehead, almost covering very dark eyebrows. He had brown eyes behind elegant spectacles and was dressed like a country gentleman in a magazine, in various shades of green, brown and beige. He inclined his head at Harry and then turned to Alice, who seemed almost dwarfed by the tall father and daughter.

'I'm afraid there's been some serious vandalism at the church,' he said, speaking to Alice but glancing at Harry. 'One of the older windows has been broken. I understand your sons were seen there this morning, Mrs Fletcher. That they were playing with a cricket bat and ball.'

'Baseball,' said Joe helpfully.

Alice's face stiffened as she turned to look at Tom. 'What happened?' she asked.

'I saw the window being broken,' said Harry. 'And the boy who did it. It was someone called Jack, John . . . ?' He glanced down at Tom for help.

'Jake,' said Joe. 'Jake Knowles.'

'He was standing on the wall when I drove up,' Harry went on. 'I saw him swing the bat and hit the ball straight through the window. I'll be speaking to his parents.'

Renshaw looked at Harry for a second. He'd completely ignored the boys. 'Please don't bother,' he said eventually. 'I'll deal with it. Sorry to disturb, Mrs Fletcher.' He nodded once at Alice then turned to Harry. 'I'm sorry I missed you this morning, Vicar,' he went on. 'But welcome, we'll have lunch soon.' Then he walked down the drive and turned to go up the hill.

After extracting a promise from Alice that she and her husband would come to dinner the following week, Jenny climbed into her Range Rover and drove away. The children disappeared again.

'I really have to go,' said Harry. 'I'm meeting someone at the vicarage in fifteen minutes. It was good to meet you all.'

Alice smiled. 'You too, Harry. We'll see you next Thursday.'

7

11 September

E VI WINCED. SOMEONE HAD BORROWED HER CHAIR AND altered the height. It forced her to lean forward across her desk at an odd angle and put extra pressure on her damaged nerve. She looked at her watch. She had to be in court in thirty minutes. She'd fix the chair when she was next in.

She opened up the story she'd saved the previous week from the *Telegraph*'s website, wondering if there was something she'd missed. Gillian Royle had just left, following her second session. On the surface, progress seemed to have been made. Gillian was taking her medication, had noticed a difference already in her ability to sleep, and had arranged her first AA meeting. She even claimed to be trying to eat. Plenty of boxes to tick. Something, though, didn't feel quite right.

Since qualifying as a psychiatrist, Evi had worked with many patients who had been struggling to come to terms with loss. She'd treated several parents who had lost children. Gillian Royle, though, was something new. There was more going on in Gillian's head than grief for her daughter. After two sessions Evi was sure of it. Her pain was too fresh, too intense, like a fire that was being continually stoked. A horrible image in the circumstances; still, something was getting in the way of Gillian's recovery, preventing her from moving on.

Evi had been lied to many times; she knew when a patient wasn't telling her the truth; she also knew when someone wasn't telling her everything.

She re-read the newspaper story. *The town of Heptonclough is in shock* . . . She'd read that bit several times, nothing new there . . . *blaze could have been caused by a gas ring left burning* . . . if Gillian had left the cooker switched on, the fire would, technically, be her fault. Was she torturing herself with guilt?

During the previous hour with Gillian, following normal procedures, Evi had steered the girl towards talking about her early years. It hadn't gone well. She'd sensed tension in Gillian's relationship with her mother and wondered if a lack of parental support had contributed to Gillian's breakdown following Hayley's death. Gillian had talked briefly about a dead father whom she could barely remember, and had gone on to mention a stepfather arriving on the scene several years later. Evi was still scanning the story on her screen. *This latest tragedy comes barely three years after the loss of Heptonclough child Megan* . . . The story moved on to a different incident and Evi closed the page down.

The more she'd probed Gillian about her childhood, the more agitated the girl had become, until she'd flatly refused to talk about it any more. Which was interesting in itself. Conditions as acute as Gillian's rarely had a single cause, in Evi's view. What was often seen as the primary cause – in this case the loss of a child – was all too often just the trigger; the final straw in a chain of events and circumstances. There was a lot more about Gillian to learn.

8

'JOE!'

It was Friday afternoon and the boys hadn't long been home from school. All things considered, it hadn't been too bad a week. Thanks to Harry, the new vicar, Jake Knowles had had a serious telling-off about the church window and, for the time being at least, he was leaving Tom alone.

Tom was wandering around the downstairs rooms, wondering where Joe was and whether he could persuade him to go in goal while he practised striking. Hearing voices through the open back door, Tom pushed himself up on to the worktop and saw his brother sitting on the wall that ran between their garden and the churchyard. He seemed to be chatting to someone on the other side. Tom picked up the ball and went out.

'Heads up, Joe!' he called from the doorway and drop-kicked the ball towards him. Joe looked up, startled, as the ball sailed over his head, disappearing into the churchyard beyond.

Tom ran at the wall and sprang up. Although the wall was high, it was old and the earth behind it made the lower part bulge out into the Fletchers' garden. Some of the stones were missing, offering plenty of hand- and footholds. All the same, Tom had never seen Joe climb it by himself before.

When he made the top, he realized he and his brother were directly above Lucy Pickup's grave, the one that had interested Joe so much last week.

'Who were you talking to?' he asked.

Joe opened his eyes wide and looked down into the churchyard. He looked left, he looked right, and then back at Tom again. 'No one there,' he said, giving his shoulders a little shrug.

'I heard you,' Tom insisted. He pointed to the kitchen window. 'I saw you from in there. You looked like you were talking to someone.'

Joe turned to the churchyard once again. 'Can't see anyone,' he said.

Tom gave up. If his brother wanted an imaginary friend, who was he to worry. 'Want to play goalies and strikers?' he asked.

Joe nodded. 'OK,' he said. Then his lips curled in a sly little smile. 'Where's the ball?' he asked.

It was a good question. The ball had disappeared.

'Crap,' muttered Tom, partly because he knew they didn't have another one, and partly because he realized this would be the first time they'd gone into the graveyard since they'd been menaced by Jake Knowles and his gang. 'Come on,' he said reluctantly. 'We'll have to go and look.'

Tom jumped down. The ball couldn't have gone far.

Well, clearly he didn't know his own kicking power because the ball was nowhere to be seen. Tom led the way and Joe followed behind, singing quietly to himself.

'Tom, Joe! Teatime!'

'Crap,' said Tom again, picking up his pace. They had less than five minutes now before their mother got steamed. 'Didn't you see where it went?' he asked Joe.

'Tom, Joe!'

Tom stopped walking. He turned to look back at the wall they'd just climbed over. It was twenty yards away. Their mother would be at the back door. So why was her voice coming from a small thicket of laurel bushes in the opposite direction?

Tom stared at the bushes. They didn't seem to be moving.

'Tom! Where are you?'

That was definitely Mum, her voice coming from the right direction, sounding 100 per cent normal and getting quite mad now.

'Tom.' A softer voice, lower in pitch, still sounding an awful lot like his mum though.

'Did you hear that?' Tom turned to his brother. Joe was watching the laurel bushes. 'Joe, is someone in those bushes? Someone pretending to be Mum?'

'Tom, Joe, get back here!'

'We're coming,' yelled Tom. Without stopping to think, he grabbed Joe's hand and half dragged him back to the wall. He leaped up and twisted round, ready to cry out, because he just knew something horrible had followed them, was ready to spring.

The graveyard was empty. Without looking down, Tom held his hand out to Joe and pulled him up.

'Oh, good of you to show up. Now come and wash your hands.'

Tom risked a quick glance in the direction of the house. Yep, that was Mum, Millie clinging to her knees. She shook her head at them in exasperation and turned back into the house. Tom realized his breathing was slowing down. It had been echoes, that was all. The old headstones had a way of making echoes sound odd.

As Tom helped Joe to the ground on the garden side, he saw his brother smiling again. Tom turned. There was the ball. Right in the middle of the garden.

'How?'

Joe wasn't looking at him but directly at the kitchen window. Tom looked too, expecting to see Millie waving from the counter.

Jesus, that wasn't Millie's face. Who the hell was in the kitchen? It looked a bit like a child with long hair, except there was something very wrong with that face. Then Tom realized he was looking at a reflection, that the child – the girl – he could see was right behind them, peering at him and Joe over the wall. He spun round. Nothing there. Back again to the kitchen window. The reflection was gone.

Tom crossed the garden and picked up the ball. He no longer had any desire to play goalies and strikers. He wanted to get inside and shut the back door. He did exactly that, even taking the key from its hook and turning it. He stayed in the cloakroom for a second, just to get his breath back, thinking about what had just happened.

That was quite an imaginary friend his brother had, seeing as how Tom could see her too.

9

18 September

'CAN I ASK YOU SOMETHING?' GILLIAN WAS SAYING.

'Of course,' replied Evi.

'I've met this woman, she's new to the town, but I've been talking to her quite a bit and she was surprised that I'd never had a funeral for Hayley. She said funerals – or, if there's no body, a memorial service – give people a chance to grieve, to say goodbye properly.'

'Well, she's right,' said Evi cautiously. 'Normally the funeral is an important part of the grieving process.'

'But I never had that,' said Gillian, leaning forward in her chair. 'And that might be why I haven't been able to move on, why I still . . . so this woman, Alice, she said I should think about a memorial service for Hayley. She said I should discuss it with the new vicar. What do you think?'

'I think it could be a very good idea,' said Evi. 'But I also think it's important to get the timing right. It would be a very emotional experience for you. You've only taken the very first steps towards recovery. We need to be careful not to do anything that would set you back.'

Gillian nodded slowly, but her face showed her disappointment that Evi hadn't immediately fallen in with her plans.

'It's still very early days,' Evi continued quickly. 'I think a memorial service would be a good thing to think about, but maybe not rush into. We could talk about it again next week.'

Gillian sighed and shrugged her thin shoulders. 'OK,' she agreed, but she looked deflated.

'And you've made a new friend?' asked Evi. 'Alice, did you say?'

Gillian nodded, brightening a little. 'She and her family built a new house just by the old church,' she said. 'I don't think people really wanted them to do it, but she seems nice. She wants to paint me. She says I have a remarkable face.'

Evi nodded her head. 'You do,' she said, smiling. Since their first appointment, Gillian's skin had cleared a little, and without the distraction of the spots, it was easier to notice the high cheekbones, clean jaw-line and tiny nose. She would have been a striking girl, before grief turned her inside-out. 'Are you going to sit for her?' she asked.

Gillian's face seemed to cloud over. 'She has three children,' she said. 'I don't mind the two boys, but there's a little girl. She's almost exactly the age Hayley was.'

'That must be very hard.'

'She has blonde curls,' said Gillian, staring down at her hands. 'Sometimes, if I see her from behind, or if I hear her in another room, it feels like Hayley has come back. It's like there's a voice in my head saying, "She's yours, get her, get her now." I have to stop myself from grabbing her and running out of the house.'

Evi realized she was sitting very still. She reached out and picked up a pen. 'Do you think you would do something like that?' she asked.

'Like what? Take Millie?'

'You say you have to stop yourself,' said Evi quietly. 'How hard is it to stop yourself?'

Gillian shook her head. 'I wouldn't do that,' she said. 'I wouldn't do that to Alice. I know what it's like, not to know where your child is. Even if it's only for a few minutes, a part of you just dies. It's just that sometimes, seeing Millie, it's like . . .'

'Like what?' asked Evi.

'It's like Hayley's come back again.'

10

19 September

THE COTTAGE WAS LITTLE MORE THAN A FEW PILES OF blackened stone. It lay at the end of a short cobbled lane and was the first house Evi came to as she approached Heptonclough. Taking a detour from her usual route, she'd followed a little-used bridle path directly west across Tonsworth moor. Duchess, a sixteen-year-old grey cob had carried her safely along tracks strewn with fallen stones, through dense copses and across moorland streams. They'd even managed to negotiate a five-barred gate with a swing handle.

The cottage had a low, dry-stone wall and a simple iron gate. It wasn't too hard to imagine a terrified toddler pushing it open and wandering away in the dark. Looking at the house, seeing how close it was to open countryside, Gillian's actions in the weeks following the fire made some sense. Evi eased back on the reins to bring Duchess to a halt.

Lord, it was hot. Duchess was damp with sweat and so was Evi. She dropped the reins and tugged off her sweatshirt, fastening it around her waist. The cottage in which Gillian Royle and her husband had spent their married life had been rented from one of the older families in the village. After the fire the couple had been offered a one-bedroom flat above the general store. Peter Royle had since moved on, was living several miles away with a new, now pregnant girlfriend. Gillian was still in the flat.

Duchess, ever the opportunist, set off towards a patch of grass growing beneath a gate opposite. Evi gathered up the reins. There was nothing here to see, no insights to be had into her new patient. Just black stones, a few pieces of charred wood and a tangle of brambles. She lifted Duchess's head and gently flicked her whip on the horse's left flank.

They passed two more cottages, each with small gardens packed with root vegetables, fruit bushes and canes of runner beans; then the houses on either side of the lane became more uniform, stone-built, with slate roofs.

Closer to the town centre, the cobbles were smoother. On both sides of the street, three-storey stone buildings towered up. Evi turned Duchess and headed up the hill, drawing closer to Heptonclough's most famous landmarks: the two churches.

The remains of the medieval building stood alongside its Victorian replacement like an echo, or a memory that refused to fade away. Even seated on Duchess, the great stone arches of the ruin towered above her. Some of the old walls soared towards the sky, others lay crumbled on the ground. Carved pillars like standing stones stood proudly, thumbing their noses at gravity and the passage of time. Flagstones, smooth and shiny with age, covered the ground, and everywhere she looked, the moor was bursting through, pushing up corners and stealing into gaps, as it tried, after hundreds of years, to reclaim the land.

The newer building was less grand than its predecessor would have been, built on a smaller scale and without the large, central bell tower. Instead, four smaller, apex-roofed turrets sat at the roof corners. About three feet high, each was constructed from four stone pillars. On the other side of the narrow street stood tall dark-stone houses.

There was no one in sight. Evi and Duchess could almost have been alone in this strange town at the top of the moors.

The large house closest to the churches was new, judging by its pale stonework and the untouched small garden at the front. On the doorstep, like the only signs of life in a ghost town, stood a tiny pair of pink wellington boots.

A high-pitched squealing broke through the silence and

something brightly coloured shot past Evi's left shoulder. Duchess, normally unflappable, gave a little jump and slipped on the cobbles.

'Steady, steady now.' Evi was tightening the reins, sitting straight and still in the saddle. What the hell had that been?

There it was again. Twenty yards away, flying along, pennants flapping. Evi urged Duchess up the hill, away from the churchyard. With any luck she'd be able to turn higher up and get back on to the moor.

It was coming back, heading straight for them. Duchess skittered backwards into the wall of a house. Evi had been thrown off balance but she grabbed a chunk of mane and pushed herself upright. 'Don't come near us,' she yelled. 'You're scaring the horse.'

She made eye contact for a fraction of a second and knew she had a serious problem on her hands. The boy on the bike knew perfectly well that he was scaring the horse.

Evi pulled hard, turning Duchess to face the hill. If the horse was going to bolt, they had to go upwards.

There was another one, travelling in the opposite direction. Two teenage boys, on high-performance bikes, riding round the high wall that circled the two churches. It was utter suicide, they were going to collide, to fall six feet on to hard, flint cobbles. The boys got within two feet of each other and then one disappeared, his bike finding some ridge that took him down into the churchyard. The remaining rider shot past Evi as she fought to get Duchess under control.

There were more of them. Four young stunt-riders, travelling at impossible speeds around the old walls, pennants flying from their handlebars, brakes screaming as they spun around corners.

'Get lost, you stupid buggers!' she managed to shout. Horses hated bikes at the best of times, the combination of silence and speed completely unnerved them. And these four were buzzing around her like mosquitoes. They kept coming back, disappearing behind the wall and then reappearing somewhere else. Here was a fifth, sneaking up behind her, cutting in front. Duchess threw up her head, spun on the spot and set off at a fast canter down the hill.

Urgent shouting. Hooves skidding. A short smack of something that might have been pain but at the time felt more like outrage.

And then silence.

Evi was lying on the ground, staring at a piece of litter that had caught between two cobbles and wondering if she was still alive. A second later she got her answer. A drop of blood landed on the stone and she watched it tremble in the breath from her mouth.

She knew there was pain waiting for her, but the part of her brain that normally took charge was spinning away, leaving her behind. She was lost amidst cold, white softness, but feeling hot – so very hot – and watching a tiny stream trickle away from her, wondering why a mountain stream should be crimson and knowing, even in that first moment, that her old life was over.

'Hold on, I'll be there in a sec!'

Someone had called to her, that last time, in a language she couldn't understand. Someone had yelled instructions at her in a Germanic tongue and she'd stared upwards, at the bluest sky she'd ever seen, and known that movement was beyond her. Might be beyond her for the rest of—

'Don't move. I'm almost done. Alice! Tom! Can you hear me?'

And then she'd been surrounded by tall, fair-haired men who'd smelled of beer and sun-cream and they'd sent words down to her, meant to comfort, to keep her calm, while they trussed her up and pinned her tight and sent her spinning away again, down the mountain . . .

'It's OK, don't try and get up. I've caught your horse, he's perfectly safe.' A man was kneeling beside her, one hand gently on her shoulder, speaking to her in a strange accent. 'I'm going to call for an ambulance but I've left my phone in the church. I can't leave you in the road . . . Alice! Tom!'

Evi raised her head and moved it slowly from right to left, up and down. There was a pounding in her forehead but her neck felt fine. She flexed her right foot inside her boot and then her left. Both did what they were supposed to. She put both palms on the cobbles and pushed. There was a sharp pain in her ribs but she knew, instinctively, that it wasn't serious.

'No, don't move.' The voice was close to her ear again. 'The Fletchers were here a minute ago. They can't have gone far. No, I really don't think you should . . .'

Evi was sitting up. The man kneeling beside her, though tall, looked too slightly built to be German or Austrian. And these hills all around her weren't mountains. They were moors, just turning the soft, deep purple of a fresh bruise.

'Are you OK?' asked the fair-haired man, who was dressed in shorts and a running vest. Boys on bikes. Duchess panicking. She'd been rescued by a passing jogger. 'Where does it hurt?' he was saying.

'Everywhere,' grumbled Evi, discovering she could speak. 'Nothing serious. Where's Duchess?'

The jogger turned to look down the hill and Evi did the same. Duchess was tied to an old iron ring at the corner of the church wall. Her head was down and her huge yellow teeth were making short work of a nettle patch.

'Thank God you caught her,' said Evi. 'Those stupid bastards. She had a nasty bruise on her foot a few days ago. Did she seem OK?'

'Well, obviously starving to death, but otherwise fine. Not that I'm much of an authority on horseflesh, I'm afraid.'

Duchess was standing squarely on all four legs. Would she be eating if she were in pain? Quite possibly, knowing Duchess.

'Are you sure you're not hurt?' asked the man, who, she noticed now, was wearing deck shoes. And the shorts weren't running shorts. They were blue and white striped cotton, almost to his knees, and the hair on the back of his calves was blond and thick.

'Quite sure,' she said, taking her eyes away from his legs. 'I'm a doctor, I'd know,' she added when he looked uncertain. 'Do you think you could help me get out of the road?'

'Of course, sorry.' The fair-haired man leaped to his feet and bent down, holding out his right hand for Evi, as if offering to help her up from a picnic rug.

She shook her head. 'That won't work, I'm afraid. I can't stand by myself. If you don't mind, can you take me under the arms and lift? I'm not that heavy.'

He was shaking his head, looking worried. 'You said you weren't hurt,' he said. 'If you can't get up by yourself I don't think I should be lifting you. I think we should call for help.'

Did he need it spelling out?

Evi took a deep breath. 'I'm not hurt now, but three years ago I had a bad accident and seriously damaged the sciatic nerve in my left leg,' she said. 'I can't walk unaided and my leg is certainly not strong enough to support my weight while I get up from these cobbles. Which are not very comfortable, by the way.'

The man stared at her for a second, then she watched his eyes fall to her left leg, unnaturally thin and ugly inside the crimson jodhpurs.

'Does this road get much traffic?' asked Evi, looking up the hill.

'It doesn't. But you're quite right. Sorry.' He knelt again and put his right arm under her shoulders. His left hand slid under her thighs and even though she'd been expecting it, had been quite prepared to be touched, she felt a shock running through her that had nothing to do with pain. Then she was upright, leaning against him, and he smelled of skin and dust and fresh male sweat.

'OK, ten yards up the hill there is a bench for weary shepherds to stop and take succour on. I don't imagine they'll mind if we borrow it. Can you make it that far?'

'Of course,' she snapped, although it was easier said than done. She had no choice but to wrap her arm round his waist. He was hot. Of course he was hot, it was a hot day and she was hot too and she probably smelled of horses. Evi moved her right leg, and her left screamed at her to stop this stupid moving business right now.

'Bugger it,' she muttered, trying without success to bring her weaker leg forward. *Come on, you useless, bloody* ...

She stumbled and almost fell again, but her companion tightened his grip around her waist, bent lower and lifted both legs clean off the ground. Instinctively, she reached her free arm up to clasp him around the neck. His face had turned pink.

'Sorry, didn't want you going down again,' he said. 'Can I carry you to the bench?'

She nodded and a second later he was putting her gently down on a wooden bench close to the church wall. She leaned back gratefully and closed her eyes. How could she have been so stupid? Bringing Duchess all this way. She could have seriously injured them both. Why the hell did life have to be so bloody difficult? She waited, eyes closed, until the tears had slipped back where they came from.

When she opened her eyes again she was alone. He'd just left her?

56

Christ, she hadn't exactly been Miss Congeniality but even so . . .

Pushing herself forward, Evi looked all around. Across the street the windows were dark and empty. A heavy stillness seemed to have settled over the moors. The bike riders had disappeared – hardly surprising given the trouble they'd caused – but where was everyone else? So many houses, so many windows and not a soul in sight. It was Saturday afternoon, for heaven's sake. Why was no one looking out to see what was going on?

Except, maybe they were. Behind one of those dark windows someone was watching her, she was sure of it. Without appearing to look, she let her eyes scan left and right. Not the faintest hint of movement that she could see, but there was someone there all the same. She turned slowly.

There it was. Movement. Way up high. Evi raised her hand to her eyes to shut out the sun. No, it was impossible. What she thought she'd seen was a shape scurrying along the top of the church. No one could be up there. She'd seen a bird. A squirrel maybe. Or a cat.

She unfastened the chin-strap and removed her hat. The pressure in her head eased immediately. She lifted her hair with her fingers, letting the air get to her scalp and soothe it.

She could hear footsteps. Her ginger-haired knight in shining stripy shorts was back, half jogging along the church path towards her, carrying a glass of water.

'Hi,' he said as he drew closer. 'I can do tea as well but that takes a bit longer. How're you doing?'

How was she doing? She'd been harassed by feral teenagers who could move at warp speed, she'd fallen off a fifteen-hands horse, had to lie in the road like a beached whale, and then, just on the off-chance that she had a shred of dignity remaining, she'd been hoisted off her feet by a ginger-haired twit who smelled like . . . like a man.

'Better, I think,' she said. 'It's always a shock, coming off a horse. Especially when you don't land on soft ground.'

He joined her on the bench. 'I'll take your word for it,' he said. 'I don't want to sound rude, but should you really be out on your own, with a weak leg and all?'

Evi opened her mouth and then closed it tight. He meant well. She looked at her watch, giving herself a second. 'Well, it's not likely to be happening again any time soon,' she said. 'The yard I ride

57

from are very strict. I'll be doing supervised trots round the manège for the next six months.'

'Well maybe . . .' He caught a look at her face and stopped. 'How far have you ridden?' he asked.

'From Bracken Farm livery yard,' she said. 'It's about four miles across the moor.'

'Shall I phone them for you? I'm not sure if they can get a horse-box all the way up here, but I can walk—'

'No.' It came out louder and firmer than she'd meant it to because she had a feeling there was a battle imminent and, bruised and shaking though she might be, it was one she had to win. 'Thank you,' she went on, forcing a smile. 'I'll be riding back in a minute.' Feeling far from ready to remount, she finished the water and put her hat back on, determined to make *I'm going now* signals, because she knew exactly what was coming.

He was shaking his head. Well, of course he was shaking his head. He was tall and strong, with full use of his limbs, and that made him the boss. 'I'm not putting you back on that horse,' he said.

'Excuse me?'

'Sorry, pet, but you're disabled, you've taken a nasty fall and you've probably got concussion. You can't ride four miles across open moorland.'

Sorry, pet! She looked down at the road so she wouldn't be able to glare at him, because the disabled aren't allowed to be angry. If she'd learned one thing over the past three years it was that. Normal people who get angry are just pissed off and that happens to us all; when you're disabled, any sign of temper means you're disturbed, you need help, you're not capable of . . .

'Thank you for your concern,' said Evi, 'but, disabled or not, I am still responsible for my own actions and I don't actually need any help to remount. Please don't let me keep you.'

She handed back the glass and eased herself sideways on the bench. It would be better by far if he were to leave her alone now.

'How?' He hadn't moved.

'Excuse me?' she repeated.

'How, exactly, given that you couldn't get out of the road by your-self and needed to be carried to this seat, do you intend to walk fifteen yards down the hill and remount a large horse?'

58

'Watch and learn.'

She pushed herself upright. The wall was only two feet away, it would support her weight as she walked downhill.

'Hold on a second. Let's do a deal.'

He was standing right in front of her. Getting to the wall by herself was possible; negotiating her way around him first probably wasn't.

'What?'

'If you agree to rest for another ten minutes and then phone me the instant you get back to the yard, I'll help you mount and walk you back to the bridle path.'

So now she was bargaining for the most basic of freedoms with a man she'd just met. 'And if I don't agree?'

He produced a mobile phone from his pocket. 'I'll phone Bracken Farm livery yard to tell them exactly what's happened. I imagine they'll be on their way over before you reach the end of the wall.'

'Asshole.' It slipped out before she could bite her tongue.

He held up the phone.

'Get out of my way.'

He pressed a series of digits. 'Hi,' he said, after a second. 'I'd like the number of a livery yard . . .'

Evi raised her hands in surrender and sat back down again. The man apologized to the operator and replaced the phone in his pocket. He sat beside her as Evi pointedly looked at her watch, knowing she was being childish and not giving a toss.

'Cup of tea?' he offered.

'No, thank you.'

'Another glass of water?'

'Only if it takes you a long time to get it.'

The man gave a low, embarrassed chuckle. 'Crikey,' he said, 'I haven't had this much success with a woman since I got drunk at my cousin's wedding and threw up over the maid of honour.'

'Yes, well, I'm feeling about as thrilled to be in your company as she must have been.'

'We went out for eighteen months.'

Silence. Evi looked at her watch again.

'So what do you think of Heptonclough?' he asked.

Evi was staring straight ahead, determined to look at nothing but the small flight of steps and the tiny street, hardly wider than the span of a man's arms, that lay opposite. She had a sudden urge to remove her hat again.

'Very nice,' she said.

'First visit?'

'First and last.'

An iron railing had been fixed into the wall to allow older, less agile people to navigate the steps. Even using it, Evi would struggle to climb steps so steep. Four steps. They might as well be a hundred.

'Are you sure you're not concussed? People aren't usually this rude when they first meet me. Later, quite often, but not right away. How many fingers am I holding up?'

Evi's head shot round, already opening her mouth to tell him . . . he was holding up both fists, no fingers in sight. He made a mock start backwards. She raised her right arm to punch him right in the face and to hell with the consequences and . . .

'You're much prettier when you smile.'

. . . realized it was the very last thing in the world she wanted to do.

'You're very pretty when you don't smile, don't get me wrong, I just happen to prefer women when they're smiling. It's a thing I have.'

She didn't want to hit him at all. She wanted to do something quite different. Even here, in the street, where the whole world could see . . .

'Shut up,' she managed.

He drew two clasped fingers across his mouth in a zipping motion, a silly, childlike gesture. His mouth was still stretched wide. She looked away before her own smile could become too . . . too much like his.

Silence again. Across the road a cat appeared. It sat on the top step and began cleaning itself.

'I've always wished I could do that,' he said.

'Aah!' She raised one finger.

'Sorry.'

Silence. The cat raised one leg and began licking its genitals. The bench they were sitting on began to shake. It was hopeless. She'd be giggling like a teenager in seconds. She turned to him, because at least then she wouldn't have to watch the cat.

'Do you live here?' she asked.

He shook his head. 'No, I just work here. I live a few miles down the hill.'

He had light-brown eyes and dark eyelashes, which were really quite striking with that fair hair. Was it ginger? Given time to think about it, ginger seemed too harsh a word for a colour that in this soft September light seemed more like . . . like . . . honey?

Glancing down, Evi caught sight of her watch. The ten minutes were up. She twisted her arm around so the watch faced downwards and she couldn't see it any more. 'What's with the two churches?' she asked.

'They're great, aren't they? Like before and after. OK, brace yourself for the history lesson. Back in the days when the great abbeys ruled England, Heptonclough had one of its own. Building work started in 1193. The church behind us was built first and then the living quarters and farm buildings later.'

He spun round on the bench, so that he was facing the ruined building behind them. Evi did the same, although her left leg had started to hurt quite badly. 'The abbot's residence is still standing,' he went on. 'It's a beautiful old medieval building. You can't quite see it from here, it's on the other side of the new church. A family called Renshaw live in it now.'

Evi was thinking back to school history lessons. 'So was Henry VIII responsible for the abbey falling into ruins?' she asked.

The man nodded. 'Well, he certainly didn't help,' he agreed. 'The last abbot of Heptonclough, Richard Paston, was involved in the rebellion against Henry's ecclesiastical policies and was tried on a charge of treason.'

'Executed?' asked Evi.

'Not far from this spot. And most of his monks. But the town continued to thrive. In the sixteenth century it was the centre of the South Pennine woollen trade. It had a Cloth Hall, a couple of banks, inns, shops, a grammar school and eventually a new church, built to one side of the old one, because the townsfolk had decided the ruins were rather picturesque.'

'They still are,' admitted Evi.

'Then, some time in the late eighteenth century, Halifax emerged as the new superpower in the wool trade and Heptonclough lost its place at the top of the tree. All the old buildings are still here, but they're mainly private houses now. Most of them owned by the same family.'

'The new church doesn't have a tower,' Evi pointed out. 'In every other respect it's like a miniature copy of the old building, but with just those four little towers instead.'

'The town council ran out of money before the new church could be finished,' her companion replied. 'So they built one small tower to house a solitary bell and then, because that looked a bit daft, they built the other three to even up the balance. They're purely decorative though, you can't even access them. I think the plan was always to knock them down and build a big one when the money was available, but . . .' He shrugged. The money to build a tower had clearly never materialized.

It was no good. Every minute she stayed increased the trouble waiting for her back at the yard. 'I'm fine now, really,' she said. 'And I have to get back. Do you think you could . . .'

'Of course.' He stood up, rather quickly, as though he had, after all, only been being polite. Evi pushed herself up. Once on her feet, her eyes were on the same level as the fair hair peeking out over the neck of his vest.

'How do you want to do this?' he asked.

She tilted her head back to look at him properly and thought that she really wouldn't mind being carried back down the hill again. A stab of pain ran down the back of her thigh. 'May I take your arm?' she said.

He held out his right elbow and, like a courting couple from the old days, they walked down the hill. Even with streams of fire running down her left leg they reached Duchess far too quickly.

'Hi Harry,' said a small voice. 'Whose horse is this?'

'This noble steed belongs to the beautiful Princess Berengaria who is riding back now to her castle on the hill,' said the man who answered to the name of Harry, and who seemed to be looking at someone on the other side of the wall. 'Do you want a leg up, Princess?' he asked, turning back to Evi.

'Could you just hold her head still?'

'Spurned again,' Harry muttered as he loosened the reins and passed them back over Duchess's head. Then he held the nose band as Evi lifted her left foot and placed it in the stirrup. Three little bounces and she was up. She could see the small boy, about five or six years old, with dark-red hair. In his right hand he was holding a plastic light-sabre, in his left was something she recognized.

'Hello,' she said. He stared back at her, no doubt thinking that she really didn't look much like a princess, certainly not a beautiful one. Being a small boy, he was probably opening his mouth right now to say exactly that.

'Is this yours?' he said instead, holding up the whip Evi had dropped and then forgotten about. 'I found it in the road.'

Evi smiled and thanked him, as he clambered up on to the wall and held it out. Harry was still holding Duchess's nose band. He led her down the short, steep hill until they reached Wite Lane. As they turned into the lane she saw the cat was following them, stepping lightly along an old wooden fence. Glancing back, Evi saw the small boy was watching them too.

Harry seemed to have run out of things to say as the cobbles became unkempt and the houses less uniform. They came to the gate at the end of the lane and Harry opened it for her, finally letting go of the nose band.

'How long will it take you to get back?' he asked. Behind his head, berries shimmered like rubies in the hedge.

'Twenty minutes if I trot most of the way and canter the last hundred yards.'

He made a stern face, like a headmaster addressing an unruly class. 'How long if you walk sedately?' The heather at his feet was the colour of mulberries. She'd forgotten how beautiful September could be.

She wouldn't let herself smile. 'Thirty-five, forty minutes.'

He looked at his watch, then fished in his pocket and pulled out a card. 'Phone me by four o'clock,' he said, passing it to her. 'If I don't hear from you, I'll be calling out the emergency services, the armed forces, the coastguard, every livery yard in a ten-mile radius and the National Farmers Union. It will be embarrassing, for both of us.'

'And very expensive for you,' said Evi, tucking the card into the pocket of her shirt.

'So call.'

'I'll call.'

'Nice meeting you, Princess.'

She squeezed with her right leg, flicked the whip and Duchess, instinctively knowing she was heading for home, set off at an active walk. Evi didn't look back. Only when she was far enough away to be sure he wouldn't see her did she sneak the card out of her shirt pocket.

A man she'd just met had insisted she call him. How long since that had happened? He'd held her in his arms. Called her beautiful. She'd wanted to snog him in a public street. She looked at the card. *Reverend Harry Laycock, B.A. Dip.Th.*, it said. *Vicar of the United Benefice of Goodshaw Bridge, Loveclough and Heptonclough.* There were contact details at the bottom. Duchess walked on and Evi put the card back in her pocket.

He was a vicar.

There simply weren't words.

11

HARRY LEANED AGAINST THE WALL FOR TEN MINUTES watching the woman ride away. Only when she and the grey horse disappeared into a copse did he turn and walk slowly back to the church. As he passed the new house he could see Alice Fletcher in her sitting-room window, talking on the telephone and watching Joe in the garden. She saw Harry and waved.

He walked through the old gateway and found someone waiting.

It was a young woman, with the grey, prematurely lined face of a heavy smoker or drinker. She wore jeans and a faded long-sleeved T-shirt and her hair was pulled back into a tight ponytail. Above the restraining band it was a greasy mouse-brown, below it stuck out at angles like straw that had been left too long in the sun.

'That was Dr Oliver, wasn't it?' she said. 'Was she talking about me?'

Harry looked back at the girl. No make-up. Clothes that weren't too clean. So, had he missed the first few seconds of this conversation? The bit where she'd said who she was and that it was nice to meet the new vicar?

'Well, she didn't mention her name,' he said after a moment. 'But now you come to mention it, she did say she was a doctor. Hi, I'm Harry Laycock.' He held out his hand, but the girl made no move to take it.

'What did she say about me?' she demanded to know.

There was something going on here that he wasn't keeping up

with. The woman on the horse had said it was her first visit to the town, hadn't she? First and last.

'Why are you smiling? What did she tell you?'

He needed to focus for a second. This girl had an issue. It was as plain as the nose on her very unhealthy-looking face.

'She didn't talk about anyone,' he said. 'She'd fallen off her horse and she was in shock. But if she's a doctor . . .'

'She's a psychiatrist.'

'A what?' Impossible to keep the surprise from his voice. That grumpy, edgy woman was a . . . blimey.

'Well, she didn't mention that,' he said, 'but if she is a psychiatrist, she wouldn't be allowed to talk about her patients with anyone, it would be—'

'I'm not a patient. I just see her sometimes.'

'Right.' Harry found himself nodding, as though he understood completely. Which he didn't.

'Are you the new vicar?'

At last, familiar territory. 'Yes,' he said. 'I'm Harry. Reverend Laycock if you want to be formal, which very few people ever are. I think it must be the shorts. And you are . . . ?'

'Did Alice tell you about me?'

'Alice?' Was it him? Had his brain just decided to take the day off?

'Alice Fletcher. From the new house.'

Light dawning. 'Are you Gillian?' he asked.

The girl nodded.

'She did mention you. I'm so sorry about your loss.'

The girl's face contracted, grew smaller, her thin lips almost disappeared. 'Thank you,' she said, as her eyes left his face and drifted somewhere over his left shoulder.

'How are you coping?' asked Harry.

Gillian took a deep breath and her eyes opened wider, momentarily losing their focus. Stupid question. She wasn't coping. And she was going to ask him why God had taken her child. Out of all the children in the world, why hers? Any second now.

'I was about to make tea,' he said quickly. 'I've got a kettle in the vestry. Will you join me?' Gillian stared at him for a second, as though tea was something out of her normal experience, then she nodded. He led her through the ruins of the abbey church and up the flagstones towards St Barnabas's, trying to remember what Alice had told him.

Gillian – Rogers, Roberts, he couldn't quite remember – had lost her daughter in a house fire three years previously. She spent her days walking the moors and wandering round the town's old streets, almost like a living ghost. Alice had met her in the abbey ruins and invited her home for coffee. It was the sort of kind, impulsive and not terribly wise thing that Alice would do. Gillian had accepted and had stayed most of the morning, half-heartedly answering Alice's attempts at conversation but mainly just watching the children playing.

The church felt chill and damp after the autumn sunshine. 'You're cleaning this church by yourself?' asked Gillian as she and Harry walked up the side aisle.

'Thankfully, no,' replied Harry. 'The diocese arranged a team of industrial cleaners. They've just finished. I'm just sorting out cupboards, finding out where everything's been stored, putting the building back to rights. Alice and the children have been helping me.'

Harry pushed open the door to the vestry and allowed Gillian to precede him inside. He would have to get some chairs in here, maybe a small table. The kettle was still warm, he'd just switched it on when he'd heard the doctor yelling at her horse. By the time he'd found teabags and mugs it had boiled. He poured on hot water, conscious of Gillian hovering just behind him, and added milk and sugar without asking whether she took either. She clearly needed both. Alice had brought over a jumbo packet of chocolate digestives earlier that day. Bless her.

He held a cup out to Gillian. She reached to take it but her small, white hand was shaking violently. The skin above her wrists was crisscrossed with scars. She saw him notice and her face flushed. He withdrew his hand and passed her the biscuits instead.

'Let's go and sit down,' he suggested, before leading the way back into the nave. He sat down on the front bench of the choir stalls. She joined him and at last he felt confident to hand over the hot drink. He sipped his own gratefully. It was thirsty work: cleaning churches, rescuing foul-mouthed psychiatrists and consoling grief-stricken parishioners. If the day continued along the same lines, he'd be breaking open the communion wine before sun-down.

'I haven't had a drink for eight days,' said Gillian, and for a second, he wasn't quite . . . Of course, Alice had mentioned Gillian had been to her GP, that she'd been referred to an alcoholics' support group, to a psychiatrist specializing in family issues. Who must, of course, be the lady he'd just met. Dr Oliver.

'Well done,' said Harry.

'I feel better,' said Gillian. 'I really do. Dr Oliver gave me some pills to help me sleep. It's been so long since I've been able to sleep.'

'I'm glad to hear that,' said Harry. He sat, his best patient-and-interested look on his face, waiting for what she was going to say next.

'Do you have faith, Gillian?' he asked, when he realized she wasn't going to talk again. Sometimes it was best to get right to the point.

She stared at him as though she didn't quite . . . 'You mean, do I believe in God?' she asked.

He nodded. 'Yes, that's what I mean,' he said. 'Losing someone we love is very difficult. Even the strongest faith will be tested.'

Her hand was shaking again. The tea would scald her. He reached out, took the mug from her and placed it on the floor.

'Someone came to see me, after it happened,' she said. 'A priest. He said Hayley was with her father in heaven and she was happy and that should comfort me, but how can she be happy without me? She'll be on her own. She's two years old and she's on her own. That's what I can't get my head around. She'll be so lonely.'

'Have you lost any family members before, Gillian?' he asked. 'Are your parents alive?'

She looked puzzled. 'My dad died when I was small,' she said. 'In a car accident. And I had a younger sister who died a long time ago.'

'I'm sorry. What about grandparents? Do you have any?'

'No, they all died. What . . .'

He was leaning forward, had taken hold of both her hands. 'Gillian, there's a reading that's given often at funeral services, you may have heard it. It was written by a bishop about a hundred years ago and it compares the death of a loved one to standing on the seashore, watching a beautiful ship sail out of sight on the horizon. Can you picture that for a second, imagine blue sea, a beautiful carved wooden boat, white sails?'

Gillian shut her eyes. She nodded her head.

'The boat's getting smaller and smaller and then it disappears over the horizon and someone standing by your side says, "She's gone."'

Tears were forming in the corners of Gillian's closed eyes.

'But even though you can't see her any more, the ship is still there, still strong and beautiful. And just as she disappears from your sight, she's appearing on other shores. Other people can see her.'

Gillian opened her eyes.

'Hayley is like that ship,' said Harry. 'She may be gone from your sight but she still exists, and in the place where she is now there are people who are thrilled to see her: your dad, your sister, your grandparents. They will take care of her and they will love her, unconditionally, until you can join her again.'

The girl's howl tore at his heart. He stayed where he was, watching her thin body sob and her tears fall on to his hands. For five, maybe ten minutes she wept, and he held her hands until he felt her pulling away from him. He didn't have tissues but somewhere in the vestry there was kitchen roll. He walked quickly back to the vestry, found it beside the sink and, returning, handed it over. She wiped her face and tried to smile up at him. Her eyes, washed by tears, were almost silver. Dr Oliver's eyes had been blue. A deep, violet blue.

In the pocket of his shorts, his mobile started to ring. He should ignore it, let it go to the answer service, get back to whoever it was later. Except he knew who it was.

'Excuse me,' he said, getting up. 'I'll be back in a sec.'

He walked a few paces down the aisle and pressed Answer.

'Harry Laycock.'

'Berengaria speaking.'

'Did you make it back safely, Dr Oliver?'

'Now that's . . . a bit spooky. How'd you do that?'

Harry glanced back up the aisle to where Gillian was staring at the floor. She was too close, she'd hear everything he said. 'Like my boss, I work in mysterious ways,' he answered.

There was a second's pause.

'Right, well, thanks for your help,' came Dr Oliver's voice. 'But Duchess and I are both back where we belong and none the worse for our adventure.'

'Delighted to hear it.' Gillian was looking at him now. She wouldn't like the interruption. The bereaved could be selfish. Not great timing, Princess. 'You take care now,' he said. 'And say hello to Duchess for me.'

'I'll do that.' The voice on the phone had fallen flat. 'Goodbye.'

She was gone. And he had to get back to Gillian. Who was no longer sitting calmly on the front choir stall but was on her feet, staring round in what could only be described as horror. It was as though something had pulled the skin on her face tighter, made it mask-like. She was striding towards him. 'Did you hear that?' she demanded. 'Did you hear it?'

'I? What?' He'd been on the phone. What was he supposed to have heard?

'That voice, calling "Mummy," did you hear it?'

Harry looked all around, astonished and a little alarmed by the change in Gillian. 'I heard something, I think, but I was saying goodbye.' He held up the phone.

'What?' she demanded. 'What did you hear?'

'Well, a child, I thought. A child outside.'

She clutched his arm, her fingers tight on his bare skin. 'No, it was inside. It was coming from inside the church.'

'There's no one else here,' he said slowly. 'These old buildings can be deceptive. Sound echoes in funny ways.'

Gillian had spun away from him, was half running back up the aisle. She reached the choir stalls and started searching them, peering down the length of first one then the other.

What on earth?

She was crossing the church, dragging out the organ stool, back again behind the altar, pulling up the cloth. He'd almost reached her when she seemed to give up. She sobbed once and almost fell to the tiled floor. Then she drew herself up and opened her mouth.

'Hayley!' she screamed.

Harry stopped. He'd heard voices in this church too. And the sound of people he couldn't see moving around. Why did he have this overwhelming urge to look behind him?

He turned. There wasn't a soul in the church but Gillian and himself.

'Let's get you home,' he said. 'You probably need to rest.' If she gave him the name of her GP he could phone him, explain what was happening, see if he could get her immediate help. He could try and call in on her himself tomorrow after morning services were done. As he reached her she clutched at him.

'You heard her, you heard Hayley.' She was almost begging him, pleading with him to tell her she wasn't losing her grip on reality.

'I certainly heard a child,' he said, although in all honesty, he wasn't that sure. He'd been listening to a change in inflexion in a woman's voice on the phone and wondering what it might mean. 'It's possible I heard the child saying "Mummy," but, you know, the Fletcher children have been playing around the church for most of the afternoon. It could easily have been Millie that we heard.'

Gillian was staring at him.

'Come on,' he said. 'Let's get some fresh air, I'll walk you home.'

Muttering a silent prayer that the Fletcher children, including the youngest, would be outside, Harry led Gillian out of the door and into the sunshine. They were halfway down the path when a toy arrow whizzed past them, making Gillian jump. Harry turned to the Fletchers' garden on his right and found himself staring into the blue eyes of Joe Fletcher. A few yards away Tom was kicking a football against the wall of the house. Their sister sat on bare earth, digging in the soil.

'Missed,' said Harry, grinning at Joe.

Joe's head shot round to see if his mother had noticed. She was hanging out washing and didn't turn round.

'Sorry,' he mouthed. Harry winked.

'Mouse,' said Millie, her gaze fixed on something just a foot or two away. Her eyes gleamed and she reached out a chubby arm.

'Millie, no, that's a rat,' called Harry. Out of the corner of his eye, he saw Alice spin round and drop what she was holding.

Tom stopped kicking as Harry jumped over the wall and landed in the soft earth of the Fletchers' garden.

'Gone,' said Joe. The rat was scurrying towards the wall. Its fat, grey tail hovered for a second in the gap between two stones and then disappeared. Harry looked back at the churchyard. Gillian had disappeared too.

12

21 September

FIRST THE WHISPERS WERE IN A DREAM. AND THEN THEY weren't. Tom had no idea when it changed, when he went from dream to real, but one minute he was fast asleep and then he was awake and the dream was slipping away. He thought perhaps there were trees, and something in the trees that was watching him. Maybe there was the church, but definitely whispering. He was totally sure about that. Because he could still hear it.

He sat up. The luminous numbers on the desk alarm clock told him it was 02.53. His parents were never up at this time. They'd be fast asleep, the house closed up for the night.

So who was whispering?

Hanging upside-down, he stuck his head into the space above Joe's bunk. His brother had his own room, right next door. He kept all his toys in it and played in it a lot, but he never slept there. Every night he climbed into the bunk below Tom's.

'Joe, are you awake?'

Even as he opened his mouth he could see that the bottom bunk was empty. The quilt was pushed back and there was a dent in the pillow where Joe's head had been.

Tom swung his feet round and dropped to the carpet. All seemed still on the dark landing. Three doors were slightly open – the doors to the bathroom, to Millie's room and to his parents' bedroom – but behind each door there was just darkness. As he stepped closer to the top of the stairs, a cool breeze swept through the house; the front door was wide open.

Had someone come in? Or gone out?

The top step gave a very loud creak. Half hoping his parents would wake up and hear him, Tom took another step and then another.

Who had been whispering? Where was Joe?

As he reached the bottom step a wind swept past him into the house. Tiny hairs on his arms stood up to make goose bumps. Then the wind was gone and the air was soft and almost warm again. No need to shiver, really, except he couldn't stop.

He knew he should wake his mum and dad. Joe's leaving the house in the middle of the night was too serious for him to deal with alone. Except when he and Joe were involved in a scrape, the blame was never shared 50:50. A good 90 per cent of it invariably came in Tom's direction and the facts of the case were rarely allowed to get in the way. If he woke his parents up now, he knew exactly who would find themselves in the you-know-what the minute Joe was found and returned home.

Tom was going to kill him this time, he really was.

He stepped outside and, for a moment, forgot that he was angry, forgot that he was getting very close to being scared. So this was what it was like then – the night-time – soft and scented and strangely warm, a place where all the colours had gone, leaving black and silver and moonbeams in their place. He took another step away from the house.

Then that feeling began to creep over him again, the one he seemed to get every time he left the house these days. Even inside the house sometimes, especially when it was getting dark outside, it could steal up on him. Some days, it seemed to Tom, the curtains just couldn't be closed quickly enough in the evening.

Someone was watching him now, he knew it, someone very close. He could almost hear breathing, he just had to hope it was his brother. Tom turned his head slowly towards the corner of the house.

Two large eyes in a pale, flabby face looked back at him. Then they were gone.

Tom ran for the house. In the relative safety of the doorway, he stopped and turned back.

A girl, about his own age if size was anything to go by, was shinning up the wall that separated the Fletchers' garden from the church land. She climbed quickly, as if she'd done it many times before, long hair trailing behind her and loose clothes fluttering in the breeze. Like Tom, she was barefoot, but her feet were nothing like his. Even at this distance they looked enormous compared to the rest of her. So did her hands.

Then Tom caught sight of something else at the corner of the house, at the exact spot from which the girl had appeared. He was ready to dive indoors when he realized it was Joe, in his red and blue Spiderman dressing gown.

'What are you doing?' he hissed as Joe came trotting towards him. 'Come back inside now or I'm getting Dad.' Glancing back up towards the church wall, he saw the girl had gone. Really gone, or just hiding? Because that's what she did. She hid and she watched.

'We're not supposed to be here, Tom,' muttered Joe.

'I know we're not,' shot back Tom. 'So let's get back inside before Mum and Dad wake up.'

Joe lifted his head. His eyes looked huge in his pale face. 'No,' he said, letting his eyes drift away from Tom to the wall. 'We're not supposed to be here,' he repeated. 'It's not safe.'

13

22 September

*M*ILLIE, THE LITTLE GIRL WITH HAIR THE COLOUR OF SPUN *sugar, was in the garden. She was wearing hand-me-down clothes from one of her brothers, dark-blue jogging trousers and a blue and white football sweatshirt. Mud clung to her as she sat on the bare earth. The nappy, peeking out over the top of her joggers, made her bottom look enormous.*

'Millie.' Her mother's voice, from inside the house. She appeared in the doorway, plastic bowl in one hand, the other on her hip in exasperation.

'Will you look at you?' she called. Millie beamed back. She tried to stand, made it halfway and then fell back on her bottom.

'Stay there for a minute, poppet,' called Millie's mother. 'I'll get you some clothes. Then we'll get the boys. Bye!' She disappeared inside the house again and the child opened her mouth to wail. Then her head shot round to face the other direction. She'd heard something.

Millie got up and set off along the rough ground, almost to the wall that bordered the property. She stopped when she was only a few inches away and looked up. A yew tree, possibly several hundred years old, grew in the churchyard so close to the wall as to be almost part of it. Millie looked up.

'Lo,' she said. 'Lo Ebba.'

14

24 September

SHE WAS TALLER THAN HE REMEMBERED, BUT EVERY BIT AS slender. She had a bridle and reins slung round her shoulders as she appeared from the horse-box. She slid her right arm under the saddle that hung waiting on a large hook and then set off down the yard. Her left arm gripped a heavy-duty steel-and-plastic walking stick as she made her slow, ungainly way across the concrete.

Harry remained still, half hidden by the low branches of a huge walnut tree, watching her limp towards the tack room. She pushed the door with her shoulder and, rather awkwardly, disappeared inside.

Was this really a good idea? It was months since he'd asked a woman out. And why on earth had he picked one he knew absolutely nothing about?

Except he did know one or two things, didn't he? Like the fact that the sciatic nerve was the longest and widest single nerve in the body, starting in the lower back and running down through the buttock and the leg. He knew that it fed the skin of the leg and also the muscles of the back of the thigh, lower leg and foot. The day he'd met Dr Oliver – Evi, he now knew she was called – he'd sat at his computer after dinner and started searching. Ten minutes later, he'd felt like he was prying.

The door to the tack room was opening and she was coming out. No longer loaded down with tack, she walked more easily, but still with a pronounced, rolling limp.

She saw him before he had a chance to move and stopped walking. Was that good or bad? Then she reached up to unfasten and remove her hat. Good? She carried on towards him and that twitch on her face could be a smile or it could be a grimace of embarrassment. Difficult to be sure and no time to make up his mind because she was feet away and he really had to say—

'Hello.' She'd got there first. *Hello* was OK, wasn't it? Better than *What the hell are you doing here?*

'Hi. Good ride?' *Good ride!* Was that really the best he could do?

'Bracing, thanks. What are you doing here?'

He pulled his right hand out of his pocket. Ten seconds into the conversation and he was already employing Plan B.

'Is this yours?' he asked, as the tiny silver bracelet with blue stones caught the light. She didn't move to take it.

'Nope,' she said, shaking her head. The hair around her temples was damp with sweat, flattened against her head by the pressure of the riding hat. She put a hand up to it and then brought it back down again. Her face was pink; five days ago it had been pale with shock.

'Did you find it on the road?' she asked.

'No. I bought it on Rawtenstall market a couple of days ago,' he confessed. Well, that was a bit high risk but it might just have paid off. The twitch around her mouth had widened, might even be verging on a smile.

'That was a bit rash,' she said. 'I don't think it's your colour.'

'You're right, I'm more of a soft-lemony man, but I needed an excuse.'

Yes, definitely a smile. 'What for?' she said.

'I was worried about Duchess.'

'Duchess?' Lips pulled straight again. Eyebrows raised. Eyes still smiling.

'Yes, how is she?' He turned to the box where the grey cob stood watching them and took a few paces towards her. 'This is her, right?'

She was following him. He could hear the clatter of the stick on the concrete. 'This is Duchess,' she confirmed. 'None the worse for

78

her adventure at the weekend. Which I haven't mentioned to anyone here, by the way.'

'My lips are sealed. How does she feel about Polo mints?'

She was standing at his side now, inches away. 'She'll bite your hand off,' she said.

Harry felt in his pocket again and brought out the thin green tube that he'd also bought at the market. In her box, Duchess whickered at him. Two boxes further down a horse began kicking against its door.

'You've done it now,' said Evi. 'Horses can smell Polo mints through the wrapper. And they recognize the paper.'

'At least someone's pleased to see me,' said Harry, unwrapping the tube and holding out the flat of his hand to Duchess. A split-second later the mint had been replaced by a good dollop of horse slobber. Now what, exactly, was he supposed to do with that? Wiping it down his jeans was not going to look good.

'I should sit down,' said Evi. 'Is that OK?'

'Of course,' said Harry, wiggling his fingers to dry them off. 'Do you need any help?'

'No,' she said. 'I just can't stand up for any length of time.' She moved the stick and set off across the yard, back to the walnut tree, under which a few plastic chairs were scattered. Harry followed close behind and held a chair-back steady while she lowered herself. He pulled up a second chair and sat beside her. Duchess's drool was starting to dry on his hand.

In the manège in front of them a rider was schooling a young horse, the same colour as Duchess but altogether finer of build. The school was surrounded by a beech hedge and the leaves were already starting to turn the soft golden-brown of newly minted coins.

'Beautiful evening,' said Harry, watching the setting sun bounce off the beech hedge and throw gold reflections on to the horse's coat. It looked like it was wearing chain-mail.

'How did you know I was here?' asked Evi.

'I've been coming every night on the off-chance,' replied Harry. The horse almost seemed to be trotting on the spot, its head tucked down so that its nose was pointing at the ground. Foam was gathering around its mouth. 'Is that horse a thoroughbred?' he asked.

'He's from Ireland,' said Evi. 'Quite beautiful, but far too young and skittish for me to be allowed anywhere near. And seriously?'

She was looking at him now, not at the beautiful young horse. Her eyes were as blue as he remembered. 'Seriously,' he said, 'I phoned the yard on Monday and asked to speak to Dr Oliver. I insisted Monday was the night you came. I mentioned Duchess and asked how she was recovering from her bruised foot and said it was really important I talk to you and were they sure you weren't there because I was certain you'd said Monday. After a few minutes of this, they looked you up in the book and told me that Dr Oliver, also known as Evi, rides on Thursdays, Saturdays and sometimes Sundays.'

Evi turned back to the manège. She had the most perfect profile. Forehead just the right length, small, straight nose, full lips, plump chin. 'That's very devious behavior for a man of God,' she said at last.

Harry laughed. 'You've obviously never heard of the Jesuits. Would it be inappropriate to ask you out for a drink?'

Clearly it would, because she wasn't smiling any more. 'Sorry,' he said. 'If you have a husband or long-term boyfriend or you just can't stand men with ginger hair then obviously I'm completely out of order and I'll – well, maybe Duchess is free on Friday night. I'll go and see.'

He half stood. He'd misjudged the entire situation and now he had to make as dignified an exit as possible.

She put a hand on his arm. 'I'm on very strong painkillers,' she said. 'All the time. I'm not supposed to drink alcohol.'

Somehow, that didn't feel like an out-and-out no. 'Well, that's fine because I'm a man of the cloth,' he said, sitting down again. 'We're not allowed to get wasted every night, so you'd be good for me. They're running a season of Christopher Lee movies in Rawtenstall. Do you like horror films?'

'Not really.' The hand fell away from his arm, but that smile was definitely back.

He shook his head. 'Me neither. Too easily scared. How do you feel about romantic comedies?'

'I'm starting to think I might be in one. Aren't vicars supposed to be celibate?'

'That's Catholic priests,' he said, managing to keep a straight face. 'Sex is definitely allowed in the Anglican church,' he went on, as she turned from him and he could see the skin of her neck start to glow. 'The guidelines say we should usually take a woman out a couple of times first. You know, for a movie, or a pizza, but I suppose I could be flexible.'

She was bright pink now and staring straight ahead as though the grey horse in the school was about to do something spectacular. 'Do shut up,' she snapped.

'Well, I would, but you haven't said yes yet and it's difficult to do this in sign language.'

She was facing him again, trying to be serious, not quite managing it. 'I called you an asshole the other day,' she said.

'Very perceptive. I like that in a woman.'

She dropped her head and looked at him sideways. It was a surprisingly childlike gesture for a woman who must be in her early thirties. 'I'm sorry I was a bitch,' she said. 'But I was on my backside in the middle of the road with limbs all over the place and . . .'

'It was a good look for you – sorry, didn't quite mean that the way it sounded – I'll shut up. Maybe I should ask Duchess out.'

'I think they'll excommunicate you for that.'

'No, that's allowed too. It's more common than you might think.'

She started to laugh, a soft, almost soundless mirth that shook her shoulders and made her breasts bounce inside her shirt. He was staring again. He leaned back in his chair and looked up. A small flock of starlings was moving across the sky. As one, the birds changed direction and, for a split-second, formed what could almost be a heart-shape in the air before switching again and heading away from them.

'I'm not a churchgoer,' she said after a moment.

Harry shrugged. 'Nobody's perfect.'

'I'm serious.' She was too. She'd stopped smiling. 'I really don't believe in God,' she went on. 'Won't that be a problem? While we're watching this romantic comedy or eating pizza or whatever?'

'I'll do you a deal, Evi,' he said, knowing that, in truth, the deal was all but done and all he had to do was close it.

'Another one?' she asked.

'The first one worked out OK. I got you back on the horse and you were still speaking to me. So the new deal is, I won't try and convert you. You don't try and analyse me.'

'How did you know?' she asked. 'How did you know what my name is and what I do?'

Harry pointed at the sky. The starlings were still there, hovering overhead, as though they knew what was happening on the ground and were hanging around to see the outcome. 'All-knowing-one on speed-dial,' he said. 'How about Friday?'

She didn't even pretend to think about it. 'OK, that would be – bugger, I mean, sorry – I have to work. I'm seeing a family in Oldham at their house. I won't be back till late.'

'Well, Saturday then – oh no, sorry, I mean bugger – I have this church thing. Heptonclough – where we met, you'll remember – are having their annual harvest shindig. You know the sort of thing, ceremonial cutting of the last wheat, dancing around naked as the sun goes down and then the harvest feast in one of the big houses.'

'Sounds a riot.'

'Well, quite. They've asked me to read a traditional prayer over the crop and say grace at the dinner. I'm invited to bring a guest, but maybe . . .' Harry stopped. Taking a date to his first official function? Was that really a good idea?

'I think it could be fun,' said Evi. 'And I'd get to see you in action.'

Harry realized he really didn't want his first date with Evi to go wrong. He gestured at his clothes. 'I'd be wearing the, you know, the regalia – dog collar, ceremonial robes. At least till after the formal stuff.'

'Can't wait.' The starlings were starting to move off, twisting back in their direction every couple of seconds, as if to check it was all still going well. And it was going well. Except he might just have messed it up.

'Now you're starting to sound kinky,' he said.

'Says the man who wants to date my horse.'

'Saturday then. Can I walk you to your car?'

She pushed herself upright. 'Thanks,' she said. 'It's next to that flashy blue thing with the soft top and all the chrome.'

15

25 September

'YOU LOOK MUCH BETTER, GILLIAN,' SAID EVI. 'I'D HARDLY have known you.'

'Thank you. I do feel better.'

Gillian's hair was freshly washed, her clothes seemed cleaner. There was even a touch of make-up around those strange, silver-grey eyes. It was possible to see, this morning, the attractive girl she'd been before her life had fallen apart.

'And you're still getting on all right with the medication?' Evi asked.

Gillian nodded. 'It's amazing, the difference it makes,' she said. Then her face darkened. 'I spoke to my mum about what you'd given me and she said I'd become addicted. That I'd have to take pills for the rest of my life.'

Well-meaning relatives with fixed views didn't always help.

'Don't worry about that,' said Evi, shaking her head. 'Addiction is always a risk but it's one we're very careful to guard against. The medicines I've given you are a temporary measure. I'll be aiming to wean you off them gradually, once we both think you can cope without them. How are you finding the AA meetings?'

Another nod. 'They're nice. Nice people. I haven't had a drink in fourteen days.'

'That's brilliant, Gillian, well done.'

Astonishing, the difference in the girl. Four weeks ago, Gillian had barely been able to string a sentence together.

'Can we talk about what you've been doing over the week,' suggested Evi. 'Have you been eating?'

'I'm trying, but . . . it's funny, Pete used to tease me about putting weight on. Now, I'm a size zero and his new girlfriend's getting fatter by the week.'

Getting conscious about her body size again. Using a modelling term – size zero – and secretly proud of it.

'Are you still in touch with Pete?' asked Evi. The subject of Gillian's ex-husband had come up briefly in two of their previous appointments. Both times, Gillian had been reluctant to discuss him and Evi hadn't been able to help thinking there was a lot of suppressed anger getting in the way of her recovery. Now, just at the mention of the man's name, Gillian's lips had all but disappeared and a small muscle beneath her left eye was twitching.

'Are you angry with him?' asked Evi, when Gillian showed no sign of responding. 'For leaving when you were grieving?'

Gillian's eyes narrowed. 'He was having an affair,' she said, looking over Evi's shoulder to the window. 'Before the fire. He was already seeing her, the woman he's with now.'

She'd thought there was something. 'I'm sorry, I didn't know,' said Evi. 'How did you find out?'

Gillian looked down at the carpet. 'Someone told me,' she said. 'A friend of mine. She'd seen them in the pub together. But I knew anyway. You always know, don't you?'

'But you were out together, the night of the fire. Maybe it wasn't too serious, this thing with . . .'

'We weren't out together,' interrupted Gillian. 'He was with her. He'd left me on my own with Hayley. Again. So I phoned Barry Robinson and asked him to babysit. Then I caught the bus into town. I was spying on my cheating husband when my baby was burning to death.'

That certainly explained a lot. No wonder the girl felt guilty. Even less wonder her husband had left. The two of them would barely have been able to look at each other without feeling overwhelmed with guilt.

'Do you still have feelings for Pete?' asked Evi.

'He's a cheating bastard,' said Gillian. 'My stepdad was the same. Most of them are. Out for what they can get and they don't care who with.'

Alarm bells were ringing in Evi's head. 'You didn't get on with your stepfather?' she asked. Gillian's stepfather had cheated? With whom?

Gillian was still looking at the floor. Her lips had tightened. She had the look of a teenager in trouble for staying out too late.

'Do you blame Pete for Hayley's death?' Evi tried again, when she realized Gillian wasn't going to talk about her stepfather. No answer. 'Are you angry with him for maybe not grieving as much as you?'

At last Gillian looked up. 'Hayley's death destroyed Pete,' she said. 'He adored her. Afterwards, he couldn't bring himself to look at me because I reminded him of her.'

'Grief often breaks up marriages,' said Evi. 'Sometimes the pain is so intense that the only way people can move on is by making a clean break.'

'Do you think I'll ever meet anyone else?' Gillian asked after a moment.

'Do you mean a man?' inquired Evi, surprised. 'A boyfriend?'

'Yes. Is it possible, do you think, to find someone that I have feelings for? Who might, you know, look after me.'

Had she met someone already? It might account for the clean hair and clothes, for the interest in the future. Someone at the AA meetings?

'I think it's quite likely you will,' said Evi. 'You're still young and you're very pretty. But relationships take a lot of emotional energy. We need to concentrate on getting you strong again.'

'I'd look for someone different to Pete, next time,' said Gillian. 'Maybe someone older. I wouldn't worry so much about how he looked. Just so long as he was nice.'

This girl wasn't looking; she thought she'd already found him.

'Nice is a good quality in a man,' said Evi. 'How are you finding the other people at the AA meetings?'

'They're OK. Is it too soon, do you think, for me to have met someone?'

'Have you met someone?' asked Evi.

The girl was actually blushing. 'No,' she said. 'Maybe. You'd think I was mad if I told you.'

'Why would I think you mad?'

'Well, it's like, he's so not my type. He was just really nice. And then, the next day, he came to see me. He stayed for nearly two hours, just chatting. There was, like, a chemistry, do you know what I'm saying?'

Evi was starting to smile too, in spite of her reservations. 'Yes,' she said, 'I know about chemistry.'

All the textbooks would say the girl wasn't ready for a new relationship but, hey, sometimes you just had to go with the flow. And she knew something herself about the difference a chance meeting could make to a life. How suddenly the darkness that was a woman's future could let in a beam of sunlight.

'But Christ, I mean, a vicar. It's just so not me.'

'A what?'

'He's a vicar. Can you believe it? I'd have to stop swearing, for one thing. And church every week. I'm not sure I could hack it.'

Evi's smile was starting to hurt. She allowed the muscles around her mouth to relax and concentrated on keeping her expression interested and friendly. 'You've met a vicar?' she asked.

'I know, I know. But there was just something about him. And he's young and he wears normal clothes and, actually, I think you might know him, I saw you . . .'

Gillian was gabbling on and Evi was no longer listening. Oh yes, there was something about him all right.

'We're going to have to stop now, Gillian,' she said, although there were still four minutes to go on the clock. 'I'm delighted to see how well you're doing.'

Gillian left the room smiling. A few weeks ago her life had been in tatters. Now she was smiling. Evi picked up the phone. Was there any possible way? None that she could see. She dialled a number and thanked the God she didn't believe in when she got Harry's answer machine.

16

26 September

AAAH-LAY-OH!

The cry came echoing up the street. A man's voice, loud and strong. A second later lots of voices answered him. Aah-lay-oh, aah-lay-oh, aah-lay-oh!

Silence. Joe looked at his brother, his eyes round as saucers. Tom gave a little shrug and tried to look as if he'd heard it all before.

Aaah-lay-oh! One voice again, coming from somewhere down the hill. Two beats of silence and then the cry struck up again. Aaay-lay-oh, aah-lay-oh, getting louder and faster like a drumbeat. It sounded as though a hundred men were just around the corner.

And then, just when Tom thought they couldn't possibly get any louder, it all stopped. There was a second of peace and then an almighty crash of metal against stone. Then another and another. Crash! Crash! Footsteps coming up the hill. Tom moved a little closer to his dad, just a small step, too tiny for anyone to notice.

The Fletchers were standing in the driveway and it was seven o'clock in the evening. It was Joe and Millie's bedtime, not far off Tom's, but tonight was the Cutting of the Neck. A very old ritual, Mr Renshaw had explained when he'd come round to invite the Fletchers, one that dated back hundreds of years. The Cutting of the Neck. At the time it had sounded cool, and Tom could tell his mum was pleased to be asked. But listening to those footsteps and that horrible scraping of sharp metal against rock, like knives being sharpened, he couldn't help but think: whose neck?

He shivered and took another step closer to his dad. At his side, Joe did the same. The sun had gone now and so had the lovely golden light that had covered the countryside an hour earlier. The sky was a cool silvery pink and, on the ground, the shadows were getting longer.

Further up the hill in the middle of the lane Tom could see Mr Renshaw in a tweed jacket and flat cap. By his side was old Mr Tobias, who'd been to visit a few times and who loved to talk to Mum about painting. Mr Tobias looked exactly like his son, just much older. Actually, they were a bit like the two churches: one tall, strong and proud, the other just the same but so very old. Then there was a woman who was also tall and smartly dressed and who looked like the two men. She wasn't so old, though, and there was something about her face that seemed to Tom sort of empty.

Next to her was Harry, looking just like a vicar, in white robes embroidered with gold and holding a large red prayer-book. Behind them stood a whole crowd, all well dressed, mainly women and girls. He hadn't known so many people lived in Heptonclough. They stood in doorways, at the entrances to alleys, leaned against the church wall or out of open windows. Tom realized he was scanning faces, looking for one that was pale, with large dark eyes, framed by long, dirty hair.

By this time, the sound of dozens of boots thudding against cobbles could be heard. And that horrible scraping noise. Over and over again, like fingernails drawn down a blackboard, like violins tuning up in a bad school orchestra, like . . .

Scythes!

The men were coming now, round the corner, heading up the hill towards them, and each was carrying a scythe: a horribly sharp, curved blade like a pirate's scimitar on the end of a long pole. As they walked, they scraped the blades against the cobbles and the stone walls.

'Oh my,' said Alice. 'Stand back, everyone.'

Tom knew she was joking, but he stood back all the same, right on to his dad's foot. Gareth Fletcher groaned and nudged his son forwards again. The leaders reached Mr Renshaw and the others at the church gate and the procession stopped. One man at the front, who Tom thought was Dick Grimes, the butcher, gave a loud cry and every man in the crowd lifted his scythe high on to his shoulders. Then total silence. Mr Renshaw gave Harry a small nod.

'Let us pray,' announced Harry and everyone bowed their heads. Joe leaned closer to his brother. 'Do you think he's got shorts on under that dress?' he whispered.

'O God, who dost shower upon us the abundance of thy mercy,' read Harry, 'and who dost cast upon the seed in the ground both the heat of the sun and the moisture of the rain . . .'

'What's he saying?' whispered Joe in Tom's ear.

'He's thanking God for making the crops grow,' Tom hissed back.

As Harry was talking, Tom caught sight of Gillian, the woman his mother felt sorry for, standing a little way down the street at the entrance to Wite Lane. Tom couldn't help it, but Gillian always made him feel uncomfortable. She was too sad. And she had a way of looking at him, Joe and Millie that made him squirm. Especially Millie. For some reason, Gillian seemed fascinated by Millie. She wasn't looking at her now, though, she was watching Harry.

'We thank thee for these great blessings,' he was saying. 'Through Jesus Christ our Lord. Amen.'

'Amen,' shouted the men with scythes and their families who'd followed them.

'Amen,' said Joe, a second after everyone else.

'Men,' said Millie from high up on her father's shoulders.

Sinclair Renshaw nodded his thanks to the vicar and then set off down the hill. The men followed him and then everyone turned into Wite Lane, heading for the fields at the bottom. Harry fell into line and, almost at the back, so did the Fletchers.

They walked along the lane and Tom had time to notice that the blackberries were getting ripe, that rosehips and hawthorn berries were glistening and that the sky ahead of them was the colour of ripe barley.

'All right Gareth?' said a man who had caught up with Tom's father. It was Mike Pickup, who lived with his wife Jenny at Morrell Farm, right up on the top of the moor. 'Nice evening for it.'

'Evening, Mike,' Gareth replied.

Mike Pickup looked a little older than Tom's dad and quite a bit fatter. The hair on his head was thinning and his cheeks were bright red. He was dressed in tweeds like the two Mr Renshaws.

At the gate of Gillian's old house Tom and his family had to step sideways to avoid horse droppings and then they carried on, through a stile and into a field. They crossed the field like a fat crocodile, heading uphill, only stopping when they reached the centre. Tom watched the men form a large circle, standing several feet apart. The others formed a larger circle around the outside. Still no sign of the odd little girl. If the whole town was here, where was she?

'I think we're going to dance,' whispered Tom's mum. His dad frowned at her to be quiet.

The Fletchers could just about see Sinclair Renshaw, standing alone in the centre of the circle. At his side, a tiny patch of the crop hadn't yet been harvested. Dick Grimes walked forward and gave Sinclair a scythe.

'Is that hay?' asked Gareth, quietly.

'Aye,' replied Mike. 'Animal feed. Only thing that'll grow this high up. Rest of the field was cut two weeks ago. We harvest by the waning moon. Always have done.'

Tom glanced up and saw the pale moon just appearing on the horizon. 'It's full,' he said.

Mike Pickup shook his head. 'Full ten hours ago,' he said. 'On the wane now. Hush.'

They hushed. In the centre of the circle Mr Renshaw took hold of the last few handfuls of hay, twisted them round in his hand and pulled them tight. He raised the scythe high above his head.

'I hav'n!' he cried, in a voice so loud Tom thought they could probably hear it on the waning moon. 'I hav'n!' he repeated. 'I hav'n!' he called for a third time.

'What havee?' yelled the men in response.

'A neck,' called Sinclair. Then his scythe flashed down so fast Tom didn't see it move, the last of the hay was cut and every man, woman and child in the field was cheering. Mum, Dad and even Millie were clapping politely. Tom and Joe looked at each other.

Then the women were scurrying around like field-mice, gathering up every last bit of hay that had been missed in the previous cutting. The men were crowding round Mr Renshaw, shaking him by the hand as if he'd done something amazing, and then turning to file out of the field. Tom watched Harry help Gillian over the stile and then the two of them walked back down Wite Lane. At the gate of her former house they stopped and stood talking together.

'When does he cut the neck?' said Joe at Tom's side.

'I think that was the neck,' said Tom. 'I think neck means last bit of the crop.'

For a second Joe looked disappointed. Then he shook his head and, when he spoke, his voice sounded older.

'I think there's more to it than that,' he said.

17

HARRY FOLLOWED THE MEN AHEAD OF HIM THROUGH A high stone archway and down a narrow cobbled alley that ran along the lower end of the churchyard. To his left were the medieval buildings of the old abbot's residence and the monks' quarters, on his right the high iron railings that topped this part of the church wall. It was the first time he'd approached the Renshaw residence; his previous meetings with his churchwarden had been in St Barnabas's vestry or the White Lion.

Unlike much of the rest of the town, the stone of the Abbot's House had been kept clean and was the pale colour of powdered ginger. Giant urns filled with wheat, barley and wild flowers stood to either side of the front door. The door had been carved with leaves and roses and looked as old as the rest of the house. It wasn't open and the men ahead walked past. They carried on, past candle-lanterns that would guide them home after dark.

High on the wall a black cat sat watching them go by and Harry had a moment to wonder if it was the same cat he and Evi had seen a week ago. The Abbot's House was huge, stretching nearly a hundred feet along the alley. Just ahead, another door lay open and the men were turning into it. Harry followed them into a large hall with high narrow windows. Trestle tables, piled high with food, had been placed down the centre, and at the far end a pulpit-like structure of almost black wood stood against the wall.

'I'll need to see the soles of your feet, Vicar,' said a well-spoken, elderly voice at his side. Harry turned to see Sinclair's father, Tobias, the oldest man in the town and, if rumour were true, the cleverest.

'Mr Renshaw,' he said, holding out his hand. 'I'm Harry Laycock. Good to meet you.'

'Likewise.' They shook hands. The men who had entered the hall first were hanging their scythes around the wall. Everywhere Harry looked, hooks were fixed into the stonework. More men squeezed in behind him. Women and girls carrying loose ears of wheat were beginning to arrive.

'And what was that about my feet?' asked Harry.

'A tradition.' Tobias smiled.

'Another one?' There wasn't really room for a conversation in the doorway. Harry had to stand very close to Tobias. He would have been as tall as his son when younger. Even now, he was almost Harry's height.

'Oh, we have plenty of traditions,' replied the older man. 'This is one of our least disturbing. I advise you to go along, save your resistance for when you really need it. You, being a newcomer to the town, give me your foot – this charming young lady will help you balance, I'm sure – and I scrape the sole of your shoe with the welcome stone. It's a religious tradition, started by the monks in the twelfth century. Far be it from you to turn your back on history.'

'Far be it indeed,' said Harry. 'And what were you saying about a charming young – oh, hello again, Gillian. Actually I think I'm OK – so, how do I do this, facing you like a can-can girl or with my back turned like a horse being shod?'

'What kinky jinxes are these?' asked Alice, appearing in the doorway with Millie on her hip. The two boys followed behind. 'Move along, Vicar,' she said. 'There's a queue.'

'The queue will have to wait, Alice,' said Tobias. 'You're next. And then your beautiful daughter. Good evening, my dear.' He reached out and ran long, brown fingers over Millie's hair.

'Just go with it, Vicar,' said another female voice, as Harry turned to see Jenny Pickup squeezing past them into the hall. 'The first time you come to the harvest feast you have your shoe scraped with a bit of old rock. My grandfather's been doing this for sixty years, he's not going to stop now.'

'Fine by me,' said Alice. With Millie still hanging on one hip, she lifted her right leg until it made a perfect right angle with her left. Her foot was directly in front of Tobias. He caught hold of her ankle in one hand and with the other rubbed a smooth stone the size of a mango across the sole of her foot.

'Impressive,' said Harry, as Alice put her foot down without so much as a wobble.

'Fifteen years of ballet classes,' said Alice. 'Your turn.'

Harry shrugged at Tom and Joe, grasped Tom's shoulder for balance and offered his foot to Tobias. A few seconds later, Tom, Joe, Millie and Gareth Fletcher had all been foot-scraped and the Fletchers and Harry moved into the hall.

'It's like an armoury,' said Gareth, looking round as the weapons count on the walls increased with every new arrival. High above the scythes hung shotguns and rifles. Some of them looked antique, collectors' items. Others didn't.

'Cool,' said Joe. 'Daddy, can I—'

'No,' said Alice.

'This was the refectory where the monks used to eat in the old days,' said Jenny, who'd stayed with them. She was wearing a long-sleeved, tight-fitting black dress. Somehow, it didn't suit her as much as the casual clothes she'd worn the day she and Harry had met. 'When my dad was young it was the grammar school.' She pointed to the carved pulpit. 'That's the old schoolmaster's chair,' she said, before turning to Harry. 'These days we just use this room for parties. Good to see you with your clothes on, Vicar.'

Harry opened his mouth with no clear idea of what he was going to say.

'What's that lady doing?' asked Tom.

At the far end of the hall the woman who'd been standing with Sinclair and Tobias earlier had climbed the steps to the old school-master's seat and was intent upon something on her lap. Around her, women were putting the stalks of straw they'd picked up from the field into large water-filled tubs.

'That's my sister, Christiana,' replied Jenny. 'Every year she's the harvest queen. It's her job to make the corn dolly.'

'What's a corn dolly?' asked Joe.

'It's an old farming tradition,' explained Jenny. 'In the old days, before we all became Christians, people believed the spirit of the

94

land lived in the crop and that, when it was harvested, the spirit became homeless. So with the last few ears of whatever crop it was, they made the corn dolly – a sort of temporary home for the spirit over the winter. In the spring, it got ploughed back into the land. I used to be jealous of Christiana when I was a kid and begged Dad to let me be queen just once. He always said if I could ever make a corn dolly like Christiana then I would be.'

'So did you?' asked Tom.

'No, it's bloody impossible – 'scuse me, Vicar. I don't know how she does it. She'll have finished it by the end of the evening. Now then, let's have a drink.'

Harry found himself being steered, along with the adult Fletchers, towards the drinks table. Around them, the hall was filling up and people were starting to spill out through a pair of wooden doors into the large walled garden beyond. Harry could see the deep turquoise blue of the evening sky and fruit trees hung with lanterns. A four-piece fiddle-and-pipe band was getting ready to play.

Along one wall had been fastened museum-style glass cases and their contents had attracted the attention of the Fletcher boys and their father. Harry joined them. The cases showed archaeological artefacts that had been discovered on the moors and preserved by the Renshaw family in their own private museum. There were flint tools from the Neolithic period, Bronze Age weapons, Roman jewellery, even a human bone or two.

He wasn't able to look for long before his attention was claimed. Over and over again, people introduced themselves to him, until he lost all hope of remembering names.

After an hour or so it seemed he'd met everyone. The hall was getting hot and he set off for the garden doors, only to pause when he saw the Fletcher boys and a few of the village children gathered around the harvest queen on her schoolmaster's throne. Over their heads he watched the quick, skilled fingers of Sinclair's eldest daughter.

She was a big woman, almost six feet tall and with a large frame. She'd be in her late thirties, he guessed, maybe early forties. Her hair was a thick dark brown and her skin was largely unlined. She would have been a good-looking woman, had there been some spark of intelligence behind those large brown eyes, had her mouth not hung open, as though she'd forgotten the norm was to keep it closed.

Maybe she had. Maybe every ounce of thought in her head was concentrated upon her hands. They were moving at an incredible speed. Binding, twisting, plaiting, over and over again her fingers twitched as the last of the hay, soaked and made supple now, was manipulated into shape. Her eyes were fixed straight ahead, not once did she look down at her work, but in the short time she'd been in her chair, a loop of about six inches long had been formed and she was now fastening long straws, twisting and weaving them into place.

'It's a Pennine spiral,' said a voice. Harry and the boys turned at the same moment to see that Tobias Renshaw had joined them. 'Corn dollies are traditional all over the UK,' the older man went on, 'but each region tends to have its own particular design. The spiral is considered one of the most difficult to craft. My granddaughter's brains all went into her fingers.'

Harry looked quickly at Christiana; her face twisted for a second but her gaze didn't falter. Neither did her hands.

'She looks like she's concentrating hard,' said Harry. 'Does she mind being watched?'

'Christiana lives in her own world,' said the old man. 'I doubt she knows we're here.'

Harry saw Christiana dart a quick look at her grandfather. He put his hands on the Fletcher boys' shoulders. 'Come on, you two,' he said, 'Let's leave Miss Renshaw in peace. We can admire her work later.'

He turned, about to guide the boys out into the garden to find their parents. Tobias stopped him with a hand against his chest.

'I think you must despise our traditions, Vicar,' he said. The pressure of his hand felt surprisingly strong for so elderly a man and Harry fought a temptation to push it away.

'Not at all,' he replied. 'Rituals are very important to people. The church is awash with them.'

'Quite so,' said Tobias, in his low, cultured voice, allowing his hand to fall. 'Events like this one hold communities together. Very few of the men here tonight work on the land any more – they have jobs in the nearby towns, maybe they're self-employed and work from home, some of them have no jobs. But the Cutting of the Neck is something they all take part in because their fathers and their grandfathers did. Through it, and other traditions like it, they feel a connection to the land. Can you understand that?'

'I was brought up in the rough end of Newcastle,' said Harry. 'We didn't see much of the land.'

'Everything you will eat tonight was grown or bred within five miles of this spot,' said Tobias. 'All the game I shot myself, although my eyesight isn't what it was. Ninety per cent of what I've eaten my entire life comes from this moor. Quite a number of people in town can say the same. The Renshaws have been self-sufficient for hundreds of years.'

'You're not fond of fish, then?' said Harry.

Tobias's eyebrows lifted. 'On the contrary, we own a trout stream at the bottom of the valley.' He gestured towards the buffet table. 'I recommend the trout pâté.'

'I look forward to it. Hi Gillian, did you need me?'

'I'll keep you just a moment longer, Vicar. Excuse us, my dear, won't you?' said Tobias. 'Run along, boys, I need a private word with Reverend Laycock.' Without waiting to be told twice, Tom and Joe scurried across the hall towards the weapons cases. Gillian moved away to the other side of the hall, but Harry could feel that she was still watching them.

'There is another town tradition you should know about, Vicar,' said Tobias. 'Again, you'll find variations all around England. A few weeks after the harvest, typically in the days leading up to Old Winter's Day in mid October, we slaughter the livestock that won't be needed next spring. Mainly surplus sheep and pigs, some chickens, occasionally a cow. In the old days the meat would be preserved to take us through the winter. These days we just fill our freezers.'

'Sounds sensible enough. Do you want some prayers to send the animals on their way to the abattoir?'

'You misunderstand, Vicar,' said Tobias. 'Your services won't be required and the animals are sent nowhere. We slaughter them here.'

'Here in town?'

'Yes. Dick Grimes and my son hold all the necessary licences between them. Dick has the facilities at the back of his shop. I only mention it because the Fletcher family live just across the road and will hear something of what's going on. A lot of the men are involved. The street outside gets – how shall I put this? – a little messy. We call it the Blood Harvest.'

'The what?'

'You heard me correctly. I'm happy to talk to the Fletchers myself, of course, but I just thought, as you seem to have something of a rapport with them, it might come better from you. If they were to visit relatives for the weekend, that might not be a bad thing.'

A few feet beyond the door to the party room, Millie sat on the floor. Oblivious to the feet and legs around her, she was stroking a cat. Her fat little hand ran down its fur, from head to tail-tip. The tail twitched. Millie caught it and squeezed. The cat jumped to its feet and stepped daintily away.

Millie looked round. One of her brothers, the one she called Doe, was very close by, looking at some weapons in a glass case. He didn't turn around as Millie pushed herself to her feet and toddled after the cat. First the cat, then Millie, stepped out of the party room and into the alley outside. No one noticed them leave.

'There you are, Harry. You seem quiet tonight. Is everything OK?'

Alice had found him at the bottom of the walled garden, on a wicker bench surrounded by old roses, nursing an empty glass.

'I'm fine,' he said, moving sideways on the bench to give her room to sit down. 'Just recharging the batteries. People rarely just chat to the vicar, you know. They always expect something more. A bit of spiritual guidance over the sherry. Maybe a discussion on where the Church of England's going. Get's a bit tiring after a while.'

Alice settled herself down next to him. He could smell the perfume she always wore. Something very light and sweet, rather old-fashioned. 'I could barely see you sitting here,' she said. 'What happened to the robes?'

Harry had taken off his robes and collar at the first chance he'd had. 'Too hot,' he said. 'And far too distinctive. I needed to blend into the background for a while.'

Alice let her head fall on to one side. It felt like a very familiar gesture, although he didn't think he'd seen her make it before. 'Did someone upset you?' she asked.

He looked at her properly, tempted to tell her about his chat with Tobias, then decided against it. Why ruin her evening too? She was looking happier tonight than he'd seen her since they'd met. He'd have a quiet word with Gareth later in the week.

'I had a date tonight,' he said, surprising himself. 'She blew me out.'

Alice's small face lit up. 'A date? How exciting.'

Harry held up both hands. 'And yet not, as it turns out.'

'I'm sorry.' Alice touched his arm briefly. 'Did she give you a reason?'

'She just left a message on my answer machine. She said work was piling up. Hoped we could get together in a couple of weeks or so if things calmed down. Didn't sound hopeful.'

'Bad luck,' said Alice after a second. 'Want another drink?'

'If I have another drink I'll be spending the night in the vestry,' said Harry. 'But we should get back to the party. Come on.'

Harry and Alice stood up and walked back through the apple trees towards the house. When they were once again approaching the crowd of people Harry became aware of urgent movement, of someone pushing their way though the throng. A second later Gareth Fletcher appeared, holding Tom's hand tightly.

'We can't find Joe and Millie,' he said. 'We've looked everywhere. They've vanished.'

Part Two
Blood Harvest

18

AS HARRY AND TOM MADE THEIR WAY THROUGH THE HALL, Sinclair Renshaw appeared in front of them.

'What's happened, Vicar?' he asked.

'The two youngest Fletcher children are missing,' replied Harry hurriedly.

'The little girl?' interrupted Sinclair, speaking softly, in spite of the music and noise in the hall.

'Yes, and her brother. Their parents have gone home to see if they've made their way there. Tom and I are—'

'One second.' Sinclair turned to look round the room. 'Father!' he called. Then he took hold of Tom's arm and steered him over to the older man. Tom could hear Harry following, but when he glanced back, he could tell the vicar wasn't happy. Harry had been told to watch Tom and look outside, and that's what he wanted to do. It was what Tom wanted to do too – look for Joe and Millie and stay very close to a grown-up he could trust.

'Father.' They'd reached the door to the alley. Outside it was too dark for Joe and Millie to be wandering around on their own. 'The youngest Fletcher child is missing,' explained Sinclair, still speaking in a low voice. 'The little girl.'

'And her brother,' insisted Harry.

'Yes, yes,' said Sinclair. 'Father, get Jenny and Christiana and search the house.' Then he lowered his voice even further. 'Lock the door,' he added.

Tobias nodded once and then made his way (quite quickly for so old a man) across the hall to where Christiana was still twisting straw. Sinclair turned back to Harry.

'How long has she – they – been missing? When and where were they last seen?'

Harry didn't know, of course, so he looked at Tom. Tom didn't know much either, and it was hard to think when the biggest man he'd ever seen was glaring down at him.

'In here,' he said. 'I was . . .' He stopped. He'd been told to keep an eye on his brother and sister while his dad fetched drinks. It was all his fault.

'What?' said Harry. 'It's important, Tom. What were you doing?'

'I was under the food table,' said Tom. 'Hiding from Jake Knowles.' He looked up at Harry, hoping he'd understand. Jake and two of his mates had come looking for him, his mum was nowhere in sight and his dad had been at the other side of the room, almost in the garden. Tom had ducked under the big white tablecloth and crawled to the other end. When he'd reached his dad, they'd crossed the room again to find Joe and Millie.

'We looked all round the room,' he said. 'And in the alley outside, and in the garden. They'd just vanished.'

As he was speaking, Tom saw Tobias Renshaw and his grand-daughter Christiana cross the room and disappear through a large wooden door.

Sinclair Renshaw continued to stare at Tom for a second, then he turned back to Harry. 'Keep the lad with you,' he said. 'I'll organize a search. We don't want everyone involved, it would be chaos. Leave it with me.'

He strode away. Harry and Tom looked at each other and headed for the open door, pushing past a woman wearing a bright-yellow sweater. Outside, the high walls seemed to make the alleyway even darker than they'd expected and Tom was grateful for the tiny lanterns on the wall.

'Your mum and dad would have gone that way,' said Harry, point-ing towards Tom's house. 'Let's go down here.'

Harry and Tom turned left and the sound of the party faded until they could hear nothing but their own footsteps. The spaces between the lanterns became wider and the alley darker. They turned a corner and reached a dead end.

'Joe and Millie couldn't have got over that,' said Tom, looking at the high stone wall in front of them.

'No,' agreed Harry. 'But they could have gone through here.'

Tom turned and felt as if his insides had fallen out. He could almost imagine he'd see them, if he looked down, lying splat on the ground. There was a tall iron gate in the churchyard wall. A padlock lay open on the ground in front of it. Beyond the gate he could see gravestones, shining like pearls in the moonlight.

Harry looked into the graveyard and then down at Tom. 'Tom, run back to the hall,' he said. 'I'll watch till I see you're safely back.'

'No, I want to stay with you,' said Tom, without thinking, because the truth was, he wanted to go into that graveyard like he wanted someone to poke a stick in his eye.

'Tom, it won't be very nice. Go back.'

It was a graveyard, for God's sake! And not just any old grave-yard, but the one at the back of their house where something decidedly odd liked to hang around. Of course it wasn't going to be nice. But Joe and Millie were in it. Somehow Tom knew it. They'd gone through this gate.

'I'm coming with you,' said Tom. 'We have to find them.'

Harry muttered something that, had he not been a vicar, would have sounded an awful lot like swearing and then picked up two of the candle-lanterns. He held one out to Tom. 'Hold this away from you,' he said. 'Hold it high.'

Tom did what he was told and then they were pushing at the gate and stepping into the churchyard.

It was so quiet, as though the world had had its volume turned down. Then Harry spoke and Tom couldn't stop himself from jumping.

'This would have been one of the monks' private entrances to the church in the old days,' he said. 'Now, we're going to walk slowly, we're going to keep to the path as much as possible and we're going to listen hard. Only I'm allowed to shout. Is that understood?'

'Yes,' whispered Tom and they set off.

They'd been walking for several minutes before Tom realized they were holding hands. And the silence felt unnatural. They should have been able to hear something, shouldn't they? Wind in the trees? Something? Tom could have almost imagined he'd gone deaf if it hadn't been for their footsteps on the path and the sound of Harry's breathing. Then Harry stopped and so did he.

'Joe!' called Harry. 'Millie!'

From somewhere nearby came a rustling sound and Harry's head shot round. 'Joe?' he called. They both waited. No one answered Harry and, after a second, he and Tom set off again.

'Tom!' called a tiny voice from a few yards further up the hill.

Harry stopped sharp. 'That was Joe,' he said. 'Where did it come from?' He let go of Tom's hand and began to turn on the spot, holding his lantern high. 'Joe!' he yelled, louder this time.

'Tom,' called the voice again.

'That was definitely Joe,' said Harry. 'Did you hear where it came from?' Harry was still turning this way and that, looking more like a gun-dog than a man, as though any second now he'd put his nose to the ground and start sniffing. Tom, on the other hand, hadn't moved.

'No, it wasn't,' he said.

'What?' muttered Harry.

'It wasn't Joe,' Tom repeated, looking back at the gate, trying to work out how far it was and if, once they started to run, Harry would leave him behind. 'Harry,' he went on, 'let's get out of here.'

Harry either didn't hear or decided to ignore Tom. He caught hold of his hand again and began to pull him away from the path and up the hill towards the Renshaw mausoleum. 'He's not far away,' he was saying. 'Stay with me, Tom. Watch where you're walking.'

Tom and Harry began to stumble across the uneven ground and soon their feet were soaked. Dew had already formed on the long grass and was gleaming silver where the moonlight touched it. The cold softness brushed Tom's legs and headstones leered up at them. They didn't look like pearls any more; they looked like teeth.

Tom fixed his eyes on the ground and concentrated on staying on his feet. Harry was going too fast and Tom wanted to yell at him to stop, that he was making a terrible mistake and that—

'Tom,' called the horrible voice, from right behind them. Tom pulled away from Harry and sprang round, ready to fight as hard as he could, because he'd had enough, absolutely enough this time and—

It was Joe. Real Joe. Half walking, half running across the grass towards them. Stepping forward, Harry had scooped Joe up off the ground and was hugging him tight, muttering, 'Thank God, thank God.' Tom was saying it too, in his head, *Thank God, thank God.* And then, suddenly, he wasn't. Because Joe was on his own.

19

'YOU'RE OBSESSING, YOU SILLY COW,' MUTTERED EVI TO herself. 'Shut it down and go to bed.' She looked at the clock in the bottom left-hand corner of her computer screen: 9.25 p.m. She couldn't go to bed at half past nine.

Would there be anything on TV? She spun herself round in the chair and glanced across the room at the set. Was she kidding? It was Saturday night. And there was nothing on her bookshelves she hadn't read at least four times.

She looked back at the screen, at the picture of Harry that she'd found on the *Lancashire Telegraph*'s website. He was wearing a black shirt, clerical collar and black jacket. The photograph was perhaps a year or two old. His hair was a little longer and in the lobe of his left ear he wore a tiny metal cross. The accompanying story told her that the Reverend Harry Laycock had been appointed to the living of the recently united benefice of Goodshaw Bridge, Loveclough and Heptonclough, and that in his previous post he'd been a special assistant to the archdeacon in the Diocese of Durham. Earlier in his career, he had spent several years working at an Anglican ministry in Namibia. He was unmarried and gave his hobbies as football (playing and watching), rock-climbing and long-distance running.

She could print the photograph off.

Except that she was absolutely, positively, not going to do anything that pathetic. She scrolled up the page and typed 'Heptonclough' into the search engine, pressing Return before she had time to think about what she was doing. The site found several entries. This wasn't obsessing, this was legitimate research. She had a patient in the town.

Heptonclough didn't make the news too often. The most recent story was the reference to Harry's appointment. She passed over it quickly before she was tempted to open it up again. *Heptonclough man fined for poaching; New bus service linking Heptonclough with nearby Goodshaw Bridge.* He lived in Goodshaw Bridge – oh, get a grip, woman. She found the story about the fire in Gillian's house, and then a follow-up article reporting that Barry Robinson had been discharged from hospital but remembered nothing about the fire. *Search continues for missing Megan; Heptonclough pub's warning to under-age drinkers . . .*

Evi scrolled back up the list. *Search continues for missing Megan.* Why did that ring a bell? The story was six years old. And – she scrolled down the list – there were several follow-up stories and one that preceded it: *Child missing on moors.*

She opened the link and read the first few lines. She'd been working in Shropshire when the story first made the news, but she remembered a young girl going missing on the Pennine moors. The search had gone on for days. The child, or the child's body, had never been found. Evi had even mentioned it in a lecture she'd given at the university – the particular stages of grief people suffer when their loss is unquantified and unconfirmed, and the difficulties of closure when hope – however unrealistic – lives on.

> Dozens of local people joined the police search for missing four-year-old Megan Connor. Megan, who wandered away from her family during a picnic, has blonde, shoulder-length hair and blue eyes. She was wearing a red raincoat and red wellington boots. Photographs are being distributed throughout the north-west, and in the meantime, Megan's family have asked the public to remain vigilant and pray for their daughter's safe return.

The picture accompanying the story showed a girl in a Snow White costume, no longer a toddler but still with the plump, soft features of the very young. If Gillian had taken part in the public search for Megan, it might explain why, three years later, she'd become obsessed with the idea that her own daughter might be similarly lost.

It was no good, she couldn't sit still any longer. For some reason the pain in her leg seemed worse tonight. She had Tramadol in her bathroom cabinet. She hadn't taken one, hadn't needed to take one, for nearly six months. Did she really want to start using them again?

20

'WHERE'S MILLIE?' SAID HARRY, PUTTING JOE BACK ON his feet. 'Joe, where's your sister?'

'I think they went up there,' said Joe, giving his brother a nervous look and pointing uphill towards the church.

'Who?' said Harry. 'Who went up there?'

'I didn't see,' said Joe, again looking sideways at Tom. 'I saw Tom go under the table and then Millie was gone.'

'Did she go outside? Did she leave the party?'

'I looked outside,' said Joe. 'I thought I saw someone coming in here, but they went too fast.'

Harry took his eyes off Joe for a second and looked towards the older boy. He really didn't like the look on Tom's face.

'Do you know anything about this?' he asked. 'Do you know who took Millie?'

Tom wouldn't make eye-contact with Harry, wouldn't take his eyes off his brother. Slowly, he shook his head.

Harry pushed himself upright. 'Hello!' he yelled into the night. 'Can anyone hear me?' They waited. 'Where the hell is everyone?' he muttered, when no one answered him. 'OK, are you two all right to come with me?'

Joe nodded immediately, followed – a second later – by Tom. Harry bent down again and picked up Joe. Leaving the lantern behind and holding tight on to Tom's hand, he set off.

'Millie!' yelled Harry, stopping every few seconds. They reached the top of the hill and stopped in the shadow of the ruined abbey, ten yards or so from the church door. Joe, tiny though he was, had become heavy. Harry lowered him to the ground.

'Millie,' he yelled and heard his own voice bounce back from a dozen different directions. 'Millie, Millie, Millie,' called the echo.

'Millie,' called a voice that was loud and clear. Definitely not an echo.

'Who said that?' asked Harry, spinning on the spot.

Joe and Tom looked only at each other. 'Has she taken her, Joe?' said Tom, in a low voice. 'This is serious. Where are they?'

'And who are they?' said Harry, who was walking backwards away from the boys towards the church. 'What's going on here? Millie!'

'Tommy,' called a high, thin voice and Tom sprang to Harry's side.

'OK, this has gone far enough, guys.' Harry made sure he wasn't yelling, but it was difficult to keep the anger from his voice. 'There is a child missing and the police will be called, if they haven't been already. Come on out now.'

They waited. In the distance a dog barked. They could hear a car engine start up. Then suddenly a high-pitched wailing broke through the night.

'That's Millie,' said Tom. 'That's really her. She's somewhere close. Millie! Where are you?'

'She's in the church,' said Joe. 'The door's open.'

Harry saw that Joe was right. The door to the church was open just a few inches. Which it shouldn't have been at this time of night. He sprinted across, aware of the boys following close behind. In through the doors he ran, pressing the light switches as he went. He ran into the nave and stopped dead. Above his head, someone was whimpering.

'Oh, God save us,' said Harry, looking up.

Tom and Joe lifted their heads to see what Harry had spotted. Way above them, on the wooden balcony rail, her little face screwed up in terror, sat Millie.

21

Dear Steve,

I'd really love your advice on something. I'm attaching two newspaper articles to give you background, although you may recall the case of Megan Connor. From what I can recall, she was never found.

I have a 26-year-old patient from the town where Megan went missing, whose daughter was accidentally killed three years after Megan's disappearance. I can't help thinking the prolonged grief my patient is experiencing might have been influenced by her memories of the earlier event.

I seem to remember the whole country was pretty traumatized by it, and it must surely have been worse in the area itself. My patient may even have taken part in the public search.

My question is this: can I bring it up in our discussions or should I wait for her to mention it herself? On the surface, she seems to be making progress but there's a lot I still don't understand. I can't help thinking she's keeping something from me. Any thoughts?

Love to Helen and the kids,
Evi

Evi checked her spelling, added a comma and pressed Send. Steve Channing was a sort of informal supervisor, a more experienced psychiatrist to whom she often turned for advice on difficult cases. Of course, he'd know from the date and time on the email that she was working on a Saturday night, but . . . well, she couldn't hide from everyone.

22

'HOW DID SHE GET UP THERE?' WHIMPERED TOM, UNABLE to take his eyes off his tiny sister, balanced precariously twenty feet above the hard stone floor of the church. No one answered him – why would they? – it was a stupid question. The only important thing was how they were going to get her down.

'Stay where you are, Millie. Don't move.' Harry was running back towards the church door. They heard his footsteps on the stairs that led to the gallery. He'd be in time, he had to be. Harry's footsteps stopped and they heard the door that separated the gallery from the stairs being shaken in its frame.

'You are kidding me,' came Harry's voice from behind the door. Then the church echoed with the sound of loud banging. Harry was kicking at the door from the other side.

'They've locked the door,' said Joe. 'He can't get to her.'

Scared by the noise, Millie looked down at her brothers. Then she held out both arms and Tom's stomach turned cold. She was going to jump to him, like she did from the back of the sofa. She was going to jump, confident that he'd catch her, like he always did. But there was no way he could, not from that height, she'd fall too fast. There was nothing, absolutely nothing they could do, she was going to fall and her head would shatter on the stone like glass.

'No, Millie, no, don't move!' Both boys were yelling up at her, watching in horror as the toddler lost her balance on the narrow ledge and tumbled forward. As Joe began to scream, Millie reached out and grabbed the rail with one hand. At the same time her feet, still wearing pink party shoes, found the smallest of footholds on a slim ledge that ran around the edge of the gallery.

'Shut up, you two, shut up now,' hissed Harry, who'd joined them again. Tom caught hold of Joe and pulled his brother to him. He hadn't realized both of them had been yelling so much. Joe clung tight and somehow the boys managed to stop screaming.

'Millie,' called Harry, in a voice that Tom could hear shaking. 'Keep still, sweetheart, hold tight, I'm coming to get you.'

Harry looked at both sides of the church and seemed to be making up his mind. Then he turned back to the boys.

'Get the hassocks – the prayer cushions,' he said. 'Get as many as you can and put them down on the floor, directly underneath her. Do it now.'

Tom couldn't move. He couldn't take his eyes off Millie. If he looked away for a second, she'd fall. Then he was aware of Joe scurrying around at his side. His brother had already taken three hassocks from their hooks in the pews and had put them on the ground beneath Millie.

Tom shot round and began gathering more from the pew opposite. As he pulled them off their hooks, he hurled them through the air at the spot where Millie would land. He threw six and then sped back to the aisle. Looking up, he positioned himself directly beneath his sister's plump legs and pink shoes and began arranging the cushions to form a soft carpet. If they could only get enough, the hassocks would break her fall.

Out of the corner of his eye Tom could see Harry pull himself up on to the window ledge and then move sideways until he could reach the gallery rail. How he was going to get up higher, Tom had no idea, but Harry climbed mountains in his spare time – if anyone could do it, he could. Tom just had to concentrate on the hassocks. Joe was following his example and throwing them over the top of the pew. As fast as they landed, Tom placed them next to the others. Millie's crash mat was getting bigger.

'No, sweetheart, no.' Harry's voice was strained with the effort of climbing. And of trying not to panic. 'Stay where you are,' he was calling. 'Hold tight, I'm coming.' Tom paused for a second and risked looking up. Harry was clinging, like a huge spider, to the carved panelling that lined the rear church wall. If he didn't slip, he'd reach the balcony rail in a few seconds and be able to climb over. Another second would take him to Millie and she'd be safe.

They were seconds he might not have. Because Millie had spotted Harry edging his way towards her and was trying to get to him. She'd moved along the ledge and was no longer directly above the hassocks. And those chubby fingers of hers had no real strength. She was sobbing hard. She couldn't hold on much longer. She was about to fall. And she knew it.

23

EVI WAS LOOKING AT GILLIAN ROYLE'S MEDICAL RECORDS. When she'd accepted Gillian as a patient, they had been forwarded to her, following normal procedure. Luckily, the GP's surgery Gillian attended had been one of the first to become fully computerized. Even the old paper-based records from the girl's childhood had, at some time, been inputted on to the system.

She'd read them already, of course, before her first appointment with the girl. Was there anything she'd missed?

'*He's a cheating bastard,*' Gillian had said. '*My stepdad was the same.*' More than once now, Gillian had become edgy on the subject of the men in her life. Several aspects of the girl's character – her cynicism about men and sex, her sense of being a victim, a sort of unspoken belief that the world owed her something – were all making Evi suspect there was some history of abuse in Gillian's past.

Evi scrolled back to the early records, when Gillian had been a child. She'd had the usual immunizations, chickenpox as a three-year-old. She'd visited her GP shortly after her father's accidental death, but no medication or follow-up treatment had been prescribed.

At the age of nine, Gillian had started to attend a different surgery in Blackburn. The change probably coincided with her mother's remarriage and the family's moving away from Heptonclough. Gillian's visits to the GP at that time had increased in frequency. She'd complained often of unspecified tummy aches, causing her to miss several days of school, but investigations had found nothing wrong. There had also been a series of minor injuries – a broken wrist, bruising, etc. It could indicate abuse. Or it could just suggest a lively, accident-prone child.

When Gillian was thirteen, she and her mother had moved back to Heptonclough. Gillian had been prescribed the contraceptive pill at a very early age – a couple of months short of her fifteenth birth-day – and had had a pregnancy terminated at the age of seventeen. Not an ideal scenario, but neither was it untypical for a modern teenager.

Oh, for heaven's sake, she had plenty of other patients. Evi stood up again. She glanced towards the bathroom. The door was open and she could see the cabinet.

It was completely dark outside. Would there be dancing up in Heptonclough right now? Evi hadn't danced in three years. Probably never would again.

24

'WE HAVE TO MOVE THE CUSHIONS,' TOM URGED HIS brother. 'Help me push them.' On their hands and knees, he and Joe began to slide the hassocks along the floor. But they didn't move smoothly across the uneven flags; as they hit bumps and nicks in the stonework, they separated.

'Keep them together,' yelled Tom, not daring to look up, as he and Joe frantically tried to push the hassocks back into place. He had no idea whether they were under Millie or not, he simply didn't dare look up because he knew if he did he'd see his sister's body hurtling towards him.

''Ow the fuck did she get up there?' said a voice from across the church. Tom glanced up to see that Jake Knowles and Billy Aspin had silently entered the building. Both were staring up at the vicar and the toddler in fascination.

Harry was getting closer to Millie, who was still clinging to the balcony rail. Something hit Tom in the face and he looked round to see Jake and Billy in the third pew down, collecting hassocks and throwing them at him.

'You're miles out, dickhead,' called Jake, his eyes fixed on Tom's but his pointed finger switching from the balcony to the floor. 'Six inches that way.'

He was right. Tom began pushing the cushions to the left, as Joe worked hard to keep them together. They were joined by Billy, who started to double them up, while Jake carried on throwing them like missiles through the air.

Then he heard a thumping noise above him and caught the scream before it left his mouth. Billy, Jake and Joe were all looking up. Harry was in the gallery, talking softly to Millie as he made his way slowly towards her. He was about five strides away . . . four . . . three . . . Tom held his breath. Harry reached out. Tom closed his eyes.

'He's got her,' said Jake. Tom exhaled as his eyes opened. There was no dead sister, bleeding on the stone floor in front of him. It was over. Jake was looking at the hassocks, scattered over the tiles.

'Suppose we have to put this lot back now,' he said.

'Boys.' It was Harry's voice, coming from above them, sounding like he'd just run a race. 'Millie and I can't get down until we find the key for this door. Can someone look in the vestry?'

For a moment, Tom couldn't remember where the vestry was. At the front of the church, he thought. He turned and stopped dead. Blinked and looked again. Nothing there. But for a second he'd been sure. To one side of the organ, her thin body pressed against the pipes, someone had been watching them. A little girl.

25

*T*HEY WERE LEAVING THE CHURCHYARD: THE MAN WHO *seemed to be in charge of the church now and Millie's two brothers. And the mother too; not Millie's mother, she was still running round the family's garden, shouting and making a huge fuss. No, this was the other mother, the one who'd appeared from nowhere just as the children and the man had left the church. She was carrying Millie in her arms as they turned down the hill.*

Millie's parents had seen them. They were running towards the group. Everyone was talking at once, looking at Millie, patting her head, hugging her close. They'd been scared, had thought they'd lost her. They'd take better care of her now. For a while.

26

2 October

'AT FIRST, FOR A FEW MINUTES, IT WAS LIKE I WAS BACK IN the old nightmare again, do you know what I mean? My little girl was lost and I had to find her. I had to go out and walk the moors, calling and calling, until I found her.'

'It's OK, Gillian, take your time. Give yourself a minute.'

'I couldn't think properly. I just wanted to scream.'

'I understand,' said Evi. 'It must have been dreadful for everyone, but especially for you.' Yet another search on the moors for Gillian: first Megan, then Hayley, now this latest – Millie, was she called?

'It was,' said Gillian.

'Take your time,' Evi said again. Should she mention the search for Megan? She hadn't heard back from her supervisor yet.

'But then it was like someone flicked a switch and I could see clearly again. The worst had already happened to me. I had nothing to be afraid of, so I was in the best position to help. I know all the hiding places around the town. I've been checking them all just about every day for nearly three years and I knew I had the best chance of finding her.'

Gillian had been out shopping since Evi had last seen her. She was wearing black trousers that looked new and a tight black sweater. Her skin was improving all the time.

'We've plenty of time, Gillian,' she said. 'Forty minutes before we have to stop. Do you want to tell me what you did?'

'I went out looking,' answered Gillian. 'On my own, in the dark, because I'm used to that. I walked along Wite Lane, past our old house, up through the fields towards the Tor. Then I came back again because I saw lights on in the church.'

'That shows great strength of character,' said Evi. 'That you were able to take part in the search, after everything you've been through.'

Gillian was nodding, still excited. 'And it felt really good, you know, when I saw Alice and Gareth and I had Millie in my arms. They were so grateful and—'

'You found the little girl?'

'Yes – well no – not exactly. I found all four of them, coming out of the church. They were all in a bit of a state. Tom was arguing with his brother about something to do with little girls. I took Millie off Tom because I was worried he was going to drop her. I didn't notice Harry at first. He was leaning against a wall and in his black clothes he was pretty hard to see.'

Evi picked up her water glass from the desk and realized she wasn't thirsty. She kept it in her hand, swirling the water around. 'And the little girl had just wandered off?' she asked.

'To be honest, no one's sure what happened. Millie's too young to tell us. The official line is that she followed some bigger children out of the party and then found she couldn't keep up.'

The glass was distracting Gillian. Evi made herself put it down. There was a paperclip on the desk. If she picked that up she'd start twisting it in her fingers. It would be another distraction.

'And the unofficial line?' asked Evi, finding herself curious.

'The family have had a few run-ins with a local gang,' replied Gillian. 'Who were hanging round while it happened, apparently. The Fletchers think perhaps they took Millie, maybe as a joke, and then it all went wrong. The police have been up but none of the boys has admitted anything. Everyone's just glad it ended the way it did.'

'And this was past nine o'clock?' Evi asked. 'Quite late for a little one to be up, wasn't it?'

'Oh, all the kids stay up late for the Cutting. It's tradition.'

'The Cutting?'

'That's what they call it. It's an old farming thing. Then a party. Everyone's invited. I was never that keen, to be honest, especially after Pete left. But then, when Harry asked me if I was going to be there, I thought, why not? Except then I was in this big panic about what I was going to wear. Not that it was a date or anything, but he had made a point of asking me if I was going to be there and . . . what's the matter? What have I said?'

The paperclip was in Evi's fingers after all. She shook her head and forced a smile. 'Nothing, I'm sorry,' she said, putting the twisted piece of metal back on the desk. 'You're in a very upbeat mood today. I can't quite keep up. Carry on.'

'So I decided to wear the cropped trousers in the end. With the yellow sweater I got in Tesco, only it doesn't look like something you'd buy from Tesco, it looks sort of classy, really. I can't remember the last time I bought new clothes. It's a good sign, isn't it, wanting to buy new clothes, to look nice again?'

Silence.

'Isn't it?' Gillian repeated.

Evi nodded. Was she still smiling? Just about. 'It's a very good sign,' she agreed.

It was an extremely good sign, wanting to look nice again. A long, floaty skirt almost to her ankles, a tight red top that would have shown off her shoulders, and a lavender pashmina in case the evening became chilly; that's what she'd been planning to wear.

'And how did you cope with the party afterwards?' she asked. 'There would have been alcohol, I'm guessing. Were you tempted?'

Gillian thought for a moment, then shook her head. 'Not really,' she said. 'There was so much going on. A lot of people wanted to talk to me, ask me how I was getting on. Jenny was sweet. Jenny Pickup, I mean – used to be Jenny Renshaw. I used to nanny for her years ago and then she was Hayley's godmother. And Harry was around a lot. Course, I didn't take too much notice of him at the party. You know how people talk.'

'Was it a late night?' Evi had imagined a late night, being driven home in that open-topped car. The night had been warm when she'd gone out into the garden just before eleven. There had been stars.

'It all finished not long after we found Millie,' Gillian said. 'The Fletcher family went home and then the rest of us went back to the Renshaws', but the band had stopped and people were starting to clear up. Odd really, because in the old days the parties could go on well into the night.'

'Did you go home?'

Gillian shook her head. 'No, I went with Harry.'

Evi reached out and lifted her glass. She put it to her lips, then licked the moisture off them. The glass went back down.

'With Harry?' she said. 'Harry the vicar?'

'I know, I know.' Gillian was almost chuckling. 'I'm still not used to the vicar bit myself. But when he took that stupid dress thing off he didn't look like a vicar at all. He was standing outside when I left and I just had a feeling he'd been waiting for me.'

'Did he say that?'

'Well, he wouldn't, would he? I think he might be a bit shy. So I asked him if he wanted to come back to the flat for a coffee.'

Evi's hand was on the glass again. 'What did he say?'

'Well, I was sure he was going to say yes but then some people came round the corner, so he said he had to make sure the church was locked up and he walked off up the hill. Course, I knew he wanted me to follow him so I waited a few minutes and then I went up too.'

'Gillian . . .'

'What?'

'Well, it's just . . . vicars have a certain code of conduct.'

Blank look on Gillian's face.

'A certain way they have to behave,' Evi tried again, 'and inviting a young woman he hardly knows up to a church at night . . . well, it doesn't feel too responsible to me. Are you sure that's what he wanted?'

Gillian shrugged. 'Men are men,' she said. 'He might wear a dog collar but he's still got a prick in his pants.'

Evi picked up the glass again. It was empty.

'I'm sorry,' said Evi, when she trusted her voice again. 'You probably think I'm prying. If you don't feel ready to talk about this, that's fine. Are you still sleeping well?'

'You think a vicar wouldn't be interested in someone like me?'

Gillian asked. The lines on her face seemed to have hardened. The lipstick she'd chosen looked too dark for her.

'No, that's not what I meant at all.'

'So why did he kiss me?'

Evi took a deep breath. 'Gillian, my only concern is whether you're ready to get involved again. Emotionally, you've been very badly damaged.'

He'd kissed her?

The girl had shrunk into her chair again. She didn't seem able to look at Evi any more.

'Do you really like him?' Evi asked softly.

Gillian nodded without looking up. 'It sounds stupid,' she said, speaking to the rug at her feet, 'because I hardly know him, but it's like I care about him. When I went in the church he was just sitting in the front pew. I went and sat down next to him and put my hand on his. He didn't pull his away. He said he was sorry about what had happened, that it must have been dreadful for me, after what I'd been through.'

'Sounds like it was pretty grim for everyone,' said Evi. Ten minutes before the end of the session. A tiny amount of time in the greater scheme of things. And yet too long to carry a picture in her head of Harry and this girl, in a dimly lit church, holding hands.

'It was like we had such a connection,' Gillian was saying. 'I felt I could say anything. So I asked him what I'd wanted to the first time I met him. How could God let bad things happen to innocent people, like Hayley? And almost to Millie. If He's all powerful, the way people say, why do these things happen?'

And me, thought Evi. What part of the great plan made me a cripple? What part of the plan whisked Harry away from me just when . . . less than ten minutes to go.

'What did he say?' she asked.

'He started quoting this prayer at me. He does that a lot, I've noticed. Incredible memory. Something about Jesus not having any hands or feet . . .'

'No hands but ours,' said Evi, after a moment.

'That's it. Do you know it?'

'I was brought up a Catholic,' said Evi. 'That prayer was written by St Teresa in the sixteenth century. "*Christ has no body now on earth but ours, no hands but ours, no feet but ours.*" It means that everything that happens here on earth – all the good things, all the bad things too – are down to us.'

'Yes, that's what Harry said,' replied Gillian. 'He said it's up to us now. He said God had a great plan, he was sure of it, but that it was a plan in outline and that it was up to us to fill in the details.'

'He sounds quite wise, this Harry of yours,' said Evi. So ridiculous. She'd only met him twice. There was no reason, really, for her stomach to feel like lead.

'I think so,' said Gillian. 'I'm going to church on Sunday. First time in years.'

Gillian turned suddenly and looked at the clock on the wall. 'I have to go,' she announced. 'I said I'd meet him at noon. I'm helping decorate the church. Thank you, Evi, I'll see you next week.'

Gillian got up and left the room. There were still eight minutes of her appointment left to run but it seemed she didn't need Evi any more. And why would she? She had Harry.

27

'*THE ASSISTANT REFEREE RAISES THE BOARD AND THERE'S only three minutes of injury time to play in this crucial top-of-the-table clash. The ball goes to Brown . . . he turns, passes to young Ewood debutante Fletcher . . . Fletcher, still Fletcher . . . a little look up . . . Green's in space . . . I think Fletcher's going all the way . . . GOAL!'*

Giving the supporters a modest wave, Tom jogged back to the centre of the pitch for the final kick-off. Less than a minute of injury time to go and victory, as they say, was in the bag. Then one of the other players turned to him.

'Tommy,' he whispered.

Tom was awake in an instant. No longer the new star striker, leading his favourite football team to victory. Just ten-year-old Tom Fletcher, lying in bed in the middle of the night. With a big problem on his hands.

Outside, the wind was racing up the moor. Tom could hear it whistling through alleyways, making windows tremble in their frames. He lay, not daring to move, with the quilt pulled up around his ears; he was used to the wind by now. In the radiator pipes he could hear the odd gurgle as the house settled down for the night. He was used to that too. From two feet below he could hear the soft ticking of Joe's breathing. Everything normal.

Except that someone else was in the bedroom with him and Joe. Someone at the end of his bed, who had just tugged at his quilt.

Completely awake now, Tom didn't dare move. The tugging could have been part of his dream, he just had to stay still, make sure it didn't happen again. He waited for ten, twenty seconds and realized he was holding his breath. As quietly as he could, he let it out. A fraction of a second later, someone else breathed in.

Still he didn't dare move. It could have been his own breath he'd heard, or Joe's. It could have been.

The quilt moved again, pulled away from his face. He could feel the night air on his cheek now and his left ear. In the bunk below Joe called out in his sleep – a muffled word that sounded a bit like 'Mummy' and then a low moan.

'Tommy.' Joe's voice. Except Joe was asleep.

'Tommy.' His mother's voice. But his mother would never scare him like this.

Tom's eyes were open. How had it got so dark? The landing light that was always kept on at night in case one of the children needed to get up had been switched off and his room was darker than it ever normally was. The furniture, the toys left scattered around, were little more than dark shadows. They were familiar dark shadows though, the sort he was used to and expected to see. The one he really hadn't expected to see was the one at the foot of his bed.

Whatever it was, it was sitting quite still, but breathing, he could see the slight movement of the shoulders. He could see the outline of the head and the two tiny points of light that could have been – almost certainly were – eyes. The shadow was watching him.

For half a second Tom wasn't capable of movement. Then he wasn't capable of anything else. He scrambled backwards, kicking against the cover with his heels, pushing with his elbows. His head slammed hard into the metal frame of the bed-head and he knew he couldn't go any further.

The shadow moved, leaned towards him.

'Millie,' it said, in a voice that Tom thought was perhaps supposed to be his. 'Millie fall.'

28

3 October

'ARE THEY OK?' ASKED HARRY, WHO'D BEEN LISTENING TO the story in fascination.

Gareth shrugged. 'Well, they're all pretty quiet,' he said. 'Tom and Joe aren't speaking but neither of them will let Millie out of their sight. Tom's developed something of a fascination with window locks, checking they're secure, wanting to know where the keys are.'

'And he says it was a little girl? Who's been watching you all?'

Gareth nodded. 'He's mentioned her before, we just didn't take much notice. There are lots of kids around town, and Tom's imagination has always been on the colourful side.'

'And where was Alice while . . .' he stopped. Did that sound judgemental?

'In her studio,' said Gareth, either not noticing or choosing to ignore it. 'She's been working on a portrait of old Mr Tobias, he's been sitting for her several times a week and she wants to get it finished before the end of the month. She heard Tom screaming upstairs but by the time she got to him he'd woken the other two and they were yelling their heads off too.'

'Any sign of a break-in?' asked Harry. 'Is it possible Tom did see someone?'

Gareth shook his head. 'The small window in the downstairs loo was open but no normal-sized person could get through it. And a child – even if one were out on her own at night – wouldn't be able to reach it.'

The two men had reached the back of the church. They stopped in front of a tall narrow door that looked as though it had been made from yew. 'Are you sure you're OK to do this?' asked Harry. 'It's not urgent. You should probably . . .'

Gareth picked up the tool-box he'd brought with him. 'It's fine,' he said. 'They've gone on a walk. Joe wanted to have a look at the Tor. I said I'd join them when we're done.'

'Well, if you sure.'

'I'm sure. Let's open this crypt.'

Harry found the right key and pushed it into the lock. 'Technically, not a crypt,' he said. 'More of a cellar. Might be handy for storage. I just want a steer on whether I need to call a surveyor in to check it's safe.' The key turned easily enough. Harry took hold of the handle and raised the latch.

'And you don't want to look round the spooky place on your own,' said Gareth.

'You're absolutely right about that. Blimey, this door is stiff. Shouldn't think it's been moved in years.'

'Oh, step out of the way, Vicar, this is a job for a man.'

'Back off, buddy, I'm on it,' said Harry. 'Here we go.'

The door swung inwards just as a bubble of sour-smelling dust burst in front of them. Harry blinked hard. Gareth cleared his throat. 'Stone me, that's a bit rich,' he said. 'Are you sure there's nothing dead down there?'

'I'm not sure of anything,' replied Harry, picking up his flashlight and stepping on to the spiral staircase that wound its way down beneath the church. The cold air seemed to steal around the back of his neck. 'Stakes and garlic flowers at the ready.'

The damp smell of the church's cellar got stronger as the two men went down. Before they were halfway Harry was glad he and Gareth were wearing fleeces. Twenty-two steps and they were at the bottom, shining their torches around. The two beams picked out massive stone pillars and a vaulted brick roof. So much bigger than either of them had expected.

'I stand corrected,' said Harry, after a few seconds. 'This is a crypt.'

If Tom had been asked a couple of weeks ago, he might have said October was one of his favourite months. Because October was when the trees started to look like toffee apples and ploughed fields turned the colour of dark chocolate. He liked the way the air tasted on his tongue, fresh and sharp like a Polo mint, and he loved the sense of expectation, as first Hallowe'en, then Bonfire Night, then Christmas drew near. This year, though, he was struggling with the whole expectation business. This year, he just didn't like to look too far ahead.

'Hold on, you two,' his mother's voice called up the hill. 'Wait for us girls.'

Tom glanced back. Joe was a few yards behind, dressed as a medieval archer with a plastic bow strung over his shoulder and a quiver of arrows on his back. He was keeping up well and singing quietly to himself. Almost thirty yards further down the hill Alice and Millie were just appearing through the fog.

'Tom, stay on the path!' called his mother.

'OK, OK!'

He carried on up.

Harry walked forward until he was in the centre of the wide, dark space. Three rows of ornate brick columns held up the vaulted ceiling. The floor was not the earth one he'd expected but was lined with old headstones like the church paths at ground level.

'Just incredible,' muttered Gareth at his side.

The two men walked on. A few yards ahead the wall to their right seemed to come to an abrupt halt and Harry's torch hit blackness. As the two men drew closer they realized an archway led through the wall. They could see nothing beyond.

'You first,' said Gareth.

'Wimp.'

Harry stepped through the black archway and shone his torch around. 'Well, I'll be . . .' he began. The underground space on the other side of the wall was even bigger than the church crypt.

'We're under the old church,' said Gareth, who'd followed close behind. 'Two churches, one massive cellar.'

'I don't imagine storage space is going to be a problem somehow,' said Harry, shining his torch round to see arched and gated alcoves against the far wall. 'I don't think this was ever just a cellar. There's too much ornamentation. I think it was used for worship. Can you hear water?'

'Yeah. Sounds a bit more than a burst pipe,' said Gareth. 'I think it's coming from over here.'

Gareth led the way; Harry followed, admiring the stonework around the walls, with its carvings of roses, leaves and insects. He saw a procession of carved stone pilgrims heading for a shrine. The flags beneath his feet were worn smooth. For hundreds of years monks had silently trod these stones. Ahead of him, Gareth had found the source of the water sounds.

'I have never seen anything like this,' he was saying.

Set into the furthest wall of the cellar was a massive stone scallop-shell. Water was streaming into it from a narrow pipe several inches above and then, almost like a decorative water feature in someone's garden, it poured over the sides of the shell and disappeared into a grille. Harry held out his hand and scooped up some of the water. It was freezing. He held it to his mouth, sniffed, then dipped in his tongue.

'Probably drinkable,' he said. 'Do you think this was some sort of massive priest hole for the monks? When enemies came they fled down here. With their own water supply they could probably hole up for weeks.'

'There are several underground streams around here,' said Gareth. 'We had to watch out for them when we were putting the house foundations in. Maybe you can bottle it.'

'Heptonclough Spring,' said Harry, nodding. 'Has a ring to it.'

'So can we discuss this whole crypt-versus-cellar business?' said Gareth, who was shining his torch into the nearest of the alcoves. 'Because I can't help thinking there are dead things yonder.'

Shapes loomed out of the fog and for a moment Tom slowed down. Then he realized there had been buildings here at one time. He was looking at their ruins.

'Tom, stop now!'

She meant it this time. There was no mistaking that particular tone and volume. He waited until his mother and Millie had caught up. Both looked tired.

The previous night, when his mother had come racing from her studio, smelling of paint and strong coffee, to find her eldest son crouched terrified behind his bedroom door, Tom had been convinced the little girl was still somewhere in the house. He'd refused to go back to bed until everywhere – absolutely every possible hiding place – had been searched.

Joe, the lying toe-rag, had refused to back him up, to admit that he too had seen the girl, had even spoken to her. Joe had just opened his eyes until they were as wide as saucers and shaken his head.

'Thank you,' said his mum. 'Now can we all stay together, please? No one is going out of my sight in this fog. OK, I think it's this way.'

With Millie on one hip, Alice set off and the boys trailed behind. Tom kept his eyes on the ground. If Joe said anything to wind him up he would land him one.

They reached the edge of a copse of trees just as the fog seemed to lift a little. A carpet of beech leaves lay before them. The trees were old and massive. Tom and his family stepped forward until they were in amongst them. The tiny cottage, straight out of a fairy tale, appeared before them.

Harry and Gareth were standing beside a small, stone-lined alcove. The entrance was covered in intricate ironwork and the gate was locked.

'Don't have the key to that one,' said Harry.

'Really not a problem, mate,' replied Gareth, shaking his head.

Beyond the ironwork the two men could see four carved stone coffins, set on shelves on either side of the alcove. Prone statues of men in clerical robes lay on each of them. The name Thomas Barwick was inscribed on the first. He'd been abbot in the year 1346. The writing on the other coffins was too worn for Harry to make it out. The men started walking back down the length of the cellar, shining their torches into each locked alcove they passed. They stopped at the last. Beyond the stone coffins, set into the far wall, was a wooden door.

'Where do you think that leads?' said Gareth. 'I've completely lost my bearings.'

Harry shrugged. He had too. 'There are some old keys in the desk in the vestry,' he said. 'Shoved to the back of one of the drawers.'

'Another day, perhaps,' said Gareth.

'I can't believe no one told me this was here,' said Harry. 'Its historical significance could be huge. There'll be coach parties visiting.'

'Maybe that's why it's been kept so quiet,' suggested Gareth. 'Does your churchwarden strike you as the sort of man who wants his town turned into a tourist attraction?'

'He doesn't own the whole town,' said Harry, annoyed. Abbots from hundreds of years ago could be interred in this very space. It was an incredible find.

'Just most of it.'

'Yeah, well he doesn't own the church. And he certainly doesn't own this.'

'Red Riding Hood's house,' said Tom, forgetting that he was sulking.

'Red Riding Hood's grandmother's house,' corrected his mother, as Millie toddled up to the cottage's front door.

Unlike the ruined buildings they'd just passed, the cottage seemed solid and in good repair. The walls were intact, the roof looked sound, the front door firm on its hinges. There were even two windows, with shutters pulled tight. And a chimney.

Alice reached out and tried the door handle. Locked. She turned back to her children and shrugged. 'Guess Grandmother's not home,' she said. 'I think this must be the cottage Jenny told us about. The one she and her sister used to play in.'

Tom shivered. He glanced at Joe, who was looking down at the ground, as though he had no interest in the cottage. A sudden thought struck Tom. What if this cottage was where the girl lived?

'Let's go,' he announced. Alice nodded and the family walked on until they came to the Tor.

'Can we climb up, Mum?' asked Joe.

'Absolutely not,' replied Alice. 'In this fog and without your father, this is as far as we're going.'

Tom was staring up at the massive pile of rocks that disappeared into cloud. There was something about the way they towered over him that made him feel nervous. And he certainly didn't like looking up, the way his mum and Joe and even Millie were doing. Turning away, he cried out before he could stop himself.

'What's the matter?' called Alice, spinning round.

'There's someone over there,' said Tom. 'In the trees. Someone watching us.'

Alice frowned and screwed up her eyes. Then she looked quickly from right to left. 'I can't see anything,' she said. 'Just trees.'

Tom moved closer to his mother. A tall, thin figure had been standing amongst the trees, watching. Once spotted, it had moved, fading back into the fog. Tom turned to glare at Joe, then stopped himself. It hadn't really looked the right shape or height to be the girl.

'Come on,' said Alice. 'We should get back. I don't think this fog is going to lift. Quick as we can, everyone.' Hoisting Millie on to her hip again, she set off towards the trees. Then she stopped. 'There *is* someone there,' she said in a quiet voice. 'Hold on a sec, Joe.'

Tom felt a lump forming in his chest. He couldn't see anything, or at least . . . his mother was reaching into her pocket. She brought out her mobile and looked at the screen. Then she pressed some keys and held it to her ear.

'Who are you phoning?' said Tom.

'Daddy,' replied Alice, before shaking her head. 'He must still be underground.'

She looked behind them once more and then set off again, heading downhill. First Joe and then Tom followed. Neither of them spoke. Every few steps Alice slowed down and looked back. After a few seconds Tom found himself doing the same thing. Just grey cloud behind. Already the Tor had disappeared.

After a few minutes, they reached the copse. The trees seemed to Tom to have grown taller since the family had last walked past them. He moved closer to his mother and realized Joe had done the same thing. No one seemed to want to speak. Even Millie was unusually silent. Alice hadn't put her mobile away. She glanced at it again and Tom could see her thumb hovering over one of the keys. It looked as if his mother was getting ready to press 9.

'Mummy, I'm scared,' said Joe in a small voice.

'There's nothing to be scared of, sweetheart,' replied his mother quickly, in a voice that seemed a bit shriller than normal. 'We'll be home in ten minutes.'

She set off again, more slowly this time, one step in front of the other. When Tom looked up he could see her eyes darting from side to side. They were in the midst of the trees now. Everywhere they turned, dark shadows surrounded them.

'Tom, poppet,' said Alice, without looking at him. 'If I were to tell you to, could you take Joe's hand and run as fast as you possibly can down the hill and find Daddy?'

'Why?' said Tom.

'He's probably still in the church,' said Alice. 'Maybe at home. Could you find him and tell him where we are?'

'What about you and Millie?'

'I'll look after Millie. I just know how fast you are. I know you and Joe could get home really quickly. Can you do that for me, angel?'

Tom wasn't sure. Run in the fog and leave his mother behind? They were almost through the trees now. The mist wasn't quite so thick lower down the moor. The outlines of Heptonclough's buildings were starting to appear. They could see further down the hill.

'Oh, for heaven's sake,' said Alice, stopping and closing her eyes. 'Oh, for heaven's sake, Tom, you scared the life out of me.'

Tom looked at his mother. She didn't look cross, she looked hugely relieved. He turned his head down the hill to see a figure a hundred yards or so away from them.

'It's Gillian,' she said. 'Out for one of her walks. Fancy being scared of Gillian.'

29

8 October

'EVI, IT'S STEVE. IS THIS A GOOD TIME?'

Evi looked at her watch. She was on her way to a children's home, to have her first meeting with a child who hadn't spoken in the ten days since the police had used their special powers under the Children Act to remove him from his home. It was a ten-minute journey. Ten minutes either side of that to get herself in and out of the car. But her supervisor had rung on her mobile. She could talk on the move.

'It's fine,' she said, gathering up her notepad and several pencils from the desk. 'I have a couple of minutes. Thanks for getting back.'

'Well, sorry it took so long, but we've been away. I only got back to the office this morning.'

'Anywhere nice?' Why did pencils permanently need sharpening? She leaned against the desk and fumbled in the drawer.

'Antigua. And yes, it was very nice. Now, this email of yours.'

'Any thoughts?' She'd found the sharpener. But holding the phone against her ear with her shoulder was going to play havoc with her back.

'You say the patient is making progress?' She could hear Steve sipping his usual strong black coffee.

'On the surface, yes,' said Evi. Two pencils sharpened, that would have to be enough. 'She's managing to curtail the drinking, the medication I've prescribed is working well, she's started to talk about the future.' OK, writing stuff, phone – yes, she had that – what the hell had she done with the car keys?

'So what's the problem?'

'I just can't help feeling there's something she's not telling me,' said Evi. Her car keys were in her coat pocket. They were always in her coat pocket. 'She's very reluctant to talk about her early life, the death of her father, the appearance of a stepfather. There are times when it's as though a curtain comes down. Subject off limits.'

'You've not been seeing her that long, have you?'

'No, only a few weeks,' said Evi, wondering if she could get her coat on without falling over. 'And I know these things can take time. It's just that the Megan Connor business struck me as being quite a coincidence. I can't help thinking it would have had an impact.'

'You're probably right. But I'd wait for her to bring it up. Let her talk about what she's happy to talk about. You're still right at the start of treatment. There's plenty of time.'

'I know. I thought that myself. Just needed you to confirm it.' The coat was on, just. Evi hung her bag from the bespoke hook on her wheelchair and checked that her stick was in its place along the back. She sank down, still gripping the phone between her shoulder and her ear.

'That's my girl,' said Steve. 'I tell you what, though, I remember the Megan case well.'

'Oh?' Evi's office door had been hung to swing outwards when she pushed it with her foot.

'Yeah, a colleague of mine took a very close interest. He was doing some work on the effects of disasters on small communities.'

'How do you mean?' asked Evi, setting off along the corridor.

'When a community suffers an out-of-the-ordinary loss, its impact can be felt for quite some time,' said Steve. 'The place gets a slightly grim reputation with the outside world and that can start to affect how people there think and behave. He wrote a paper on the subject, it looked at places like Hungerford, Dunblane, Lockerbie, Aberfan. I'll try and dig it out for you.'

Evi turned the corner and nearly ran into a group of three colleagues chatting in the corridor. They stepped aside and she nodded her thanks. 'The *BMJ* did a piece on it too, not long ago,'

Steve was saying. 'After a disaster, up to 50 per cent of the population can suffer from mental distress. The prevalence of mild or moderate disorders can double. Even severe disorders like psychosis increase.'

'But you're talking about major disasters, surely? Earthquakes, airplanes coming down, chemical plants exploding. Severe loss of life.' Evi passed a woman and child in the corridor, then a porter.

'True, and I'm not trying to suggest that a couple of dead children can compare in any real way. But the Megan case was very high-profile. You should still expect there to be an impact on the community's mental health. On some level the people up there will feel responsible. They'll feel tainted.'

'So what happened previously could, albeit subconsciously, be affecting my patient's recovery?'

'I wouldn't be in the least bit surprised. You might want to find out more about what actually happened when your patient's daughter died. Read some old newspapers, talk to the GP in question. It'll give you a point of reference. You can compare what she's telling you with what you know about the facts. See if there are any discrepancies. You mustn't be confrontational, of course, but sometimes we learn more from what our patients don't tell us than from what they do. Make any sort of sense?'

Evi had reached the main door of the hospital. Some idiot had left a pile of packing crates at the top of the disabled ramp. 'Yes, it does,' she said, glaring at the crates. 'Thanks, Steve. I'm going to have to go now. I have to give somebody a serious bollocking.'

30

10 October

'To EVERYTHING THERE IS A SEASON, A TIME FOR EVERY purpose under the sun,' read Harry. His voice, rarely low-pitched, bounced around the empty church. 'A time to be born and a time to die; a time to plant and a time to pluck up . . .'

A scuffling noise behind him. He stopped. A quick glance over his shoulder told him he was still alone in the church. He'd said goodbye to Alice ten minutes ago, to Gillian three or four minutes after that. Both had been helping him put the finishing touches to the harvest decorations. He'd have seen anyone come in. You didn't miss much, standing in the pulpit.

'. . . a time to pluck up that which is planted,' he continued, his eyes scanning the rows of pews although he was sure the noise had come from behind him. 'A time to kill and a time . . .' He stopped again, not liking the feeling he was getting between his shoulder blades, the feeling that any second now, someone behind him would reach out and . . .

He glanced down at his notes again. Ecclesiastes, chapter three, always went down well at harvest time. People liked the simple beauty of the piece, its sense of balance, of completeness.

'Time to die,' said a small voice from just behind him.

Harry kept his eyes fixed on the gallery and waited. In the nave something creaked, but old wood does that. For a second he

142

wondered if the Fletcher boys had crept into the church again, but it hadn't sounded like either of them. He allowed his eyes to fall down to his hands. They were clutching the wooden rail of the pulpit rather tighter than appeared manly. Without making a sound, he spun on the spot.

The chancel looked empty, but then he hadn't really expected anything else. Someone was having some fun with the vicar. He turned back to face the front of the church again.

'. . . and a time to heal . . . a time to weep and a time to laugh,' he read out, in a voice that would be too loud, even tomorrow, when the church had people in it. In an empty church, it sounded a bit crazed.

'Time to kill,' whispered the voice.

Oh, for the love of . . .

Harry didn't bother with the steps, he swung his legs over the pulpit rail and dropped to the floor. The voice had been just feet away, he was sure of it. There was no time for anyone to disappear. Except they had. No one in the choir stalls, no one in the small space behind the organ, no one hiding behind the altar, no one in the . . . he stopped. Could someone be in the old crypt? Could sound be travelling upwards somehow?

'Everything all right, Vicar?'

Harry stopped and turned to face the new voice. Jenny Pickup, Sinclair's daughter, was standing halfway down the aisle watching him with a look of bemused interest on her face. Harry felt his own face glowing. For some reason, Jenny always seemed to find him a bit of a joke.

'Have you ever heard of a secret way into this building, Jenny?' he asked. 'Maybe into the cellar beneath us? That local kids might know about?'

She shook her head. 'Not to my knowledge,' she said. 'Why, has anything gone missing?'

'No, nothing like that,' said Harry quickly. 'It's just I was running through the sermon for tomorrow and I swear I heard someone repeating what I was saying.'

Jenny was wearing a pale-pink sweatshirt that suited her, and riding breeches tucked into black boots. 'This building echoes in odd ways,' she said after a moment. 'It's well known for it.'

'It really didn't sound like an echo,' Harry replied. 'It sounded like a child. In which case I need to find him before I lock up.'

Jenny had walked forward. Her eyes were moving slowly round the building. 'Let me lock up for you tonight, Vicar,' she said.

'You?'

'Yes,' she nodded, a small, slightly sad smile on her face. 'I came to have a quick word with you. And then I wanted to spend some time here on my own. Would that be OK, do you think? I promise to make sure there's not a soul here when I leave.'

'If you're sure,' he said.

'No problem. Let me walk outside with you. It's a beautiful evening.'

Harry collected his jacket and then the two of them walked into the vestry. Harry couldn't resist a last look back around the nave. Empty.

'Do you need to borrow my keys?' he offered.

'No, it's OK, thank you,' Jenny replied, as they walked outside. 'Dad lent me his. He'll probably pop back himself later, just to make sure I really did lock up and all the lights are out.'

A Land Rover pulling a long, low trailer had stopped outside Dick Grimes's shop, near the church entrance. The driver jumped out, followed by a black and white collie. He went to the back of the trailer and unfastened the rear door. The dog ran up the ramp and a dozen sheep stumbled out. Harry and Jenny watched the dog herd them around the vehicle and towards the barn behind the butcher's shop.

'You're not a countryman, are you, Vicar?' she said to him.

They watched the sheep disappear into the barn, then the driver and collie reappeared and jumped back into the cab. As the vehicle drove off around the corner, a woman had to step close to the wall to avoid being hit. It was Gillian.

'No,' said Harry, turning back to Jenny. 'But I'm learning fast.'

'It's all done humanely,' she said. 'And the animals don't suffer the stress of a long journey.'

'I don't doubt that for a second.' Harry glanced up the hill. Gillian was still there. 'Don't think I disapprove,' he went on. 'I just need to get used to it.'

'The men all come up to our house afterwards,' said Jenny. 'We do a supper and the pub usually provides a keg or two. It would be great if you could join us.' Jenny was twisting her car keys in her hands. Her fingers were long and slim but reddened and a little rough, maybe from riding horses in bad weather.

'Thank you,' said Harry, acutely conscious of Gillian just yards away but determined not to look at her again. 'That's very kind,' he went on. 'And next year I'd love to. But I have a big day tomorrow. I probably should get an early night.'

'Next year then.' Jenny had been working. Her short fingernails were dirty and there was straw on her sweatshirt.

'I wish Gillian would go home,' said Harry. 'It's getting cold and she never seems to wear a proper coat.' Evi's fingernails had been short too, but very clean and polished. Funny, the things you noticed.

Jenny glanced over Harry's shoulder. 'Gillian's been looking a lot better lately,' she said. 'We've been worried about her for some time. She really didn't seem to be coping.'

'She suffered a terrible loss,' said Harry.

Jenny took a deep breath. 'I lost a daughter too, Vicar. Did you know that?'

'I didn't,' he replied, turning away from Gillian to meet Jenny's hazel eyes. 'I'm so sorry. Is that what you wanted to talk to me about?'

'In a way. It was ten years ago, so I've had more time, I suppose. But there's not a day goes by when the pain isn't there. When I don't think, what would she have been doing today? How would she look, now that she's eight, or nine, or ten?'

'I do understand,' Harry said, although he knew he didn't, not really. No one could appreciate that sort of pain unless they'd lived through it.

'Are you nervous about tomorrow?' Jenny was asking him.

'Of course,' he replied truthfully. 'I've led worship in my other two parishes and that went fine, but here's different somehow. Probably because the church has been closed for so long. I haven't managed to find out yet why that was.'

'That's what I wanted to talk to you about. Can we sit down for a second?'

Harry found himself following Jenny to the old shepherds'

bench where he'd sat with Evi. She still hadn't called him back.

Jenny was twisting her car keys in her hand. 'It'll be fine tomorrow,' she said. 'I think you'll have a good turn-out. People are ready to start using the church again.'

'Why did they stop?' he asked, realizing she needed a direct question.

She wasn't looking at him. 'Out of respect,' she said. 'And also out of sadness. Lucy, my daughter, died in the church.'

And no one had thought to warn him? 'I'm so sorry,' he said.

'She fell from the gallery. It was my fault. We weren't even in the church, we were at Dad's house and I was talking to someone – to Gillian and her mother, as it happened. They used to work for us. I didn't see Lucy wander off.'

'From the gallery?' said Harry. 'You mean like Millie Fletcher almost did the other week?'

Jenny nodded. 'You can understand now why we were all so upset by that. It just seemed the most dreadful, stupid joke. Those boys, I don't know what goes on in their heads . . .'

'I'm so sorry,' said Harry. 'Please, tell me about Lucy. She just wandered away when you weren't looking?'

'We started searching, of course, but we looked in the house – it's a big house – and then the garden, then the lane outside. It never occurred to us that she might have made her way into the church. And up all those steps. By the time we found her, she was cold. And her skull, her little skull was just . . .'

The blood was draining from Jenny's face. Her whole body was shaking.

'I'm so terribly sorry,' repeated Harry. 'I had no idea. All this . . . opening up the church again, it must be very distressing for you.'

'No, it's fine, I'm ready.' Jenny was still pale, but the trembling seemed to be slowing down. 'I asked Dad not to mention what happened,' she was saying. 'I wanted to tell you myself.'

'That was very brave of you. Thank you.' It certainly explained a lot. He'd been told that ten years ago the parishioners had suddenly stopped using the church. When the incumbent vicar retired, the diocese had formally closed the building. Only when the parish had been united with two others had the decision been taken to reopen. He'd had no idea what had really lain behind it all.

At the top of the lane, Gillian was still hovering. Jenny saw his eyes flicker and turned her head to look up the hill.

'I was godmother to Gillian's daughter,' she said. 'A couple of months before the fire, I gave her all Lucy's old clothes, including some really precious ones that Christiana had made. It felt like a big step forward for me, like I was getting ready to move on. And then Hayley was dead too and all the clothes were burned. It was almost like I'd lost Lucy again.'

Harry couldn't think of anything to say.

'There was a little pyjama set. Christiana embroidered it herself with all the Beatrix Potter characters. It was so beautiful. I thought I was so brave giving it away.'

Again nothing to say. He was hopeless, in the presence of grief, completely hopeless.

'You're a good listener,' said Jenny, getting to her feet. 'I'm going back inside now. Good luck tomorrow.'

'Would you like me to come with you?' He stood up.

'No, thank you,' she said. 'I'll be fine. I've never been afraid of ghosts.' She smiled at him and turned to walk back towards the church.

31

'OH GOD, LISTEN TO IT, GARETH, IT'S STILL GOING ON.'
The gentle, rocking motion that had lulled Tom to
sleep and kept him there had stopped. His dad had
parked the car and his mum was talking in that low voice she used
when she didn't want him or Joe to hear what she was saying.
Normally it was a signal to listen all the harder, but Tom really
didn't want to be any more awake than he already was. He just
wanted to sleep.

He heard movement and thought perhaps his dad had turned
round in his seat to look at the children. 'They're flat out,' he said,
whispering like their mother had done. 'We'll just carry them in.
They won't know anything about it.'

'But listen to it. It's making me feel sick.'

Tom didn't want to hear anything. There was a dream somewhere, a good one, if he could only find his way back to it. But he
was listening all the same. He couldn't help it. What was that noise?
Like someone was moaning. No, not just one person, lots of people,
crying in dull, low voices. Were they people, though? They didn't
sound like people. *Rooarrk*, they were saying, over and over again,
Rooaark. Tom couldn't explain why, but it was making him feel
guilty.

'We'll put them in bed and put some music on,' said his father.
'Come on, we won't be able to hear it as much inside.'

The car door opened and Tom could feel cold air on his face. And

148

the noise became louder. Not just *Rooarrk* but other sounds too. *Naaaa! Naaaa!* Somewhere close by, men were shouting, laughing, yelling instructions to each other. Tom really, really didn't want to listen to it but the din was seeping its way into his head, like water through a sponge. Then someone was reaching over him and he could smell his mother's lily-of-the-valley perfume. The soft wool of her sweater brushed his face and he thought perhaps he was reaching up a hand towards her, to pull her down closer. Then she moved away.

'We can't leave Tom out here,' she said. 'How are we going to do this?'

Leave Tom?

'I'll lock the car door,' said his dad. 'We'll be thirty seconds. Come on, let's get on with it.'

The scent of Tom's mother faded. He heard the car door being closed softly, the beeping sound of the remote key and then the locks themselves clunking down. Tom opened his eyes. He was in the car, sitting by the window of the rear seat. Alone.

The car was parked in the driveway of their house. He could see lights in the downstairs rooms. The front door was open. His parents would be carrying Joe and Millie up to bed and then his dad would come back for him. The family often did this when they were out quite late, like tonight, when they'd been to Granny and Grandad Fletcher's house for dinner. Tom closed his eyes and prepared to drift off again.

But how could he sleep when something close by was miserable and frightened? Over and over again something was moaning. It had made his mother feel sick. It was making Tom want to cry. Then there was a scream. A loud, piercing scream and he was wide awake again.

Tom turned his head to look up the hill. Across the road, the buildings around the butcher's shop were brightly lit. He could see movement, men walking around, carrying large bundles on their shoulders.

His seatbelt was still tight around him and he reached down to unfasten it. The car was locked and there were child locks on the rear doors, but he knew he could climb over the seats and open the front door. He could be in the house in five seconds. Five seconds between leaving the locked car and getting inside the house.

The shouting and screaming seemed to be getting closer. Maybe it was just louder. Either way, five seconds seemed too long. His dad would be back soon. He shrunk down in his seat, wanting to close his eyes again but not quite daring. He really wanted his dad back. He raised his hands to press them against his ears.

Was there something just outside the car? Something scraping softly against the paintwork? Tom held his breath. There was. Something was moving around outside. He could hear it. He could almost feel the vehicle rocking. Without daring to move his head, he glanced at the door. Still locked. No one could open it without the key. Could they?

He had to scream for his dad. Yell his head off. Except the night was full of screams. No one would hear his. The horn! His dad would hear that. He just had to lean forward, he could reach it from the back seat. His dad would hear and come running. Tom sat upright and got ready to spring.

A small hand appeared at the window, not six inches from his face.

Tom knew he'd cried out. He also knew no one had heard him. He tried again and nothing came out. He couldn't move either. He just had to watch.

The hand was the wrong colour. Hands aren't that colour. They aren't red.

The hand began to move downwards, leaving a trail of something that looked like red slime. Tom could see the mark left behind by the base of the thumb and then five wavering lines as the thumb and fingers squeaked their way down the glass. He watched the arm and then the wrist disappear below the rim of the window. The palm had almost disappeared from view and then the fingers waggled at him, like a wave.

He was up, across the front seat, reaching for the horn. A face was staring in through the windscreen. Tom opened his mouth to yell but it was as though all the oxygen had been sucked out of the car. He couldn't breathe, so he couldn't shout.

What was it? What the hell was it? A girl, he thought, she had long hair. But her head was far too big. And her face was like the figures Joe sometimes made from plasticine. Her eyes were huge and her lips were full, red and damp. The worst thing, almost, was her skin. It was so pale. It hung loose on her bones as if it was too big for her and it really didn't look like skin at all. It was like the stuff you get when wax runs off candles and then hardens and goes all white and wrinkly. She looked like someone had dipped her in melted candle wax. But her skin wasn't the worst thing. The worst thing was the lump on her neck that pushed up against her face and pulled the neckline of her dress out of shape. As she stared at Tom through the windscreen, the lump almost seemed to be moving by itself and he had a sudden vision of the rest of her body below the neck of her dress: lumpy, putty-soft, and with veins standing out against wax-like skin.

He'd found the horn and was pressing with all his strength, terrifying himself with the sound but simply unable to take his hand off it. Then he was out of the car. He didn't know how he'd done that. He only knew he was outside. The drive was hard through his slippers, the night was filled with the sound of torment and the creature from a nightmare was between him and the front door.

He realized he was screaming. Then he was running. Then he was screaming in his mother's voice. And his dad's voice. He was yelling 'Tom, Tom, where are you?' and she was chasing him, she was coming after him and run, it was all he could do, run, run, run.

And hide.

Everything was quiet. Cold. Wet. He had no idea where he was, but he knew he was somewhere dark and damp. He was lying down, but had no idea whether he'd fallen or just run out of breath. He was panting as if he'd never get enough air in his lungs ever again. Something hard was digging into his ribs but he didn't dare move.

'Tom!'

His dad's voice. He was close by. Except . . . was it? Was it him?

'Daddee.' A soft voice, low and teasing, like a kid playing hide and seek. A voice that sounded – oh God – exactly like . . .

'Tom, where are you?' called his dad.

No, no, Dad, no. It's not me!

'Daddee . . .'

'Really not funny, Tom. Come out now.'

'Gareth, have you found him?' His mother's voice, from further away. She sounded as if she was crying. Was it her? It sounded like her, but . . .

Footsteps. Heavy footsteps close by. Too heavy to be . . .

Tom was on his feet. He was in the graveyard and his dad was ten feet away. He'd seen him, was coming towards him. Then Tom was being carried across the graveyard and suddenly there was his mum and they were inside and that horrible moaning noise was so loud in his head. He could see his mother's face trying to talk to him but the noise was too loud. They were in the sitting room and his dad had put him down on one sofa and his mum was leaning over him, holding on to him and trying to say something, but he couldn't hear because the sounds in his head were just too loud. Then she started to cry and Tom could see tears running down her face, but he couldn't hear her crying because all he could hear, all he would ever hear again, was this horrible, horrible howling.

And then he realized who was howling.

'Tom, angel, please stop crying, please stop.'

He had stopped. His mum just didn't seem to have noticed. She was on the sofa too now and had pulled Tom on to her lap. He wasn't much smaller than she was and he never sat on her knee any more, but he was so glad to be there with her arms wrapped tight around him. Then there were footsteps at the bottom of the stairs and his dad appeared in the doorway.

'They're fine,' he said to Alice in a soft voice. 'Both still asleep.'

Gareth crossed the room and knelt down on the rug in front of Tom. Then he reached up to stroke his son's forehead.

'What happened, matey?' His dad asked, running his hand over Tom's head.

He told them, of course. Why wouldn't he? They were his parents, the people he trusted more than anyone else in the whole world. It hadn't occurred to him that there are some things parents can't bring themselves to believe.

32

11 October

*'All creatures of our God and King
Lift up your voice and with us sing.'*

T
HE CHURCH WAS CLOSE TO FULL AND THE PEOPLE OF
Heptonclough weren't shy about using their voices. Harry
scanned the congregation. Jenny Pickup was standing beside
her husband, two rows from the front. Her face seemed composed.

One or two men in the congregation, on the other hand, looked
as though they might be nursing hangovers, and he wondered how
many of them had been involved in the festivities of the previous
evening. Ritual slaughter on Saturday night; church the next morning. Ah well. He lived among farmers now.

He hadn't spotted the Fletchers yet. Alice had assured him they
would be well away from Heptonclough the night before but, even
so, their house was just too close to the barn Dick Grimes used as
the town abattoir. When he'd arrived an hour earlier, Harry had
spent five minutes walking up and down the road. *The street outside
gets – how shall I put this? – a little messy*, Tobias had said. Either it
had rained in the night or the clean-up operation had been thorough.
There was no trace of what had taken place the night before.

The hymn was drawing to an end. There was Gareth, halfway down
on the left side of the aisle. Alice was by his side. One of her hands

153

held a hymn book, the other was on Tom's shoulder. Her eldest son seemed to be staring at his feet. None of them were singing.

'I've been asked two questions rather frequently over the past three weeks,' said Harry. He was in the pulpit and most faces were looking his way; always a good sign. 'The first is: "'Ow're you settlin' in, Vicar?" The second: "You're not a countryman, are you, lad?"'

A few quiet titters around the church.

'The answer to the first is: very well, thank you, everyone's been very kind. To the second: no, I'm not. I'm not a countryman. But I'm starting to get it.'

In the crowded church, only three people were sitting in the front left-hand pew: Sinclair, his father Tobias and his elder daughter, Christiana. In the old days this would have been the Renshaw family pew. To all intents and purposes, it still was.

'We can all get great comfort from the sense of living in an ordered universe,' continued Harry. 'Up here, among the hills, where the land plays such an important part in our lives and where the seasons govern so much of what we do, it's perhaps easier to feel a sense of harmony with the world than we might do in our towns and cities.'

In the soft light of the church, Christiana Renshaw's large, regular features looked almost beautiful, and very like those of her younger sister. She was looking not at Harry but at an apple in one of the window flower-arrangements. She was sitting several feet away from her grandfather.

'There is a reason,' said Harry, 'why the passage I just read to you is so popular at harvest time, at christenings and weddings, even at funerals. At important times in our lives we like to be reminded that we are part of a great plan, that there is a purpose. And that everything has its place and its time. Our reading today, Ecclesiastes, chapter three, verses one to eight, conveys that better than just about any other biblical piece I can think of.'

Gillian was sitting eight rows back, immediately behind the Fletcher family. Even from a distance, Harry could see that her hair had been washed and that she was wearing make-up.

'So it's rather strange then,' he continued, 'that the rest of Ecclesiastes should be the least understood book of the entire Bible.'

The service was almost over. The congregation was singing the offertory hymn, Dick and Selby Grimes, the church's two sidesmen, were carrying round the collection plates and Harry was preparing for Holy Communion. He'd prepared everything the afternoon before, opening the wine and decanting it. All he needed to do now was pour the wine into the chalice. He took the stopper off the decanter, poured some wine into the cup and added water. He took the wafers of the host and placed them on the silver tray. He would carry them round and distribute them. Sinclair would follow him with the wine.

Harry raised the plate into the air. The priest is always the first to receive Holy Communion. Next would be Sinclair and the organist, then the rest of the congregation. Behind him he could hear the sidesmen marshalling people into place.

'The body of our Lord Jesus Christ, which was given for you, preserve your body and soul unto everlasting life.' He took a wafer from the plate. 'Take and eat this in remembrance that Christ died for you, and feed on Him in your heart by faith with thanksgiving.'

Harry put the wafer into his mouth. The organist had finished playing and was crossing to take his place beside Sinclair. The church had fallen silent. Harry could hear the first row of communicants settling themselves at the chancel rail. He should phone Jenny and Mike later, make sure their first service hadn't been too difficult. He'd pop round if necessary. He lifted the chalice. Could he smell something strange?

'The blood of our lord Jesus Christ,' he said, 'preserve your body and soul unto everlasting life. Drink this in remembrance that Christ's blood was shed for you and be thankful.' Harry brought the chalice to his lips. The sun outside came streaming through the window above the altar. For a second the solid-silver chalice looked as crimson-red as its contents.

'The blood of Christ,' he whispered to himself. The cold of the silver met his lips.

Outside, rooks were flying around the roof. He could hear them calling to each other. Inside the church, all was still. The congregation was hushed, waiting for him to rise and begin the sacrament.

Slowly, very slowly, Harry put the cup back down on the altar.

There was a white linen napkin just within reach. He grasped it and clutched it to his mouth. He was going to gag, any second now. He picked up the cup again and walked as quickly as he could without spilling its contents to the vestry. He pushed the door open with his shoulder then kicked it shut behind him. He got to the sink just in time.

Red liquid splattered across white porcelain as Harry realized he was retching. And that the entire congregation could hear him. He turned on the cold tap and ran water over his hands. Then he raised them to his face.

'Vicar, what's wrong?'

Sinclair Renshaw had followed him into the vestry. Harry cupped his hands and allowed them to fill with water. He brought them up to his face and drank.

'Vicar, are you ill? What can I do?'

Harry turned, lifted the chalice and held it out to his church-warden. 'Another tradition?' he asked. His hand was shaking. He put the cup down again.

Sinclair glanced at the cup, then turned and walked swiftly away. He closed the door of the vestry and walked back until he was standing close to Harry.

'Is this how it all ends?' asked Harry. 'You let the blood run freely on Saturday night and then the next day you drink it?'

'What on earth's the matter?' asked Sinclair.

Harry was pointing at the cup. 'That isn't wine,' he said, his hand still shaking. 'It's blood. Not the symbolic kind – the real thing.'

'Surely not?'

'Taste it yourself. I did.'

Sinclair took the cup and carried it to the light. He raised it to his face and took a deep breath through his nose. Then he dipped his forefinger into the liquid and examined it closely. Harry watched, unable to read the expression on the older man's face. After a second or two, Sinclair rinsed his hand under the tap and then turned back to face him.

'Have a drink of water,' he said. 'Take a moment to compose yourself.'

Then he turned again and crossed the room. On a shelf, he found a second chalice, an older, slightly tarnished one, and rinsed it out in the sink. Opening a cupboard door – Sinclair clearly knew his way around the vestry – he took out a new bottle of wine. Harry found a chair and watched as Sinclair found a corkscrew and opened the wine. He poured it into the chalice and sipped it.

'This is fine,' he said. 'Are you able to continue?'

Harry couldn't reply. *The blood of Christ, shed for you.* Blood harvest.

'Vicar!' Sinclair's voice was still low, but he wasn't standing for any nonsense. 'I can tell everyone you've been taken ill. Would you prefer me to do that?'

Harry was on his feet again, shaking his head. 'No. I'll be fine,' he said. 'Thank you.'

'Good man. Say the blessing here, just with me. It'll help calm you.'

He was right. Harry took a deep breath and said the familiar words. He raised the cup to his lips before he had time to think about what he was doing and drank. Still wine.

'Feeling better?' asked Sinclair.

'Yes, thank you. We should . . .' He gestured towards the vestry door. He had no idea what everyone outside would be thinking by now.

'One moment.' Sinclair's hand was on his arm. 'After the service I'll take care of that.' He gestured towards the first cup, the one still filled with . . . 'A stupid practical joke,' he went on. 'People had a lot to drink last night. Please accept my apologies.'

Harry nodded and the two men left the vestry. Harry picked up the plate of wafers and crossed the chancel to where the first communicant was still kneeling patiently.

'The body of Christ,' he said, placing a wafer on the outstretched hand before him. 'The body of Christ . . . The body of Christ.' He continued down the line and behind him could hear Sinclair administering the wine. 'The blood of Christ,' he was saying, 'the blood of Christ.

Harry wondered if he'd ever be able to take pleasure in those words again.

33

"WINE, HARRY?'

'Thanks. Do you have any white?' Harry took off his coat and looked for somewhere to hang it. Coat-hooks in the Fletcher house always seemed occupied.

'Give me a minute.' Gareth crouched down and opened the fridge.

'Something smells good, Alice,' said Harry, taking a large glass from Gareth. The kitchen table was set for Sunday lunch. Millie, in her high chair, nibbled on a breadstick. There was no sign of the boys.

The bowl of the glass felt very cold. The liquid inside was reassuringly pale in colour. He sipped it. Definitely wine. Millie offered him her breadstick. When he shook his head, she dropped it on the floor.

'We're having Southern Baked Chicken,' replied Alice. 'Crispin' up nicely.'

'What was the problem during Communion?' asked Gareth, pouring a glass of the white wine for Alice and red for himself. 'We wondered where you'd gone.'

'Oh, the wine was corked,' said Harry, as he and Sinclair had agreed he would. What had happened was best kept between the two of them. He bent down to find Millie's breadstick. 'Seriously nasty, vinegary stuff,' he went on.

'It all went pretty well, though,' said Alice. 'You had a full house and nobody went to sleep.'

'And I'm sure they all found it a deeply fulfilling spiritual experience,' said Gareth. 'Ignore my wife. She's American.'

'Like you ever set foot in a church before you married me,' retorted Alice. 'Were you even baptized? Where's your breadstick, poppet? Oh, did the vicar steal it? Bad vicar.'

'I was dipped into Rawtenstall reservoir by my left ankle,' said Gareth. 'It made me invincible.'

Something was wrong here. Alice and Gareth were trying too hard. Something about the smiles and the banter felt forced. Come to think of it, neither looked like they'd had much sleep.

'Can I do anything, Alice?' Harry offered.

'You could find the boys. It usually takes about ten minutes to get them to the table, so be firm.'

Taking his glass with him, Harry began a search of the house. The downstairs rooms were empty of children so he headed upstairs. 'Boys,' he called when he reached the top step. 'Lunch is ready.'

There was no reply, so he walked towards two doors at the end of the landing. He knocked gently at the first and pushed it open. Joe sat in the middle of the carpet, surrounded by tiny toy soldiers.

'Hey, buddy,' said Harry. 'Mum says lunch is ready.'

Joe looked back down and moved several of his soldiers to new positions.

'I heard you being sick,' he said. 'In church. Everyone heard.'

Great, thought Harry. 'Well, I hope it won't put anyone off their lunch,' he said. 'Are you coming down?' He stepped back to the doorway. The room next door must be Tom's.

'They died, didn't they?'

Harry walked back into the room and crouched until his head was almost on a level with Joe's. The child hadn't taken his eyes off his game of soldiers. *Time to die.*

'What do you mean, Joe?' he asked. 'Who died?'

Joe raised his head and looked back at Harry. There were dark shadows under his eyes.

'Who died, Joe?' he asked, keeping his voice as soft as he could.

'The little girls in the church,' replied Joe.

'Joe, were you in church yesterday afternoon?' asked Harry. 'Did you hear me talking to Mrs Pickup?'

Joe shook his head. He didn't look as though he was lying. In any case, Jenny had told him about her daughter when she and Harry had been outside.

'Harry, boys, lunch,' called Alice from the bottom of the stairs. Harry began to push himself to his feet.

'Not that one,' muttered Joe, talking to his soldiers this time. 'Everybody knows about that one. I meant the other ones.'

Harry was back down on his knees again. 'Which other ones?' he asked. 'Joe?'

Joe looked up at him again. He was the sweetest-looking boy Harry had ever seen, with his pale freckled face, blue eyes and red hair. But there was something in those eyes that didn't look quite right.

'Is nobody in this house hungry?' yelled Alice.

Harry got to his feet. 'We have to go, buddy,' he said, pulling Joe to his feet and steering him towards the door. On the landing a noise behind them made them turn. The door to Tom's room was pulled open. The room beyond was in darkness, the curtains drawn. Tom appeared in the doorway, crossed in front of them and walked heavily down the stairs. It was the first time he had ever ignored Harry.

'Mummy, after lunch can we do the lanterns?' said Joe.

Alice was leaning across the table, cutting Millie's chicken into smaller pieces. She glanced at Tom and then at Harry. A frown line had appeared between her eyebrows. 'I'm not sure, sweetie,' she replied. 'Not everybody likes Hallowe'en. We can't upset the vicar.'

'I'm fine with pumpkins,' said Harry, watching Alice look nervously back at Tom. 'I'll give you a hand if you like, Joe,' he went on. 'Although, given how talented your mum and dad are, I'll probably be a big disappointment.'

'We do trick-or-treating on Hallowe'en,' said Joe. 'You can come with us if you like.'

'Actually, Joe, I haven't promised anything yet.' Alice was looking at Tom again. Her eldest son's plate hadn't been touched. 'What do you think, Harry?' she said, turning to him again. 'Is Heptonclough likely to celebrate Hallowe'en?'

'Oh, I'd put money on it,' Harry replied. 'Everything OK, Tom?'

'Tom has to go and see a special doctor,' announced Joe. 'Because he's been making up stories about monsters and last night he was historical.'

'What?' said Harry.

'Joe, that will do,' said Gareth at the same time.

'Tom had a bad dream,' explained Alice quickly. 'We got home late and the lane was very noisy. It was our fault for leaving him in the car.' She turned to her eldest son and ran a finger along the back of his hand. 'Sorry, angel,' she said. Tom ignored her.

'Come on, Tom,' said Gareth, 'eat some lunch.'

Tom's chair clattered loudly on the wooden floor as he pushed it back and jumped to his feet. 'It wasn't a bad dream!' he yelled. 'She's real and Joe knows who she is. He lets her into the house and when she kills us all it will be his fault and I bloody hate him!'

He'd left the room before either of his parents had time to react. Alice stood quietly and followed him. Gareth drained his glass and poured himself another. Joe was looking at Harry with big blue eyes.

Half an hour later, Harry left the Fletchers' house. After sending Joe and Millie off to play, Gareth had told him about the previous evening. Neither he nor Alice had ever seen anything of the girl that Tom continually talked about. Alice was taking him to the doctor in the morning.

The sky was threatening rain again as Harry walked down the drive. He stopped as he reached the family car. Someone had washed part of it. The driver's door and bonnet were dusty and mud-spattered, but the rear window and the panels immediately below it were clean as a whistle. There were even marks in the dust where someone might have run a cloth. There was also, in the top corner of the rear window, a faint mark that might just have been a fingerprint. A red one.

34

16 October

THE KNOCK ON THE DOOR STARTLED HIM, EVEN THOUGH he'd been expecting it. Harry got up and turned down the music. As he stepped into the hallway he could see two tall figures behind the glass of his front door.

Mike Pickup, Jenny's husband and Sinclair Renshaw's son-in-law, was dressed in a tweed jacket and cap in muted colours, brown corduroy trousers and a knitted green tie. The man at his side wore a dark-grey pin-stripe suit that looked as though it had been hand-made. Neither was smiling.

'Good evening, Vicar,' said Mike Pickup. 'This is Detective Chief Superintendent Rushton.'

The detective gave Harry a brief nod. 'Brian Rushton,' he said, 'Lancashire Constabulary. Pennine Division.'

'Good to meet you,' said Harry. 'Please, come in.'

His visitors followed him into the study. Harry bent to remove the slumbering ball of ginger fur from one of the armchairs and then waited until both his guests had taken seats. The study was the largest room in his house. It was where he worked, received visitors, and sometimes held small prayer meetings. Thanks to the presence of two large Edwardian radiators, it was also the warmest room in the house; and invariably, where he found the cat.

He put the animal on the floor and gave it a shove under the desk. 'Can I get you both a drink?' he offered. 'I have Irish whiskey,' he went on, indicating the bottle already open on his desk. 'There's beer in the fridge. Or I can put the kettle on.'

'Thank you, no,' said Pickup, answering for both. 'But don't let us stop you. We won't take up too much of your time.' He stopped, clearly waiting for Harry to sit down. The detective chief superintendent, who was in his late fifties and whose dominant features were his narrow, slate-coloured eyes and heavy dark eyebrows, was slowly looking around the room.

Harry took the chair nearest the desk. He wasn't entirely surprised to see the cat reappear and leap on to the arm of the detective's chair.

He started to get up again. 'I'm sorry,' he said. 'I'll get rid of him.'

'No, you're fine, lad. I'm used to cats.' Rushton held up one hand to keep Harry in his seat. 'Wife has two at home,' he said, switching his attention to the cat. 'Siamese. Noisy little buggers.' He reached up to stroke the cat behind its ears. The responding purr sounded like an engine being fired up.

'I, on the other hand, am not used to cats,' said Harry. 'That one seems to have adopted me.'

Rushton raised his enormous eyebrows. Harry shrugged.

'Maybe it's part of the fixtures and fittings of the vicarage,' he explained. 'Or just an opportunist stray. Either way, it was waiting for me when I arrived and has been refusing to leave ever since. I haven't fed it, not once, it just won't go away.'

'Does it have a name?' asked Rushton.

'That bloody cat,' answered Harry truthfully.

Rushton's lips twitched. Mike Pickup cleared his throat. 'Vicar, thank you for seeing us at short notice,' he said.

Harry inclined his head in his churchwarden's direction.

'The truth is I only heard from Brian less than an hour ago myself,' Pickup continued. A glance was exchanged between the two men, then Pickup turned back to Harry. 'Brian and I are old friends,' he said, as Harry hid a smile. The tomcat was curled up on the officer's lap, purring like a traction engine as Rushton's large hand ran the length of his body.

'Mike came to see me last Sunday evening,' Rushton said. 'After the incident during the harvest service.'

'Jenny and I had lunch at her father's house after the service,' explained Mike. 'I'm afraid we were curious about what happened during Communion. Sinclair obviously didn't want to discuss it, but Jenny pressed and in the end he gave in and told us. He seemed to think it was just a stupid practical joke that we could all forget about, but after what nearly happened with the Fletcher child a couple of weeks ago, I really wasn't happy. After lunch I went back to the vestry. Sinclair had poured the contents of the chalice away and washed it, but he'd forgotten about the decanter. I took it to Brian. He promised to have his lab look at it. Discreetly.'

'I see,' said Harry.

'Brian phoned me this evening to tell me the results,' continued Mike. 'It was pig's blood, which is pretty much what we expected. We slaughtered a number of animals on the Saturday and, as you may know, when a pig is killed the blood is drained and saved. It's used for making black pudding. Someone must have got hold of some – it wouldn't have been hard – and then found their way into the church.'

Rushton leaned forward in his seat. 'Reverend Laycock,' he said. 'I understand you got everything ready for the harvest service late on Saturday afternoon. Who could have had access to the church between the time of your leaving it and the Sunday-morning service?'

Harry looked at Mike, reluctant to mention Jenny in front of her husband. Mike opened his mouth to speak.

'My wife was in the church for about a quarter of an hour after Reverend Laycock left,' he said. 'Sinclair lent her his keys. I joined her at around four thirty and we both had a good look round the building. She told me you'd suspected children or someone of hiding in the church, Vicar. Is that right?'

'It is,' admitted Harry. 'Someone was messing around in there. I probably shouldn't have left Jenny on her own, but she did insist.'

'Jenny was fine,' said Mike. 'It was good of you to allow her some time. And the church was empty when we left. We made sure of it.'

'Who else has keys to the church?' asked Rushton.

'Normally, only the vicar and the churchwardens, possibly the cleaner, would have keys to a church building,' replied Mike. 'At present we don't have a cleaner. To my knowledge, only the vicar, Sinclair and I have keys now.'

'Reverend, I'm not a churchgoer myself,' began Rushton.

'Nobody's perfect,' said Harry automatically.

'Quite,' said Rushton. 'But Michael here tells me it's customary for the priest to take Communion first, is that right?'

Harry nodded. 'Yes, always. The idea is I'm in a state of grace myself before I administer the bread and wine to the other communicants.'

'Would most people know that, do you think?'

'I guess so. People who attend Communion regularly, anyway.'

'What's on your mind, Brian?' asked Mike.

'Well, it seems to me we have two possibilities. Either someone has a personal grudge against the vicar, and he was the one meant to be upset by the incident. Or the culprit didn't realize the Communion wine would be tasted by the vicar first. Because if you'd taken that cup straight to the congregation, I bet you'd have got to around half a dozen before the first two or three realized what was going on. Then you would have had a problem on your hands. Can you think of anyone who might have a reason to play this sort of trick?'

Harry thought for a moment, because he knew it was expected of him. 'I can't,' he said. 'I've been wondering if maybe someone didn't want the church to be opened again. Or perhaps I've upset someone since I've been here without realizing it.'

'You haven't,' said Mike. 'Actually, people are rather taken with you.'

'What we'd like you to do, Reverend,' said Rushton, 'is to let us take your fingerprints so that we can check the decanter for any that don't match yours.'

'I'm happy to do the same, if it helps,' said Mike, before turning to Harry. 'Vicar, we need to think about church security. I'll arrange to have the locks changed first thing in the morning. Make sure there are just the three sets of keys available.'

'Fair enough,' agreed Harry.

'Good. I can have the new keys ready for you the day after tomorrow. Come and have some lunch in the White Lion with me. Shall we say one o'clock?'

Taking fingerprints was the work of a few minutes and then the two men said goodnight and left. Harry returned to his study. He looked at the drinks cabinet. He'd had enough. He felt something warm moving between his ankles and looked down. The cat was rubbing its body against his jeans.

'I hate cats,' grumbled Harry. He bent to pick it up. It lay in his arms, purring, comfortingly warm.

Half an hour later the cat was fast asleep. Harry hadn't moved.

35

19 October

EVI PARKED HER CAR IN THE ONE REMAINING SPACE. THE huge hangar-style building of Goodshaw Bridge fire station was twenty yards away. She got out of the car and found her stick.

'I struggle with stairs, I'm afraid,' she explained to the fire officer at the reception desk. 'Is there a lift I could use? Sorry to be a nuisance.'

'No problem, love. Give me a minute.'

The fireman led her along the corridor. She tried to keep up but her back had been giving her trouble for days. Constantly leaning on her stick was putting too much pressure on the muscles on one side of her body and they were pressing against nerves. She should be using her chair more. It was just . . .

They reached the lift and went up one floor, then back along the corridor. Maybe on her way out she could just slide down the pole.

Ahead, her guide stopped at a blue door and rapped on it. Without waiting for a response he pushed it open. 'Lady to see you, chief,' he announced before glancing back at Evi. 'Dr . . . er?'

'Evi Oliver,' she managed through gritted teeth. 'Thanks so much.'

Inside the room, two more firemen were standing, waiting for her.

'Dr Oliver, good morning,' said the taller, older of the two, holding out his hand. 'I'm station chief Arnold Earnshaw. This is my deputy, Nigel Blake.'

'It was very good of you to see me,' said Evi.

'No problem. If the fire bell goes, you won't see us for dust. Until then, we're all yours. Now then, how about a coffee?' He raised his voice. 'Where you going, Jack?'

Evi's guide reappeared, double-checked that his two superiors still took their tea milky with three sugars each and happily agreed to make Evi a white coffee.

All three sat down. Evi would have liked a moment to get her breath back but both men were watching her, waiting for her to begin.

'I explained on the phone that I was interested in finding out more about a fire that occurred in Heptonclough a few years ago,' she began. 'It's in connection with a case of mine, but I'm sure you'll understand I can't give you details. It's a matter of patient confidentiality.'

Chief Earnshaw nodded his head. His colleague, too, looked interested, happy to help. She wondered if firemen were bored a lot of the time, actually quite welcomed distractions.

'The fire was in the late autumn, three years ago,' said Evi. 'In a cottage in Wite Lane, Heptonclough, did I mention that?'

Earnshaw nodded and patted a manila file on his desk. 'It's all in here,' he said. 'Not that we really needed to look it up. That was a bad one. A little lass died.'

'Were you there?'

'Both of us,' said Earnshaw. 'Every one of our regulars and a few of our volunteers as well. What can we tell you?'

'I understand that once the fire is contained, there are two basic questions that you need to answer,' said Evi. 'Where the point of origin was and what was the cause of the fire?' Gillian still hadn't told her how the fire had started. If it had been due to negligence on her part, or her husband's, it might go some way towards explaining her anger, or her guilt. Both men were nodding at her.

'Is that a good place to start?' she asked.

Blake leaned forward. 'You need three things to make a fire, Dr Oliver,' he said. 'You need heat, a fuel source such as paper or

168

gasoline, and you need oxygen. Without any one of those, no fire. Do you understand?'

Evi nodded.

'In most circumstances, we can take the oxygen bit for granted. So, what we're looking for is a combination of heat and fuel. After that, fire travels sideways and upwards from its point of origin. If a fire occurs at the foot of a wall, you'll see the burn patterns spreading up and away from it in a V shape. Are you with me?'

Evi nodded again.

'Some things in a house, like synthetic materials or stairways, can distort this, but as a rule of thumb you track the fire damage back to the point at which it was greatest and then look for the heat-and-fuel combination. At the Wite Cottage fire, the point of origin was pretty clear, even though the upper floor eventually collapsed. It was the kitchen, the area around the cooker.'

'And do you know how it started?' asked Evi.

'Largely guesswork,' replied Blake, 'because the damage in the area was so extensive. But we understand cooking oils were kept around the cooker, never a good idea. We suspect a pan was left with a gas flame underneath. It happens a lot with omelette pans. People make an omelette, concentrate on tipping it on to a plate without breaking it and they put the pan down, forgetting they've not turned the gas off. The pan gets hotter and hotter until the oil left in it catches light. If a plastic bottle of olive oil was close by, the plastic would melt and the oil run out. You can see how . . .'

'Yes, of course,' said Evi, making a mental note to move the bottles of cooking oil she kept close to her own hob.

'In this case, though, the real problem was the Calor gas,' said Earnshaw. 'The cottage wasn't connected up to the mains gas supply, so the family used a cooker that was powered by Calor gas. It's not uncommon in rural areas, but in this case, the family had three spare canisters stored in a small room just to one side of the cooker. Once they caught fire . . .'

'I see,' said Evi, wondering if she really had the nerve to ask her next question. 'I know this is a difficult question and please excuse me for asking it, but did you ever consider the possibility of arson?'

Earnshaw leaned back in his chair. Blake was frowning at her.

'We always have to consider arson,' said Earnshaw after a while.

'But on this occasion, there was nothing to cause us any undue concern. The fire had an easily identifiable point of origin.'

'One that could be readily explained,' chipped in Blake.

'Had it started in a wastepaper bin in a bedroom,' said Earnshaw, 'or if we'd found a trail of petrol around the house, it would have been a different matter.'

'The house was rented, so there was no possibility of insurance fraud,' said Blake.

'And the couple lost their child,' said Earnshaw, as though Evi should have thought of that herself. The arson-to-disguise-accidental-death theory wasn't going anywhere. Evi began to think she might be outstaying her welcome.

'I do understand that,' she said. 'I know I'm asking insensitive questions. I'm sorry I can't explain why.'

'Hiding evidence of arson really isn't that simple,' said Blake. 'Arsonists often use matches and then just throw them away, thinking the fire will destroy them.'

'And it doesn't?'

Blake shook his head. 'Match heads contain something called diatoms,' he said. 'Single-celled organisms containing a very tough compound called silica. Silica survives fires. Sometimes we can even identify the brand of match used.'

'I see,' said Evi. 'I've got one last question, if I may, then I'll leave you in peace. How soon after the fire was extinguished did you realize that the child's body had been completely destroyed?'

The two men looked at each other. Blake's frown had deepened.

'The fire burned for several hours, I understand,' Evi went on. 'Even after it was extinguished, you would have had to be sure the structure was safe.'

'The upper floor collapsed,' said Blake.

'Yes, exactly,' said Evi. 'So you would have had to search through the wreckage, it must have taken quite some time, before you were sure.' And all that time, Gillian had been traipsing over the moors, willing herself to keep believing. 'Before you were sure the fire had obliterated the child's body.'

'Dr Oliver, it's very rare for bodies to be completely destroyed in fire. Very rare indeed,' said Earnshaw.

'I'm sorry, I don't quite . . .'

'People who imagine otherwise don't know their chemistry,' said Blake. 'When bodies are cremated, they're exposed to temperatures of around 1,500° Fahrenheit for at least a couple of hours. Even then, you'll still find human remains among the ashes. Most structural fires, particularly in a residential house, don't burn hot enough or long enough to destroy a body. The house itself just doesn't provide enough fuel.'

'In this case, of course, the fire did get very hot because of the Calor gas acting as a fuel supply,' said Earnshaw.

'And is that why the little girl's remains . . .'

'We found her the next day,' said Blake. 'Very little left, of course, but even so . . . What made you think her remains weren't found?'

Evi's hands had flown to her mouth. 'I'm so sorry,' she managed. 'I've been completely misinformed.'

'What we found was very similar to what we'd expect after a cremation,' said Blake. 'Ashes and bone fragments. They were identified as human. There wasn't really any doubt that we'd found the child.'

'And what happened to the remains?'

'They were given to the family,' said Earnshaw. 'To the mother, from what I can remember.'

36

21 October

'WHY DO YOU THINK YOUR PARENTS WANTED YOU TO see me, Tom?' asked the doctor with sleek dark hair and thick black eyelashes. Evi, he'd been told to call her. She looked like one of his sister's Russian dolls, with her pale, heart-shaped face and big blue eyes. She was even wearing the same colours as Millie's dolls: a red blouse with a violet scarf.

Tom shrugged. Evi seemed nice, that was the worst thing, nice in a way that made him want to trust her. Trust her was something he really couldn't do.

'Has something been worrying you?' she was asking him now. 'Is anything making you anxious in any way?'

Tom shook his head.

Evi smiled at him. He waited for her to ask him another question. She didn't, just kept looking and smiling at him. Behind her head, a large window showed a sky so dark it was almost black in places. Any minute now it was going to tip it down.

'How are you getting on at your new school?' she asked.

'OK.'

'Can you tell me the names of some of your new friends?'

She'd tricked him, she'd asked him the sort of question he couldn't answer with a yes, no, OK or a shrug. Friends were OK,

172

though, he could talk about friends. He could talk about Josh Cooper, he was OK.

'Are any boys at school not your friends?' she asked, when they'd talked about boys in Tom's class for a few minutes.

'Jake Knowles,' Tom answered, without hesitation. Jake Knowles, his arch enemy, who had somehow found out that Tom was seeing a special doctor and had made his life extra miserable about it for days now. According to Jake, Tom was destined for the madhouse, where they tied you up and kept you in a padded cell and sent electric shocks through your brain. The special doctor would see he was nuts and send him away and he'd never see his mum and dad again. Worst of all, he wouldn't be able to look after Millie. He wouldn't be able to keep an eye on Joe.

'Do you want to talk to me about what happened a week ago last Saturday?' Evi was asking him now. 'When something frightened you and you ran into the churchyard?'

'It was a dream,' said Tom. 'Just a bad dream.'

37

*M*ILLIE HAD CLIMBED DOWN THE BACK STEPS INTO THE garden. *She pushed herself upright and looked all around. When her eyes found the yew tree her little face lit up. She set off towards it.*

'Millie!' Tom had appeared at the back door. 'Millie, where are you going?' He jumped down and crossed the garden to his sister in three strides, then bent to pick her up.

'Millie shouldn't be out on her own,' he said, as she started to squirm and he carried her back to the door.

Millie looked back at the yew tree as she was carried indoors and the door was firmly closed behind the two children. She wasn't allowed to be alone any more, not even for a minute.

38

23 October

'SCHIZOPHRENIA IS QUITE RARE,' SAID EVI. 'ONLY AROUND 1 per cent of the population develop it, and it's only in a very few of those cases that we see an onset of symptoms before the age of ten. Most importantly, neither you nor your husband have any family history of the illness.'

It was Evi's first meeting alone with Alice Fletcher, in the family's large, colourful sitting room. The two boys, both of whom she'd already met individually, were at school, Millie upstairs napping. So far, it was proving to be an unusual meeting. From the outset, Alice had almost seemed determined to charm her son's psychiatrist. She'd shown an interest in Evi personally, which patients, normally rather self-obsessed, rarely did. She'd tried to make her laugh, had even succeeded a couple of times. And yet it was so clearly a facade, and a fragile one at that. Alice's hands had shaken too much, her laughter had seemed forced and before the meeting was twenty minutes old she'd broken down and confided her fear that Tom was suffering from COS, or child-onset schizophrenia.

'But these voices . . .' she was saying.

'Hearing voices is just one symptom of schizophrenia,' said Evi firmly. 'There are quite a few others, none of which Tom appears to have.'

'Like what?' demanded Alice.

'Well, for one thing, his emotional reactions seem quite normal. I've seen no evidence of what we call thought disorder. And other than his insistence on this little girl – who he still hasn't mentioned to me, by the way – there's no sign of any delusional behaviour.'

Alice Fletcher interested her, Evi decided. A long way from her own home, she, more than the rest of the family, might be expected to find it hard to settle in Heptonclough. The question was, how much of the children's problems were the result of their picking up on the mother's anxieties?

'Even when schizophrenia is diagnosed in childhood,' Evi continued quickly, 'it's nearly always preceded by other diagnoses.' She started ticking them off on her fingers. 'Attention Deficit Hyperactivity Disorder, Bipolar Mood Disorder, Obsessive Compulsive Disorder. Do you know what any of these conditions—'

'Yes,' interrupted Alice. 'And the OCD, the obsessive compulsive thing, that fits too. Tom goes round the house every night, checking and re-checking the locks on all the doors and windows. He has a list. He ticks things off one by one and he won't go to bed until he's gone through it. Sometimes he gets up in the night and starts running through the list again. What's that all about?'

'I don't know yet,' said Evi. 'But I have noticed Tom's anxiety about his little sister. Joe shares it too, incidentally, although he may just be picking up on Tom's fears. Have they seen something on the news, do you know, something to make them especially anxious about her right now?'

Alice thought for a moment, then shook her head. 'I doubt it,' she said. 'They only watch children's television. Several times I've found him asleep on Millie's bedroom floor.'

Evi glanced down at her notes. 'Just to come back to this little girl, for a while,' she said. 'Because from what you've told me, most of what's bothering Tom seems to centre around her. Is it possible that there is someone in town who just looks a bit odd, maybe behaves in a strange way? Have you thought about that?'

Alice nodded. 'Of course,' she said. 'And I have asked a couple of people. Not many, I don't want everyone to know what we're going through, but I did have a quiet word with Jenny Pickup. And with her grandfather, Tobias. They've lived here all their lives. They'd never heard of anyone remotely fitting the description Tom gives.'

Alice paused for a moment.

'Besides,' she continued, 'Tom talks about this little girl as though she's barely human, the sort of thing we see in nightmares. This is a strange town, Evi, but harbouring monsters? How likely is that?'

39

27 October

HARRY WAS GETTING CLOSER TO THE TOWN. THE silhouettes of the great stone buildings were bigger every time he turned another bend in the road. Over his left shoulder a firework burst in the sky. He slowed the car a fraction more. He'd always loved fireworks. Maybe on 5 November he'd drive up the moor again, park the car and watch the fireworks exploding from a hundred different bonfire parties, stretching all the way across the Pennines.

The tarmac of the road gave way to cobbles and he turned the last corner that would bring him into town. Gold stars burst in the sky to his left and he was looking at them, not at the church, as he drew up and parked. He switched off the engine and got out of the car.

He'd been visiting one of his oldest parishioners. Mrs Cairns was in her nineties and almost bed-ridden. Afterwards, her daughter and husband had insisted he eat with them. By the time he left it was nearly nine o'clock and he still had to collect the church accounts from St Barnabas's.

His feet had just made contact with the smooth stones of the church path when he knew something was wrong. He'd never considered himself a particularly sensitive man, but this feeling wasn't one he could ignore. He knew he had to turn round and face the ruined church. And he really wasn't sure he could bring himself to do it.

He had turned. He was looking. He just didn't believe what he was seeing.

The ancient ruins of the abbey church were still there. The great arches still soared upwards, towards the purple sky. The tower, tall and forbidding, cast its shadow across the ground. Everything was just as it had been since the day he'd arrived. Pretty much as it had been for several hundred years. Only the figures were new. Sitting in window frames, leaning against pillars, sprawled along the top of arches, squeezed into every conceivable gap in the stonework were people. They sat, stood, leaned, sprawled, still as statues, mouths leering, eyes staring, surrounding him. Watching.

40

29 October

THE INTERMENT OF TWO-YEAR-OLD LUCY ELOISE PICKUP, only child of Michael Pickup and Jennifer Pickup née Renshaw, was the last entry in the burial register. Harry flicked back to the beginning. The first entry recorded the burial of Joshua Aspin in 1897. A church register had to be closed and taken to the diocesan record office when the oldest entry was 150 years ago. This one hadn't got there yet. He was about to close the book when he spotted the Renshaw name again. Sophie Renshaw had died in 1908, aged eighteen. The words *'An innocent Christian soul'* had been entered after the basic details. Harry glanced at his watch. It was eleven o'clock.

He turned the page and spotted names he recognized: Renshaw several times, Knowles and Grimes more than once. There it was again, halfway down the third page. Charles Perkins, aged fifteen, buried on 7 September 1932. *An innocent Christian soul.* He looked at his watch again. Three minutes past eleven. Harry leaned back in his chair and glanced round the room. No damp running socks drying on the radiator; the draining board was clear of used tea-bags.

A sudden noise from the nave made him jump and almost over-balance. He lowered his chair until all four legs were firmly on the ground. No one could be in the main body of the church. The

180

building had been locked when he'd arrived, he'd opened just one door, to the vestry, and that was less than three yards away. No one could have entered without him seeing them. And yet what he'd just heard had been too loud to be the random creaking of old wood. It has sounded like . . . like scraping metal. He stood up, crossed the room and opened the door into the nave.

The church was empty, of course, he hadn't expected anything else. It just didn't feel empty. He stepped backwards towards the vestry, his eyes roaming the chancel, looking for movement. He was listening hard. It was almost a relief to close the door. He might as well admit it, he just didn't like this church. There was something about it that made him feel uneasy.

Scared, you mean. This church scares you.

He looked at his watch again. It was ten minutes past eleven and his visitor was indisputably late. Could he wait outside? Not without looking a complete prat, he couldn't. He picked up his mobile. No messages.

He jumped again as a knock sounded on the vestry door.

Evi pulled up behind Harry's car. Using her stick as a lever she pushed herself out of her own. It was a long walk to the vestry door and using her chair was the only really sensible option. Her stick would fold up and slot along the back, the briefcase would sit on her lap, she'd be able to push herself across those smooth old flagstones in a matter of seconds. Faster than many people could run. And Harry would see her in a wheelchair.

She locked the car and began the slow walk up the path. She walked for two minutes, keeping her eyes firmly on the ground, wary of uneven stones. When she stopped for a breather a shadow caught her eye. The sun was throwing the outline of the ruined abbey on to the grass in front of her. She could make out the tower and the three arches that ran up one side of the nave. She could see the arched gap where a stained-glass window had once shone. What was left of the window ledge was fifteen feet above the ground. Should someone really be sitting on it?

Using the stick for balance, she turned and looked at the ruin. What in the name of . . .

Life-sized figures, wearing real clothes but with heads fashioned from turnips, pumpkins, even straw, filled the ruined church. Evi counted quickly. There had to be twenty or more of the things. They sat in empty window frames, lay across the top of arches, leaned against pillars; one had even been tied by its waist to the tower. It dangled, high above the ground. Unable to resist, Evi took a step closer, then another, taking herself almost within the confines of the church. They were guys, exceptionally well made from what she could see. None of them slumped, lifeless and flattened, the way guys normally did. Their bodies were solid, their limbs in proportion. They appeared remarkably human; until you looked at their faces, on each of which was carved a wide, jagged grin.

Not really liking to turn her back on them, Evi glanced towards the Fletcher house. At least two of the upstairs windows would get a pretty good view of the newly decorated abbey. Tom Fletcher and his brother would have to look out on this when they went to bed.

Her left leg was telling her she'd been still for long enough. She put her stick forward and, glancing back every few seconds, continued up the path.

She was flushed. There was a frown line running vertically down her forehead that he hadn't noticed before. Her hair was different too, sleek and dark, just reaching her shoulders and so shiny it looked wet.

'You should have phoned from the car,' he said. 'I'd have come out to help.'

Evi's lips stretched into a smile but the frown line was still there. 'And yet I managed,' she said.

'So you did. Come in.'

He stepped back and allowed her into the vestry. She made her way across to the two chairs he'd positioned close to the radiator and clutched the arm of the nearest one. She lowered herself slowly and then folded the stick and put it by her side. She was wearing a scarlet woollen jacket with a plain black top and trousers, and she'd brought a soft, spicy scent into the vestry with her. And something of the autumn morning too, a smell of leaves, of wood smoke, a crispness. He was staring.

'I can make coffee,' he offered, turning his back and moving to the sink. 'Or tea. There's even some Hobnobs somewhere. Alice never visits without bringing a packet over.'

'Coffee would be great, thank you. No sugar. Milk, if you have it.' He'd forgotten how sweet and low her voice was when she wasn't annoyed with him. He glanced back. How could eyes be that blue? They were so blue they were almost violet, like pansies at twilight. He was staring again.

He made coffee for them both, listening to rustling behind him as she opened her case and took out papers. Once she dropped a pen, but when he jumped round to pick it up, she'd already found it. The pink in her cheeks was fading. His own face felt far too hot.

He handed her a mug, took his own seat and waited.

Harry looked every inch the priest this morning: neat black clothes, white clerical collar, shiny black brogues. There was even a pair of reading glasses on the desk.

'Thank you for seeing me,' she began. He said nothing, just inclined his head at her.

She held out a sheet of paper. 'I need to give you this,' she said. 'Alice and Gareth Fletcher have authorized me to speak to you. To discuss as much of their case with you as seems appropriate.' Harry took the paper from her and looked at it. The glasses stayed on the desk. He was far too young to need reading glasses anyway. They must just be for effect. After a second or so he put it down and picked up his mug.

'I'm also speaking to several teachers at Tom and Joe's school,' she continued. 'To the headmaster of Tom's old school. And to their GP. It's normal practice when treating a child.'

She waited for Harry to respond. He didn't. 'Children are so affected by their environments that we have to know as much as we can about their surroundings,' she went on. 'About what impacts on their lives.'

'I've become fond of the Fletchers,' said Harry. 'I hope you can help them.'

So different, this morning. So completely unlike the man she'd met.

'I'll certainly do my best,' she said. 'But it's very early days. This is really just a fact-finding mission.'

Harry put his mug down on the desk behind him. 'Anything I can do,' he said, as he turned back.

So cold. A different man. Just wearing the same face. Still, she had a job to do.

'Tom was referred to me by his GP two weeks ago,' she said. 'He was presenting with extreme anxiety, difficulties at school, trouble sleeping, aggressive behaviour – both at school and at home – and even the possibility of psychotic episodes. Taken together, these are all very troubling symptoms in a ten-year-old boy.'

'I know his parents have been very concerned,' said Harry. 'As have I.'

'I don't know how much you know about psychiatry, but—'

'Next to nothing.'

Jesus, would it kill him to smile? Did he think this was easy for her?

'The normal procedure is to see the child first, to establish some sort of rapport – even trust, if possible. If the child is old enough, which Tom is, I try to get them to talk about what their problems are. To tell me why they think they've been referred to me, what's worrying them, how they think it might be addressed.'

She stopped. Harry's eyes hadn't left her face but she could read nothing from his expression.

'It hasn't worked too well with Tom yet,' she said. 'He's really quite skilled at saying the minimum he can get away with. When I try and steer him towards talking about the various incidents – with this odd little girl, for example – he just clams up. Claims it was all a bad dream.'

She paused. Harry nodded at her to continue.

'Then I try to bring in the rest of the family,' she went on. 'I observe how they interact with each other, try to spot any tensions, any sign of discord. I also take a full family history, medical and social. The aim is to get as complete a picture as possible of the family's life.'

She stopped. This was proving even harder than she'd expected. 'I'm following,' said Harry. 'Please go on.'

'There's always a physical examination,' said Evi. 'Of the referred child and any siblings. I don't carry it out myself, I find it interferes with the rapport I try to create with them, but Tom, Joe and Millie have all been examined by the GP.'

Harry was frowning. 'Are you allowed to tell me what he found?' he asked.

Evi shrugged. 'They're fine,' she said. 'Physically, they're all healthy children, with no significant medical issues, all developing normally. I've carried out a couple of evaluation tests myself with them. If anything, in terms of speech, cognitive functioning and general knowledge, Tom and Joe seem particularly well developed for their ages. Both would seem to be of above average intelligence. Does that accord with what you've observed?'

'Completely,' said Harry, without pausing to think. 'When I met them they were bright, funny, normal kids. I liked them a lot. Still do.'

The Fletchers were his friends. He wouldn't be able to be entirely objective. She'd have to win his trust too.

'It might also be worth mentioning that the GP found no evidence of abuse with any of the children. Either physical or sexual. Of course, we still can't rule it out entirely, but . . .'

He was glaring at her. Maybe he needed a reality check.

'When a child is as disturbed as Tom appears to be, it would be irresponsible to ignore the possibility,' she said, knowing her voice had hardened. Something in Harry's eyes flickered back at her.

'The most significant feature of their case, for me,' continued Evi, consciously trying to lower and soften her voice, even though he was starting to piss her off, 'is that the family's troubles seem to date from their moving here.'

Definitely something in his eyes.

'Tom's record at his old school was exemplary,' she said. 'I've spoken to his former GP, his old football coach, even his old scout master. They all report a normal, well-adjusted, happy child. Yet the family moves here and it all goes wrong.'

Harry had dropped his gaze. He was staring at the floor now. He looked sullen. Did he imagine she thought he was to blame?

'Mental illness in children rarely has a single identifiable cause,' she said. 'Anything pertaining to the Fletchers' new environment could have acted as a trigger, woken up some dormant condition inside Tom. It would be really helpful to know what that trigger was.'

'Is this where I come in?' he asked her, glancing up.

'Yes,' she said. 'You're new here too. You're probably in a better position than anyone to spot a possible catalyst. Can you think of anything?'

Harry took his time. Could he think of anything? The Fletcher family had moved to a town that hadn't welcomed newcomers for over ten years and where ritual slaughter was an excuse for a good night out. Where whispers came scurrying out of nowhere. And where someone poured pig's blood into a Communion chalice. Could he think of anything? Would he know when to stop?

'This is an unusual town,' he said at last. 'People here have a way of doing things that's all their own.'

'Can you give me any examples?' Evi had opened a small notepad and held a pencil between the fingers of her left hand. The hair on the right side of her head had been tucked behind one ear. Such a tiny ear. With a ruby stud.

'The first day I came here I saw the two boys being menaced by a local gang,' he said. 'Slightly older boys. Some of them teenagers.'

'On bikes?' she asked quickly.

Puzzled, Harry shook his head. 'Not at the time. Although I have since seen one or two of them riding around on bikes. They can certainly move at speed when they put their mind to it. And they're agile. I'm sure I've seen figures climbing around among the abbey ruins, even on the church roof. We haven't been able to prove it but we're pretty certain they were responsible for what happened to Millie Fletcher a couple of weeks ago.'

'And they were threatening Tom and Joe, that first day?'

Harry nodded. 'They broke a church window, tried to put the blame on the boys.'

'It wouldn't be the first time a close-knit community turned on outsiders,' said Evi. 'How have people here been with you?'

Harry thought about it for a second. 'Well, on the face of it, quite friendly. There are some nice people here. But there have been strange things happening.' He stopped. Did he want to tell Evi about the whispers he heard in the church? About what someone had tricked him into drinking? That a house of God scared him? 'Nothing I really want to go into,' he went on, 'but it wouldn't surprise me to hear that someone with a rather malicious sense of humour had been trying to frighten the boys.'

'That's it.' Evi was leaning forward in her chair. 'That's what I sense from Tom. Fear.'

A silver chain around her neck was glinting in the soft light of the vestry.

'What's he afraid of?' Harry asked.

'Normally when a child is afraid, we look close to home for the source,' replied Evi, 'but there's no indication that Tom is afraid of his family.'

She was wearing make-up, which she hadn't been when he'd met her previously. He hadn't realized quite how beautiful she was.

'We have a test,' she was saying. 'We call it the desert-island test. We ask the child to imagine he's on a desert island, way out in the middle of the sea, miles away from everything and completely safe. And we ask him to choose one person to be on the island with him. Who would he choose, out of all the people in the world?'

You, thought Harry, I think I might just choose you. 'What did Tom say?' he asked.

'He said Millie. His little sister. When he was asked to choose a second person he chose his mum. Then his dad.'

'Not Joe?'

'Joe was his fourth choice. I did the same test with Joe. He said the same thing. Millie first, his mum and dad next, then Tom.'

'Interesting that they both picked Millie.'

Evi dropped her eyes and turned a page of her notebook. Her dark hair swung down, covering her face. She turned another page and found what she was looking for. 'Then Joe said something that really puzzled me,' she continued, glancing back up at Harry. 'He said, would there be a church on the island, because if there was, he didn't think Millie should go.'

The radiator didn't seem to be working as well as it had been. Harry felt his fingers growing cold. *They died, didn't they? The little girls in the church.*

'I'm fine, really. I can manage,' said Evi.

Harry was holding open the vestry door. She stepped out and he allowed it to close behind her. 'I don't doubt that for a minute,' he said. 'But I see all my visitors to the gates. Can I . . .'

187

He was holding out his right elbow. She shook her head. 'I'm fine, thank you,' she said again.

They set off and Evi was acutely conscious of her stick tapping on the path between them. It took almost a minute to walk the length of the church. They turned the corner and she heard herself take a sharp breath. She'd forgotten that the ruined abbey had a new congregation. She stopped moving, glad of the excuse to rest for a moment.

'What on earth are they, Harry?' she asked, realizing she'd used his name for the first time that morning. 'I can't tell you the shock I had when I arrived.'

'Be glad you're not seeing them in the dead of night,' said Harry. 'I did. Came back to collect the church accounts and nearly had heart failure.'

Evi looked from one bizarre figure to the next. Some male, some female, one – oh cripes, that was the worst, the size of a small child. Then, conscious of Harry waiting patiently by her side, she started moving again.

'I know it's nearly Bonfire Night,' she said, 'but why so many guys? I've never seen such a collection.'

'They're not guys,' said Harry. 'They're bone men.'

Evi's head flicked from the ruins to the man at her side and then back again. 'Bone men? As in rag-and-bone men?' she asked.

Harry shook his head. 'Oh, it's more literal than that. They're called bone men, apparently, because a large part of their make-up is exactly that.'

She stopped again. 'You're going to have to explain.'

'Well, it's another Heptonclough tradition. They have a lot of them up here. This one dates back to the Middle Ages, when there was a charnel house adjoining the church. Every thirty years or so, graves would be opened, the bones dug up and placed in the charnel house. When it was full, they were burned. On a bone fire, which later became known as a bonfire. I had the full history the other day from my churchwarden's father, whom I'd like to describe as a delightful old man, but that would be pushing it. So I can tell you as much as you want to know about our friends over there, and probably more. For example, they're all made following the same pattern that old Mr Tobias devised himself fifty years ago.'

'This is all rather gross. What sort of bones. Surely not hu—'

'Well, let's hope not. Although I wouldn't be entirely surprised. They're fashioned mainly from natural materials. Most of the framework is willow and they're stuffed with straw, hay, corn, old vegetables. Each family in the village provides at least one. It's their way of getting rid of the year's rubbish – old clothes, paper, bits of wood, anything organic, especially bones. Which they have rather a lot of at this time of year because they've just finished slaughtering livestock for the winter. They freeze, dry and salt the meat, boil up the bones for soup and jelly, and then, well I guess they just don't have enough dogs. If you'd phoned me when you got here like you promised I could have met you and spared you the shock.'

Evi was still looking round the ruin. 'It must be one hell of a bonfire,' she said.

'I think they *are* the bonfire. Must be quite a sight, although I think I might give it a miss. And don't worry about saying "hell" on sacred ground. I'm becoming surprisingly open-minded.'

Was she imagining it or was that a glimpse of the old Harry? 'I'll bet you are,' she said. 'Is the fire here? On church property?'

'Over my dead . . . although maybe I should be careful what I say. No, it's in a field not too far away. You'd have ridden past it the day we met. It's where they held a sort of harvest ceremony a few weeks ago.' He stopped.

'The one you asked me to?' she said softly.

'Yes, the night of our aborted first date.'

She had nothing to say. She had to start walking again. She had to get in the car and drive off. Before . . .

'You look lovely, by the way,' he said.

. . . before he said something like that.

'Thank you,' she managed, letting her eyes fall to his feet and then rise back up to his face. 'You look like a vicar.'

He laughed briefly and seemed to pull away from her. 'Well, what you see is what you get, I suppose,' he said. He set off walking again, a little ahead of her this time. Then he stopped and turned back. 'Was that the problem?' he asked.

'Problem?' she stalled. No, Harry, that hadn't been the problem.

'Is that why you changed your mind?' he said.

She hadn't changed her mind. 'It's complicated,' she said. What could she possibly tell him? 'I can't even explain.'

The smile that had been dancing around at the corners of his mouth faded. 'There's really no need,' he said. He was holding his arm out again. She took it. 'If you change it back again, you know where I am.'

She really hadn't changed it in the first place. They were almost at the churchyard entrance. Two or three minutes away from saying goodbye. The sudden appearance of the woman took them both by surprise.

'What are you doing here?' she demanded, glaring at Evi.

Harry was startled. He'd been engrossed with the woman at his side. He hadn't noticed the other one standing just beyond the church wall.

'Hello, Gillian,' he said, cursing his luck. He'd wanted to take his time saying goodbye to Evi, to see if maybe . . . 'Did you need to see me?' he went on. 'The vestry's open. Actually, it shouldn't be. I'm supposed to be locking it up every time I leave the building. I guess I was distracted.' He smiled down at Evi. She wasn't looking at him any more. Her eyes were fixed on Gillian. He felt the pressure of her hand on his arm lighten. He pressed his own arm closer to his ribcage and laid his free hand on top of hers.

'Why are you here?' demanded Gillian again, taking her eyes off Evi's face only to glare at her hand, now trapped on Harry's arm. 'What were you saying?'

'Gillian, why don't you wait . . .' he began.

Gillian's head jerked up. 'What was she saying? She's not supposed to—'

'No, I'm not,' interrupted Evi. 'I'm not allowed to talk about my patients – ever – without their permission. So I don't do it. I came here to see Reverend Laycock about something else entirely.'

'We weren't talking about you,' said Harry, feeling the need to be perfectly clear. He looked from Gillian to Evi. The younger woman looked angry and bewildered. Evi just looked sad. A sudden thought struck him. Oh good grief.

'Actually, Gillian, I have a meeting at one of my other churches in fifteen minutes,' he said. 'Sorry, clean forgot. If you need to talk, you could phone me at home this afternoon. Excuse us now. I have to see Dr Oliver to her car.'

Gillian walked up the path away from them and stopped, just out of earshot. Harry walked Evi out of the churchyard and the few yards to her car. 'This problem we have,' he said, keeping his voice low. 'You know, the one that's getting in the way of our first date.'

Evi was fumbling in her bag. She didn't answer him.

'Did we just encounter it?' he asked.

She'd found her keys. She pressed the remote control and the car unlocked. He released her arm and moved in front of her to open the car door. She still wasn't looking at him but had turned back to the abbey ruins.

'It's not really any of my business, I know,' she said, folding up her stick and dropping it on the passenger seat. 'But is it not odd, to have all these figures on church property?' Her briefcase went in the car too. She seemed determined not to look at him. 'I'm just think-ing about the Fletcher boys,' she went on. 'I imagine this is a pretty scary sight when it's dark.'

'Oh, trust me on that one,' said Harry. Well, if she was refusing to look at him, he could stare all he liked. There was a tiny freckle just below her right ear.

She'd turned – and caught him. 'So can't you . . .' She left the question hanging.

'Evi, I've only been here a few weeks. If I start throwing my weight around now it could be disastrous for my tenure here.'

She opened her mouth, but he stopped her. 'Yes, I know. I'm putting my career before the welfare of two young children and I really feel quite bad about that, but the fact is I am not solely in charge of this property. I can talk to my churchwardens, see if the figures can't be taken down sooner than planned. I can speak to my archdeacon. If he supports me I can probably stop it happening next year.'

The fingers of her right hand had closed on top of his on the driver door. 'I'm sorry,' she said, 'I don't mean to give you a hard time. But they'll be here for another seven days.'

'No. They'll be here for four.' Did she realize she was touching him?

'Bonfire Night's on—'

'The good folks round here don't light their bone fire on November the fifth,' he answered. 'Apparently they don't set much store by defeating the Catholic plot to blow up parliament. They party on the second of November.'

'All Souls' Day?' she asked him.

'I thought you weren't a churchgoer? But you're right. November the second is All Souls' Day, when we pray for the departed who may not yet have reached God's kingdom. Only up here they call it something else. They call it Day of the Dead.'

41

31 October

THERE OUGHT TO BE A BIG MOON ON HALLOWE'EN. IT FELT right somehow. The moon Tom was looking at now, rising so quickly he could almost see the trail of silver light it left behind, wasn't quite full but looked huge in the sky all the same. It was the ghostly galleon of poems, gleaming down at him from just above the tallest archway in the abbey ruin.

Hallowe'en was usually a pretty big thing in the Fletcher house, probably due to Tom's mother being American. Not this year, though. Nobody celebrated Hallowe'en in Heptonclough; everyone was too busy getting ready for the Day of the Dead celebrations on the second of November. So the Fletcher children had one solitary jack-o-lantern sitting on the sitting-room window ledge, facing the garden where no one but them could see it.

Tom was sitting at the window in his room, hidden behind the curtain. When he did that, nobody could see him. Just lately, it was proving a useful way of finding out all sorts of things he wasn't supposed to know.

Like, for instance, that his mother had been trying hard to get all the bone men taken down from the ruins. Joe and he had counted twenty-four of them that morning, five more than when they first appeared. His mother absolutely hated them and had been on the phone to Harry just ten minutes ago. She'd come very close to falling out with him.

Twenty-six. He'd just counted twenty-six bone men around the abbey ruins. There'd only been twenty-four this morning. Sometime during the day two more had been added. Excellent!

That morning, at breakfast, Joe had asked if they could make one of their own. Their mother had said a very firm no, glancing at Tom nervously, but he honestly wouldn't have minded. He thought they were quite cool, even funny in their way. There was one with jodhpurs, a pair of old wellies and a riding hat. One of its hands held a stick that was supposed to be a riding crop and it had a kid's stuffed fox, like Basil Brush, under one arm.

Oh shit. Oh Jesus. One of them just moved. Tom blinked, rubbed his eyes, looked harder. One of the bone men – made up of nothing but clothes and old rubbish – was crawling along one of the walls. He got ready to jump down, to run and fetch his parents. Then stopped. It was gone. Had he imagined it?

If he had, he was still doing it, because there was another one, climbing through the lowest window of the tower. It was the one Joe thought was the funniest, the one wearing a lady's flowered dress and a big straw hat. Tom could see the hat, almost as clear as daylight, wobble on the figure's head. Then it jumped into the shadows and disappeared.

What the hell was going on? Were they all going to get up and move? Tom was kneeling upright now, not caring if someone saw him, actually hoping they would. Another movement, over by the outside wall. Then two of them, moving together – or was one carrying the other?

'Dad!' he called, as loudly as he dared, knowing Millie was asleep across the hall. 'Dad, come here.'

Then a hand touched him and he almost leaped through the glass. Thank God, someone was here, someone else could see. He tugged the curtain aside to see who had come into his room.

Joe. Tom reached down a hand, pulled Joe up beside him and tugged the curtain round them both again. 'Look at the abbey,' he told his brother. 'The bone men are alive.'

Joe pressed his face to the glass and looked. The two boys watched one of the bone men run across the grassed area that used to be the nave. It disappeared behind a pile of stones. Tom turned to Joe. Who didn't look in the least bit surprised. Tom felt the excitement in his ribcage plummet.

'It's her, isn't it?' he said in a low voice. 'The bone men aren't moving by themselves. She's moving them.'

Joe turned away from his brother, getting ready to climb down from the ledge. Tom stopped him, holding so tightly to his arm he knew it had to hurt. Joe muttered something his older brother didn't catch. Tom didn't think. He just shoved him hard. Joe's head cracked against the glass and then he fell on to the carpet.

Later, when Joe had been declared out of danger of dying, more's the pity, and was tucked up in bed with hot chocolate and stories and a huge great fuss on the part of his mother, and Tom had been told to stay in his room for the rest of the decade, he finally worked out what Joe had said, just before he'd been clobbered.

'Not posed tell,' he'd muttered. Which in Joe-speak meant: not supposed to tell.

Part Three
Day of the Dead

42

2 November

'GO IN PEACE TO LOVE AND SERVE THE LORD,' SAID Harry. The organ began to play the recessional and Harry stepped down from the chancel. The Renshaws, as always, were first to leave church. As Christiana stood to follow her father and grandfather out of the pew, she appeared to be clutching something in her right fist.

Harry went into the vestry, crossed the room and unbolted the outside door. Stepping outside, he walked quickly to the rear of the church, just in time to shake Sinclair's hand as he left the building. Christiana held out her hand without looking at him. Nothing in it now. Next came Mike and Jenny Pickup. Jenny's eyes were damp and she carried a small bouquet of pink roses. A week earlier Harry had put a blank book by the church door, inviting parishioners to write the names of people they wanted remembered during the service. Lucy's name had been at the top. 'Thank you,' Jenny said. 'That was lovely.'

The rest of the congregation followed, each needing to take the vicar by the hand, thank him and tell him something of their lost loved ones. Almost at the back came Gillian, who never seemed to miss a service these days, which he supposed he should be glad about, one more Christian soldier and all that. Hayley, too, had been remembered during the service. Harry shook Gillian's hand and, knowing she had no grave to honour, almost bent to kiss her cheek. Except the last time he'd done that she'd turned her head at the last second and their lips had met. It had been an awkward moment, which his hastily muttered apology had done little to smooth over.

A middle-aged, red-haired woman followed Gillian out, and she was the last. Harry walked back into the church. Checking that the nave was empty, he set off up the aisle. Someone had scattered rose petals.

He glanced up. They could almost have been dropped from the balcony. They lay at the exact spot where little Lucy Pickup had died, where Millie Fletcher had almost fallen. Harry remembered Christiana's clenched fist as she left the building. Leaving the petals where they were, he walked quickly up the aisle and into the vestry once more. He checked that the outside door was locked and started to undress. Three minutes later, he was stepping out on to the path again, bracing himself against the cold and locking the vestry door behind him.

'And tha's a quick-change artist as well, lad.' One of his parishioners, a man in his seventies, was walking towards him. His wife, his parents and two brothers were buried in the churchyard, he'd told Harry earlier.

'I'm a man of many talents, Mr Hargreaves,' replied Harry, leaning against the church wall to stretch out his hamstrings.

'Tha's not goin' up ont' moor, is thee, lad? Tha'll take off in this wind.'

'Ah never knew vicars 'ad legs,' chortled a woman, hobbling her way up behind Stanley Hargreaves.

'Healthy body, healthy soul, Mrs Hawthorn,' replied Harry. 'Sorry I can't show you a better pair.'

Harry jogged slowly past the two elderly people. As he left the churchyard, he saw Alice taking Millie to their car. He should really have a word with her. He jogged down the hill a few paces and saw that Alice was now talking to the woman with dyed red hair who'd followed Gillian from church.

'So beautiful,' the woman was saying, reaching out to touch Millie's curls. 'I had one just like her. Breaks my heart to see her.'

Millie squirmed away from the woman, hiding her face against her mother's shoulder, just as Alice spotted Harry. He approached slowly, not wanting to interrupt, unsure how welcome he was going to be.

'They grow up so quickly,' Alice said.

'Mine never grew up,' the woman replied. Unable to reach Millie's face any more, she patted the child's shoulder. 'You take good care of this little one. You never know how precious they are till you've lost them.'

Alice gave up the effort to smile. 'Yes, I'm sure,' she said. 'Well, there's the vicar. I must just say hello. It was nice to meet you.' The woman nodded at Alice and then, with one last stroke of Millie's head, set off down the hill.

'Don't know who that cheery soul was,' said Alice in a low voice, as Harry approached. He glanced at the woman's retreating form and shook his head. 'She was in church just now,' he said, 'but I've never met her before. Listen, about last night . . .'

Alice held up her hand. 'No, I'm sorry. I do understand how difficult it is for you. It's just . . .' She stopped. 'I can't help thinking there's something seriously wrong with Tom.'

She bent into the car and put Millie into her child's seat before buckling the strap round her daughter. Harry leaned closer to the car in the hope that it might offer some shelter. The perishing wind was getting up his shorts. 'I really doubt that,' he said. 'And getting yourself worked up won't help him.'

'That's exactly what Evi said,' replied Alice.

Harry couldn't stop. His legs were starting to shake and he had a pain in his chest, but the minute he stopped running the sweat on his body would start to chill down.

He was two miles above the village. Ten minutes after setting off, he'd found an old bridle path and followed it to the road. He'd gone up, climbing higher and higher, until the wind was almost lifting him off his feet. Now he was heading for home.

The walls and hedges offered some shelter, but when the wind hit him full on he almost felt as if he'd stopped moving. His wristbands were soaked through and the cold air was hurting his lungs. This was insane. Even the view was wasted – his eyes were watering so much he could barely see the ground beneath his feet.

High above the trees to the east soared the massive Morrell Tor, a huge collection of gritstone boulders balanced precariously on top of each other. Formed naturally, but once believed to be man-made, tors were particularly common in the Pennines. Morrell Tor, Harry had learned, was notorious locally. Legend had it that in days gone by, unwanted and illegitimate babies would be tossed from its heights, to shatter on the rocks below and be carried off by wolves and wild dogs. Today, it presented a serious problem for sheep farmers, who went to great lengths to keep their livestock away from it. On nights with strong winds, it was said, a singing among the rocks would lure a dozen or more to their death.

He realized he'd stopped running. And that he was freezing. He had to get home, shower and change, then attend an old folks' lunch in Goodshaw Bridge. And he had a phone call to make. In another few yards he'd be able to follow a footpath along the edge of a field, to bring him out at the end of Wite Lane.

He squeezed through the gap between two tall boulders and set off again along the field edge, heading downhill, keeping his eyes on the ground. At the corner he climbed the low wall into the stubble field beyond. In less than a minute he was at the lowest end. He jumped over the stile and down into Wite Lane. Almost home.

Huddled in front of the burned-out fireplace of the Royle cottage was the thin, trembling body of a girl. Gillian. Twenty yards away he could hear her crying. Except it wasn't really crying. Keening. That was the only word for it: a high-pitched, heartbreakingly sad keening. The Irish called it the song for the dead.

43

'IT'S OK, IT'S OK.' HE'D PUSHED OPEN THE GATE, WAS stepping up the overgrown path. 'Come on, love, let's get you home.' He walked through the space where the front door used to be. Gillian didn't look up. She remained hunched over, clutching something to her chest. He crossed the uneven ground and bent down beside her. She looked up at him then and he fought a temptation to pull back. For a second the look in her eyes had scared him, had made him think that something essential inside her had slipped out the back way.

'Come on,' he said, 'let's get out of here. Come on, pet, you're freezing.' Gillian was only wearing a thin sweater and her wrist felt colder than stone. He put an arm around her waist and pulled her to her feet.

She continued to sob as he guided her out through the gate and half led, half dragged her along Wite Lane. The churchyard and street were deserted and his was the only car in the lane. He steered Gillian across the road and opened the passenger door. He never locked the car in Heptonclough and his keys were still in the vestry, with his clothes. He reached into the car, pulled out his coat and wrapped it round her shoulders.

'Get in,' he told her. 'I need to grab my bag from the vestry, then I'll drive you home.'

Shivering, he ran up the churchyard path, pulled the key out of his shorts pocket and opened the vestry door. His bag was where he'd left it. Grabbing a sweatshirt, he pulled it over his head. He was about to leave when something made him stop and turn.

Someone had been in here. The door to the nave was open. It hadn't been when he'd left, he was sure of it. Harry took a step towards it. It would have been one of his churchwardens, Mike or Sinclair. They were the only other people who had keys now. And yet they'd formed a habit, over the last few weeks, of telling him when they were going to be in the building. He'd seen both of them less than an hour ago. Neither had mentioned plans to come back. Still, it could only be . . .

He stopped in the doorway, knowing that his heart was beating too fast and his breathing was too shallow, and telling himself it was the result of a fast run over hill country. Not his churchwardens then. Neither Mike nor Sinclair would have taken every single hassock from the pews and thrown them around the building. Harry stepped into the chancel. Dozens of cushions: on the carpet, caught between the organ pipes, on the choir stalls, everywhere but where they should be.

Harry walked forward, knowing that this wasn't just about the hassocks, that there was more for him to find, and that it was only a matter of seconds before he did. He wasn't breathing too fast any more, he was struggling to breathe at all.

Something was growing, fungus-like, in his throat, pressing against its sides, blocking the airway as he reached the centre of the chancel and turned to look down the aisle. He was ready to be shocked. Just not that shocked. He wasn't prepared to see a small child, broken in pieces, beneath the gallery.

Millie Fletcher! He'd seen her wearing that sweater.

For a few seconds it was impossible to do anything but stare. No air at all was getting into his body now. His head would start to spin at any moment. He began to walk forward, clutching the ends of pews like a toddler unsure on its legs. As he reached the halfway point, he realized he was trembling in relief, not fear. And he was breathing again. Not Millie, thank God, thank God, it couldn't be Millie – or any real child, for that matter – because no part of a child's anatomy was made up of vegetables. Oh, thank God.

A turnip, still bearing the crude drawing of a child's face, had smashed apart on the flagstones. The wicker construction of the figure was in pieces. It was the smallest of the bone men, brought inside and dressed up in Millie's sweater. The shivering running through his body began to feel less about relief and more about outrage. The message couldn't be clearer. This was intended to be Millie, to show Millie broken to pieces on the church floor, as she so nearly had been on the night of the harvest festival, as Lucy Pickup had been before her. What in the name of God was going on here?

Conscious that Gillian was still waiting for him in the car, Harry reached the figure and crouched down. He couldn't just leave it there. He stretched out an arm to start gathering the pieces together and stopped himself just in time.

Evidence.

From the vestry he brought a large black bin-liner and the Marigold gloves left behind by one of the cleaning team. Wearing the gloves, he gathered the pieces together, including the pink and orange sweater, and put them all in the black bag. When he was done, he tied a knot in the top and stood up.

He had to let the police know. Teenage prank or not, Millie was two years old and had already been put in real danger once. And this really wasn't funny. Plus, changed locks or not, someone was still getting in and out of the church whenever they wanted to.

Gillian didn't ask what had taken him so long; she hardly seemed to have noticed. Harry turned the heater up to full blast and set off down the hill. It only took two minutes before he pulled up outside the town's post office and convenience store. Gillian lived in a flat above it.

She hadn't moved. In her lap she clutched a small, pink soft-toy. He switched off the engine and climbed out. His shoulders were starting to ache.

'Gillian, pet.' He was leaning in, not really wanting to touch her again but suspecting it was inevitable. 'You're home now. Come on, let's get you inside.'

Still she didn't move. Swallowing his irritation, Harry slid his arm around her shoulders. She came willingly enough then, leaning against him as she slipped clumsily out of the car. As they crossed the street, Harry noticed two women watching them.

The outside door wasn't locked. He took Gillian's hand and pulled her up the narrow stairway with its worn, dirty carpet. At the top, he turned to her. 'Keys?' he enquired. She shrugged.

He pushed the door and it swung open with a waft of unwashed laundry and stale air. Either the flat wasn't much warmer than the day outside or he was well on his way to catching a chill.

He steered Gillian towards the sofa and crossed quickly to the electric fire. Switching it on to full, he turned back to the girl. She was sitting at the edge of the sofa, staring at the wall in front of her. The toy in her hands was a rabbit.

'Gillian, you need a blanket. Where will I find one?'

She didn't answer and he turned away from her. If she looked at his face, she'd see how annoyed he was. Angry with her, angry with himself, angry with the old folks of Goodshaw Bridge who, even now, would be glancing at their watches, and very angry with the sick bastard who thought he could scare him by dressing up a pile of bones and twigs.

Gillian's flat wasn't large. He soon found the kitchen and then the bedroom. He caught a quick glimpse of a floor covered in clothes, empty glasses scattered around and a greasy dinner plate on the bedside table. He pulled the duvet off the bed.

Back in the living room, Gillian had curled herself up on the sofa, still clutching the rabbit. He put the duvet over her and returned to the bedroom for a pillow. He tucked it under her head and crouched down until he could look her in the eyes.

'Gillian, I need to call someone,' he said. 'Someone who can come and look after you.'

Silver-grey eyes gazed back at him. 'You,' she croaked. 'I want you to look after me.'

He shook his head. 'I have to be somewhere. I'm late already and you need someone who can look after you properly, not a man you hardly know.'

Gillian pushed herself up on to one elbow. She took one hand off the pink toy and reached up to her hair. 'Stay,' she said, stroking her hair to neaten it. She pushed herself up higher and held her hand out to Harry. 'Stay,' she repeated. 'We could, you know . . .'

'Do you want me to call Dr Oliver?' he offered, leaning back on his heels so that he was just out of reach. 'It might help you to talk to her.'

Gillian was upright on the sofa now, glaring at him. Make-up was smeared on her cheeks. Her nose was red from the cold. 'Is she your girlfriend?' she demanded.

'Of course not,' he said, knowing it was true but feeling as if he was lying. 'I've only met her a few times.' No, that wasn't good enough. It was unfair to all three of them. 'But I do like her,' he added.

'I thought you liked me,' she wailed.

'I do,' he answered. When had she taken hold of his hand? 'But I'm too old for you and . . .'

'I don't care.'

'. . . and you need to get well again before you start any sort of relationship.' He had to get his hand back. He had to retreat to a safe distance.

'I could get well quickly if I had you, I know I could.'

He had to tell her. She had to know it was never going to happen.

'Gillian, I know how difficult today must have been for you, seeing people visiting graves, having others around to comfort them. Believe me, I know what it's like to be alone.'

'I'm not a slag, you know. There hasn't been anyone since Pete.'

'I don't doubt that. But trust me, that is not the way to get over Hayley. What about your GP?'

It wasn't going to work. She was taking a deep breath, getting ready to . . .

'You have no idea!' she screamed at him.

She was right. He had no idea. He was completely out of his depth.

'What about a friend?' he offered. 'Is there anyone who lives nearby?'

'She won't leave me,' said Gillian, speaking to a point somewhere in the middle of his chest.

'Who won't? Do you mean Hayley?'

She nodded. 'She's dead, I know that,' she said. 'I've known for a long time, but she won't go away.' She grabbed his hand again. 'She's haunting me.'

'Gillian . . .'

Her head shot up. Her eyes looked terrified. 'Please help me,' she begged. 'You can do something, I know you can. Make her go away. You can do a – what do you call it? – an exorcism.'

The girl was unbalanced. She needed serious help.

'Gillian, I'm going to call someone. You can't—'

'Listen to me.' She'd grabbed both his hands now, had fallen off the sofa and was kneeling in front of him. 'This is the Day of the Dead, right? When lost souls who can't find their way to heaven come back to where they used to live. I never used to believe in all that, but I do now. She was here today. She took the toy, Pink Rabbit, and put it in our old house. I found it just now, where the kitchen fireplace used to be.'

'Gillian . . .'

'She talks to me all the time. I hear her voice, calling "Mummy, Mummy, help me." It doesn't matter where I am. In here, asleep, out on the moors, she's always there, always talking to me. "Mummy, Mummy," she says, "find me." She moves things around, here in the flat, leaves little presents for me. Every time I turn round, every time I wake up in the night, I think she's going to be there, just as she was the last time I saw her, in her Beatrix Potter pyjamas.'

Harry realized he was shaking.

'She's with me every day. She's driving me insane.'

'Gillian, you know, don't you, there are no such things as ghosts?'

There was a loud banging on the outside door.

'Sit down,' he told her. 'I'll go and see who that is.' She was still holding his hand. She clung on, unwilling to let go, but Harry headed towards the door and she had little choice. Overcome with relief at being away from her, even for a few minutes, he jogged down the stairs and pulled open the door. The middle-aged woman with the dyed-red hair was standing outside.

'Vicar.' She inclined her head and stepped forward, clearly expecting him to move aside and let her in. 'Edith Holcome phoned me,' she said. 'She saw you bring Gillian home. Said I should probably get down here.' She moved forward again.

'Are you a friend of Gillian's?' asked Harry. Had reinforcements arrived after all?

'I'm her mother. Gwen Bannister. Nice to meet you, Vicar. Don't worry any more, I'll look after her now.'

Her mother? Oh, thank God.

'Well, if you're sure . . .' Had he left anything upstairs? Did it matter? Were his keys in his pocket? Yes.

'She's extremely upset,' he offered, not wanting anyone to go up those stairs unprepared. 'I think she may need to see a doctor.'

'I know, I know, I've seen it all before.' The woman had pushed her way past him and was already halfway up the stairs. 'I lost a child too and did I fall to pieces? We had more backbone in my day.'

Could he go? Darn right he could.

Without looking back, he slipped out of the door and ran across the street to his car. He'd left his coat behind but it seemed a small price to pay. He looked at his watch. If he drove as though all the devils in hell were after him and spent less than two minutes in the shower, he'd still be twenty minutes late. He really had no more time to waste.

So why was he picking up the phone?

Duchess's hooves were clattering on the concrete of the livery yard when Evi's phone started to ring. She reached inside the pocket of her coat and glanced at the screen. Oh!

'Evi Oliver,' she said, as Duchess edged closer to her box.

'Hi, it's Harry Laycock,' said the voice on the phone. She'd known who it was. His name had appeared on the digital screen. Just the one word: Harry.

'Oh, good morning.' Was that right – friendly but with a faint note of surprise? 'How are you?'

'Fine,' he said. 'In a bit of a rush. Listen, I've been thinking. This bonfire thing. I think you should go. I mean come. Come with me.'

He was asking her out. Was he? 'You told me you were going nowhere near it,' she pointed out.

'I've changed my mind. There's something not quite normal going on up here, Evi, and I need to know what it is. And if you really want to get to the bottom of what's bothering Tom Fletcher, I suspect you do too.'

She could see him? That night? 'I'm not sure, Harry,' she said. 'It seems a bit . . .'

'I could pick you up at six thirty and drive you up there. Help you over the rough ground. Not that you need any help, I fully understand that. And it wouldn't be a date, or anything. Strictly professional, you know – work – for both of us.'

'Thank you, I know what professional means. I was going to say, it seems a bit intrusive. The Fletchers might think I'm spying on them. Maintaining trust is really important when you're working with a family.' Oh, shut up, you silly cow, you're going to talk him out of it.

'I've already spoken to Alice. She's fine with it. And we're both invited for supper afterwards but, I repeat, it's definitely not a date.'

'Yes, I got that bit too. I quite understand.' A date with Harry. She was going on a date with Harry. Duchess started backing away from the box, was twisting round on the concrete. 'Look, you've caught me on the hop a bit,' Evi said. 'It might be a good idea but I'd have to talk to Alice myself. Can I call you back this afternoon?'

'Of course. Now I really have to run. I'll talk to you later.'

He was gone – and what in the name of all that was wonderful was she going to wear?

44

A S QUICKLY AS HE COULD, BUT NOT FORGETTING TO watch out for anyone who might be lurking, Tom ran through the churchyard entrance, skirted round the ruins, past the church and into the graveyard, then dived behind a stone to get his breath back.

It was four thirty, and a few stripes of orange and pink in the sky showed where the sun had been not five minutes earlier. The cloud cover was thickening rapidly. The light would fade fast now. He hadn't much time.

He set off again, keeping as close as he could to the boundary wall. If anything happened, he could be over it and in through the back door in seconds. She was fast, Tom knew that, but he was fast too.

At Lucy Pickup's grave he crouched low again. Someone had left a bunch of tiny pink roses on it and – it looked so sad somehow – a small cream teddy bear with a pink ribbon round its neck. He remembered, then, the reason why the town had its bonfire tonight instead of on November the fifth; November the second was the Day of the Dead. Harry had told them all about it. It was the day when people remembered and honoured all those they loved who were dead now. In Heptonclough people visited their graves, prayed for them, left presents. They honour their dead in Heptonclough, Harry had said.

Tom looked all around. Still enough light. And he was very close to the wall.

Yew trees are no good for climbing, anyone could tell you that. They don't grow that tall and their branches don't get thick enough. But this tree had just one strong branch that hung out over the Fletchers' garden. If Tom was careful, if he didn't worry about a few scratches, he could make his way on to it.

He had about ten, fifteen minutes. His mother thought he was doing homework and she'd warned Joe and Millie not to come near him. Fifteen minutes might be enough.

Climbing up, Tom was shocked to discover how much of his house could be seen from the tree. He could see Joe crawling along the back of the sofa with his machine gun tucked under his arm. Tom could even see quite a lot of the upstairs rooms too. There was his mum in the bathroom, reaching into the cupboard for one of Millie's nappies. All of which made him wonder. Did she sit here, on this branch, watching them? Yew trees never lose their leaves. Tucked up in here, if she kept still, she could watch his family for hours and they'd never know.

Round his neck, tucked into his sweatshirt to keep it safe, he had his dad's digital camera. He knew how to set the flash, how to focus and how to zoom in and out. He'd practised all yesterday evening, taking pictures of Millie dancing around the living room, and then his dad had showed him how to download them on to the computer. Tom was going to wait until the little girl appeared and take photographs. As many as he could. And then they'd have to believe him. If he could show them pictures they'd know he'd been telling the truth. That he wasn't mad. Best of all, *he'd* know he wasn't mad.

In a couple of hours it could all be over.

45

'SO WHAT'S THE PLAN, REVEREND? KICK OFF WITH SOME voodoo rites before a spot of ritual sacrifice, quick break for a hot-dog and then zombies rising around midnight?'

'I don't think you're taking this seriously,' replied Harry, guiding Evi round two girls who were clinging to each other in the middle of the road. One of them had the glassy-eyed look of the seriously intoxicated. Ahead of them a pink and green firework exploded in the sky. For a second, he could see the sparks reflected in the clouds. Then darkness again.

'Am too,' said Evi. 'I did a project in my first year on crowd psychology. I love seeing it in action.'

A boy in his late teens appeared from one of Heptonclough's numerous stone alleyways and lurched towards them. An unlit cigarette dangled from his mouth. 'Godda light?' he enquired, before looking into Harry's face. 'Oh, sorry, Vicar.' He stumbled away down the hill. Evi gave a soft laugh.

The town was more crowded than Harry had seen it before and he'd been forced to park almost a quarter of a mile down the hill. He'd offered to drop Evi off at the church, so that she could wait for him on the shepherds' bench, but she'd refused and now they'd joined the others who were walking up the hill towards the bonfire field. The night was heavy with the smell of gunpowder and wood smoke.

Every few seconds, people who were able to move faster passed

213

them. Most turned to nod, wish Harry good evening and stare curiously at Evi. And he really didn't blame them. In a dark-blue quilted coat the exact colour of her eyes and a matching hat, she might just be the prettiest girl any of them had seen in a long time.

'What are your professional observations so far?' he asked.

Evi stretched her neck to look round, then peered up at him. 'Everything you might expect,' she said. 'Kids are excited, so they're playing up. That makes the parents a bit tetchy – they're scared of losing them in the dark, so they'll be over-protective, a bit anxious. That'll manifest itself as bad temper.'

There was that tiny freckle again, just below her right ear.

'The older kids will be drinking more than usual,' she went on. 'Those old enough to get away with it will be in the pub. The younger ones will have bottles of cider tucked away in dark corners. There's potential for arguments, even violence, but probably not for another couple of hours.'

If he kissed that freckle, he'd be able to feel the curve of her ear on his cheek, and her hair would tickle his nose.

'The main problem,' she said, 'is that events like this create a certain sense of expectation. Everyone's waiting for something to happen. People are in a state of anticipation, and if they're disappointed in some way, then that's when the trouble will start because they'll need a vent for their frustration. Are you even listening to me?'

'Most certainly,' he said, knowing he was grinning like a fool. 'Are we still talking about the bonfire?'

The Fletchers left the house just before seven, tucked up in all their warmest clothes. Millie was in her mother's arms, Joe on his dad's shoulders and Tom had been told, several times by both parents, that if they lost sight of him for a second they'd cut off his toes. The camera was round his neck.

He'd managed twenty minutes in the churchyard before his mum had appeared at the back door yelling for him. He'd scrambled down the wall and run across the garden, with one hand over the camera to protect it. Once his mother had got the necessary telling-off out of her system, Tom had told her he'd been taking pictures of the sunset for a school project. She'd seemed happy enough. So was he. It hadn't been a wasted twenty minutes. Oh no. Not wasted at all.

As they reached the top of the hill, Harry suspected Evi was starting to tire. She was less talkative and her pace had noticeably slowed. Why hadn't she let him drive her up? And would she bite his head off if he suggested stopping to rest for a moment?

'Can we sit down for a sec?' asked Evi.

Cute as a button and stubborn as a mule. She was going to be so much trouble; he really had no business being this happy. He steered her over to the shepherds' bench and they sat down together. Most of the townsfolk had already turned into Wite Lane. He could hear the roar and crackle of the fire and see a faint orange glow above the buildings. Turning to check uphill, he saw that the bone men had all been removed from around the abbey. Apart from the one that he'd handed over to Detective Chief Superintendent Rushton a couple of hours ago. The one that would be checked for fingerprints and other trace evidence over the next few days. He and Rushton had both agreed to say nothing to the Fletchers until they knew more.

'Was Alice OK when you spoke to her?' asked Harry. His busy day had continued and he hadn't been able to answer the phone when Evi had called him earlier. A short message had told him where to pick her up.

'Yes, she seemed fine.' Evi was still breathing hard, her cheeks pink. 'She seemed pretty certain the children all wanted to go to the bonfire. Tom's developed a keen interest in photography, apparently, and wants to get some good shots. And one of her friends from the town has promised her that nothing sinister happens.'

'First time for everything,' muttered Harry.

'Sorry?'

Harry shook his head. 'Nothing, go on.'

'So we decided that, as long as nothing upsets or scares them, doing things as a family will be good for them. And then she insisted I join you all for dinner. She's sweet.'

'Nice to see thee with a young lady, Reverend.'

Harry turned from Evi to see three elderly women, including the one who'd admired his legs earlier. She was looking from him to Evi with an evil grin on her face. 'I always says how vicars should be married,' she finished. That wasn't a grin, it was a leer. Evi gave a soft snigger at his side and he felt his cheeks glowing. Lucky it was dark.

'No, no, Mrs Hawthorn,' he called. 'Dr Oliver is a colleague. All strictly professional.'

Minnie Hawthorn's two friends had joined in. All three of them stood grinning at him like something from a pantomime version of *Macbeth*. Witch Hawthorn looked at Evi, then back at Harry. 'Aye lad,' she agreed, nodding her woollen-capped head. 'Ah can see that.'

Tittering, the three of them followed the crowd along Wite Lane, Minnie Hawthorn glancing back at the last second. Did she just wink at him?

'There's no fooling the old crones,' said Harry quietly.

'We should get on,' said Evi. 'I'm fine now. And we haven't even seen the Fletchers yet.'

'Hang on a sec. While I have your full attention, there's something else you should know.'

A loud bang made them both jump. A shower of gold shot into the air over Evi's head and disappeared into ever-thickening cloud. The ruined walls of the old abbey stood out sharply against the brief flash of light. They looked strangely empty without the bone men, although one of them seemed to have been left behind.

Harry dropped his eyes to look directly at Evi. 'I bumped into Gillian today,' he said.

As predicted, Evi's face stiffened. She opened her mouth and he held up one hand to stop her. 'I know you're not allowed to talk about her,' he said, 'but there's nothing to stop me from doing it, so just listen.'

Yes, there was definitely still one of the bone men left in the ruin, he could see a figure in the window of the tower. He had to concentrate, this was important. He made himself look down at Evi, not too difficult really. 'She was in the grounds of her old house, close to hysterical,' he said. 'Clutching one of her daughter's toys. I had to drive her home, but she was barely functioning. Her mother arrived after a few minutes, which was—'

'Her mother?'

'Yes. I only met her today. She was quite happy to take over, so I left. But the thing is, we all thought Gillian was getting better. People say she's improved enormously over the last few weeks, pretty much since she's been seeing you, but today I was worried. She talks about her daughter in a way that doesn't seem normal. She said the girl was haunting her. She wanted me to carry out an exorcism.'

Evi was looking at the bench. He couldn't see her eyes. Another firework hit the sky. He'd been mistaken about the figure. The tower window was empty.

'I just thought you should know,' he said.

'Thank you,' said Evi, to the bench.

Harry took a deep breath. 'And also,' he said, 'I hope it goes without saying that even if she weren't seriously emotionally damaged and obviously in need of ongoing professional help, that never in a million years would I even consider . . . do I really need to say it?'

'No,' whispered Evi.

'Thank you.'

'But . . .' She looked up.

'Why is there always a but?' asked Harry, wondering if holding hands might count as unprofessional.

'Let's just say, hypothetically, that I could see a potential conflict of interest in my treatment of a patient,' said Evi. 'The correct procedure would be to find a colleague suitable to take over the case. But that can't always happen instantly. And the wishes of the patient have to be taken into account. They may not want to be referred. And as long as someone remains my patient, his or her interests have to remain my priority.'

'Understood.' Harry stood up and held out his hand to Evi. She took it, rose to her feet and then took his arm again. They crossed the now empty street and turned into Wite Lane.

The bone men were in a circle around the bonfire, being held upright by people who were dressed in black with black paint on their faces. 'It's just face paint,' Tom's mum kept saying to no one in particular. 'Look, that's Mr Marsden from the paper shop.' Tom knew his mother meant well but she was wasting her breath. He knew they were people dressed in black. But when they kept to

217

the shadows they could hardly be seen at all. As they'd walked past the family just minutes earlier, it had almost looked as if the bone men were moving by themselves. Now they were standing around the fire, bone men at the front, shadow men standing behind them. Then, forming another circle some distance back were people from the town. Tom and his family had stayed behind in the lane. Joe was still on his dad's shoulders and Tom was on the wall, just behind his mum, who was starting to mutter about how long the rain was going to hold off. He could see easily over the heads of the crowd to the circle of bone men and the fire in the middle. It really was the coolest thing he'd ever seen.

It was hard, taking his eyes away even for a second, but he had to keep looking round. She was here somewhere, he knew it. She wouldn't miss this.

As Harry and Evi crossed the street a bicycle ridden by a boy dressed all in black and with a black face came speeding past them. Sparklers blazed from the handlebars. He glared at Harry, before speeding away down the hill.

'Friend of yours?' asked Evi

'Hardly,' Harry replied. 'That's Tom Fletcher's number-one enemy, a boy called Jake Knowles. I got him in trouble the day I arrived here. He's never forgiven me. And he's the prime suspect in the Millie-on-the-church-gallery debacle.' Harry thought for a second. Had Jake Knowles been responsible for the effigy of Millie in the church? It was disturbed behaviour, even by the standards of a delinquent schoolboy.

'I think he's one of the boys who scared Duchess the day I fell off,' said Evi. 'I recognized the bike.'

'Figures.'

There were no streetlights in Wite Lane. Torches, old-fashioned ones with real flames, had been fastened to walls and fences to light the way. Harry could smell the kerosene as they walked past. As the cobbles gave way to weeds, Evi stumbled and fell against Harry.

'You know, I'm sure it would be easier for you if I put my arm around your waist,' he offered.

'Nice try, Vicar. I need a few drinks before that one will work.'

'I thought you didn't drink.'

She had a little smile on her face like a cat. 'I said I'm not supposed to. I never said I didn't.'

Harry laughed. 'Finally, my day is starting to pick up.'

No sign of her so far, but Tom knew she'd be extra careful with all these people around. She'd be in the shadows somewhere, behind a wall, maybe on a low roof. Looking through the camera lens made it easier for him to search. There was less chance of being distracted and no one could tell that he was doing anything other than waiting for good photographs. He was still on the wall. How people could stand closer to the fire than he was, Tom had no idea. Its heat on his face was just about tolerable, but the crowd in the field were only yards away from the blaze. Then there were the shadow men, closer still, and then – although he didn't suppose they would mind the heat – the bone men themselves. What were they waiting for? Harry and Evi had joined them and they were all just standing, waiting.

Harry was beginning to understand what Evi meant about a sense of expectation. He could see it in the faces of those around him, like people in a sale queue, waiting for the shop doors to open. They were trying to talk to their neighbours, making an effort to look unconcerned, but their eyes kept flicking to the grim circle in the field – who must surely be about to burn up, they were standing so close to the fire. In fact, they seemed even closer than when he and Evi had arrived, as though the fire was drawing them in. A sudden movement to his right caught his attention. He turned. Gillian was standing three yards away, very close to the gate of her old house, staring directly at him. She was wearing his coat.

The bone men were drawing closer to the fire. Tom had been watching them, he'd even let the camera fall loose around his neck. Very slowly, the people holding them were taking small steps forward. How could they? How could they stand the heat? The noise of the crowd was dying down as well. One by one, it seemed, people were falling silent and turning to watch the bone men move steadily closer to the flames.

219

'Harry, listen to me.'

Evi was talking to him, in a low voice that he struggled to hear above the roar of the fire. He tore his gaze away and bent lower.

'I'm not happy,' she said directly into his ear. 'Something's going to happen.'

He stretched up and looked back at the fire. The whole town, it seemed, was gathered around it in a massive circle. Less than a dozen people – including him and Evi, Gillian and the Fletcher family – were still in the lane. 'What?' he said, bending back down to her. 'What's going to happen?'

'I think they're building up for some sort of dare-devil stunt,' she said. 'I think most of these people know what it is and I think it sometimes goes wrong. Since we arrived tonight I've seen two people with fairly serious burns on their faces. And people are nervous. Look at them.'

She was right. Couples had moved closer together. Parents were holding tightly to children. Men with beer glasses in their hands had stopped drinking. All eyes except his and Evi's were on the fire. On the circle of men around it.

They were waiting. Tom didn't know what for. He'd given up trying to take photographs, he didn't want to miss what was going to happen next. Not far away from them a kid starting crying – for a second he thought it was Millie. Another three, possibly four steps and those bone men would be in the fire. They were made of straw and old rags, how could they possibly—

One of them was on fire. A stray spark must have caught it, because what a second ago had been a human-shaped figure was now a mass of flames being held high in the air.

'We honour the dead!'

Tom didn't know where the shout came from, but as it rang out across the moor the flaming bone man was flung high into the air. It landed almost on the summit of the fire and within seconds had melted into the whole. Someone higher on the moor, maybe on Morrell Tor, released a firework. It shot into the sky and it seemed as though the dead man's soul was heading upwards.

Another of the bone men was alight and flying through the air.

Another firework. Then a third bone man and a fourth. More fireworks. The crowd watched as, one by one, the bone men caught fire and were thrown on to the bonfire. As each one took to the air, the same shout went up.

'We honour the dead!'

Some of the bone men must have had fireworks in their pockets, because coloured sparks started to shoot out of the fire in all directions. People in the crowd began to squeal and turn away. Just in front of Tom, his dad pulled Joe off his shoulders and put him on the ground. Alice, with Millie in her arms, took a step back and Tom felt his dad pull him down off the wall. Then the fire collapsed into the ground.

'What in the . . . ?'

Harry stepped forward, leaving Evi behind by the wall. He was vaguely aware of Gareth Fletcher instructing his family to stay where they were. The two men strode forward until they could step up on to the fence and get a better view.

'I can't believe what I'm looking at,' Harry heard himself saying.

'How the bugger did they manage that?' asked Gareth.

Where the bonfire had blazed not seconds ago there was now a great, gaping hole in the ground. The fire had become a pit filled with flames. Coloured sparks from fireworks shot out in every direction and Harry could still make out several human-shaped forms.

'I think we've just glimpsed the gateway to hell,' said Gareth.

Harry watched as the men who had held the effigies turned from the fire at last, were handed spades from onlookers and began to shovel waiting piles of earth on to the fire. Others joined in, some using spades, others their bare hands.

'They built the fire over a pit,' said Gareth. 'They must have put some sort of floor over the top and then built the fire on it. When the foundation burned through the whole thing collapsed.'

'They're burying the dead,' said Evi. Harry turned, startled. She was beside him on the fence. For a moment he wondered how she'd managed it and then realized that a woman who could mount a horse could probably climb a fence. 'Look what they're doing, throwing earth on to the bones. It's what we do at a burial.'

221

'Weirdest thing I've ever seen,' said Gareth. 'What do you think, Doc?'

Evi seemed to think about it for a second. 'Personally,' she said, 'I'm glad it was no worse.'

46

*T*HE BLINDS IN THE WINDOW WERE STILL OPEN. THAT DIDN'T
happen much any more. Normally Tom closed them even before
it got properly dark. The whole family, apart from Millie, were
in the kitchen. The father stood closest to the window, talking to the man
who looked after the church. At the table sat a young woman with dark
hair and large eyes. They were drinking and talking. They looked happy.
Where was Millie?

Tom had climbed up on to the kitchen counter. He was staring out
at the darkness. Then he reached up and pulled down the string that
lowered the blind. The scene disappeared.

Had they locked the door?

47

'I CAN'T BELIEVE JENNY DIDN'T WARN ME ABOUT THAT,' SAID Alice.

'Maybe she didn't want to spoil the surprise,' said Gareth. 'Tom, will you get down from there? What will you have, Evi?'

Gareth turned away from his eldest son to look at Evi, which gave Tom just enough time to lower the blind on the kitchen window. He noticed that Evi was watching him as he went to the other window, climbed up on to the worktop and did the same thing. Had he checked that the front door was locked?

'So can we have a bone man next year?' Joe asked, for what felt like the tenth time that evening. Joe thought that if he asked a question often enough then sooner or later he'd get the answer he wanted. Frequently, it worked.

'Not if it means your father gets his testicles roasted,' said Alice, as Joe dissolved into giggles. He couldn't hear that word without cracking up. 'I think there must be a lot of singed eyebrows in Heptonclough tonight.'

'Not to mention other parts,' said Harry. 'Thanks, mate.' He took a lager from Tom's dad and opened it, drinking straight from the can.

'Come on, Joe,' said Alice, 'it's time for you to go up. Tom, you've got fifteen minutes.'

'I want to look at my photographs first,' Tom said.

'Did you get any good ones?' asked Evi.

A sudden thought struck Tom. 'I think so,' he said. 'You can come and look at them with me if you want.'

Tom's mum turned round in the doorway. 'Tom, sweetheart . . .' she started.

'Thanks,' said Evi. 'I'd like to. If that's OK, Alice?'

'Of course,' said Alice. 'But the computer's upstairs, is that all right?'

'Yup,' said Evi, standing up. Her stick had been leaning against the ironing-board cupboard. She took hold of it and started to follow Tom out of the room.

'Are you . . .' began Harry.

'Yes,' said Evi, looking at him with what Tom guessed was supposed to be a glare, but honestly, if she thought that was scary, she should take a few lessons from his mum.

Tom ran up the stairs with Evi following behind. He could hear the soft tap of her stick on each step. By the time he reached the top he could hear her breathing. His mum had told him that Evi was probably in pain a lot of the time and that it was very brave of her not to show it or complain. Tom supposed his mother was right. He could never keep quiet when he'd hurt himself and as for Joe – well, the whole world knew about it.

He led the way along the landing to his parents' room, where the computer was kept, and they both sat down. Tom connected the camera to the hard drive and uploaded the photographs he'd taken that evening. He hadn't had chance to look at any of them himself yet.

'These are ones I took of the bone men when they were still in the abbey,' he said. Downstairs, Harry laughed. Evi's head twisted to face the door, then turned back to Tom again.

'They're good,' she said. 'I like the way you can see the moon just starting to come up in that one. And the colours in those three are great. You've really captured the sunset well.'

Tom knew she was buttering him up, but it was still nice to hear. The pictures were good, his mum often said he'd got her eye for composition, but it wasn't the shots of the abbey he needed Evi to see. He'd brought her upstairs to show her . . .

'Who's this?' said Evi.

Feeling his heart start to beat faster, Tom clicked on the picture

Evi was looking at and enlarged it. There it was. Evidence. The little girl that nobody believed in, captured on camera. The trouble was . . .

'Is it Joe?' asked Evi. 'No, it's bigger than Joe. Another friend?'

. . . the figure in the photograph, skulking behind one of the taller headstones, just wasn't clear enough. Knowing who it was, Tom could just about make out the strange old-fashioned dress she'd been wearing and her long hair, but to someone seeing this picture for the first time, it could be anyone. Tom closed the shot down and pulled up the next one.

He'd stayed in his position in the yew tree for nearly twenty minutes, getting cold and stiff, and had been about to give up when she'd appeared. He'd watched her enter the churchyard down at the bottom end and make her way up. She moved fast and she came silently. She'd stopped when she was three feet away from the wall and had crouched there, watching their house. Hardly daring to breathe, Tom had taken one photograph after another.

'There she is again,' said Evi. 'Is it a she? Not sure. That could be hair, could be grass, hard to tell. Oh look, there again. These are good, Tom,' she said, giving him a sideways glance. 'Shadowy figure in the graveyard, very atmospheric. Oh look, there's another one.'

Downstairs, someone opened the front door. 'Someone's come in,' he said. 'I need to get Dad.'

'Tom, what's the matter?' said Evi in alarm. 'Where are you . . . ?'

Tom jumped to his feet and crossed the room.

'Tom,' called Evi, 'it probably *was* your dad. Or Harry, getting something from the car. Why are you . . . ?'

Tom wasn't hanging around to listen to whatever Evi had to say to him. Knowing it was rude, but that some things are just more important, he ran across the landing to the top of the stairs. He was right, the front door was about three inches open. He hadn't checked it, why hadn't he checked it? He ran down, hearing a faint tap on the landing behind him. At the bottom he pushed the door shut and locked it.

Was she inside even now? Tom shot into the dining room. No one under the table. The curtains. Holding his breath and standing at arm's length, he tugged them apart. The window ledge was empty. She couldn't have gone into the kitchen, his dad and Harry were there. There hadn't been time for her to go upstairs. If she was in the house, she'd be in the living room.

'Tom!' Evi had reached the top of the stairs. He pretended he hadn't heard her and pushed open the living-room door.

'Buddy, what's going on?' Tom's dad and Harry had left the kitchen.

'I heard the front door,' Tom said. 'Someone's come in.' He saw Harry look at his dad, his dad's lips tighten.

'Double-check the kitchen for me, Harry, would you?' said Gareth, without taking his eyes off Tom. 'Make sure the back door is locked.'

'OK,' said Harry, and Tom heard him walk back along the hall-way to the kitchen. His dad came into the room and walked to the nearest window. He pulled the curtains back, then did the same thing with the far window. 'It's OK,' he said. He was standing directly behind the one sofa Tom couldn't see around. 'Do you want me to do the dining room?'

'I did in there,' said Tom in a small voice.

'Probably just the wind,' said his dad.

Tom nodded. His dad was right. This time, at least, it was probably just the wind.

He went back upstairs and he and Evi looked at his pictures until his mum called Evi down for supper and told Tom to go to bed. Five of the shots he'd taken showed the girl, but none of them were clear enough to prove she was anything other than a normal child. All the same, Evi had seemed unusually interested in her. She'd kept asking Tom who she was. He'd told her he didn't know, that he hadn't known anyone else was in the churchyard. She'd pretended to believe him, but Tom suspected they both knew what it was really all about. Sometimes it seemed that he and Evi were playing a game, dancing around each other, waiting to see which one of them would give in first.

It was a pity that he hadn't got a clear shot, but not a disaster. The important thing was that the girl appeared on film. That meant she was real and he wasn't mad. Tom couldn't describe the relief of knowing that. And he was going to try again.

48

'THANK YOU, I HAD A LOVELY TIME,' SAID EVI.

Alice kissed Evi on her cheek and then reached up to do the same to Harry. Gareth was standing with his hand on the front door.

'Al, have you seen my keys?' he asked.

'Oh, I've probably hidden them from you again in your jeans pocket,' replied Alice, giving Harry a small hug.

'They were hanging up,' said Gareth. 'Just next to yours. I have to leave at six.'

'Better get looking, then,' said Alice. She smiled at Evi. 'My husband loses his keys on a daily basis,' she said. 'Often we find them on the roof of the car. Frequently, the garden wall. Even, on one occasion, in the butter dish.'

'I'll see you tomorrow, Gareth,' said Harry, taking Evi's arm as Gareth turned from the front door and disappeared inside the house.

'Thanks again, Alice,' he said. One last smile from Alice and then she closed the front door. Evi heard the sound of a key being turned as she and Harry walked down the drive.

Harry started the engine and reversed out of the drive into the lane. For a minute or two they drove in silence. It would take them twenty minutes to get home, twenty-five if the roads were busy, and at this rate they probably wouldn't speak all the way there. Evi had been watching Harry's reflection in the passenger window. She

228

turned to face him. She had to find something to say, even something really lame.

'They're nice people,' she said. Yep, that was pretty lame, even by her standards.

Harry stepped on the brake and the car slowed down. At the side of the road a lone sheep looked up lazily from the grass she was chewing.

'Who are?' said Harry, steering round the corner and picking up speed again.

'The Fletchers.'

'Oh yeah, sorry,' he said, glancing at her. 'I was thinking about something else. How did you find Tom tonight?'

Evi thought about it for a second. How had she found Tom? Still puzzling, was the honest truth.

'Alice said she'd mentioned schizophrenia to you,' said Harry, when she didn't reply straight away. 'Is it possible?'

'Tom isn't psychotic,' Evi said. Harry had shaved that evening. She could see the small scars of a rash just above the collar of his coat.

'What about these hallucinations?' he said, glancing at her again. 'Alice said he hears voices in his head.'

'Actually, he doesn't,' she replied. 'He doesn't hear them in his head.'

Ahead of them they could see the headlights of another vehicle. Harry pulled over on to the grass verge, inches from the wall. They sat, waiting for the car to reach them. Now that he was looking directly at her, Evi was finding it hard to maintain eye-contact.

'Tom's voices, according to everything Alice has told me, come from outside of himself,' she continued, dropping her eyes to the wooden trim of the dashboard. 'They come from round corners, behind doors. And always from the same source. A young girl who he thinks is watching the family, whispering to them – to him, in particular – muttering scary, threatening things.'

The approaching car drew level, flickered its headlights at them and passed by. Harry released the handbrake and set off again.

'He's trying to prove to us that this weird little girl of his is real,' said Evi.

'How is he doing that?' Harry asked. 'Wait, don't tell me. Has he been trying to take her photograph?'

Evi nodded. 'He showed me over twenty shots he'd taken tonight. Five of them show a small, indistinct figure, huddling against stones.'

'Who did he say it was?'

They turned another bend and caught sight of Heptonclough, already some way below them, twinkling in the dark like a city from a fairy tale.

'He said he didn't know,' replied Evi. 'That he hadn't known anyone was there. He was lying, of course, the figure was the focal point of the shots. Tom would have had to know he or she was there. I suspect he's got some friend of his to skulk around in the churchyard, pretending to be this girl. But the point is, it's clever and it's rational. It suggests to me he knows the little girl isn't real but still needs us to believe in her. He deliberately takes pictures he knows will be ambiguous.'

'So he didn't actually claim it was the girl?'

Another bend, another glimpse of the dark landscape below.

'No. He still hasn't admitted her existence to me. So I couldn't mention her either. I have to wait from him to do that. Why are we heading up the moor?'

'Short cut,' said Harry. 'What if she *is* real?'

Evi thought for a second and then smiled at his profile. 'According to his parents, Tom talks about this girl in terms that suggests she's not human,' she replied. 'And, by the way, there are no short cuts across the moor. Are you kidnapping me?'

'Yep,' he said. 'What about someone who looks unusual? Tom only sees her at night, from what I understand. He could be getting confused. What if there is someone who likes to hide, play tricks on people, maybe somebody a bit disturbed?'

They climbed higher and the darkness spread itself around them like a pool of black ink, flowing across the moors. From somewhere below a firework exploded. As the sparks died away, Evi could see the dark outline of trees against the sky.

She thought for a second and then shook her head. 'Only Tom sees and hears her. Where are we going exactly?'

'What if Gillian hears her?'

'Gillian?'

'Gillian hears her dead daughter calling to her. She swears it's Hayley's voice. Did she tell you that?'

Gillian had never told her that. No, she'd said, *I never see her.* Never *see* her?

Harry was slowing the car. He switched the headlights on to full beam and turned off the road. They were driving across the open moor now, along the faintest hint of a farm track. Ahead of them seemed to be . . . nothing.

'She says someone comes into the flat,' he continued, slowing to a crawl as the car began to bump and jolt over the uneven ground. 'Someone moves things around, especially Hayley's old toys.'

They'd reached a small open area of land. Harry switched off the engine and headlights. The sudden absence of noise was startling, the disappearance of light even more so. At her side, Harry became little more than silhouette and shadow, and yet, for some reason, it was even harder to look at him.

'Gillian and Tom are my patients for a reason,' said Evi. 'They both have problems.'

He was moving – impossible not to catch her breath – but he only reached up to the car roof and unlocked it. The soft leather folded back and the night, shimmering with wood smoke and gunpowder, wrapped itself around her like a cool blanket. Above Evi's head, the sky was the colour of damsons and the stars seemed to have moved a light year or two closer to earth.

'Tell me when you get cold,' he said, settling back into his seat. A second of silence and then: 'What if I've heard her?'

She risked a proper look. 'What?' He was leaning back in his seat, hands behind his head, staring at the sky. Whatever he was about to tell her, it was something he wasn't comfortable talking about.

The night air felt damp in Evi's nostrils; rain wasn't far away. A volley of violet stars hurled themselves into the sky, distracting them both for a second.

'Your eyes are that colour,' said Harry. 'And, yes, I've heard voices too. Eerie disembodied voices, coming from nowhere.'

And he hadn't thought to mention it. 'When?' she asked, pushing herself a little more upright in the seat. 'Where?'

'When I've been alone,' he said. 'Only in Heptonclough, though.

Only in and around the church. I'll bet Tom doesn't hear his voices at school, does he?'

Evi leaned back again. 'I need to think about that one,' she said. 'What are we doing up here, exactly?'

'I found this spot a couple of weeks ago,' said Harry, as he leaned forward to switch on the cassette player. It started to hiss as he pressed the Play button. 'We're about twenty yards from the edge of Morrell Tor, the highest spot on the moor. I promised myself I'd drive up here and watch the fireworks.'

He was nuts. And she had to stop smiling, she was just encouraging him. 'You're three days too early,' she pointed out.

He turned to her, his arm sliding along the back of her seat. He was inches away. She could smell the beer he'd drunk at the Fletcher's. 'In three days I couldn't have been sure of having you with me,' he said. 'Do you dance?'

'Do I what?'

'Dance. You know, move your body in time to music. I chose this track specially.'

Evi listened for a second. 'Dancing In The Dark,' she said in a soft voice. 'My mum used to play this. Where are you . . .?'

Harry had climbed out of the car and was walking round the front of the bonnet. He held open her door and offered his hand.

Evi shook her head. Definitely nuts. 'I can't dance, Harry. You've seen me. I can barely walk by myself.'

As though he hadn't heard, he reached across her to turn up the volume. Then he'd taken her by both arms and was lifting her out of the car. Evi opened her mouth to tell him it wouldn't work, she hadn't danced in years, they'd both end up sprawled on the ground, but with his arm wrapped tightly around her waist, she found she could walk quite easily across the few remaining feet of farm track and on to the rock of the Tor. He took her right hand in his, his other arm stayed round her waist to hold her up. His jacket wasn't fastened. His hand felt like ice. Holding her tightly against him, he began to move.

The old-fashioned cassette player seemed to distort the music somehow, making the drumbeat louder, more insistent than she remembered. And it was ridiculously loud, they'd be able to hear it in the town . . . but impossible to worry about that, to think about anything but Harry, who danced like he was born to it, holding her up without effort, singing softly in her ear.

The wind blew her hair across his face, he tossed his head and pulled her into the curve of his shoulder and still they kept moving, swinging backwards and forwards in a four-time movement, on the hard rock of the Tor. And she'd thought she'd never dance again.

'The singing, dancing priest,' she whispered, when she sensed the track coming to an end.

'Played in a band at university,' said Harry, as the vocals faded and the notes of the saxophone curled out across the moor. 'We used to do some Springsteen covers.'

The sax drifted away. Harry dropped her hand and wrapped both arms around her. She could feel the heat from his neck against her face. This was insane. She could not get involved with him, both of them knew that, and yet here they were, on what felt like the tip of the world, clutching each other like teenagers.

'I've had a very weird day,' he whispered, as a new track started.

'Want to talk about it?' she managed.

'No.' She felt a soft brushing on her neck, just below her ear, and couldn't stop herself shivering.

'You're cold,' he said, straightening up.

No, I'm not. Don't let go of me.

He stepped back, one arm dropped away, he was taking her back to the car. She stopped him with a hand on his chest. 'I'm not cold,' she said. 'Why are you a priest?'

For a second he looked surprised. 'To serve the Lord,' he replied, looking down at her, then up at the sky. 'Was that rain?'

'No,' she said, shaking her head. 'I need more than that. I need to understand what makes a man like you become a priest.'

He was still smiling but his eyes looked wary. 'That's a lot to ask on a first date. And that was definitely rain. Come on, back in the car.'

She allowed him to lead her back to the passenger seat and hold the door open until she was sitting down again.

'You said this wasn't a date,' she pointed out, as he joined her in the car and twisted round in the seat to refasten the roof in place.

'I lied,' he muttered, locking the hood and switching on the engine. Then he seemed to change his mind and switched it off again.

'I never intended to become a minister,' he said. 'I come from a working-class family in Newcastle who weren't churchgoers and it simply never occurred to me. But I was bright, I got a scholarship to a good school and I met some very impressive teachers. History was my thing, religious history in particular. I became fascinated by organized religion: its rituals, history, art and literature, symbolism – everything really. I did religious studies at university, not theology.'

She waited for him to go on. 'What happened?' she asked, when he didn't. 'You had a road-to-Damascus moment?'

He was drumming his fingers on the steering wheel, he wasn't comfortable talking about this. 'Sort of,' he said. 'People kept telling me that I'd make a good priest. There was just this little problem of faith.'

The rain came from nowhere, thudding down on the soft roof of the car like small stones. 'You didn't believe?' she asked.

He ran a hand through his hair. 'I was almost there,' he said. 'I could tell myself that I believed in all the distinct parts, but they were still just a whole load of separate theories. Does that make any sort of sense?'

'I think so,' said Evi, although it didn't really.

'And then one day, something happened. I . . . saw the connection.'

'The connection?'

'Yep.' The engine was on again, he was reversing away from the Tor's edge. 'And that is all you're going to see of the inner man for one night, Dr Oliver. Fasten your seatbelt and prepare for take-off.'

They drove down the moor at a speed that had Evi wishing she believed in a deity she could pray to: for her own personal safety. She didn't dare try to talk to him again, to say anything that might distract him. Besides, she'd just been ridiculously indiscreet. How could she tell herself she wasn't involved with him, when she knew that the skin of his neck smelled of lime and ginger, and the exact point on his chest her lips would touch if she leaned towards him?

Within minutes of the rain starting, small streams were racing down the sides of the road. A quarter of an hour later, they'd left the moor and were depressingly close to her house.

'So where do we go from here?' asked Harry as he turned into her road.

'I'm seeing Tom later this week,' she said. 'He seems to be relaxing more around me now. Maybe he'll open up a bit. If he'd just admit the existence of—' Harry had stopped the car outside her building.

'I wasn't talking about the Fletchers,' he said, in a voice that seemed to have dropped an octave.

'I should go,' she said, bending down to find her bag. 'I have an early start in the morning and . . . it was a good suggestion about tonight. Thank you, I think it will help.' She turned her back on him and found the door handle, conscious of being watched. She was going to have to do this quickly, she could call goodnight over her shoulder as she walked up the path. It was a short path, hardly two yards to the porch.

The engine fell silent. Behind her, Harry's door was opening. He was much faster than she was, he would make it round the car before she was even standing up. Yes, there he was, holding out a hand, and was there any point in telling him she could manage? Probably not, and in any event, this was a new Harry, with darker eyes and who seemed to have grown taller; a Harry who didn't speak, whose arm was around her waist as he hurried her along the path, through the downpour, to the shelter of the porch. Definitely a new Harry, who'd turned her to face him, whose fingers were reaching into her hair and whose head was bending towards her as the world went dark.

Oh, this couldn't be a kiss – this was a butterfly, bruising its wings against her mouth, settling lightly on the curve of her cheek, the point where the smile begins.

Was this a kiss? This soft stroking of the lips? This crazy feeling that she was being touched everywhere?

And this certainly couldn't be a kiss, not now that she was spinning away into a place lined with dark velvet. Hands were tangled in her hair – no, one was at the small of her back, pressing her closer. The rain against the porch roof felt like drums in her head. Fingers stroked the side of her face. How could she have forgotten the smell of a man's skin; or the weight of his body, pushing her against the wall of the porch? If this was a kiss, why were tears burning in the back of her eyes?

'Do you want to come inside?'

Had she said that out loud? She must have done. Because they weren't kissing any more, just close enough for it to make no difference and his breath was swirling around her face like warm mist.

'There's nothing I'd like more,' he said, in a voice that was nothing like Harry's.

The keys were in her pocket. No, they were in her hand. Her hand was reaching out for the lock; his was closing around it, slowing her down.

'But—' he said.

Why was there always a but?

He'd brought her hand back, was holding it to his lips. 'We still haven't done the pizza or the movie,' he whispered. She could barely hear him above the rain.

And you are a priest, she thought.

'And I really don't want to rush this.' He released her hand and tilted her chin upwards so that she was looking directly at him.

'That's rather sweet,' she said. 'And more than a little womanly.'

At that, Harry was back, grinning at her, scooping her up and holding her tightly against him. 'There is nothing remotely womanly about me,' he hissed into her ear, 'as I fully intend to prove before too much longer. Now get inside, you baggage, before I change my mind.'

When the phone rang, Harry's first thought was that he'd only just fallen asleep and that it would be Evi, asking him to come round. He turned over in bed, unable for the moment to remember which side the phone was on. You know what? Sod it. Sod the pizza, sod the movie, sod everything, he was going.

No, that side had the clock. It was 3.01 a.m. He turned over and reached out. He could be dressed in two minutes, at her place in ten. By 3.15 he could be . . .

'Hi,' he said, pressing the phone against his ear.

'Vicar? Reverend Laycock?' It was a man's voice. An elderly man.

'Yes, speaking,' he said, his stomach cold with disappointment. He'd be going out after all, but not to a woman's warm bed.

Someone was dying. Sex or death – the only reasons to call someone in the middle of the night.

'Renshaw here. Renshaw senior. My son asked me to call.'

Tobias Renshaw, his churchwarden's father, ringing him in the
small hours?

'My son apologizes for not calling himself, and for waking you,
but I'm afraid you're needed at St Barnabas's straight away. You'll
see the police vehicles in the lane. When you arrive, you should
make yourself known to Detective Chief Superintendent Rushton.'

49

3 November

SIMBA, MILLIE'S BLUE TEDDY BEAR, LAY ON HIS BACK AT THE bottom of the stairs. When Tom had seen him last, not five hours ago, he'd been clutched in his little sister's arms. So either the soft toy had developed a taste for midnight strolls or something was very wrong. Tom ran across the landing to Millie's room. The cot was empty.

Downstairs, a door slammed shut. Tom glanced towards his parents' room. No time to do anything but yell as he ran across the landing, down the stairs and through the kitchen. He'd heard the back door. Whoever had Millie had only just left the house.

He felt a rush of cold air as he dodged his way around the kitchen table. The back door had bounced open again and the wooden floorboards of the cloakroom were wet. It was still raining hard outside and, even in the doorway, looking out over the mass of mud that was the back garden, the wind battered against him, sending volleys of ice-cold raindrops to soak his pyjamas.

His eyes weren't used to the darkness yet. He screwed them up and could just about make out the churchyard wall and the laurel trees behind it. From the direction of the yew tree and Lucy Pickup's grave, he heard a grunt.

Someone was out there. Someone with Millie.

'Dad!' he yelled. No answering shout. No choice really. He had to go out.

The relentless rain over the past few hours, together with all that had fallen over the previous day or two, had turned the garden into a swamp. Thick black mud surged over Tom's feet as he stepped away from the shelter of the back door. A few more steps and he could see better. A black figure was trying to climb the wall but it was carrying something in one hand, something that looked like a large, black hold-all.

'Dad!' he yelled, as loud as he could, trying to send his voice in the direction of the house but not wanting to take his eyes off the figure at the wall. 'Dad!'

His dad would never make it in time. Tom ran forward, sinking almost to his knees in mud, and was just in time to catch hold of one of the climber's retreating legs. The girl – because who else could it be? – began kicking at him, but she was losing her grip on the wall. She made a grab upwards and gave one last kick that caught Tom off guard. Her booted foot connected with the side of his face and he let go. She gave a sort of leap and then she was lying spread-eagled over the top of the wall, kicking wildly as she scrabbled to her feet. She was almost away, but the black hold-all she'd been carrying was still at the foot of the wall.

She looked from it to Tom and then, with a sharp movement of her head, down at the wall she was standing on. She staggered, almost fell, and then jumped down on the other side.

The wall was moving. It wasn't possible, but it was happening. The bulge of stones, which for years had held back tons of earth, seemed to swell. Tom watched first one stone, then another, then several, topple from the top and fall into the garden. Through the gap they left behind, earth began to spill over from the churchyard. One of the gravestones seemed to be sliding closer. Tom wanted more than anything to run but something was rooting him to the spot.

The bulge swelled more, like a pregnant woman about to give birth to something hideous. The black figure on the other side of the wall took a few steps back as more and more of the earth started to slide away.

Then the wall just burst apart like a tower built by a toddler.

Stones flew everywhere and black liquid poured out in a thick torrent. The headstone nearest the wall – Lucy Pickup's stone – slipped closer and closer and then fell, cracking in two as it landed not three feet from Tom. Earth poured over the slope where the wall had been and a stench of drains and rotting things almost choked him.

The girl was continuing to back away. Tom took a step forward and something landed heavily beside him, missing him by inches and throwing him off balance. Falling to the ground, he recognized the edge of a coffin, a fraction before the wood collapsed completely and revealed its occupant.

The skull grinned at Tom with tiny white teeth. Pieces of flesh, like old yellow leather, still clung to it. Tom scrambled away from the corpse, feeling the scream build inside his head and knowing that if he let it out he might never be able to stop.

A fresh flood of earth poured down on him, filled with pale-coloured objects that he knew could only be bones. He threw back his head and got ready to let the scream out when a beam of light hit his face and an arm grabbed his shoulder. Tom whirled round. A small figure, wearing a yellow raincoat with its hood pulled up tight and carrying a flashlight, knelt beside him. It was Joe.

Tom pushed himself to his feet. Everything in his head was yelling at him to get back to the house, wake his mum and dad, call the police. As he set off for the back door, Joe pulled him back.

'No, wait,' Joe shouted, straining to make himself heard above the wind. 'We have to find her.'

'It's too late,' Tom yelled back. Up in the churchyard there was no sign of the dark figure. 'She's gone. We have to get Mum and Dad.'

Joe shone the flashlight on the ground around their feet. Tom wanted to yell at him to stop. It was all so much worse when you could see it properly. The skull, now broken away from the rest of the corpse, lay a few yards away. Lucy's tiny statue had fallen along with the rest of her grave. Pieces of coffin were scattered around. He saw what he thought was a human hand, the finger bones clenched in a fist.

Joe seemed to be looking for something. At last, the torch flickered on the black bag which the intruder had tried to escape with. It was half buried beneath a pile of mud and stones. With a cry, Joe ran towards it and started tugging at the handles. Still desperate to get away, Tom had a sense that this might be important. Gingerly, he picked his way over to help.

With a glooping noise, the bag came free and the boys staggered backwards, still clinging to the straps. Joe dropped to his knees and started to tug at the zip. Squeaking with frustration, he finally managed to wrench it back. Then, in the pale light of the torch, Tom could see him grinning. He dropped to his knees beside his brother and peered inside. Millie lay in the bag. As the boys watched, her eyes flickered open. She blinked up at her brothers in astonishment as raindrops began to fall on her face.

50

SOMETHING WAS THUDDING LOUD INSIDE HARRY'S CHEST. Not his heart, though, his heart never made this sort of racket. Should he say something, tell them he knew the identity of one of the dead children?

It was almost painful, this pounding against his ribs. If it was indeed his heart, he had a serious problem. Hearts weren't supposed to beat this hard.

He couldn't say anything now, he'd sound ridiculous, hysterical even. Tomorrow would be soon enough. He glanced down to make sure he would step on matting, and moved away from the cordoned area. The white-clad figures around him got back to work.

The Fletchers' back garden was a quagmire. Harry followed in Detective Chief Superintendent Rushton's footsteps, along the loose-weave steel path that had been laid over the mud. Above their heads a makeshift PVC shelter was holding back the worst of the weather. Powerful lights on steel poles had been positioned in the four corners. Now that he was facing the house, Harry could see lights on in the downstairs windows. The blinds and curtains had all been drawn.

'As crimes scenes go, this is as bad as it gets,' said Rushton as they walked back towards the house. 'We're working in the dark, in shocking weather, the mud's close to a foot deep in places and it looks like there was quite a lot of contamination of the site before we got here.'

One of the white-clad figures was moving slowly round the out-side of the inner cordon, taking photographs. Another figure, which Harry thought might be a woman, was using a measuring tape. She stretched it from the wall to the smallest of the three bodies, then began scribbling, or maybe drawing, on a clipboard hanging around her neck.

'The forensics people you see have just arrived from Manchester,' explained Rushton. 'We don't have that sort of specialism locally. Luckily, the first officer on site was a bright lad. He sealed off the area until the team could get here. Did the same up in the churchyard.'

Harry looked up. More white figures could be seen on the other side of the stone wall. Up there, too, efforts were being made to control the weather. An awning had been stretched across metal poles. One of the officers was struggling to fasten plastic sheeting around the edges. In this wind it was close to hopeless.

'What are all these people doing?' Harry asked.

'The photographer is recording the scene before the trace-evidence people can get to work,' said Rushton. 'He'll take pictures from every angle, then he'll climb up into the graveyard and do the same. That girl over there, she's sketching. She'll measure how everything is situated in relation to everything else and then it'll all be fed into a computer. We'll get a very accurate model that we can use if we ever need to go to court. The main task tonight will be removing the bodies, intact if possible, and getting them to the pathology unit. Along with everything else that might be relevant. The coffin will go, of course, any bits of clothing, hair and so on. We'll take casts of any footprints. Looks like they've started already.'

Rushton was pointing to a spot not far from the house. A man was kneeling on a mat of chequer-plated aluminum, pouring liquid on to the ground in front of him.

'The other two bodies could have come from graves on either side of Lucy's,' suggested Harry. 'I can't tell you whose they were, but there'll be a plan somewhere.'

'We have it already,' said Rushton. 'Family graves on both sides, three people recorded as being in the one, four in the other. All adults. And from what we can see so far, those graves are still intact.'

'Is it possible they've been in the ground a long time?' asked

Harry, knowing it wasn't. None of the corpses he'd just seen was properly skeletonized. 'In a much earlier grave that no one knew about? This churchyard is hundreds of years old. There must be ancient graves all over this hill. Headstones got removed, people forgot who was in the ground.' He stopped. He was gabbling. And clutching at straws.

'Well, we can't rule it out for now,' said Rushton. 'But frankly, the team think it unlikely. And you have to see their point. Did they look like ancient corpses to you?'

Harry looked back over his shoulder. 'Do the Fletchers know what's going on?' he asked. 'They've been under a lot of pressure lately, it won't be the best—'

'Oh aye, they know,' said Rushton. 'It was the kids that brought the wall down.'

'What?'

'I haven't had chance to speak to the parents yet, so I've only had half a tale,' said the detective, 'but it seems the two boys were out in this weather, climbing the wall. They had their younger sister in a hold-all, apparently. Looks like some sort of attempt at running away from home. Job for Social Services, if you ask me. Where are you going?'

Harry was heading back along the path to the house. A hand fell on to his shoulder. 'Hold your horses, lad. You can't go in yet. The family GP is in there and the two youngsters are talking to one of my DCs. Let's just leave everyone to do their jobs for a minute, shall we?'

Harry knew he wasn't being given a choice.

'You're familiar with the layout of this part of the churchyard, Reverend?' said Rushton, as they started walking again. 'Both churches, old and new, were built at the top of a steep hill, so a lot of terracing had to be done to create the graveyard. The wall we're looking at was built several hundred years ago, from what I'm told, but it was a lot higher on this side than on the church side. Are you with me?'

'Yes, I know that,' said Harry, as they reached the edge of the Fletchers' property and turned to leave the garden. 'Gareth Fletcher has mentioned it to me a couple of times. He wanted to get a surveyor in, he was concerned about the stability of the wall.'

'He was right to be.' The two men were at the side of the house. Another massive awning had been stretched across from the house to the church wall, creating a dry space for the forensic team to store equipment. Unable to reach them, the weather seemed determined not to be ignored. Raindrops thundered down on the plastic roof while the wind kept it in constant, noisy motion.

'I'm told there's an underground stream that runs beneath the church,' Rushton continued, removing his overalls and indicating that Harry should do the same. 'Ordinarily that's not a problem, but when there's been heavy rainfall, like over the past few days, the church cellar gets flooded. The land around here gets boggy. Did you know?'

'Yes.' Harry was balanced on one foot, struggling to take off a boot that was too tight and looking round for his own shoes. 'Gareth and I had a walk around the boundary a couple of weeks ago. I agreed it didn't look too stable, but there's a process I have to go through when any work needs to be done on church property. I'd already set the wheels in motion but these things typically take weeks, sometimes months.'

'Well, Brian, is it my granddaughter's grave?'

Harry and Rushton both turned to see that Sinclair Renshaw had entered the tent from the Fletchers' driveway. The fingers of his right hand clutched a cigarette. Harry had never seen him smoke before.

'It looks that way,' said Rushton. 'I'm very sorry.'

Sinclair nodded his head, just once.

'Do Jenny and Mike know?' asked Harry. 'Do you want me to—'

'I've asked they not be told until the morning,' Sinclair interrupted him. 'Christiana has made coffee in the vestry. You should come up. It's warmer in there.'

Harry pulled his own jacket back on. 'What happens now?' he asked Rushton.

'Well, strangely enough, there is a protocol in cases like these,' replied the detective, indicating that they should leave the tent. 'When remains are uncovered on church property, they have to be removed from site and examined by a police-approved pathologist. If he determines the remains are ancient bones, a lot of them apply the hundred-year rule: they're simply returned to the minister in charge – in this case, you – and it becomes your responsibility to re-inter them.'

'Yes, I think I knew that,' agreed Harry, 'although it's not a situation I've ever come across before.'

'It's certainly never happened here,' said Sinclair.

'On the other hand, if the remains are, shall we say, fresher, we have to confirm their identity,' added Rushton. 'Make sure the body really is the person whose name is on the headstone. Do you follow me, Reverend?'

'Yes, of course,' said Harry.

'Once identity is confirmed, we hand the remains back jointly to you and the family and let you arrange for re-interment.'

'Another funeral,' said Sinclair, running his hand over his face. 'It will be too much for Jenny. How can any mother be expected to bury her child twice?'

51

'WE SHOULDN'T RULE OUT A BREAK-IN,' SAID HARRY. 'Tom could be telling the truth.'

Gareth was holding a coffee mug between his palms. Both hands looked unnaturally white, the fingers blue-tinged. Harry felt himself shivering in sympathy. He could hear the creak of the central-heating system, but the events of the night seemed to have brought a chill indoors.

'No sign of one,' Gareth answered him, shaking his head. 'Front door was locked, no windows open or broken. The back door was open, but we keep the key in it and the bolt's at the bottom. Tom could have opened it by himself.'

'Where did he get the bag from?'

'By the front door. I had it ready to take with me in the morning.'

Harry thought for a moment and then turned to walk back along the corridor to the door. Under the window he could see trainers, shorts, socks – Gareth's gym kit had been emptied out and left behind. Footsteps behind told him Gareth had followed. Through the coloured glass of the front door Harry could see two white figures, ghostly in the orange streetlight. They walked across the road carrying what looked like a stretcher between them. As Harry turned back to Gareth he caught sight of grey dust around the front door handle.

'What's that?' he asked.

'The police have already dusted for fingerprints,' replied Gareth.

'They've done all the ground floor and Millie's room. I think they were just covering themselves. They didn't find anything.'

'What about Joe?' asked Harry. 'What does he say happened?'

'Joe heard Tom yelling and got up,' said Gareth. 'He heard banging around downstairs, put his waterproofs on – showing great presence of mind for a six-year-old – and went out. He saw Tom lying in the mud and helped him carry the bag, with Millie in it, back to the house. I'd got up for a pee, realized the back door was open and come down. Got the fright of my life. All three of them, soaked to the skin and covered in mud. Tom started yelling about this little girl of his, Alice was all for rushing them to A&E, I took a look outside and realized I'd better get the police on the blower. Just what have they found out there?'

'Not clear yet,' lied Harry. He'd been asked not to mention the full extent of what had been discovered in the garden. 'I'm sorry about the wall. If I'd had any idea . . .'

Gareth was staring at the row of three hooks that hung by the front door. 'That's funny,' he said.

'What is?' asked Alice, who was halfway down the stairs. Harry turned to smile at her and couldn't bring himself to do it. That wasn't a face someone could smile at.

'My keys. They were missing earlier, remember?' said Gareth. 'Did you find them?'

Alice shook her head. 'They were probably there all along,' she replied.

'They weren't. I checked after the kids had gone to bed. I had to dig out my spare set to use in the morning. How could they have got back here?'

Alice looked from Harry to her husband. 'Tom could have . . .' she began.

'Why would Tom hide his dad's keys?' asked Harry, trying to curb his impatience – they didn't know everything he did. 'If he'd wanted to open the front door in the night there were other sets he could have used, weren't there?'

Alice nodded. 'Mine were there,' she said, glancing up at the hooks. 'They still are. And he didn't open the front door. It was locked when we came down.'

'He thought someone had come into the house earlier this

evening,' said Harry. 'He was upstairs with Evi and came rushing down in a panic. Remember? He made us check the ground floor.'

'Exactly,' said Gareth. 'We checked. No one was in the house.'

'No, they weren't,' said Harry. 'Question is, were the keys?'

52

'THREE HUMAN SKELETONS,' THE PATHOLOGIST SAID, 'almost certainly the remains of very young children, but I'll get to that presently.'

Harry was hot. The room was smaller than he'd expected. Having been invited by Rushton to be present at the pathologist's examination – the remains were all still technically his responsibility – he'd hoped to be able to position himself in the furthest corner. It wasn't going to be. No one was getting too far away from the action today – there just wasn't the space. A stainless-steel counter, almost a metre wide, ran around the perimeter of the room. The floor was tiled and appeared to slope downwards, allowing for easier sluicing towards the central drain. Above the counters, glass-fronted cupboards lined the walls. Three gurneys were positioned in the centre of the room. They left little room for the pathologist, his two technicians, the team of three police officers and himself. Twice already, Harry had had to side-step, finding himself in the way. He looked at his watch. They'd been in the lab less than five minutes.

'The one we have here,' continued the pathologist, stepping up to the first gurney – Harry had been introduced to him fifteen minutes ago but couldn't recall his name – 'St Barnabas number one, we'll call it for the time being, has been in the ground the longest. We can see almost complete skeletonization, with just the remains of muscle and ligament holding together the bones of the thorax and the abdomen.' He began walking round the gurney, heading for the skull. 'The right arm appears to have broken away at the shoulder when the grave was disturbed,' he said, 'and part of the ulna from the left arm hasn't been recovered yet. A couple of the metacarpals from the left hand are also missing. The brain and the internal organs will be long since gone, of course. We found some traces of fabric around the upper body and two tiny white buttons that had fallen into the ribcage.'

'Lucy Pickup was buried ten years ago,' said Rushton. 'Is that consistent with . . . ?'

The pathologist held up one hand. 'The rate of skeletonization is highly variable,' he said. 'It depends on the soil, the success of the embalming process if any has taken place, depth of burial and so on. The soil in the area where the bodies were found is alkaline, which would normally slow the rate of decomposition; on the other hand, this is a very young child. Very little body mass. On balance, I'd say a burial timescale of between five and fifteen years.'

'We're going to need a bit more than that, Raymond,' said Rushton, who'd positioned himself at the foot of the gurney, directly opposite the pathologist. Raymond, that was his name. Raymond Clarke, one of the approved pathologists on the police list.

'How old would you say she is?' continued Rushton.

'I'm only just getting started,' replied Clarke. 'And we don't know whether number one is a she yet. As to age, that shouldn't be too much of a problem. Based on the skeleton we have an estimated height measurement of 87 cm, which would put our little friend here in the fifteen-to-thirty-six-month bracket. Then we look at the rate of ossification.'

'Fusion of the bones?' asked Rushton.

Clarke gave a single nod of his head. 'Ossification occurs in eight hundred points of the body and can offer some very useful clues as to age,' he said. 'An infant is born without carpal bones in the hand, for example. Then we have the cranium. There are five major bones in a newborn's skull, which gradually fuse along specialized joints called sutures. The newborn also has a number of fontanelles or spots of soft membrane on the skull. On our friend here they've closed over, suggesting a child of at least twenty-four months.'

'Between two and three, then?' asked Rushton. 'Could be Lucy.'

'Very possibly,' said Clarke. 'So now we look at the injuries sustained to the corpse.'

Harry wondered if anyone else was as hot as he. Why would a pathology room be warm? You'd expect the opposite, surely, to keep the bodies in good condition. The two detectives Rushton had introduced him to – he was blowed if he could remember names – were standing like a couple of statues a few inches to his left. One of them, tall and very thin, looked to be in his late thirties. His hair was as thin as the rest of him and he appeared to have no eyelashes. The other detective was a year or so younger and powerfully built. Neither looked as uncomfortable as Harry felt. Maybe they'd just had more practice hiding it.

'I've received the coroner's report into the death of Lucy Pickup,' Raymond Clarke continued, turning away from the corpse to a lap-top computer. He peeled the surgical glove off his right hand and hit a key to activate the screen. 'It's all here if anyone wants to look. It refers to severe blunt-force trauma to the right posterior part of the skull, specifically the parietal and occipital bones, following a fall from around fifteen feet on to solid flint flagstones. Displaced fractures of the skull caused considerable internal bleeding and the force of the impact would have sent severe destructive shock waves through the brain. Death would have been almost instantaneous.'

Rushton and the taller of the two detectives closed in around Clarke. All three men peered at the computer screen. Harry stayed where he was. He already knew how Lucy had died. She'd fallen, tumbled to her death in his church, and her little skull . . .

He was looking at that skull now. The pathologist could take as much time as he liked, he knew it was Lucy. 'In addition,' Clarke was saying, 'the spinal cord was broken in two places, between the third and fourth lumbar vertebrae and slightly higher, between the fifth and sixth thoracic vertebrae. There was also a femoral shaft fracture on the right leg.' He turned away from the computer, caught Harry's eye for a second and then stepped back to the gurney. 'If we look at the head of little miss,' he said, 'and yes, gentlemen, I'm coming round to the idea that she was a little miss, we can see the extent of the trauma to the skull.' Pulling his glove back on, Clarke slid his hand under the skull and turned it so his audience could see where the skull bones had collapsed. 'These injuries are pretty much consistent with a fall from a considerable height,' he said. 'I haven't had chance to properly examine the spine yet, but if we look at her right leg, the break across the femur is quite visible. Can you see?'

'Could that have occurred last night?' asked the stockier of the detectives. He was a sergeant, Harry thought. A sergeant called Russell. Luke Russell.

'Not impossible,' said Clarke. 'But if you look at the X-rays taken for the coroner's post-mortem, the lines of breakage are very similar. Later on today, we'll take more X-rays. We can compare the two, just to be on the safe side.'

'If her body was subjected to a post-mortem examination,' asked the tall, thin detective, whom Harry thought was the more senior of the two, 'wouldn't it be obvious? Don't you have to cut the chest open, remove the organs?'

'Yes, indeed,' said Clarke. 'A full internal post-mortem involves cutting through the ribcage and removing the breastplate. The internal organs are taken out, examined, put inside a biohazard bag and replaced inside the chest cavity. The top of the skull is sawn open so the brain can be examined. All very difficult signs to miss.'

'So . . .'

'Unfortunately, not much help to us here because a full internal post-mortem wasn't done on Lucy Pickup, just an external examination. It's always a bit of a judgement call, whether or not to go the whole way and open the body up. The circumstances surrounding the death are taken into account, quite often the wishes of the family are considered. My guess is that the examiner at the time didn't feel the full Monty was merited. What we do have, though, are signs of the embalming work done.'

Clarke turned to one of his assistants, 'Pass me that bag, please, Angela,' he said. The older of the two lab assistants took a clear plastic bag from the counter behind her and handed it to him. He held it up to the light, beckoning the officers closer. To Harry, at the back, the bag looked empty.

'What we have in this bag,' said Clarke, 'is an eye cap. Can you see? Looks a bit like a very large contact lens. Embalmers use them to keep the eyelids closed, make the deceased look like they're sleeping peacefully.' He reached a gloved hand inside the bag and removed the translucent plastic disc. 'We found this lodged inside number one's skull,' he said. 'It would have been placed on the eye with adhesive to keep the eyelid in place.' He returned it to the bag and handed it back to his assistant.

'We also found traces of wire in the jaw,' he said. 'Consistent with the type used by embalmers to keep the lips together. And if you look at the skull, gentlemen—' He moved back to the body on the gurney. The others followed and gathered at the head end. Harry moved just close enough to show willing. Clarke was pointing out where the fractured pieces of the skull lay separate from the head. 'If you look carefully,' he said, 'you can see where the skull appears to have been glued together in places. Repairing an injury in that way is classic embalming procedure. It's all about preserving the body and making it as presentable as possible for the relatives in the days leading up to the funeral. Interestingly, this is the only one of the three showing any signs of embalming. We'll send tissue off for analysis, of course. Formaldehyde is pretty nasty stuff, tends to hang around for a while.'

Clarke stepped away from the body, peeled off his gloves and dropped them in a biohazard disposal bin. Reaching up, he took a new pair from a dispenser. 'We can also do a DNA analysis to be absolutely sure,' he said, pulling on the gloves. 'I understand the parents are coming in this morning, but if you ask me, I'm 95 per cent certain this is the little lady whose grave was disturbed last night. This is Lucy Pickup.'

No one spoke. Above their heads the fans of the air-conditioning unit suggested a coolness in the room that Harry just did not feel.

'Right,' said Clarke, and Harry almost expected to see him rolling up his sleeves. 'That's the easy bit over with. Now let's have a look at her two friends, shall we?'

DS Russell glanced over at Harry, as if wondering how he'd respond to any suggestion of disrespect. Harry dropped his eyes. When he looked up again, the pathologist had turned to the second gurney. The others gathered round.

'This child is a very similar size,' said the detective inspector. 'How sure can you be that this isn't Lucy Pickup?'

'These remains haven't been in the ground for ten years,' replied Clarke, without even pausing to think. 'I'd be surprised if they've been in soil for more than a couple of months. Completely different state of preservation.'

Harry stepped closer and DS Russell moved aside to allow him to approach the gurney.

'Number three is the same,' said Clarke, indicating the third trolley. 'Can you see?'

'Not skeletonized at all,' said Rushton. 'They still have skin. They look . . .'

'Dry?' suggested Clarke, nodding his head. 'They should. They're mummified.'

Harry looked from one child to the next. They were, as the pathologist said, completely dry, as though something had sucked all the moisture from their bodies. Their skin was shrivelled, dark as old leather, wrapped like cling-film over their small bones. Their scalps still had hair, there were tiny fingernails on their hands. 'Incorruptible,' he murmured to himself.

'There are no bandages,' said DS Russell. 'I thought mummies were wrapped in bandages.'

'Mention mummies and everyone thinks of Ancient Egypt,' said Clarke. 'But strictly speaking, a mummy is just a corpse whose skin and organs have been preserved by exposure to something like chemicals, extreme cold or lack of air. The Egyptians and a few other cultures created their mummies artificially, but mummies occur naturally the world over. Most typically in cold, dry climates.'

'It can't happen in the ground?' asked Rushton.

Clarke shook his head. 'Not in normal soil, anyway. There's a property in peat bogs that prevents oxygen getting to the body and so halts the process of decay. That's why we find so many preserved bodies in peat.'

'Could these be peat bodies?' asked Rushton.

'Doubt it. No sign of staining. My guess is that these two were kept above ground, somewhere cold and dry, where the oxygen supply was limited. Some time within the last two or three months – we can have an entomologist check insect activity, give us a clearer idea – they were moved from wherever they'd been kept and put in the grave with Lucy. If I were you, gentlemen, I'd be asking why.'

For a few seconds, there was no sound in the room but breathing.

'St Barnabas number two would have been around 105

centimetres tall,' continued Clarke, 'putting her in the three-to-five-year age bracket. From what I can tell from the skull sutures, she'd be in the upper half of that scale, maybe around four. Our best friends, though, in these cases, are the teeth.' He indicated the area around the jaw bone. 'Primary dentition consists of twenty teeth commonly known as the milk teeth. These start to erupt at around six months and are usually fully through by three years old. From about twenty-four months onwards, the adult teeth start to form underneath the milk teeth.' He ran a gloved finger along the jaw bone. 'Milk teeth start to be lost at around five to six years old,' he continued. 'Of course, this does vary quite considerably from one family to the next, but a child who has lost several of their front milk teeth is likely to be at least seven or eight. The adult teeth come through in an order that looks random but isn't. This makes it relatively easy to age the skull of a young child. There are even some pretty good charts I can show you, once we've got the bones clean and can see the teeth properly.'

'Any idea at this stage?' asked the DI, whose name Harry simply couldn't remember. Dave? Steve?

'Tricky until we do the X-rays, but from what I can tell, number two appears to have a full set of milk teeth, suggesting a child between four and six years old.'

'Boy or girl?' asked Rushton. Both detectives looked at the senior officer, then back to the body.

'This was a girl,' said Clarke. 'Thanks to the mummification I can say that with some confidence.'

'Is anyone else thinking what I'm thinking?' asked Rushton, looking at the ceiling.

'I think we all are, boss,' said DS Russell.

I'm not, thought Harry.

'Anything I'm missing?' asked Clarke, looking from one man to the next.

'Megan Connor,' said Rushton. 'Four years old. Local child. Disappeared on the moors not far from here six years ago. Biggest case of my career. Massive man hunt. We didn't find a trace.' He turned to Harry. 'Ring any bells, Reverend?'

Harry nodded. 'I think so,' he said. The story had dominated the news for quite a few weeks. 'To be honest, though, I hadn't connected the case with this area. I hadn't realized exactly where it happened.'

'Not two miles above Heptonclough,' said Rushton. 'Lass wandered off from her parents on a family picnic. Never seen again.' He turned quickly back to the pathologist. 'Any clothes found with the body, Ray?'

'Yes. This one was wearing waterproof clothes,' replied Clarke. 'Raincoat and wellingtons. Just one wellington found, though. It's over here. Size . . .'

'Size ten, red,' said Rushton, who was staring down at the dead child. 'The raincoat is red too, hooded, printed with ladybirds. Am I right?'

'Yes,' said Clarke. 'They've been removed and bagged.'

'I see those clothes in my dreams,' said Rushton. 'Where are they?'

'They're over here,' said Clarke. He turned and walked round the third gurney to the counter. A series of large, clear plastic bags lay in an orderly row. He picked up first one, then another and held them out to Rushton. Both had been labelled with lettering and numbers. Rushton took the bag containing one small wellington and softly shook his head.

'She was also wearing jeans and some sort of sweater,' said Clarke. 'Underwear too. Should help with identification.'

'I find myself relieved she was buried wearing her clothes, lads,' said Rushton, still unable to take his eyes off the wellington. 'What does that say about me?'

No one replied.

'Any thoughts on cause of death, Dr Clarke?' asked the thin-haired detective. 'The skull bones seem to be . . .'

'Yes, don't they,' agreed Clarke. 'Very similar injuries to the first child. Severe blunt trauma to the skull, mainly the parietal and frontal bones, and in this case we have a fractured right clavicle or collar-bone, a mid-shaft humerus fracture on the right arm and a distal fracture of the right radius bone. Certainly consistent with a fall, although whether this was before or after death it's very difficult to say.'

'So both these children fell from a considerable height?' said Rushton. 'How sure are you about number two? Could her bones have been broken some other way? Could she – could both of them – have been beaten?'

'Unlikely, if you look at the pattern of injuries,' said Clarke. 'Number one suffered trauma to the rear of her skull, to her spine and to her right leg, all consistent with falling from a height and landing on her back. Number two's injuries are all down the right side of her body, again consistent with a fall and landing on her right side, possibly putting out her right arm to brace herself. When children are beaten, their injuries are more random. They tend to be concentrated around the head and upper torso, although you might see trauma on the arms if the child tries to defend itself. There are no obvious defence wounds on either of these two.'

'Could these breaks have happened last night when the grave opened up?' asked the DI.

'Can't rule it out,' said Clarke. 'There's no sign of these bones starting to heal so the breaks definitely occurred very close to death or post mortem. But you had a lot of wet soft ground, and from what I've been told, the remains tumbled rather than fell; a height of – what – six feet.' He looked again at the damage to number two's skull. 'I rather doubt it, gentlemen,' he said. 'Everybody ready for number three?'

No, thought Harry.

The group around the gurney broke apart and moved away, collecting together again at the third and final corpse. Harry was the last to take his place.

'Disturbing similarities,' Clarke was saying. 'Another very young female child, remains largely mummified. What I can see of teeth and bone development suggests an age of between two and five years old. Her height would indicate . . .'

'She was clothed last night when I saw her,' interrupted Harry. 'What happened to . . .'

'Taken off and bagged,' said Clarke, narrowing his eyes and looking more closely at Harry. 'Why?'

'Can I see it?' asked Harry.

'What is it, lad?' asked Rushton.

'I'm not sure,' said Harry. 'It was dark last night. I probably wasn't thinking straight. Is it possible to see the nightdress, or whatever it was?'

Clarke nodded at the younger of the two lab assistants, who crossed to the counter and checked a number of plastic bags before lifting one and carrying it across. Harry took the bag and held it up to the light.

'It's a pyjama top,' said the lab assistant. She was a young woman, hardly more than twenty-five, slim, with short dark hair. 'We need to scrape away the surrounding soil, check it for any trace evidence and then we'll wash it,' she went on. 'It'll be a lot easier to see when we've done that.'

'Just the top?' asked Harry.

'That's all they've found so far,' replied the girl. 'The bottom half could turn up later today. It's quite a distinctive garment, though. Handmade, from what I can tell. No label or washing instructions and these animals seem to have been hand-embroidered.'

'They were,' said Harry, looking at the tiny figure of a hedgehog.

'What's on your mind, Vicar?' asked Rushton.

Harry turned to the pathologist. 'Could these be the remains of a twenty-seven-month-old little girl?' he asked. 'Been dead for about three years?'

'Well, certainly nothing to suggest otherwise,' said Clarke.

'What's going on?' said Rushton. 'Who do you think she is?'

'She's a child called Hayley Royle,' said Harry. 'Her mother is a parishioner of mine. She was thought to have died in a house fire three years ago.'

Everyone in the room was looking at him. Suddenly he wasn't hot any more. A cold stream of sweat was running down his spine.

'The pyjamas were a hand-me-down,' Harry continued, turning back to Lucy's corpse. 'From that child's mother, strangely enough,' he went on. 'Her aunt made them, they're unique.' They were all staring at him. He was probably making no sense whatsoever. Then Rushton turned to the pathologist. He didn't speak, just held his hands up in a mute question.

'There's no evidence of fire damage that I can see,' said Clarke. 'How severe was the fire?'

'It burned for hours,' said Harry. 'The house is just a shell now. The child's body was never found.'

The police officers were shooting glances at each other.

'The mother was convinced the child didn't die in the fire,' continued Harry. 'She believed Hayley had got out of the house somehow, had wandered away on to the moors. Looks like maybe she did.'

'Holy crap,' muttered DS Russell. 'Sorry, Vicar.'

'No problem,' said Harry. 'If this child didn't burn, how did she die?'

Clarke seemed lost for words.

'Did she fall too?' asked Harry, thinking of course she did. Hayley had fallen from the gallery of his church. Like Lucy had. Like Megan Connor had. Their blood would be on the stones, the police would look later in the day, they'd find traces of it. He closed his eyes. Millie Fletcher had almost become a fourth.

Clarke was talking again. 'Yes, I'm afraid she may have done. She has injuries to her skull, facial bones, ribs and pelvis. She fell from a height and landed on her front.'

'Oh, I think we can stop pretending these children fell,' said Rushton.

53

'I T CAN'T BE HAYLEY,' SAID EVI, SPEAKING IN A LOW VOICE, even though the two of them were alone in a corner of the hospital's main reception. 'Her remains were found.'

'No,' said Harry, still uncomfortably hot in his black shirt and jacket and tight clerical collar. 'According to Gillian, there was no trace . . .'

'Yes, I know what she's told you. She said the same to me. But she was lying. Oh shit, this is so inappropriate.' Evi sat back in her chair and ran a hand over her face. 'I really shouldn't be talking about this,' she said.

Harry sighed. 'Isn't there some exception to the rule, whereby if you believe someone's life is at risk, you can break confidentiality?' he asked.

'Well, yes, but even so . . .'

Harry put a hand on the arm of Evi's wheelchair. 'Evi, I've just seen three dead infants, all of whom died in a very similar manner, two of whom should never have been in the grave in the first place. I really don't think normal rules apply any more.'

Evi looked down at the floor for a second, then seemed to make up her mind.

'I went to see the firemen who were on duty when Gillian's house caught fire,' she replied, without looking up. 'They found Hayley's remains the next day. Just ashes and bone fragments, very similar to what you'd have left after a cremation, but definitely human remains. The bones were examined.'

Harry felt as if she'd just hit him in the stomach. 'Well, if that's the case, I was wrong,' he said. 'The good Dr Clarke's going to love me.' They would all love him. 'I was sure I'd heard Gillian talk about what Hayley was wearing that last night,' he went on. 'And after Jenny told me it was handmade by her sister, well, there didn't seem any doubt.'

Evi looked as worried as he felt. 'Gillian must have been mistaken,' she said. 'Severe trauma can play tricks with people's memories. Maybe she gave the pyjamas to someone else and forgot. If they're unique, they'll still help identify the body.'

'Maybe,' agreed Harry. 'The trouble is, the cat's out of the bag now. The police will have to talk to her. I'm not sure how she'll cope with it.'

'I can go up now,' said Evi. 'I've cleared all my appointments for today.'

Harry heard footsteps approaching. When he looked up, Rushton was standing in the doorway. 'We're ready to go and see Mrs Royle now, Reverend,' he said. 'Are you fit?'

'Of course,' said Harry. He stood and turned to Evi. The back of her chair had two handles, one on either side of her shoulders. 'May I?' he offered.

'Don't even think about it,' she snapped. 'Let's go.'

54

GILLIAN SEEMED TO SWAY IN THE DOORFRAME AS HER EYES fixed on Harry's. 'You didn't tell me you were coming this morning,' she said, before shooting a sly glance at Evi.

'Gillian, this is Detective Chief Superintendent Rushton,' Harry said. 'I'm afraid we need to talk to you. Is it OK if we come in?'

Gillian's eyes opened a little wider, then she turned and walked back up the stairs towards her flat. Harry allowed Evi to go up next and then followed. Rushton brought up the rear.

The flat seemed to have been tidied since the previous day. Harry hoped it hadn't been for his benefit.

'What's going on at the church?' Gillian asked, as they all entered the small living room. 'There've been police cars there all morning.'

Through the window behind Gillian, Harry could see the main road winding its way up the hill towards the church. The rain of the previous night had left a thin mist behind. The edges of the buildings that lined the road seemed to be fading, as though rubbed out by an eraser.

'That's partly why we're here,' said Harry. 'Something happened at the church last night.' He turned to Rushton. 'Detective Chief Superintendent, do you mind if I . . . ?'

'No, please go ahead,' replied Rushton, sinking into an armchair.

Harry waited for both Gillian and Evi to sit. Evi took the other armchair, Gillian sat in the middle of the sofa. Harry dropped down until he was half sitting, half leaning beside her. 'Gillian, something's happened which might cause you some distress,' he began. 'That's why I asked Dr Oliver to come.' Gillian's eyes drifted to Evi, as if only just noticing that she'd followed them up, then moved back to Harry.

'Do you remember telling me about the night your old house caught fire?' asked Harry. 'About the night Hayley was killed?'

Gillian said nothing, just nodded once, her eyes not leaving Harry's face. He began to wonder if she'd started drinking again. There was something not quite . . . 'Do you remember the pyjamas she was wearing?' he continued.

At that Gillian drew herself up. Her eyes flickered into focus and she glanced from Harry to Rushton. 'What's happened?' she asked. She was starting to look frightened.

'Mrs Royle,' said Rushton, leaning forward. In the small room, they all seemed uncomfortably close to each other. 'Early this morning we found the remains of a small child wearing pyjamas very similar to the pair you described to Reverend Laycock. Is there any possibility you were mistaken about what your daughter was wearing?'

'You found her?' Gillian had pushed herself forward on the sofa, was on the verge of leaping up.

'A child was found,' said Harry, putting his hand gently on Gillian's arm. Out of the corner of his eye, he could see both Evi and Rushton getting ready to stand up. 'But we don't see how it could possibly be Hayley.'

'I knew it.' Her fingers were clutching his hand. 'I knew she hadn't burned. Where was she? What happened to her?'

'Mrs Royle.' Rushton's voice was loud enough to silence Gillian for a second. 'I've seen the report of the chief fire officer who attended the blaze at your house. According to that, your daughter's remains were found. They were released into your possession shortly after the fire.'

'No,' snapped Gillian, glaring at Rushton.

'No?' repeated Harry.

Gillian's head spun back to face him. 'What they gave me wasn't Hayley. I know it wasn't.' She turned to glare at Rushton again. 'They were trying to palm me off with a handful of ashes. I know

264

she got out of the house. Stop looking at each other like I'm mad, I know what I'm talking about.'

'Gillian, what happened to the ashes that the firemen gave you?' asked Evi. 'What did you do with them?'

Gillian stood up so quickly Harry almost overbalanced. He watched her cross the room and disappear into the kitchen. A cupboard door was opened and objects moved around. He turned to Evi, who gave a little half-shrug. Then Gillian was back, carrying a metal jar in both hands. It looked like – it looked like what it was – an urn. Harry got to his feet.

Gillian crossed the room and stopped at the small coffee table that sat in the middle of the carpet. She dropped to her knees and swept one hand across the top. A magazine and her purse fell to the floor.

'Gillian, no!' called Evi, a fraction of a second before Harry realized what the girl was about to do.

'Oh, dear me,' muttered Rushton, pushing himself to his feet.

Gillian had removed the lid of the urn and upended it. The ashes were pouring out, creating a small cloud above the table. Harry could hear hard objects falling on to the wood. Something grey, about two inches long, fell on to the carpet near his feet.

'This is not Hayley!' yelled Gillian. 'I would know.'

Evi was next to Gillian on the carpet. One arm was around the younger woman's shoulders, the other had taken hold of Gillian's hand, was trying to hold it back, stop her from hurling the ashes around the room.

'It's OK, I've got her.' Harry's hand touched Evi's for a split second, then he was lifting Gillian up and taking the empty urn from her hand. She relaxed instantly and turned to face him, sobbing against his shoulder. God in heaven, what had he started?

'Don't touch that please, Dr Oliver,' Rushton was saying. Harry turned his head, aware of Gillian's hair clinging to his face. Evi, still kneeling on the floor, had picked up the urn and looked as though she were about to sweep the ashes back inside it. 'I'll do it,' Rushton said, taking the urn from her.

Four heads turned as they heard the front door opening and foot-steps climbing the stairs. Taking a firm hold on Gillian, Harry managed to coax her back to the sofa. He pushed her gently down and then turned back to Evi. She was still kneeling on the carpet. Not waiting for permission, he put his hands on her waist, lifted her and helped her back to the armchair she'd been sitting in.

'Thanks,' she muttered. Her bottom lip seemed to be shaking. Behind her, he saw Gwen Bannister, Gillian's mother, standing in the doorway, taking in the scene. Rushton had begun clearing away the ashes. Gillian was sobbing again, her head on her knees, her blonde hair trailing to the floor. Evi had picked up her bag and was fumbling inside it. Harry half expected the newcomer to turn and leave.

'Detective Rushton, I'd like to give Gillian something to make her feel better,' said Evi. 'Have you any more questions for her?'

'Not for now,' replied Rushton. 'I'm going to take these ashes away with me, have them re-tested. From what I can gather, three years ago the tests just confirmed they were human bones. I think we need a bit more certainty than that.'

'Perhaps Gillian can rest for a while,' suggested Evi, who was trying to stand up again.

Gwen crossed the room and took hold of her daughter's hand. 'Come on, love,' she said, pulling Gillian to her feet. 'Come and have a lie down.'

As the two women disappeared into Gillian's bedroom, Harry breathed a sigh of relief. 'Do you need Gillian to identify the pyjama top?' he asked. He knew it was in Rushton's briefcase, bagged and labelled.

Rushton shook his head. 'I don't think she's a reliable witness, do you? What about the woman who made them? Did you say it was Christiana, Sinclair's eldest?'

Harry nodded. 'So Jenny told me. The pyjamas were made for Lucy. She thought they were too good to throw away and a few years after Lucy died she gave them to Gillian for her daughter.' Harry stopped. Clothes made for one dead child had been given to another. Both had ended up in the same grave.

'What a ruddy mess,' said Rushton, who seemed to be sharing Harry's thoughts. 'Right, I'd better get up to the Abbot's House. See if I can find someone there who's still coherent enough to talk sense.'

'I'll come too,' said Harry. 'At least to the church. I need to find

266

out exactly what state the churchyard's in. My archdeacon is going to need a report. What about you, Evi?'

Evi glanced towards the bedroom door. 'I really should stay for a bit,' she said.

'Will you phone me when you're done?' asked Harry. He gave her a quick smile and turned to leave. Rushton followed him out, with the remains of a dead human in his arms.

55

'HAVE YOU BEEN IN TOUCH WITH MEGAN CONNOR'S parents?' asked Harry, as he and Rushton walked towards the Fletchers' house. At the top of the hill, the mist was thicker. It almost seemed to be seeping out of the stone, hanging in corners and under roof gables. It carried the scents of the moor with it; he could smell wet earth and, in spite of all the rain, a trace of wood smoke from the previous night.

'Aye, they're on their way,' nodded Rushton. 'Live in Accrington now, moved away a couple of years after it happened. I'm seeing them in an hour. Wish I had more answers to give them.'

Harry could remember seeing news coverage of the Connors' tearful appeal for their daughter's safe return. It had been the lead story on the evening news for several days. The police search had spread the breadth of the country and sightings of Megan had been reported as far afield as Wales and the south coast. And yet she'd been not half a mile from where she went missing.

'What I'm struggling with,' said Harry, 'is that the pathologist was so positive the two girls we think were Megan and Hayley couldn't have been in the ground for more than a few months. So their bodies were kept somewhere – for six years in Megan's case, three years in Hayley's. They were both local children; common sense would suggest it was somewhere round here.'

On the Fletchers' driveway were several police officers, and a short distance away was another, more casually dressed group that Harry realized with a sinking heart were journalists.

'Be with you in a second, people,' called Rushton to the police team. 'You're asking me if we carried out a proper search when Megan went missing, is that right, Reverend?'

'Sorry, I don't mean to . . .' The journalists had spotted them, were starting to edge around the police tape in their direction.

'The answer is yes, we most certainly did,' said Rushton in a low voice, glancing at the reporters. 'We had over fifty officers here at one point, and most of the town turned out to help. We didn't just search the town, we searched the entire moor. Every ruin, every water-pumping station, every bush and pile of rocks. We used cadaver dogs that are trained to home in only on decomposing flesh. They found two fresh corpses. One was a rabbit, up in that old cottage that belongs to the Renshaw family. The other was a domestic cat. They're trained to leave animal remains alone, so it didn't hold us up too much.'

'So how . . . ?' Harry left the question hanging.

'We also had a chopper fly over the whole area, with equipment that can detect the heat of a rotting body. It found us a badger, a deer, several more rabbits and a peregrine falcon missing one wing. No little girls.'

'DCS Rushton . . .' One of the reporters, a young man in his twenties, was peering around a woman constable, trying to get a better view of Harry and Rushton.

'So I'm inclined to think that if the dogs and the chopper and half the county of Lancashire traipsing around the place didn't find Megan, it's because she wasn't here when we did the search. Hayley, of course, we didn't look for, because no one knew she was missing.'

Other than her mother, thought Harry. One of the detectives from the post-mortem was walking towards them. It was the older and more senior of the two, the one with thinning hair and invisible eyelashes. The one who was called something like Dave or Steve.

'Give me two more seconds please, Jove,' said Rushton.

Jove?

'One of the questions I'll be asking now is why no one spotted little Lucy's grave being disturbed. Although until your friends the Fletchers built their house here, that particular part of the graveyard wasn't directly overlooked. Someone working quietly, at night, being

269

careful to cover their tracks, well, I can see how they might have got away with it. And if they were blessed with fog like this, they could probably have gone about their business in broad daylight.' He turned back down the hill and faced the reporters.

'Press conference at three, ladies and gents, I'll be happy to talk to you then,' he called. 'Right, my lovely lads,' he said, squaring his shoulders and addressing his colleagues. 'What have you got for me?'

The thin-haired detective, whom Harry had just learned was named after a Roman god, took Harry's place at Rushton's side and indicated that they should walk back up the hill towards the churchyard. Harry and the sergeant he remembered from the post-mortem followed. No longer in surgical scrubs, the sergeant's powerful build was more evident. His trousers stretched tightly around his waist.

'You'll get a better view up here,' Jove explained, as they walked through the entrance and along the church path. Harry couldn't see the top of the tower. Even the crests of the higher archways were lost in grey mist. 'They've taken the awnings down for as long as the rain holds off,' he continued. 'Trying to take advantage of the day-light.' He looked up. 'Such as it is.'

'Anything else shown up yet?' asked Rushton. The four men were walking fast, passing the church and turning towards the tented area close to the wall. A uniformed constable stood guard at the doorway.

'Other half of the pyjamas,' said Jove in a low voice. 'With some evidence of blood-staining. They've been sent to the lab. So have a couple more bones. Couldn't tell you what they were, but they looked tiny. Oh, and you know the grave on the right-hand side of the collapsed one, as you look at the house, belongs to a family called Seacroft?'

'Aye,' encouraged Rushton.

They'd arrived at the police tent. The constable stepped back and allowed them inside. Harry was the last. The polyurethane walls only covered three sides. He could see directly down into the Fletchers' garden. Three crime-scene investigators were working down there. Two of them seemed to be carrying the stones that had been dislodged from the wall over to the edge of the garden. A tiny stone statue of a child had been placed among them. The blinds in the house windows were still drawn.

'Well, the coffin can be seen now,' said Jove. 'There you go, nice bit of oak panelling. We didn't spot it last night, but most of the side is in plain view, as you see.'

Harry looked at wood, stained with damp, crumbling in places. 'We can't leave it like that,' said Jove, 'so we're going to lift it and get Clarke out here to have a look. Anything suspicious and the whole lot goes down the lab.'

'Very good,' said Rushton. 'We need to do the same with the other side. Has someone filed an exhumation request?'

'I think so, sir, but I'll check.'

'There's a massive cellar beneath the church,' said Harry, unable to keep quiet any longer. 'Cold and dry. The sort of place you might expect to produce mummified bodies. It's been shut up for years. Did you search it when you were looking for Megan?'

'We did.' Rushton gave a nod. 'Sinclair unlocked it for us. All the old sarcophagi were opened up. We took the dogs down too. Not a sniff, if you'll pardon the expression. They did get quite excited in the church itself for a while, on the steps leading up to one of those old bell towers.'

'And?' prompted Harry, turning to look at the church. Only the closest of the four towers, the one on the south-west corner, could be seen from that angle.

'Three dead pigeons,' said Rushton. 'I could smell 'em myself before I was halfway up the stairs.'

'Will you check the cellar again?' asked Harry. 'They were local girls. They were taken from here and found here. They must have been kept somewhere nearby.'

Rushton barely glanced at him. 'Thank you, Reverend, the force has some experience of conducting murder investigations.'

A radio started crackling. Jove pulled the receiver off his belt and turned away from the group. 'DI Neasden,' he muttered. After a moment, he turned back to his chief. 'Needed in the house, Guv'nor,' he said. 'They've found something.'

'How long will she be out for?' asked Gwen Bannister.

'Hard to say,' replied Evi. 'Temazepan is a very mild sedative and

271

I didn't give her much. Someone a bit fitter, maybe with greater bodyweight, would just feel very drowsy, maybe a bit spaced out. Gillian must be exhausted to have fallen asleep so quickly.'

Gillian's face had relaxed, lost some of the tension of the past half-hour. She looked younger, softer. One arm was stretched out across the pillow. The long-sleeved T-shirt she'd been wearing had ridden up almost to her elbow. Evi reached out, gently took hold of Gillian's arm and raised the fabric a little higher.

'I thought she was getting better,' said her mother, looking down at the livid, fresh scars across the girl's forearm. 'She's improved, since she's been seeing you.'

'These things take time,' said Evi. 'It's still very early days.'

Gwen turned to the door. 'Come on, love, you shouldn't be standing up. What do you say to a brew?'

'That would be good,' said Evi. 'It feels like a long time since breakfast.'

'Tea or coffee?' Gwen left the bedroom. Evi paused for long enough to tuck Gillian's injured arm inside the bedclothes and to pull the quilt a little higher up around her shoulders.

'Tea please, milk, no sugar,' she called out softly, as she walked back into the living room. The mist outside was definitely getting thicker. When they'd arrived at Gillian's flat, it had been hovering over the higher reaches of the moor and the upper parts of the town. It had crept lower since. She could just about make out parts of the ruined tower. Nothing beyond.

Evi turned from the window and sat down. The coffee table in front of her looked as if it had been smeared with fine dust. She heard the sound of the kettle boiling, of water being poured, the fridge door opening. Then Gwen returned, carrying a tray with two mugs of tea and a plate of biscuits. She stopped and looked down at the table surface, registering the significance of the dust.

'Doesn't seem quite right, does it?' she said, without straightening up. 'Should I wipe it down, do you think?'

'I'm really not sure,' said Evi. 'Perhaps leave it for now. I'll try and get in touch with that police officer before I go. I'll ask him what we should do.'

Gwen bent down and put the tray on the floor. She offered the plate of biscuits to Evi.

'I don't think Gillian can be left on her own today, I'm afraid,' said Evi, biting into a biscuit and regretting it. It was soft and lay like damp cardboard in her mouth. 'I can call in again later when she's awake, but she needs someone with her. If you aren't able to stay, I can arrange for her to be admitted. To hospital, I mean. Maybe just overnight.'

Gwen shook her head. 'It's OK. I can stay with her. I'll take her back with me tonight. I suppose we can put up with each other for once. Ruddy 'orrible biscuits. Sorry, love.'

'You're not close?' ventured Evi. Gillian so rarely talked about her mother, she really had no clear idea of the relationship between the two.

Doubt flickered across Gwen's face. 'We do well enough,' she said. 'Gill ran a bit wild for a time. Things were said on both sides. I expect you and your mum have your fallings out at times.'

'Of course,' said Evi. 'Is there just you at home?'

'Aye. Gillian's dad died in a nasty car accident a long time ago. My second marriage didn't last. But I expect you know all that already, don't you?'

Evi smiled and dropped her eyes.

'I heard they dug up some bodies last night in the churchyard,' said Gwen, finishing her biscuit and reaching for another. 'Bodies that shouldn't have been there, I mean. Is it true?'

'I'm sorry, I haven't been told much about it,' said Evi.

'Little kids, I heard. Is that why you're here? Do they think it's Hayley they found?'

'There was some talk of that being a possibility,' said Evi, wondering how much more vague she could make that sound. 'But of course . . .' She gestured towards the coffee table, at the dust that seemed to be moving now, as though stirred by a breeze neither of the women could feel.

'How could it be Hayley when Hayley's been in a jar in the kitchen for the past three years?' finished Gwen.

'When you came in,' said Evi, 'Gillian was saying that the ashes weren't Hayley. Do you know why she felt so certain of that?'

'She always refused to believe it,' said Gwen. 'Even when the remains were confirmed as being human, she wouldn't accept it. As though someone else could have burned to death in the house without her knowledge.'

Gwen sat chewing her biscuit for a second. Evi sipped scalding tea and waited.

'I sometimes wonder if it was my fault,' said Gwen, after a second. 'Whether I should have got help for her a long time ago. But in those days, we didn't have any namby-pamby counselling rubbish – no offence, love – we just got on with it.'

'You thought Gillian might have needed help some time ago?' asked Evi. 'Did she have problems at school?'

'Just the usual teenage stuff,' replied Gwen, putting her mug down on the carpet and brushing biscuit crumbs off her fingers. 'Smoking behind the bike sheds, sneaking days off. No, I'm talking about what happened to her little sister. When Gillian was twelve. She must have mentioned it.'

Gwen was staring at Evi now. The lines around her jaw seemed to have hardened. Then she picked up the mug again and drank too much. When she lowered it, Evi could see damp splashes around her mouth.

'I'm sorry,' said Evi cautiously, as the other woman ran a finger around her lips. 'I don't think Gillian ever mentioned a sister.'

Gwen leaned forward and put her mug down on the coffee table. 'You should ask her,' she said.

'I appreciate your advice,' said Evi, 'but we only talk about what Gillian wants to bring up. It wouldn't be fair to spring a subject on her. If Gillian had a sister, I have to wait until she wants to talk about her.'

'Well, you might be waiting for a long time,' said Gwen. 'She certainly never wanted to talk to me about it. But maybe you should know, especially if . . .' She looked at the coffee table, where her mug sat amidst a soft film of ash. 'Gillian had a little sister called Lauren,' she went on. 'She fell downstairs when she was eighteen months old. Someone left the stair-gate open – Gillian most likely, although she never admitted it. Lauren tripped over the bar and went from top to bottom. She hit the slate tiles on the hall floor. Lived for three days but never woke up. I never saw her eyes open again.'

'I'm so sorry,' said Evi. 'How terrible for you both, and then to

274

lose Hayley as well.' Another child had fallen to her death?

'Aye. And after that, my marriage didn't last long. John was the one who found her, you see. He never got over it.'

Evi's mobile beeped. A text message. 'Excuse me,' she said, finding her phone in her pocket and looking at the screen. The vicar could text – after a fashion. Six question marks, followed by two Xs and an H.

'I have to go now,' said Evi. 'Thank you for your confidence. I'll pop back in a couple of hours. Gillian might be awake then, and we can decide what to do. Is that OK?'

56

AT THE CHURCH DOOR HARRY STOPPED, ALLOWING THE three officers to walk ahead of him. The reporters were still hovering. Rushton and the two detectives walked past them without responding to their questions and disappeared inside the Fletchers' house.

'Is it true?'

Harry turned. The tall, heavy-set man had appeared like a genie from out of the mist, had maybe even been waiting behind the church for a chance to catch Harry alone.

'Hello, Mike,' he said. 'How are you and Jenny doing?'

'Is it true? Did they find two other kids in Lucy's grave? Both with their heads bashed in?' Mike Pickup was breathing heavily. His face seemed redder than usual and the muscles around his jaw were trembling. 'Has some sick bastard been using my daughter's grave . . . ?'

Harry put his hand on the other man's arm. 'Come on,' he said. 'There's coffee in the vestry.' Pickup showed no sign of moving. 'I'll tell you what I can,' Harry added. It had the desired effect and Mike allowed himself to be led along the last few yards of path and through the open vestry door.

Harry's inner sanctum had been invaded. Two police officers leaned against one wall, drinking coffee. Another was examining plans on Harry's desk. Christiana Renshaw was washing mugs. The vestry had become the incident room.

Harry took a coffee from Christiana and nodded his thanks, then led the way into the chancel. He walked down the steps into the nave and stopped at the first pew. He and Mike both sat down.

'I'm breaking police confidentiality by telling you this,' said Harry, 'because I think you have a right to know.' The coffee had been brewed some time ago, it wasn't that hot. Harry took two gulps, to give himself time rather than because he wanted to drink.

'The remains of three small children were found last night,' he began. 'All of them appear to have tumbled from Lucy's grave when the wall collapsed. One of them has been more or less identified as Lucy, depending upon the DNA sample, which I believe Jenny gave this morning. The identities of the other two aren't known as yet.'

'That little lass Megan, from what people are saying,' said Mike. 'I took part in the search for her. Didn't do a scrap of work for two days. I had all the lads out as well.' He put the mug down on the prayer-book shelf in front of him and fumbled in his pockets. 'I felt for her parents,' he went on. 'I know what it's like to lose a child.'

'How's Jenny doing?' asked Harry, as Mike removed a packet of cigarettes from his pocket and sat looking at them.

'She's been closeted with her dad and old Tobias all morning,' replied Mike. He tipped the packet upside-down; Harry could hear the soft pat of the cigarettes falling against cardboard. 'Family confab,' said Mike, turning the packet the other way. 'Nothing to do with me, of course. I'm not much more than the hired help.' He opened the cigarette packet, allowing the contents to fall into his hands.

'Grief affects people in different ways,' said Harry, surprised by the bitterness he could hear in the other man's voice. 'I've heard there's a special bond between fathers and daughters.'

Mike held a single cigarette between his finger and thumb. As Harry watched, it started to bend. Mike's eyes were shining. He was taking deep, slow breaths, as though fighting to prevent himself from breaking down. He began shaking his head. The cigarette in his hands was broken, useless.

'She wasn't even mine,' he said. 'What do you make of that, Harry?'

'Not biologically yours, you mean?' Harry asked.

Mike was still shaking his head. 'Jenny fell pregnant shortly after

I met her,' he said. 'We weren't even going out at the time, it was obvious it couldn't be mine. She never told me who the father was. Just a silly mistake, she said, not even a relationship, except she didn't want to get rid of it. I kind of admired her for that. But there was no way Sinclair was going to let any daughter of his be a single mother.'

'So the two of you got married?'

'Four hundred acres of farmland I got for my trouble. And two thousand ewes. I come from a farming family, Harry, over near Whitby, but I've got three older brothers. It was the only chance I'd ever have of getting my own farm. Irony is, I'd probably have married Jenny anyway. I was halfway to being in love with her.'

The mug in Harry's hands was cooling rapidly, as though Harry was soaking up all its warmth.

'And you accepted Lucy as . . .'

'There was never any question of it. I adored her from the moment I first saw her. And after a while I forgot; I just forgot she wasn't really mine. I never got over her death. If we'd had more kids maybe. Now, I doubt I ever will.'

The door from the vestry opened and two uniformed officers, a man and a woman, came into the church. They stopped when they saw Harry and Mike, muttered an apology and retreated back into the vestry. Mike watched them go, then stood up. 'What happened to them, Harry?' he said, not taking his eyes from the vestry door. 'What happened to the other two kids? How were they killed?' Two broken cigarettes lay on the stone floor.

'The exact cause of death hasn't been—' began Harry, getting to his feet and stepping out into the aisle.

Mike turned to face him. 'Don't give me that. No disrespect, Vicar,' he said. 'You were at the bloody post-mortem this morning. Had their heads been bashed in?'

Harry took a deep breath. This had been a mistake. He shouldn't have allowed himself to get drawn in. 'There was some evidence of head trauma in both cases,' he began, 'but we really need to wait—'

'Like Lucy?' demanded Mike.

'The pathologist thought the injuries could be consistent with falls,' said Harry. Rushton would kill him.

'Like Lucy?' repeated Mike.

'That's really all I can tell you, I'm afraid,' said Harry.

Pickup glared at him for a second longer. 'I'm grateful for your time, Vicar,' he said. 'I won't keep you any longer.' He nodded at Harry and then set off towards the front of the church. He passed into the vestry and out of sight. Harry's mobile issued three sharp beeps. He pulled it from his pocket. Evi had arrived at the church and was wondering where he was. He set off in Mike's footsteps.

'They'll be leaving now, I expect.' The voice startled him. Harry turned to see Christiana watching him. Her voice was like Jenny's, only softer and sweeter. He didn't think he'd ever heard her speak before.

'I'm afraid the police will be here for quite a while yet,' replied Harry. 'It's upsetting, I know. But necessary.'

'Not the police. The Fletchers.' She always wore dresses, he noticed. Tailored dresses, in fabrics that looked expensive. They fitted her perfectly and Harry wondered if she made them herself, like she'd made Lucy's pyjamas.

'The Fletchers?' repeated Harry. 'Why would the—' He stopped. Christiana's hair was loose this morning, held back from her face with an Alice band. It was long, past her shoulders, unusual on a woman in her forties. She was standing close to him now, closer than felt really comfortable, as though she didn't want to be overheard. He could smell the old-fashioned floral scent she wore and was suddenly reminded of the day she'd scattered scented rose petals beneath the gallery.

'So many little girls,' she said. 'Tell them to go, Vicar. It's not safe here. Not for little girls.'

57

'SO WHERE DO YOU THINK THE CHILDREN WERE PLANNING to go last night, Mrs Fletcher?'

'That's assuming they were planning to go anywhere,' Harry jumped in, before Alice could open her mouth. 'According to Tom, he was trying to rescue his sister.'

Evi watched the blonde social worker look down at the notepad on the kitchen table, gathering her thoughts. 'Yes,' the woman said, after a second. 'From this mythical little girl of his.' She looked up again at Alice. Her lips were a bright, glossy pink. 'Have they ever tried to run away before?' she asked.

'Again, assuming they were running away,' said Harry. 'In my experience, children don't run away in the middle of the night, especially when it's pissing it down with rain. They go in the day, usually when they've been told they can't have any sweets or have to tidy their bedrooms, and they rarely get further than the corner of the street.'

'Exactly how much experience do you have of children running away, Mr Laycock?' asked the social worker. Evi raised her mug to her lips to hide a smile. This was as far from a laughing matter as it was possible to get, and yet there was something about Harry in pugilistic mode that tickled her.

'Does anyone want more coffee?' asked Alice. Nobody answered her. Four mugs sat on the table in front of them. With the exception of Evi's, which was occasionally being used as a screen, none appeared to have been touched.

The kitchen door opened and Joe appeared. Everyone turned to him.

'Mummy, I need a wee,' he said, glancing curiously from one grown-up to the next. His lips twitched in a faint smile when he saw Harry. Alice stood up. 'Stay downstairs, poppet,' she said, indicating the door to the rear of the room. 'Can you squeeze behind Harry?'

'I want to get my remote-control Dalek,' answered Joe, not moving from the doorway. His mother shook her head.

'Not till the policemen have finished, sweetie,' she said. 'Is Millie OK?'

'She's building a tower with Tom,' answered Joe. 'With firewood.'

'Oh good,' muttered Alice, as Joe turned and left the room.

'The upstairs of our house is still officially a crime scene,' said Alice, to no one in particular. 'I haven't been allowed in Millie's room today. I've had to dress her in Joe's clothes.'

'They haven't found any evidence of this so-called break-in then,' said the social worker. Hannah Wilson, she'd introduced herself as, arriving just seconds after Harry and Evi had knocked on the door of the Fletchers' house. She was in her early thirties, on the plump side and with generous breasts squeezed inside a low-cut, tight-fitting sweater. A long, single chain of stones lay against her breast bone, emphasizing the depth of her cleavage. For nearly twenty minutes now, Evi had been waiting to see Harry's eyes fall to it. So far, he'd managed to resist.

'Alice's husband's keys were missing,' Harry pointed out.

'Keys go missing all the time,' answered Hannah. 'You'll need a bit more than that if you're going to prove attempted child abduction.'

'How about two unidentified bodies in the mortuary at Burnley General?' said Harry. 'Both pulled out of the Fletchers' back garden last night. Sorry to be so blunt, Alice.'

Alice shrugged her shoulders and glanced over at Evi. Evi half smiled back, knowing she ought to try and rein Harry in a little. A visit from Social Services was standard procedure following any incident when police were called out and children deemed at risk. If Harry pissed this woman off, it could turn personal. Hannah

Wilson might start flexing her own muscles and the Fletcher family would find themselves caught in the middle.

'Well, we don't know at this stage whether what the police are investigating outside had anything to do with the family here,' said Hannah. 'In the meantime, my sole concern is for the welfare of the children.'

'So is mine, actually,' interrupted Alice.

'And you have to admit Tom's story doesn't quite stack up.' The social worker looked from Harry to Alice to Evi, as if daring one of them to challenge her. 'Tom's face is quite badly bruised. If I understood you properly, Mrs Fletcher, he says he got it when the little girl, who was running away with his sister, kicked him.'

'That's what he told me,' said Alice.

'But from what I understand from his earlier descriptions of the girl, she doesn't wear shoes.'

Nobody spoke. Evi dropped her eyes to the table, mentally kicking herself for not spotting that first. The kitchen door opened again. It was Tom this time, the purple bruise vivid against the pale skin over his cheekbone.

'Mum, Millie's spilled her juice on the sofa,' he said. Alice sighed and started to get up.

'I'll do it,' offered Evi, rising and picking up a dishcloth. 'You finish up here, Alice. I'm sure Mrs Wilson must be nearly done by now.'

Evi followed Tom into the living room. She could hear heavy footsteps moving around upstairs and people talking in low voices. Joe was at the far end of the room, peering around the drawn curtains to see what was happening in the garden outside. Millie, looking impossibly cute in a pair of denim dungarees that had been rolled up at the ankles, waved a stick of kindling wood at her and nearly tumbled backwards into the empty fireplace. Tom rushed forwards and caught her before her head could bang against the hearth.

'Hi, cutie pie,' said Evi, when the toddler was safely on her feet again. The little girl appeared to have been crying. The skin around her eyes looked red and sore. 'Where's this sticky mess?' Evi asked.

'Der,' said Millie, indicating the middle sofa. Evi found the juice and ran the damp cloth over the seat. She could feel Tom's eyes on her.

'How are you feeling now, Tom?' she asked. 'Still tired?'

Tom shrugged. 'Who's that woman?' he asked. 'Is she a doctor, like you?'

Evi shook her head. 'No, she's a social worker. She's here to find out what happened last night and make sure you and Joe and Millie are OK.'

'Do I have to talk to her?'

Evi perched on the arm of the sofa. 'Do you want to talk to her?' she asked.

Tom thought for a moment, then shook his head.

'Why not?' asked Evi, noticing that Millie was watching the conversation, her gaze going from one speaker to the next as though she understood every word. Over at the window, Joe had gone quite still.

Tom shrugged again and dropped his eyes to the pile of firewood on the carpet.

Evi stared at him for several seconds, then made a decision. 'Why have you never told me about the little girl, Tom?' she asked. Tom's eyes widened. 'I know you showed me her photograph last night, but you didn't tell me who she was.' Out of the corner of her eye, Evi could see Joe at the window. He wasn't peering through the gap in the curtains any more, he'd turned to look at them. 'Is it because you think I wouldn't believe you?' she continued in a soft voice.

'Would you?' asked Tom.

'I spend a lot of time talking to people,' said Evi. 'And I can usually tell when they're lying. They give themselves away in all sorts of little ways. I've watched you closely when we've been talking, Tom, and I don't think you're a liar.' She let herself smile, which really wasn't difficult when you looked at Tom. 'I think you've told me the odd little fib now and then, but most of the time you don't lie.' Tom was holding eye contact. 'So if you tell me all about this little girl, and if you tell me the truth, I'll know.'

Tom looked over at Joe, then down at Millie. Both stared back, as though waiting for him to begin. Then he started to talk.

'She's been watching us for a while now,' he said. 'Sometimes, it's like she's always there . . .'

58

'WHAT'S AN EMERGENCY PROTECTION ORDER?' ASKED Harry.

'It's a court order,' replied Hannah Wilson. 'It allows children to be taken into care for their own protection. They're effective immediately.'

Harry sat back down, moving his chair closer to Alice. She was sitting quite still; he might almost have thought she wasn't listening, had it not been for the trembling in her fingers.

'Have you discussed this with Dr Oliver?' asked Harry. 'As the family psychiatrist I'd have thought she'd be the obvious person to consult.'

'Dr Oliver can submit a report, of course,' replied Wilson. 'I'm sure the magistrate will take it into account.'

Harry was about to respond – quite what he would have said, he hadn't quite decided – when they heard footsteps coming down the stairs. They could hear Rushton's distinctive voice, then the front door opening and closing. The footsteps turned in the direction of the kitchen then stopped.

'This is something the family need to know,' they heard Rushton say, in a voice that was low but firm. Then he came into the room, knocking on the door politely as he opened it. He was followed by DI Neasden and a female constable. Neasden didn't look happy.

'Sorry to interrupt, Mrs Fletcher,' said Rushton. 'Need a word, if I may.'

Alice seemed to be bracing herself for another blow. 'OK,' she said. 'Do you need to see me alone?'

Rushton looked quickly round the table, avoiding Neasden's eyes. 'Oh, I think we're all friends together,' he said. ''Ow do, Hannah. You on your way out?'

'Have you found something?' asked Harry.

'I think so,' replied Rushton. 'What time's your husband home, Mrs Fletcher?'

Alice seemed to have lost her ability to think quickly. She glanced at her watch, then at Harry. 'He said he'd be a couple of hours,' she said after a moment. She turned to the kitchen clock on the wall behind her. 'A site inspection he couldn't get out of. He should be back any time now.'

'Good,' said Rushton. 'And you might want to get a locksmith up here. See if these locks can't be changed.'

'What is it?' asked Alice.

Rushton pulled out the chair Evi had just vacated and sat down. Behind him, DI Neasden, his lips pressed tightly together, leaned back against the tall kitchen cupboard. The constable remained by the door, softly closing it behind her.

'You remember we found some footprints in the garden last night,' began Rushton. 'Our forensics people took casts of them.' He turned to the man behind him. 'Have you got it, Jove?' he asked.

DI Neasden had been carrying a thin, blue plastic wallet. With obvious reluctance, he pulled a stiff sheet of A4 white paper from it and handed it to his boss. Rushton turned it to face Alice and Harry. It was a photograph of a footprint in mud.

'We know the prints must have been left in the garden late last night,' said Rushton, 'because of all the rain you had up here. If they'd been left earlier in the evening, they'd have been washed away. So we know at least one person apart from your children was out there round about the time the wall came down.'

Hannah leaned forward to study the print.

'We took several casts of footprints last night,' said Rushton, 'and a whole load of photographs, but this one is the most clear.' He turned to Harry. 'You remember me mentioning that the constable who was first on the scene was a bright lad?'

Harry nodded.

'Brighter than I thought, it turns out,' continued Rushton, 'because he spotted this print, knew the rain would compromise it and put an upturned bucket over it until the crime team could get here. They were able to take some very good photographs and make a good cast.'

'They've made a cast of this?' asked Alice. 'What with – plaster?'

'Dental stone, I believe,' answered Rushton. 'A very tough, durable sort of plaster.' He pointed to the footprint. 'This here's probably a size seven, maybe an eight,' he said. 'Not the most helpful to have, frankly, because it could be a tall woman or a small-footed man. You're a size four, I understand, Mrs F?'

Alice nodded. 'And Gareth's a—'

'A ten, yes, we know. We took casts of his prints as well. Matched them to the boots he was wearing when he went outside. These prints are quite different. Much cruder tread on them. Can you see?' Rushton ran his finger around the outline of the print.

Harry leaned forward to get a better look. Horizontal ridges ran across the print. From the shadows on the photograph they looked deep, the sort of ridges you might see on a boot made for walking through deep mud.

'Looks like a bog-standard wellington to me,' he said. In the instep arch between sole and heel, he could just about make out an incomplete shape, maybe two-thirds of a gently rounded triangle. 'Is that a manufacturer's logo?' he asked.

'Yes, indeed,' said Rushton. 'And although it's difficult to see, I'm told the letters immediately below it say "Made in France". Shouldn't be too difficult to track down the make and manufacturer.'

'But you knew about the prints in the garden last night,' said Alice. 'Why have they suddenly become so—'

'Ah,' interrupted Rushton. 'But last night we didn't know about the matching one upstairs.'

'Boss, we really shouldn't be . . .' said DI Neasden.

Rushton held up a hand to silence him. 'There are three young children in this house,' he said. 'They need to know this.'

'Excuse me,' said Alice in a low voice. 'Matching one upstairs?'

'On the landing,' said Neasden, with a resigned look at his boss.

'Right outside your daughter's room. I'm afraid whoever was in your garden last night was in your house first.'

Alice's fingers rose to her face. It would have been difficult to say which had the least colour.

'Yes, I know, lass,' said Rushton. 'Very upsetting, but it means we're getting somewhere.'

'I looked last night,' said Alice, who didn't seem to want to believe it. 'I didn't see any sign that anyone had—'

'No, you wouldn't,' replied DI Neasden. 'It's what we call a latent print. Just about invisible to the naked eye and typically left by shoes that are quite clean.'

'You see, lass, shoes pick up traces of whatever we walk on,' said Rushton. 'It's called Locket's Law or some such.'

'Locard's Exchange Principle,' interrupted Neasden with the first smile Harry had seen on his face. 'Every time two surfaces come into contact there's potential for the exchange of physical materials. We carry away something of what we encounter, everywhere we go.'

'Yeah, that's it.' Rushton nodded his head in his DI's direction. 'So, as I was saying, every time we walk on something – dust, mud, carpet and so on – tiny particles cling to the soles of our shoes and then when our shoes come into contact with a clean, dry surface, such as your floorboards upstairs, Mrs F, they leave a faint print behind. We find them – when I say we, I mean my clever lads and lasses – in the same way we find fingerprints. We dust with fingerprint powder and then lift the print with adhesive tape.'

'Just the one print indoors?' asked Harry. Rushton turned to the inspector for confirmation.

Neasden nodded. 'We're pretty certain there's nothing else,' he said. 'I don't doubt there could have been more last night, but there was a lot of coming and going in the house, even before we got here. Any others were probably lost. Doesn't matter though. One's enough.'

'You OK, Alice?' asked Harry.

Alice seemed to be getting some of her colour back. She nodded. 'Actually, it's a bit of a relief,' she said. 'It means Tom wasn't lying.' She was silent for a second. 'He's probably been telling the truth all along,' she added.

Harry smiled at her and turned back to Rushton. 'Can you trace the boot to its owner?' he asked.

'There's a good chance.' Rushton nodded. 'We also, very conveniently, have a tiny gash in the right side of the sole, can you see?' He tapped the side of the photograph with his right index finger. Harry saw a small indentation, only half a centimetre long. 'Also, according to our lab, there are wear patterns visible. If we find the boot in question, we can prove the wearer was in your house and garden. Which, given the lack of any sign of a break-in, is why I brought up the subject of changing the locks. Perhaps think about a burglar alarm while you're at it.'

'I'll ring Gareth,' said Alice, getting to her feet. 'He can bring some new locks home with him.'

'Very wise,' agreed Rushton. 'But just hold on a sec, lass. I'm afraid that's not all. You should probably sit down.'

Alice looked at the kitchen door. 'I really need to check on the kids,' she said.

'Evi's with them,' Harry reminded her, wondering if the social worker would offer to go and see if the children were OK. She didn't. Alice took her seat again.

'Where do you do your dry-cleaning, Mrs Fletcher?' asked Rushton.

'My what?' asked Alice.

'Dry-cleaning. There's a couple of places down in Goodshaw Bridge, do you use either of those?'

'I suppose I would,' agreed Alice, 'if I ever had anything to take. But I probably use dry-cleaners once a year.'

There was a moment's silence, while Rushton and Jove exchanged glances.

'I have three children,' Alice continued, as though worried they might not believe her. 'I paint for a living and my husband is a builder. As a general rule, if something won't wash, I won't buy it.'

'Sound thinking,' said Rushton, nodding his head. 'My suits cost a fortune to keep clean, according to the wife. So, have you ever tried these home dry-cleaning kits? You know, when you shove everything in a bag with a load of chemicals and put it in the tumble-dryer?'

'I've never heard of such things,' said Alice.

'So you won't mind if Stacey here and her colleagues have a quick look round your cupboards, make sure there's nothing you've forgotten?'

Alice thought about it for a second. 'Be my guest,' she said. 'You won't find them very tidy.'

Rushton turned and nodded to the WPC. She left the room.

'We're struggling with the dry-cleaning connection,' said Harry.

'The floor's yours, Jove,' said Rushton, leaning back in his chair. In the hallway, Harry could hear the sound of the front door opening and closing as someone, he guessed the WPC, left the house.

'The crime-scene investigators found something in your garden last night that puzzled us,' said DI Neasden, speaking to Alice. 'We thought it was just a tissue of some sort at first but we photographed it, bagged it and took it to the lab, as we do.'

The front door opened again. Footsteps were coming towards the kitchen.

'About thirty minutes ago, we got a phone call from them, saying they've managed to identify it,' he continued. 'It's an essential part of a home dry-cleaning kit. A sort of cotton pad, soaked in stain-removing chemicals, that you put into the tumble-dryer with your clothes. If you do your dry-cleaning at home, that is.'

'I'm going to have to talk to the wife about them,' said Rushton, who was leaning back quite precariously by this stage.

'Yes, thanks, Boss. Anyway . . .'

The kitchen door opened and the WPC was back, with two colleagues, both male. 'OK to start in here, sir?' she asked. Rushton nodded, lowering the front legs of his chair to the floor again.

'The utility room's through there,' said Alice, indicating the back door. The two uniformed men left the kitchen, while the WPC knelt down and opened the cupboard under Alice's sink.

'Where was I?' said DI Neasden. 'Right, the dry-cleaning pad. Obviously, we wonder what it's doing in your garden. It has a strong residue of chemicals clinging to it and it wasn't particularly wet or muddy when we picked it up, suggesting that, like the footprints, it was left in your garden last night. The lab also say they've found traces of the same chemical in your husband's gym bag.'

'The dry-cleaning pad was in the bag,' said Harry. Everyone ignored him.

'Any reason why your husband might have a dry-cleaning kit in his gym bag?' asked DI Neasden.

Alice shook her head. 'Gareth can't work the washing machine,' she said.

'Now, dry-cleaning fluids have a very distinctive smell,' said Rushton, who seemed unable to keep quiet any longer. 'You must know, Reverend, all your lovely robes must have to be professionally cleaned.'

Harry nodded. 'Quite takes your breath away when you take them out of the plastic covers.'

'And when we took the sheets off your daughter's bed, we just got a whiff of something. Well, Jove did, to be honest. Very good nose.'

'How has she been today?' asked Neasden. 'Have you noticed anything unusual? The GP took a look at her last night, didn't he?'

'He did,' said Alice, who was starting to look frightened again. 'I probably should just go and see . . .'

'I'll go,' said Harry, getting to his feet. He stepped back from the table and stopped. He didn't want to leave, he wanted to hear where this was leading.

'The doctor said she seemed fine,' continued Alice. 'A bit drowsy, but otherwise OK. He wasn't worried about her, just asked me to bring her in later today.'

'Any coughing? Runny nose? Red eyes?' asked Neasden.

Alice nodded. 'She has been rubbing her eyes a lot. What's happened to her?'

'The thing that puzzled us most about your son's story,' said Rushton, 'because something was telling me he wasn't lying, was how this intruder could get a small child into a hold-all without her yelling merry hell and waking the entire house up. It's starting to make a bit more sense now.'

'I still don't see . . .' Harry had moved as far as the door.

'The principle component of these dry-cleaning pads is polyglycolether,' said DI Neasden.

'What?' said Alice.

'Miss off the fancy first bit,' said Rushton. 'Ether is what we're talking about. Been used for donkeys' years as a pretty crude anaesthetic. I'm sorry to say it, but it looks like someone held a pad soaked in ether against Millie's face. It almost certainly wouldn't have worked with an adult, probably not even on one of your lads, but given how small she is and the fact that she was sleeping anyway, it was probably just sufficient to keep her drowsy enough to put her in the bag.'

Alice gave a tiny cry and set off towards Harry.

'I'm going,' he muttered, and pulled open the kitchen door. Four strides took him to the door of the living room. He pulled it open, knowing that Alice was hot on his heels. Evi and the three children were sitting on the floor. Four faces, impossible to say which was the prettiest, turned to him. He was still trying to decide when Alice squeezed past him.

'Um, um,' called Millie, her little face lighting up, before squawking in annoyance as her mother scooped her up and pressed her against her chest.

Rushton and DI Neasden came into the room.

'Right then,' announced Rushton. 'Schoolboy Superhero Tom and his trusty sidekick, Joe the Invincible, I think we need another word with you two.'

59

'PERHAPS THEY'LL PUT A PLAQUE FOR US HERE AFTER we're dead and gone,' said Harry. 'Are you cold?'

'Why?' asked Evi. 'Are you going to offer me your coat?'

Harry carried on staring straight ahead. 'I'll share it,' he offered.

Evi waited for him to turn towards her, to grin. He didn't move.

'You look tired,' she said, although the truth was he didn't just look tired. He looked thinner, older. The man she'd met in the hospital that morning hadn't been the Harry she knew. Someone else had taken his place. Someone else was still there.

'Yeah, well, I spent the first half of the night thinking about you,' he said, still keeping his eyes fixed on the building across the street. 'Then I got a phone call.'

Evi knew from the empty feeling in her stomach that it must be the middle of the day, but the sun hadn't made it through the mist yet. So high on the moor, she could almost feel it, cold and clammy, stealing its way into her lungs.

'I really need to see how Gillian is doing,' she said, knowing the last thing she wanted to do was to go back into that flat. She pushed herself forward on the bench and looked down the hill. 'Walk me to my car?' she asked.

'No,' he said, leaning back against the wall, folding his arms.

'No?' Last night he'd kissed her, danced with her; now he couldn't even be polite?

'You need to take five minutes,' he said, turning to look at her at last. 'We both do. A tiny spot of reflection in a very unusual day.'

'You're not going to get all vicary on me, are you?' risked Evi. 'If you make me bow my head I'll start giggling.'

'How your patients take you seriously is beyond me.' At least he was smiling again, she was getting through to him.

Movement down the hill caught her eye. She raised her head to look over Harry's shoulder just as he turned. Alice's car was reversing out of the driveway. In the back seat, a small face was watching them. A hand waved. Then the car began moving forwards, past the police cordon and down the hill. Rushton and DI Neasden climbed into a dark-blue estate car and set off after the Fletchers.

'Will Millie be OK?' asked Harry.

'I'm sure she will,' said Evi quickly. 'The redness around her eyes and nostrils won't last much beyond today. She might be a bit tired and grumpy for a couple of days, at worst.'

'Will they find traces of ether in her bloodstream?' asked Harry.

'Almost certainly,' said Evi.

Someone else was emerging from the Fletchers' house. Hannah Wilson, the blonde social worker.

'Miss Pissy down there was talking about something called an Emergency Protection Order,' he said. 'Do we need to worry?'

'I'll phone her boss when I get back,' said Evi. 'Make sure I'm kept informed about any applications to the court. Good job keeping your eyes away from her cleavage, by the way.'

'Blondes don't do it for me. Will you oppose one?'

Evi thought for a moment as Hannah Wilson climbed into a small red hatchback and drove away. 'If I think it necessary, Harry, I'll apply for one myself,' she said. 'No, don't fly off the handle. Those children *are* at risk. Given the events of last night, I don't think anyone can doubt that any more.'

'But snatching them away from their mum and dad will—'

'An EPO doesn't mean taking them away from their parents, it just gives the local authority power to keep them from harm. Gareth Fletcher has parents living close by, is that right?'

Harry nodded. 'I think so,' he said. 'In Burnley.'

'Well, then a magistrate might decide that the children should go and stay with their grandparents for a while, with Alice and Gareth's full consent and cooperation, of course.'

'For how long?'

She shook her head. 'Impossible to say. EPOs usually only last a few days but they're often followed by a longer-term care order. Oh, stop glaring at me. I have never believed the children's parents are part of the problem. But there *is* a problem.'

'Rushton is going to have officers watching the house,' said Harry.

'And how long will that last? He won't have the manpower to watch them indefinitely. And even if those children in the graveyard do turn out to have been murdered, if there is a psychopath up here preying on little girls, they've still been dead for years. They're not likely to find the person responsible all that quickly.'

Harry said nothing. She was right.

'And while they carry on looking, the Fletcher children remain at risk.'

She was still right. Reluctantly, Harry gave a faint nod.

'I had a good long chat with Tom just now,' said Evi. 'He's finally started talking to me about this little girl of his.'

'And . . .'

'Well, I'm pretty certain he's not lying. Someone has been frightening him and I think, maybe, what you said last night was right. Someone is playing a rather mean practical joke. Maybe dressing up in some sort of Hallowe'en costume. She tends to appear at night, so he never gets a particularly good look at her. A lot of the time, he says, he doesn't actually see her properly. Just catches glimpses, hears her calling things to him.'

'Does he think she put Millie on the church balcony back in September?'

'Yes, he's convinced she did.'

'And he thinks she took Millie last night?'

She turned back. Was it her imagination or had Harry moved closer on the bench?

'At first he did,' she said. 'But when we talked about it, he realized it couldn't have been her. The intruder he describes is just nothing like the little girl – much taller, for one thing, and wearing very different clothes. Miss Pissy Knickers, as you like to call her, was smart enough to spot that whoever kicked Tom did it with a booted foot.'

'I said nothing about knickers. I have no interest in Miss Pissy's undergarments. What's going on here is something to do with the church. I'm sure of it.'

'The church?'

'We know for a fact that one of those children – Lucy Pickup – died in the church. Millie Fletcher almost did. I'll bet the other two did as well. They're taken up to the gallery and dropped.'

Evi gave herself a moment to take that in. 'Four little girls,' she said. 'Who would do such a thing?'

'They're dropped from the gallery and then their bodies are stored in the crypt. If Millie had fallen that night, if we hadn't found her in time, she'd have been taken down there as well. That was probably the plan for Lucy, too, but Jenny found her very quickly.'

Evi felt a tickling sensation between her shoulder blades. She clutched both her upper arms to stop the shiver breaking out. 'That's quite a leap you've just made there, Vicar,' she said.

'You were a good Catholic girl once. Ever heard of the Incorruptibles?'

Evi thought for a second then shook her head. 'Can't say I have.'

'I thought of it in the post-mortem, earlier. When I saw Megan and Hayley. Their bodies had been preserved. Hardly any decomposition at all.'

'I'm listening.'

'It's a Catholic and Orthodox Christian belief that certain human bodies, typically those of very pious people, don't decompose after death,' said Harry. 'Something supernatural, the work of the Holy Spirit, keeps them perfect. They become known as Incorruptible.'

'Incorruptible in soul and in body?' asked Evi.

He nodded. 'It's one of the signs that indicate a candidate for canonization,' he went on. 'I can give you countless examples. St Bernadette of Lourdes, Saint Pio, Saint Virginia Centurione, any number of popes.'

'But from what you told me, mummification, which is basically what we're talking about, occurs naturally.'

Harry gave a soft laugh. 'Of course it does,' he said. 'I'm not trying to claim the work of the Holy Spirit in this case, far from it. It just got me thinking.' He turned to face her. His eyes were blood-shot and there were lines on his forehead she hadn't noticed before. 'You see, if you're not taking the supernatural route,' he continued, 'you can argue that one of the reasons why so many members of the clergy, relatively speaking, have so-called incorruptible bodies is that their remains were stored in the places most likely to produce mummification – cold, dry church crypts with airtight stone coffins. Like the one almost directly below us.'

Evi couldn't stop herself glancing down. 'You've told Rushton this?' she asked.

'Yep. He's sceptical at the moment, because the crypt was thoroughly searched in the days after Megan disappeared. But he's going to have to go down there again now. If they look carefully enough, they'll find traces.'

'He's going to want you on the force,' said Evi, trying for a smile.

Harry was still looking at her. 'I find him uncomfortably tactile,' he said. 'Always touching me on the shoulder or the arm. Do you think he fancies me?'

Evi gave a little shrug. 'Can't think of any reason why he wouldn't,' she said.

'Good answer. Are you busy tonight?'

She made herself turn her face away. 'No,' she said slowly. 'But . . .'

'Why is there always a but?' said Harry.

Evi turned back. 'I can't stop seeing Gillian right now,' she said. 'The timing is all wrong. And it doesn't take a genius to see she's nuts about you.'

'And that's my fault?' He'd taken hold of her hand, was tugging at the glove. She could feel his fingers on her wrist. She tried to pull away, he held firm.

'Maybe not,' she said. 'But whether it is or isn't your fault, it's still your problem. Cheer up, there's probably a guideline you can refer to. Women have been falling for the curate for centuries.' The glove was being peeled off her fingers. She caught her breath.

'Never the right ones,' he said, his hand closing around hers. 'And what do you mean, maybe not?'

'You have a great deal of charm, Vicar. I can't believe you save it all for me.'

'Well, that's where you're wrong. You – and Detective Chief Superintendent Rushton, of course.' His index finger had slipped inside the sleeve of her jacket. 'You have such soft skin,' he muttered.

'If that child they found last night does turn out to be Hayley,' said Evi, taking hold of his hand and pulling it firmly away from hers, 'I can't begin to predict how Gillian will react. I can't stop seeing her, not even . . .'

She stopped. It didn't really need saying.

'If the child they found last night does turn out to be Hayley,' said Harry, leaning back on the bench again, 'I'm going to have to bury her.'

60

9 November

'YOU WERE RIGHT, REVEREND. THEY WERE KEPT IN THE crypt. In the third tomb along from the front. We found traces of hair and blood, from both of them. Other bodily fluids as well. Even a button.'

'God rest their souls,' replied Harry.

'Quite.' Rushton's voice down the phone was unusually subdued. 'Of course, we searched that tomb back when we were looking for Megan and it was empty then,' he went on. 'So she was obviously kept somewhere, possibly even in the killer's own house, while we were searching, then moved after all the fuss died down.'

Harry looked at the clock. Six o'clock in the evening. Was there any point calling Evi? It was four days since she'd even bothered answering the phone.

'We also found traces of blood in the main part of the church,' continued Rushton. 'What do you call it, the nave?'

Harry muttered something.

'From just underneath the gallery. The stones had been washed clean but we dug some of the mortar out from in between them,' Rushton was saying. 'We managed to match it to both girls.'

'And they've been confirmed as Megan and Hayley?'

Rushton sighed. 'Aye. We got the results of the DNA tests a couple of days ago. Not that any of us really had any doubts. We're still waiting to hear about the remains in the urn that was given to Gillian Royle. God help us if that's another missing child.'

'Quite,' said Harry. 'Any suspects?'

'Several leads we're following,' replied Rushton.

Harry waited. 'What about the effigy I found beneath the gallery?' he asked when he realized Rushton was going nowhere further.

'We've spoken to the family who made it,' admitted the detective. 'They say they went to find it on the night of the bonfire and couldn't. Claim to have no idea how it could have got into the church. There are a couple of prints that don't match anyone in the family so they could well be telling the truth. The sweater was Millie Fletcher's, though, her mother identified it.'

'Then how?'

'Stolen from the washing line is our best guess. Wouldn't have been difficult, that garden's very accessible. I've increased police presence in the town for the next few weeks, we'll be keeping a close eye on the house.' He gave another deep sigh. 'We're talking to young Tom Fletcher and his psychiatrist about this little girl that seems to have been hanging around,' he said. 'We need to track her down.'

'She must live in the town,' said Harry. 'It can't be that hard.' Rushton had been talking to Evi. Everyone got to see her but him.

'Trouble is, young Tom's imagination is on the powerful end of the spectrum. He talks about this girl as if she's barely human. We can hardly do a house-to-house search for a monster in human form.'

'Guess not.'

'And we've identified the source of the footprint found in their garden that night. A wellington, as we thought, size eight, rubber soled, made in France. Unfortunately, several thousand pairs are imported every year and there are more than a dozen suppliers in the north-west alone. It's going to take some time.'

As soon as he'd hung up, Harry tried to call Evi. He got her answer machine and left a message. Then he walked through his quiet house, opened the back door and went out into the garden. On a damp, moss-covered bench beneath a bare magnolia tree he sat down and tried to pray.

Part Four
Longest Night

61

17 December

'FOR WHAT IT'S WORTH, VICAR, I THOUGHT THAT WAS better than the first one. Shorter. Less standing around in the wind.'

Harry turned to see that Tobias Renshaw had crept up on him through the mourners that were gathered in the large hall of the Renshaws' house. It really wasn't his day. After Lucy's second interment, in a new grave, lower down the hill than her first, he'd raced back to the church, cassock flapping, to try and catch Evi before she disappeared – again – and had practically fallen over the gang of journalists lurking by the church door. He really wasn't in the mood for this obnoxious old bugger. He made a point of looking round the room.

'I'm not sure Mike is back from the graveside yet,' he said. 'I might pop out and look for him. He seems to be taking this quite hard.'

'Who?' asked Tobias. 'Oh, Jenny's husband. Never really took to him. Always struck me as being on the make. Still, she seems happy enough. How's the lovely Alice and her charming daughter? I saw them in church just now. Haven't they come back?'

'Detective Chief Superintendent,' said Harry in relief as Rushton appeared behind Tobias. 'Good to see you.'

'All right, lad.' Rushton nodded at him then turned to the older man. 'Mr R.,' he said. 'My condolences.'

'Yes, yes,' said Tobias. 'Can I get anyone a drink? You'd think there'd be a hardship fund, wouldn't you, for when a second funeral becomes necessary?' Harry and Rushton watched the old man walk away towards a drinks table.

'He's harmless enough,' said Rushton in a low voice.

'If you say so,' said Harry, without the energy even to try to hide his feelings. 'I'll tell you what puzzles me, though.'

'What's that, lad?'

'Doesn't everything round here – the land, the farms, all the property – doesn't it belong to Tobias? He's the oldest Renshaw, after all. Yet Sinclair always seems to be completely in charge.'

'It was all made over to Sinclair a few years ago,' replied Rushton. 'From what I can remember, Tobias was ready to retire and Sinclair wouldn't take over unless he was given a free rein.'

Harry could smell smoke and coffee on the other man's breath. 'He made his father sign over control?' he asked.

'Oh, that sounds worse than it was. It would all have come to Sinclair in the end. The property is – what do you call it? – entailed. The oldest male always inherits. Now then, I'm glad I've caught you. A quiet word, if I may.'

As Harry allowed himself to be gently propelled into a quiet corner of the old school room, he caught sight of Gillian watching them.

'We've had the results of the latest DNA test,' said Rushton quietly. He too had spotted Gillian. 'You know, the one done on the burned remains Mrs Royle had in her kitchen cupboard? It took longer than we'd have liked, but anyway, it's back now.'

'And?'

'Result. Perfect match to our friend Arthur.'

Harry sighed. There was a bottle of Irish whiskey on the drinks table but it wasn't even midday and he had a busy afternoon. 'So let me get this straight,' he said. 'The remains Gillian Royle had in her kitchen cupboard all this time were actually those of a seventy-year-old man called Arthur Seacroft who was originally buried next to Lucy.'

'Well, strictly speaking, just the remains of part of his right leg,' said Rushton. 'The rest of him is still in the grave. Ah, thanks, love, very nice.'

Christiana Renshaw had approached, carrying a tray of sandwiches. Rushton helped himself to two. Harry shook his head, then waited until Christiana had moved away to the next group.

'So someone dug up Arthur's grave,' he said, 'helped themselves to one of his limbs, broke into Gillian's house that night, abducted Hayley, left Arthur's leg behind in her cot and then started the fire.'

Rushton chewed for a few seconds and swallowed. 'You have to admire their nerve,' he said. 'Without some trace of charred human remains in the house, the firemen would have been suspicious. Finding nothing would have given credence to Gillian's claims that her daughter didn't die in the fire. There would have been a serious search. We'd have found them in the crypt. Arthur's right leg put paid to all that. We didn't look for Hayley. Another serious error for me to account for when I meet my maker.'

'Hindsight's a wonderful thing,' said Harry. 'I've seen the report into the fire. Gillian showed it to me. The fire investigators had no reason to suspect arson.'

Rushton said nothing. He carried on eating but his actions had an automatic look about them. 'We've also had the entomologist's report back,' he said after a minute. 'Goes on at length about egg-laying and hatching cycles, cheese graters, skuttle flies, coffin skippers – sorry, lad, I don't do bugs. The long and short of it is that he thinks Megan and Hayley joined Lucy in the ground in early September.'

'About the time the church was reopened,' said Harry.

'Exactly.' Rushton finished his first sandwich and got to work on his second. 'Whoever was responsible wasn't prepared to take the risk of the three being found when the new vicar decided to explore the crypt. So they were moved to the graveyard, which is the best place I can think of to stash away a body or two. He or she wasn't counting on the Fletcher boys and their midnight escapades.'

At the far side of the room, Christiana reappeared. Her tray of sandwiches had been replenished.

'Christiana knows more than she's telling us,' said Harry.

Rushton turned to look at Christiana. She moved slowly, but rather gracefully for such a tall woman. 'Aye, so you say, lad,' he said. 'But when I talked to her she just said who wouldn't be worried, after two other girls were found to have died the exact way Lucy did. And after Millie Fletcher so nearly went the same way. You have to admit she has a point. And before you ask, she volunteered to give us her fingerprints – they weren't on the effigy you found, or on the wine decanter Mike brought in back in October.'

'Oh, you're probably right,' admitted Harry. 'I'm jumping at shadows.'

'You know I saw her the morning after we found the bodies?' Rushton said. 'To ask her to identify the pyjamas?'

Harry nodded.

'I showed them to Jenny and Christiana. Jenny wasn't sure – well, she was very upset that day, but Christiana, now, she was quite something. She brought her workbasket out and showed me the patterns she'd used to make the animals, all those years ago. And then she told me the exact colour and reference number of each embroidery silk she'd used. She's an odd one, but bright as anything in her own way.'

'Any news on the wellington boot?' asked Harry, then waited until Rushton had finished his sandwich.

'Hit a dead end,' said Rushton. 'I'd hoped we might be able to pin it down to a particular batch, but no such luck. If we find the boot itself, we can match it, but a lot of people wear wellies around here.'

As Rushton was speaking, Harry caught sight of Gillian again. She raised a glass of colourless liquid to her lips and swallowed most of it. Rushton followed his glance and the two of them watched Gillian make her way towards the drinks table. She reached out, swaying slightly, and took hold of a bottle.

Gillian's initial reaction to learning that Hayley was indeed one of the three corpses unearthed by Tom Fletcher had been one of jubilation at being proven right: her daughter hadn't died in the fire, as she'd always claimed. That had been quickly followed, though, by ongoing torment, as she seemed unable to stop herself imagining the final hours of her daughter's life. Even without talking to Evi, Harry knew that Gillian's recovery had taken a severe setback.

He took a quick look around the room. Her mother was nowhere to be seen. 'Will you excuse me?' he said to Rushton.

The older man nodded. 'Aye, go on, lad,' he said. 'Although, frankly, I'm not sure there's much you can do for that one.'

62

'OK, HERE ARE THE RULES,' SAID EVI, LOOKING DOWN AT three alert, interested faces in front of her. They were in the family interview room at the hospital. The Fletcher children were sitting opposite her in three miniature, brightly coloured armchairs.

'In this box there are some funny masks and also some quite scary ones,' she went on. 'So as soon as anyone starts to feel scared, or anxious or worried in any way, we can stop. Joe and Millie, if you want to go over to the table and draw, or play with the toys in the box, that's fine. If you'd rather stay and help Tom, that's fine too.'

'I want to draw,' said Joe.

Evi indicated the low table, already set up with paper, coloured pens and crayons. In the corner of the room sat Alice and Detective Constable Liz Mortimer. Evi had asked them both not to distract the children or make them self-conscious. Behind a large mirror on one wall of the room, DC Andy Jeffries was watching and making notes.

'OK, Tom,' said Evi. 'Are you ready to have a look in the box?'

Tom nodded, looking anxious but also, Evi thought, quite enjoying the attention. Evi lowered herself to the carpet. Kneeling for any length of time was a seriously bad idea, one she'd pay for later, but it was unavoidable in this case. She took the lid off the cardboard box, conscious of Alice watching from under a canopy formed by her left hand, a magazine on her lap. Evi reached inside. 'I think this one is . . .' She peered quickly at the mask she was bringing out. 'Scooby Doo,' she said, holding up a cartoon dog's face.

Tom smiled and visibly relaxed. 'Can I try it on?' he asked.

Evi handed it over as Millie wriggled off her armchair and headed straight for the box. Tom put the Scooby Doo mask over his head and turned to look at himself in the large mirror. Alice looked up, smiled and turned back to her magazine. Millie had picked up the box lid and was balancing it on her head.

'Right,' said Evi, reaching into the box again. 'Next one is Basil Brush. Can I try this one?'

'We're going to the pantomime tomorrow,' said Tom. 'In Blackburn. It's a school trip.'

The exercise was one it had taken several weeks to set up. The idea had occurred to Evi shortly after Tom had first confided in her about the strange little girl. After listening to his descriptions, she'd explained to the investigation team her theory that someone, probably an older child or young teenager, had been hanging around the house and had even crept inside on at least one occasion, wearing some sort of carnival mask. If they could pin-point the mask used, the police might have some chance of tracking down where and to whom it had been sold. It was a long shot, especially as there was no proof that Tom's little girl was in any way connected to the attempted abduction of Millie, but it was one the police were willing to try.

Having decided to go ahead, the investigation team had gathered together every party, carnival and Hallowe'en mask they could find in the shops and on the internet. Evi had already discarded some that bore no relation to Tom's description and had arranged the funnier, less threatening ones so that they came out of the box first.

Tom was reaching into the box himself now, turning round with each new find to see how it looked in the mirror. Millie was copying her brother, getting the elastic tangled in her hair. Joe was studiously ignoring both of them. Gradually, the masks became darker, scarier, no longer made with children's parties in mind.

'Mum, look,' called Tom. He stood up tall, an oversized mask over his head. The mask seemed to depict a male, East European peasant with drooling mouth and very little brain.

'What?' said Alice, looking up from her magazine. 'Oh, very nice.'

'You know who I am,' prompted Tom. 'The servant from *The Young Dracula*. The one who makes them bat-bogey porridge for breakfast.'

'Yeah, I must get some of that,' agreed Alice. 'Any nicer ones in there?'

Tom turned back to the box as Millie waddled over to her mother with an Incredible Hulk mask pulled over her face. It was upside-down.

Thirty minutes later, Tom had reached the bottom of the box and Evi was ready to admit defeat. On the plus side, none of the children appeared to have been disturbed by the exercise. Tom had treated it like a huge game, trying on every mask, even making Evi put on several. Millie, too, had joined in the fun, although she'd grown tired a while ago and was now sitting on her mother's lap. Joe had completely ignored both his siblings and had concentrated instead on his drawing. He'd been working on the same picture for over half an hour now. He was just a little too far away for Evi to see what it was.

The clock in the corner of the room said it was twenty-five past six. 'I'm afraid we're going to have to stop now,' said Evi, glancing at the large mirror. 'Tom, thank you. That was very brave of you. And it was very helpful. Thank you, Millie.' She glanced over at Alice and DC Mortimer in the corner of the room. Alice raised her eyebrows in a silent question. Evi shook her head. Alice stood up, Millie in her arms. The child's eyes were glazed and she snuggled in close to her mother.

'Worth a try, I suppose,' muttered the detective, getting to her feet.

'Come on, boys,' said Alice. 'What did we do with coats? Joe, are you done?'

Evi had almost forgotten about Joe. The boy had been so quiet all the time she'd been interacting with Tom and Millie. Now he stood up, examined the drawing he'd been working on and then carried it over to her. He held it out.

Evi took it, feeling her ribcage tighten. The drawing was exceptionally good for one done by a six-year-old. It showed a figure dressed in pale blue, with long fair hair and over-sized hands and feet. The head seemed large too, whilst the eyes looked huge and heavy lidded. The full-lipped mouth hung open and the neck was terribly misshapen. A movement at Evi's side told her that Tom, too, was looking at his brother's drawing. Alice and Millie drew close.

'Ebba,' said Millie, her eyes brightening as she reached for the drawing. 'Ebba.'

'That's her,' said Tom in a small voice. 'That's what she looks like.'

63

'ALL THREE OF THEM? ARE YOU SURE?'

'Perfectly,' said Evi. 'Joe drew her, Tom and Millie both recognized her. Millie even had a name for her. Ebba, she called her. She's quite real, this Ebba person. The police just have to find her. Are you playing Springsteen?'

'A man can dream. Hang on, I'll turn it down.' Harry picked up the remote control and the music faded. 'So what is she?' he asked. 'A kid, a dwarf?'

'Hard to say. Tom showed me on a height chart roughly how tall he thought she was. About 140 centimetres, which would put her on a par with an eight- or a nine-year-old child. But if Joe's drawing was accurate, her hands, feet and head are disproportionately big. That might suggest an adult with stunted growth. And she appears to have some sort of lump, maybe a goitre, on the front of her neck.'

'If someone like that lives in Heptonclough, people will know about her.'

'Exactly. And she must live there. There are no other towns close enough.'

'There are quite a few farms dotted about, some of them pretty isolated. She may come from one of them.'

'The detective who was there mentioned that. He's going to talk to his boss about getting a couple of officers to start visiting homes.'

'They took all this seriously? I mean, at the end of the day, it was a six-year-old kid's drawing.'

'I don't think they have much else to go on, do you?'

'What did Joe have to say about her?'

'Nothing. I talked to him for a good five minutes on his own, but he wasn't saying a word. Tom thinks he's made her a promise that he won't talk about her, but drawing her picture doesn't seem to count.'

'Could she have threatened him?' asked Harry.

'Possibly. Although I rather doubt it. Joe doesn't show any sign of being frightened of her. He wasn't stressed by the conversation, just silent. And Millie greeted her picture like she was an old friend.'

'So Tom has been scared to death of someone his brother and sister are fine with? How likely does that seem?'

'Tom's quite a bit older,' said Evi. 'In many ways he's starting to think like an adult. Joe and Millie, being younger, might be more likely to accept Ebba.'

'What is that you're calling her?' asked Harry.

'Ebba. It's Millie's name for her. Could be anything, of course – Emma, Ella, who knows? The point is, she's real.'

'And how's she getting into the house?'

'Well, she isn't any more, according to Tom. He's hasn't seen her since the night the wall came down. Now that Alice and Gareth have tightened up their security, she can't get in. He thinks she might still be watching them when they're outside, but he can't be sure.'

'Come round,' said Harry, scared at how much he wanted her to. No reply.

'I'm cooking,' he tried, when there was still no response.

'You know I can't do that,' she said.

Inside Harry, something snapped. 'I don't know anything of the kind,' he said. 'All I know is that for the first time in my life, I'm losing my grip on what's happening around me. I have reporters pouncing on me every time I go out, I hardly dare answer the phone any more. Everywhere I turn I find a police officer. I'm starting to feel like I'm a suspect myself.'

'I understand that, but—'

'I'm dealing with a level of grief that is unprecedented for me, I have corpses of children tumbling out of the ground and my only friends in this place are heading for nervous breakdowns. I find effigies of children in the church, I've been tricked into drinking blood . . .'

'Harry . . .'

'And the one person I've met who could help keep me sane refuses to have anything to do with me.'

'Effigies? Blood? What are you talking about?' Her voice had dropped. She sounded as if she was holding the telephone away from her ear. Harry heard a soft knocking sound. Had the cat knocked something over?

'Evi, if I thought you weren't interested, I wouldn't be pestering you,' he said, looking round the room. No sign of the cat. 'I promise you, I'm not that pathetic. Just tell me I'm out of line and I'll leave you alone. But I don't think that. I think you feel the same way I do, and . . .' The knocking sounded again. There was someone at the door.

'What do you mean, you've drunk blood?'

'Look, can we just forget that crap for a minute and talk about us? Come for dinner – nothing else, I promise. I just want to talk. '

'Harry, what haven't you told me?'

'I'll tell you everything if you come round,' he offered.

'Oh, don't be so bloody childish,' she snapped at him. 'Harry, this is serious. Tell me what happened.'

'There's someone at the door,' he said. 'I'm going to have to answer it. If you're not here in half an hour, I'm coming to you.' He put the phone down.

Muttering curses, Harry walked down the hall. He could see a tall, dark shape through the glass of the front door. Wondering what the record might be for speed of dispatching an unwanted parishioner, Harry pulled the door open.

Detective Chief Superintendent Rushton stood on his doorstep, one hand clutching a bottle of Jameson. He lifted it into the air. 'Couldn't help noticing your own bottle was looking a bit depleted last time I was here,' he said. 'So I brought my own.'

64

18 December

'HEY, YOU.'
Harry looked up. He'd heard footsteps approaching, had just assumed it was yet another police officer prowling around his church. And now, even before he'd opened his mouth to say hello, he was up, striding across the vestry, heading for the young woman who might be wearing the same violet colour as her eyes, only it was impossible to be sure because he'd already taken her in his arms, was far too close to focus on what she was wearing, and she was smiling up at him . . .

Dream on, Harry. He hadn't moved from his desk, was still staring stupidly across the room, and yes, she was wearing violet, a large, loose sweater over tight black jeans tucked into long boots; and that was a very unclerical thought he was having about those boots on bare legs.

'You didn't come,' she said, one hand on the doorframe, the other holding the door ajar.

Harry leaned back in his chair. Five seconds it would take him to cross the room, kick the door shut and put the fantasy into action. 'The other love of my life turned up with a bottle of Irish,' he said. 'After an hour, driving really wasn't an option for either of us; and I hope he's been suffering all day as well.'

'DCS Rushton?' she asked, as her cheeks glowed a little pinker.

'The very same.' Would it be five seconds? He could probably do it in four, if he leaped over the desk.

'How was he?' She stepped forward, collecting her stick from where it had been leaning against the doorframe, and allowed the door to fall shut.

If he leaped over the desk, he'd be sick.

'Terrified he's going to be forced into early retirement before the case is solved,' he said. 'At a complete loss to know what to do next. I told him I knew just how he felt and the two of us poured each other another drink.'

Her smile faded as footsteps approached outside. Harry waited to see if they were heading for the vestry but they continued on down the path.

'I need you to tell me what's been going on here,' she said. 'It's important.'

Harry sighed. He really, really didn't want to get into all that now with Evi. All he wanted to do was step forward, pull her away from that door and . . .

She let her head fall on to one side, looked him directly in the eyes. 'Please,' she said.

'OK, OK.'

In as few words as possible, he filled her in about every weird thing that had happened to him since his arrival in Heptonclough: the whispered, threatening voices; his constant sense that he wasn't alone in the church; the smashed effigy that bore a remarkable resemblance to Millie; and his own personal favourite: drinking blood from a Communion chalice. When he'd finished, she was silent.

'Can I sit down?' she asked, after a moment.

He pulled a chair in front of the desk and she sank into it, a frown of pain creasing her forehead. Then she looked up at him. 'Are you OK?' she asked.

He shrugged. 'Can't answer that one in a hurry. Does any of it make any sense?'

She shook her head. 'Not really. But I think I'm getting closer to finding out who Ebba is. That's why I came up. My laptop's in my bag. Could you get it, please?'

Harry retrieved Evi's large, black leather bag from where she'd left it by the door and put it on the desk in front of her. While she pulled out and switched on the slim computer, he brought a chair round the desk so that they were sitting side by side. Evi opened up a window and turned the screen so that Harry could see it. It was a page from a medical reference site. His eyes went to the title at the top.

'Congenital hypothyroidism,' he read and turned to her for confirmation. She nodded.

'Once Tom had Joe's drawing to jog his memory, he was able to give me a very detailed description of the girl,' she said. 'The goitre is what really gives it away, though.'

'What is it, exactly?' asked Harry, who'd been scanning the text beneath the heading, unable to make much sense of the medical jargon.

'Basically, a shortage in the body of the hormone thyroxin,' said Evi. She was just inches away from him. He could smell her sweet, warm scent, too delicate to be perfume, maybe soap, body lotion. He had to concentrate.

'Thyroxin is produced by the thyroid gland in the neck,' she was saying. 'If we don't have enough of it we can't grow properly and we can't develop as we should. The condition is rare now, luckily, because it can be treated, but in the old days, it was quite common, especially in certain parts of the world.'

'Can't say I've ever heard of it,' said Harry, shaking his head.

'Oh, you will have,' said Evi. 'The less politically correct name for it is cretinism. I think Tom's friend – shall we call her Ebba, it makes life a bit easier – is what we used to call a cretin.'

Harry rubbed both temples, thinking for a second. 'So, she's what?' he asked. 'A child?'

'Not necessarily,' said Evi, with a tiny cat-like smile on her face. 'People with the condition rarely grow taller than about five foot so an adult could easily appear much younger. And they usually have the mental age of children, would act in a childlike way. Do you need some paracetamol?'

'If I take any more I'll rattle. How is it caused?' asked Harry. 'Is it genetic?'

'In some cases,' said Evi. 'But mainly the causes are environmental. For the body to produce thyroxin we need iodine, which we get primarily from food. In the days when people grew their own food and fed on local livestock they were much more vulnerable. Certain soil conditions, typically remote mountainous regions like the Alps, were deficient in iodine. So if you lived in an area where there was no iodine in the soil, your thyroid gland would swell up in size to suck up as much iodine as possible. That's what causes the goitre on the neck.'

'We're a long way from the Alps,' said Harry.

'Parts of Derbyshire were very vulnerable not too long ago,' replied Evi. 'Derbyshire neck was quite a well-known medical condition. Look.'

She changed the screen and Harry was looking at a picture of a woman in late-nineteenth-century dress. A massive swelling on her neck pushed her head out of position, forcing her to look upwards.'

'That's a goitre,' said Evi, indicating the lump. 'And we're really not so far from the Peak District here, are we?'

'So the girl that's been frightening Tom is a local woman suffering from this condition? I can't believe no one's mentioned her.'

'It does seem odd,' agreed Evi. 'But the Fletchers are still very new. Maybe people were just being discreet.'

Harry thought for a moment. 'I need coffee,' he said, standing up and crossing to the sink. Kettle in hand, he turned back. 'And you say the condition can be treated?'

'Absolutely,' said Evi, nodding her head. 'That's what's puzzling me. Newborn babies are routinely screened these days. If they're found to be deficient in thyroxin, it can be administered artificially. They have to take it all their lives, but their development will be normal.'

Harry switched the kettle on and found clean mugs.

'The only explanation I can think of is that she was born to relatively uneducated parents who haven't maintained her treatment,' continued Evi. 'Maybe they suffer from it themselves. I spoke to DCI Rushton this morning, suggested he start looking at outlying farms and farm-workers' cottages. Whoever this family are, I'm guessing they don't come into town too often.'

'OK, big question now,' said Harry, spooning instant coffee into the mugs. 'Could this girl – woman, whoever – be responsible for the deaths of Lucy, Megan and Hayley? For the threat to Millie?'

317

Evi flicked the screen back again. 'I've spent most of today finding out everything I can about the condition,' she said. 'There's no evidence I can see of these people behaving in violent or aggressive ways. Even Tom doesn't think it was she who tried to abduct Millie now. He claims it was a much bigger person.'

'It was dark, he was scared,' said Harry. 'He could have got confused.'

'Yes, but it doesn't feel right somehow. These people are known for their gentleness, their harmlessness. Even their name suggests that. The word "cretin" is believed to come from the Anglo-French word "*Chrétien*".'

'Meaning what?' asked Harry, as the kettle came to the boil and switched itself off.

'Christian,' said Evi. 'Cretin means Christian. It's supposed to indicate the sufferers' Christ-like inability to commit sin.'

He really couldn't concentrate this morning. 'How so?' he asked.

'They don't have the mental capacity to distinguish right from wrong, so nothing they do can be considered sinful in the true sense of the word. They remain innocent.'

Harry almost shook his head and stopped himself just in time. He was never drinking again. 'That doesn't mean they can't do anything wrong, just that they don't know they're doing wrong,' he said. 'What if this Ebba person likes the look of little blonde girls, sees them as some sort of plaything, and it all . . . oh, hang on a minute, this is ringing bells.'

'I'd say the last thing you need right now is bells ringing in your head.' She was laughing at him.

'What I need right now can't be discussed in a house of God,' he replied. She was right though, he could really do without a hangover today. 'Innocent Christians,' he said, as though trying out how the words sounded in his mouth. Then he had it. 'Innocent Christian souls,' he said. 'We need the burial register.'

'Sorry?'

Harry was already reaching into the cupboard where the register was kept.

'Look,' he said, when he'd found the right page. 'Sophie Renshaw, died in 1908, aged eighteen, described as *An Innocent Christian soul*.'

'There's another one,' said Evi. 'Charles Perkins, died in 1932, aged fifteen. How many are there?'

He counted quickly. 'Eight,' he said. 'Six girls, two boys, all under twenty-five at the time of death.'

'The condition's more common in females,' said Evi. 'You think all these people could have been like Ebba?'

'I wouldn't be in the least bit surprised. I even remember that old bugger boasting about it. "Ninety-five per cent of the food I've eaten my whole life comes from this moor," that's what he said to me. I'll bet the soil up here's – what did you call it?'

'Iodine deficient. We really need to find her, Harry.'

65

THE COACH STOPPED AND FIFTY EXCITED CHILDREN LEAPED to their feet. Through the steamed-up windows Tom could see the huge banner and posters outside King George's Hall and the massive lights of Blackburn's Christmas decorations. *The Snow Queen*, bit of a girly pantomime but who cared? It was an afternoon off school, and then tomorrow – the Christmas holidays.

Tom felt himself being pushed towards the front. 'Climb down carefully,' Mr Deacon, the headmaster, was saying. 'I do not want to spend my afternoon in Accident and Emergency.'

Grinning to himself, Tom stepped down to the pavement. A second coach had pulled up on Blakeymoor Street and the Key Stage One children were climbing down. Most of them had never been on a school trip before and they gazed around, mesmerized by the Christmas lights. As Tom watched, Joe jumped out, making light work of a step that was half the size he was. He caught Tom's eye and waved.

Following the line, unable to keep from jumping up and down as he went, Tom made his way into King George's Hall.

66

'DO YOU THINK WHERE IT HAPPENS IS IMPORTANT?' ASKED Evi, as Harry walked her back through the church. 'That of all the high places in the world small children can be thrown off, it has to be this one?'

'I'm sure of it,' he replied. 'This is the killing ground.'

Evi allowed her eyes to travel upwards, to the gallery that was almost directly above them. 'That's revolting,' she said.

Harry looked up too. 'There's something wrong in this church, Evi. I think I knew the first time I set foot in it.'

He felt her fingers brushing softly against his hand.

'Buildings absorb something of what goes on in them,' he continued. 'I wouldn't expect everyone to agree with me, but I'm sure of it. Normally, churches feel like peaceful, safe places because they've taken on decades, sometimes centuries of hope, prayer, goodwill.'

'Not this one?' Her fingers were closing around his hand.

'No,' said Harry. 'This one just feels like pain.'

For a second they didn't move. Then, just as he knew she was going to, Evi turned and reached up to him. It was just a hug, he knew that, a moment of comfort, but it was impossible to be this close to her and not bend his head down to the skin at the side of her neck, to find that freckle, to press his face against her hair and breathe in deeply. Then she moved in his arms, pulled back her head, and it was completely out of the question that he not kiss her.

Moments passed and the only thing he could think of was that the world couldn't be too bad after all because Evi was in it; and would he be damned for all eternity if he picked her up, laid her gently down on the pew beside them and made love to her for the rest of the afternoon?

Then Evi made a gasping sound that had nothing to do with passion. She'd stiffened in his arms, had pulled away from him, was staring over his left shoulder. Cold air on the back of his neck told him the front door of the church was open. He stepped back and turned.

Gillian stood in the open doorway. For a second Harry thought she was going to faint. Then it looked as though she might hurl herself at them in rage. She did neither. She simply turned and ran.

67

MILLIE WAS IN THE DOORWAY, WATCHING SOME CHICKENS strut up and down in the lane. Across the drive, her mother was unloading shopping from the car. She straightened up and headed for the door.

'Will you go back inside?' she said to the toddler, bending down towards her. 'It's freezing.' She squeezed past the child and disappeared. A moment later her hands caught hold of Millie round the waist. 'I mean it,' she said, as she lifted her daughter up and took her out of sight. 'You'll fall down those steps.'

For a moment the doorway was empty and then the mother appeared again. She crossed quickly to her car and found the last of the bags. As she straightened up and pressed the button on the thing in her hand that would lock the car, the child appeared in the doorway again. She stole a brief, sly look at her mother before turning to the chickens that had wandered into their garden. Then she climbed down the steps to the drive.

The car hadn't locked itself. The mother pressed the button twice, three times and then gave up, using the key to lock the car instead, just as Millie set off across the lawn. The mother crossed the drive and went inside. The front door closed. Silence.

Nothing to see, nothing to hear for a minute, maybe two. Then the front door was pulled open and the woman, her face white and her hands clutching her upper arms, appeared in the doorway. 'Millie!' she called, as though afraid to shout too loudly. 'Millie!' she called again, a bit louder this time. 'Millie!'

68

'WHERE DID YOU FIND THESE?' ASKED HARRY.
'Environment Agency archives,' said Gareth
Fletcher. 'Watch those crisps, I'll get throttled if I get
grease on them.'

Harry put his crisp packet down and leaned over the maps.
'Catchment maps,' he said. 'I've never heard of them.'

Gareth lifted his pint and drank. A week before Christmas, the
White Lion in the middle of Heptonclough was busy and even at
nearly five o'clock in the afternoon the two men had been lucky to
get a table. Harry almost wished they hadn't, that he and Gareth
Fletcher had been forced to reschedule the chat they'd had planned
for days. He'd wanted to help Evi find and talk to Gillian. That was
not something she should have to face on her own.

'No reason why you would,' said Gareth. 'The water authorities
produce them. They show the countryside from the point of view of
the water resources.'

'And that means what, exactly?' asked Harry. Across the room, a
party of office workers were in high spirits. Several wore paper hats.
When they stood up, most seemed unsteady on their feet.

Evi had refused to let him go with her. Gillian was her patient,
she'd said, her responsibility.

'Most maps are about roads, towns and cities, right?' said Gareth.

'Right,' agreed Harry.

'This one is about rivers. See, this is the river Rindle. Starts as a

324

spring way up in the hills and gradually makes its way down to where it joins the Tane. All these other streams and rivers are its tributaries.' Gareth leaned across the map, pointing out faint, wiggling lines with his finger. 'They all feed into it and it gradually gets bigger and bigger. The area they all cover is called the catchment.'

'OK, got that,' said Harry, who'd been watching a dark-haired girl with a purple paper hat who reminded him of . . . how soon could he phone her? Was she with Gillian right now? 'And the water authorities need these because . . .' he prompted, forcing himself to concentrate.

'If a stream dries up, if it gets polluted, if there's a fish kill, or a flood threatening, the authorities need to know where it is and what other water-courses it's going to impact upon.'

'OK.' *I could be struck off for this, Harry,* she'd said to him, as they'd argued at the church gate. *You have no idea how serious it is.*

'The modern maps are easier to read, all the different catchments are coloured differently,' Gareth was saying. 'This one must be eighty years old. It does, though, have something the more modern ones don't. This one shows the underground streams. Even some of the deeper aquifers. It dates back to the days when people dug their own wells and needed to know where they might strike lucky.'

'Still following,' said Harry. *She trusted me, and I've let her down in the worst possible way.*

'Now, you can see how a fairly sizeable subterranean stream starts right up here, just below Morrell Tor, and winds its way down through the village, feeding quite a few wells as it goes, probably all abandoned and covered over by now, and eventually goes under the church.'

'We saw it that day we went exploring. The monks had turned it into a sort of drinking fountain.'

'Exactly. Now, as we know, it disappears into a grate, running under the cellar, and – this is the important bit, are you concentrating?'

'Oh, I'm riveted.' *If anything happens to her it'll be my fault.*

'Just after it leaves the church foundations, it forks in two. The main stream continues down, through the graveyard, under the Renshaws' garden and then on down the moor. The other part heads west and follows the line of the church wall.'

'Seriously weakening it?'

'In my view, yes. If you ask me, there's not a lot of point rebuilding that wall until you can divert that offshoot of the stream.'

'If we block it off, will the water continue down the hill with the rest?'

'Probably, although I'd need to check it out with my friends in water resources. Do you want me to do that before you speak to God about releasing the funds?'

'Yes, thank you. What's this?' In an attempt to take his mind off what might be happening with Gillian and Evi, Harry had been trying to spot places he knew around the town on the map. He'd found Wite Lane, had followed the track he sometimes ran along up the hill. He was pointing at a double circle within a rectangle.

'Looks like a bore hole, an old drinking well,' said Gareth. 'Although why there'd be one way up there I have no idea.'

'It's just below the Tor, isn't it? Wasn't there an old mill up there?'

'That's right. I'll bet this is inside that hut. The one the kids call Red Riding Hood's cottage.'

Harry nodded. He knew the one. 'Belongs to the Renshaws,' he said. 'DCS Rushton was telling me how they searched it when they were looking for Megan Connor. I don't think he mentioned a bore hole.'

'If it's been covered over and forgotten about, he might not have known it was there,' said Gareth, finishing his pint. 'There are wells and bore holes all over the place that nobody knows about. Another one?'

'I think I'm still drunk from last night,' said Harry. 'One more won't make much difference.'

Gareth grinned. As he stood up both men heard the tinny notes of the Bob the Builder tune. 'Mine,' said Gareth, pulling his mobile from his pocket.

Gareth continued walking as he held the phone to his ear. He made it as far as the bar then turned on the spot, shot a quick look at Harry and left the pub, pushing aside two boys who looked barely old enough to drink.

For a second Harry didn't move. Then he got to his feet. It would be a problem at Gareth's work, he told himself, nothing important. The noise in the pub seemed to have increased. Over at the office-party table girls were squealing, and blowing on the paper trumpets that came out of crackers.

He took a step towards the door.

Millie would be fine. She'd been shopping with her mother that morning, the last big shop before Christmas, nothing could happen at the supermarket. A waitress was walking from one diner to the next. 'Sherry trifle?' she was saying. 'Who ordered the sherry trifle?' Even the till at the bar seemed unnaturally shrill.

'Merry Christmas, Vicar,' people called after him as he made his way through the crowd. He ignored them. Millie would be fine. She was never allowed out of her mother's sight these days. Someone dropped a glass just behind him, he might even have knocked it over himself. It shattered on the tiled floor.

He pushed at the door; the cold evening air hit him and so did the silence. He took a deep breath and looked around. It was completely dark. Gareth was fifteen yards further up the hill, about to get into his truck, and for a moment Harry just wanted to let him go. He didn't want him to turn round; he didn't want to see that look on anyone's face again as long as he lived.

'Hey!' he shouted, because for the life of him he'd forgotten what the other man was called.

Gareth turned back. There it was again, that look: sheer terror. He opened his mouth and Harry could just about make out what Gareth was croaking at him. Not Millie then, Millie was OK after all.

Joe was the one who'd gone missing.

69

'OK, THEN, THIS IS WHAT WE KNOW.' DETECTIVE CHIEF Superintendent Rushton stopped and cleared his throat. He had to look at the top of Alice's head, her eyes were staring down at a stray cornflake on the kitchen table.

'Joe was definitely still in King George's at the interval,' continued Rushton, 'which took place from three fifteen to three forty-five. The front-of-house manager was quite definite about timings. Joe was bought an ice cream and more than one little lad remembers seeing him in the toilet queue. What we can't be certain of is whether he was still in the theatre for the second half.'

'Who the hell was sitting next to him?' said Gareth. He hadn't stopped moving since he and Harry had walked through the door. He paced the floor, he rocked back and forth on his heels, he wandered from room to room, shouting his thoughts out to whoever might be listening. Alice, in sharp contrast, had barely moved in three hours. Her face seemed to be getting paler and smaller by the minute.

Harry looked at his watch – almost eight o'clock. He pulled his phone from his pocket and checked the screen. No messages.

'Well, that's the thing,' said DI Neasden. 'The kids didn't have allocated seats, they all swapped round at the interval. One or two of the little ones got scared of the baddie up on stage and went to sit next to the teachers. The theatre wasn't completely full, so there were empty seats. No one we've spoken to can definitely remember seeing Joe during the second half. We've checked with the event stewards; there were three of them on duty and none of them remember seeing a young lad wandering round by himself.'

'The school didn't know for certain he was missing until they got all the kids back on the coaches and did a head count,' said Rushton. 'This was at ten to five. The staff went back into the theatre to search, and gave up after another thirty minutes. We were notified at twenty-five past five.'

'He could have been gone two hours by then,' said Gareth, pushing his way past DI Neasden to get to the sink. He ran himself a glass of water, raised it to his lips and put it down again. He turned as the kitchen door opened and Tom came in. The boy stood in the doorway, looking from one adult to the next. No one seemed to know what to say to him. Then Jenny Pickup appeared behind him, paler and more dishevelled than usual, with Millie in her arms.

'Come on, Tom, love,' she said. 'Let's leave everyone to talk. Shall we play on the computer?'

Tom opened his mouth as if to say something, but his bottom lip began to tremble. He turned and ran from the room, just as Millie started squealing to get to her mother. Alice stood and held out her arms. She took her daughter and dropped down into her seat again, as though the effort of standing was just too much.

'I'll stay with Tom,' muttered Jenny.

'Thanks,' said Gareth. 'I'll come through in a sec. They should probably be in bed.'

Harry checked the screen of his mobile again as Jenny slipped out of the room.

'OK then,' said Rushton. 'Next thing we did was have a look at the CCTV footage. Not the easiest of tasks; it's a big building. As well as the pantomime, they had a conference in the Northgate Suite and the café-bar was as busy as you'd expect a few days before Christmas.'

'And?' said Gareth, pouring the water down the sink.

Rushton shook his head. 'The cameras in the foyer didn't pick up anything. Of course there were a lot of people milling around in the interval and it's not impossible he slipped out behind someone else, but the school had a member of staff standing by the doors to

329

prevent exactly that. She's adamant no child went past her and she seems pretty reliable.'

'What about other doors?' asked Harry.

'Including the staff entrance and the fire doors, there are nine exits from the building,' answered Rushton, 'some covered by cameras, some not. We did pick up one image that we want you to have a look at. Have you got it, Andy?'

Detective Constable Andy Jeffries, who looked more like a teenage hoody than a member of the Lancashire Constabulary, had his laptop ready on the kitchen table. He pressed two keys and then turned the screen to face Alice. Gareth approached the table and leaned over the back of his wife's chair. Harry moved closer. They watched as a clip of CCTV footage started playing. They were looking at one of the corridors in King George's Hall. Two members of staff walked towards the camera and, as they disappeared from view an adult and child came on screen, walking out of shot. The adult was wearing a baseball cap, trousers and a thick quilted jacket. The child was similarly dressed in an oversized baseball cap and a large, blue plastic raincoat. They walked to the doors, the adult with one arm around the child, and then disappeared outside.

'What do you think?' said Rushton.

'Let's see it again,' said Gareth.

The clip was played again. 'Impossible to be sure,' said Gareth, after they'd seen it a third time. 'Right sort of height for Joe, right build, but we just don't get any sort of look at his face. What do you think, Al?'

For a second Alice didn't react. Then she shook her head.

'We're going to be running that clip on the news tonight,' said Rushton. He looked at his watch. 'In just over an hour. Asking them to come forward. If it was nothing to do with Joe, we can rule them out.'

'Is that a man with him?' asked Harry. 'Woman? Teenager?'

'Anybody's guess,' said Rushton. 'We've got people trying to enhance the image, but when all you're working with is the back of someone's head it's tricky. Of course, these two might have nothing to do with Joe. We've got officers talking to all the bus drivers who were working that patch this afternoon. Taxi drivers too, in case the

330

lad managed to sneak some money out. Needless to say, his picture's been sent to all stations in the area, along with a description.'

Harry put his phone on the table in front of him. 'What about cameras around the town?' he said. 'Don't we all get caught on camera about a hundred times a day? If that's true, some of the ones around Blackburn must have picked Joe up.'

'We've got a team going through them all,' said Rushton. 'It'll take a while, as I'm sure you can imagine, but you're right, some of them will have spotted him.'

'Can we help?' said Harry. 'If it's a question of manpower. We can sit and look at TV screens.'

'It's a good thought,' said Rushton, 'but these things need to be done by people not emotionally involved. Your place is here, with the family. Right, where was I?' He glanced down at his notes. 'We've got officers working their way through Blackburn town centre, asking in all the shops that are still open. They're all carrying his photo.'

'Joe wouldn't just go off with a stranger though,' said Gareth. 'If he left King George's with someone, it would have to be someone he knew.'

'Quite possibly,' said Rushton. 'On the other hand, he is a very young lad. And people can be very convincing. We've also been talking to all his classmates. If Joe had any plans, he might have mentioned them to someone. Right, I need to get back to the station now. When the news bulletin goes out, the phones will go bananas.' He reached out and patted Alice's shoulder. 'Keep your spirits up, lass,' he said, getting to his feet. 'Someone will have spotted him.'

'Hold on a second,' said Harry, pushing back his own chair. 'What you're doing in Blackburn looks very thorough, but what about here?'

Rushton was frowning at him. 'Here?' he said.

'Who's looking here? I've seen no sign of a search going on outside. And we still haven't found this girl Tom's been talking about.'

'Blackburn's twelve miles away, Harry,' said Rushton. 'I doubt he ran away from the theatre only to make his way back home on his own.'

'And you think Joe's disappearance is just coincidence?'

said Harry. 'That it's not connected to what's going on up here?'

Rushton seemed about to speak and then changed his mind. 'Word outside, Reverend,' he muttered, indicating the door to the hall. Harry stood and followed Rushton out of the room. They crossed the hall towards the front door, with Gareth close behind. Rushton opened his mouth to object.

'Last time I checked, he was my son,' said Gareth, folding his arms across his chest.

'Three dead children were found in the garden of this house,' said Harry. 'And now another one is missing. This cannot be a normal abduct—'

'Those children were girls, quite a bit younger than Joe,' shot back Rushton. He glared at Harry for a second, then seemed to relax. 'I'll bring a team up in the morning,' he said. 'We'll get the dogs out, I'll see if the chopper's available, we can look for this little girl of Tom's. But tonight, I have to concentrate my resources on where the chances of finding the lad are greatest. He's somewhere in Blackburn, I'm sure of it.'

70

'FEELING BETTER?'
　　Evi wiped her nose and drew the handkerchief under her eyes so her make-up wouldn't smudge too badly. 'Yes,' she said, although she wasn't. 'I'm sorry.'

After the incident in church, Evi had driven straight to Gillian's flat. There had been no response to her continued knocking. In the end, the woman from the shop beneath the flat had told her that Gillian had caught a bus not ten minutes earlier. Evi had had no choice but to return to work. Not long after she'd arrived, she'd taken a phone call from the police, telling her about Joe's disappearance. She had cancelled her appointments for the rest of the day and then driven for nearly an hour to reach her supervisor Steve Channing's house. His wife was a partner in a large firm of accountants and they lived in an old manor house in the heart of the Forest of Bowland.

'No need,' he said. 'Now, ready to talk?'

She nodded.

'The police aren't connecting Joe's disappearance with what's been happening in the town?' said Steve. 'With what nearly happened to his sister twice?'

Evi shook her head. 'No. They're saying because he went missing in Blackburn and because he doesn't fit the victim profile, it's unlikely to be directly connected. The officer in charge of the case thinks the media coverage in the town recently has provoked Joe's abduction. He thinks someone caught a glimpse of him on TV and took a fancy to him. It's feasible, I suppose.'

Steve stood up and walked to the window. Across the street, porch lights lit up a row of stone cottages. Christmas trees stood in several of the windows. At the end of the street, a stone bridge led over a narrow river. Earlier, Evi's arrival had coincided with that of a flock of geese. They'd landed noisily on the riverbank. Evi thought she could still hear them as they settled down for the night. Then she could hear something else. A faint beeping noise coming from her handbag. Someone was trying to phone her again.

'What do you think?' Steve asked her.

She couldn't answer the phone, she could not talk to Harry right now. 'It seems too much of a coincidence to me,' she said, forcing herself to concentrate. 'And it would be just stupid to ignore the possibility that whoever killed the girls has got Joe. I wonder if DCS Rushton is afraid to admit the connection because it means he's responsible, at least partly. If he hadn't screwed up on the earlier cases, the killer wouldn't still be at large.'

Steve stepped away from the window and sat down again. 'That's a bit harsh, but you could be right,' he said. 'So what do you think is going on?'

'I can't imagine, Steve,' she said. 'It's not just three murders and an abduction. We've also had blood in the Communion chalice, an effigy hurled from the church gallery, homes broken into, disembodied voices, and a seriously handicapped woman sneaking around and terrifying people. None of it makes any sense.'

Steve just looked at her.

'Millie Fletcher fits the victim profile,' said Evi. 'I think she was targeted from the beginning, from when her family first moved into town. But why on earth would someone who had killed twice, who planned to kill again, play so many stupid tricks? It's almost as though they were trying to . . .' she stopped.

'Go on,' encouraged Steve.

'Warn people,' she finished, because Steve was looking at her in that particular way of his and she knew he wasn't going to let her get away without answering. 'But that makes no sense. Why would the killer try and warn the people who were in a position to . . .'

'Go on.'

Oh, why couldn't she think clearly? Joe's disappearance had sent her straight into panic mode. 'The killer wouldn't warn them,' she said at last. 'The killer isn't responsible for the tricks.' She ran a hand through her hair. 'Christ, it's obvious,' she went on. 'All this time we've thought we've been looking for one person. We're not, we're looking for two.'

'Now you're getting somewhere,' said Steve, an annoying smile on his face. 'The killer of the little girls, who may have Joe, and the person who's been trying to warn those in a position to protect them. Or, in Gillian's case, not warn her, because it's too late for that, but tell her what really happened. What did the voice keep saying to Gillian? "Mummy, Mummy, find me"? Maybe she was supposed to take that literally – find the grave.'

'How does Harry fit into it?' Evi asked. 'He's not a parent.'

'Harry is responsible for the church,' replied Steve.

'The killing ground,' whispered Evi, as a sudden vision of Joe's pretty, pale face and long, skinny limbs swam in front of her. She blinked hard to get rid of it.

'Exactly,' said Steve. 'Now, it seems to me the killer cannot be this woman you've been calling Ebba. Someone with a severe case of congenital hypothyroidism just wouldn't have the mental and physical capacity to plan and carry out three abductions and murders. Let alone catch a bus to Blackburn and take a young boy from King George's Hall. Agreed?'

'Yes,' said Evi. 'Yes, of course. You're right. But she could be the one who's been trying to warn people.'

Steve was leaning towards her. 'Think about what these voices have been saying. What did she say to Tom? "*Millie fall*"? He took it as a threat, but turn it around and it could just as easily be a heads-up. Now then, when did you last take your medication?'

Evi had to smile. 'I missed my six o'clock fix,' she admitted. 'In too much of a hurry to get here.'

'Can I get you something?'

'No, really, it's not too bad. I'm trying to lower the dose anyway. Steve, if Ebba had nothing to do with the abductions, if she's been trying to warn people, she probably knows who the killer is.'

Steve nodded. 'Seems to me that if you find Ebba, you find your abductor. If you find her before the killer can get Joe to the church, you might be in time to save him.'

71

HARRY OPENED THE DOOR TO THE CHURCH CRYPT. THE stale smell of things long since forgotten came stealing up towards him. He picked up the flashlight and the box of tools he'd brought from his car.

The darkness below seemed to have grown denser. Rushton and his team would be up here as soon as it was light. They'd be able to turn the church and the crypt upside-down. It would be stupid for him to do anything that might jeopardize that search. On the other hand, dawn was eleven hours away. Joe could be down there now.

But it had been so much easier to walk down those steps when it was daylight outside, when he hadn't been alone and before the corpses of murdered children started turning up. Last time he'd stood here, evil hadn't come close enough to stroke him on the back of the neck. He shone the torch down. It was a powerful beam, but even so he couldn't see more than a dozen steps. He was still on the first.

The door key was in the lock. If he went down and left it there, someone could close the door softly, turn the key and . . . the key went into his pocket. He took a deep breath, pulled his shoulders back. This was ridiculous. He was a grown man. It was just a cellar. Was this to be the night he learned he was a coward?

In the beam of the torch the darkness seemed to be moving, as though gathering its forces, waiting for him to dare, knowing

336

he probably wouldn't. He was a man of God. In a church. Was this also to be the night he learned his faith was a sham?

'Though I walk though the valley of the shadow of death, I will fear no evil,' whispered Harry, and immediately felt worse. Anyone listening would know he was lying. He was very afraid. 'I will fear no evil,' he tried again, 'for you are with me.'

He was still on the top step and Joe, tiny six-year-old Joe, could be below, cold and terrified, trapped in one of those stone chests.

'For you are with me,' repeated Harry. He hadn't moved. 'Oh, fuck it,' he said, and went down.

72

'TAKE IT EASY,' SAID STEVE, LEANING DOWN AND speaking to Evi through the window of her car. 'It's a long way and there's a hard frost forecast.'

She didn't need telling that. She could see Steve's breath spiralling away into the darkness. The frost was already starting to gleam on the dry stone walls that lined the narrow road. 'I'll be careful,' said Evi. 'And thank you.'

Seeming reluctant to let her go, Steve crouched lower and leaned both forearms on the window ledge. 'A couple more things occur to me,' he said. 'These girls were taken for a reason. When children are abducted, the obvious motive is to fulfil a sexual need.'

Evi had to bite her lip. Joe was there again, hovering like a little ghost in the driveway. 'I know this child, Steve,' she said. 'He has dark-red hair and freckles and—'

'Stop it.'

Evi blinked hard.

'His mother can weep about his red hair and freckles. You have to stick to the facts if you're going to be any use to him. Now, Megan and Hayley were both found wearing the clothes they were last seen alive in. Does that suggest sexual abuse to you?'

'Makes it less likely,' agreed Evi. 'So if the killer's motive isn't sexual, we're looking for something else?'

'Second, the place they're killed is important. There is a reason why they're dropped from the church balcony.'

'I agree,' she said. 'So does Harry. He thinks it's all about the church.'

'Third, there is a link between these victims, including Joe,' said Steve. 'Whoever took them had a connection with all of them. Otherwise, he or she would have gone much further afield to find their victims and in doing so would have reduced the chances of being caught. He or she stuck to home ground, suggesting to me it couldn't be just any girls, it had to be those particular ones. Find the link and you'll find the killer.'

'Or find Ebba.'

'Exactly. Will the GP talk to you, do you think?'

Evi shrugged. 'I have no idea,' she said. 'He might think I'm ambushing him when I turn up at Saturday-morning surgery.'

'Well, you have to give it a try.'

'I know. Are your knees up to prolonged crouching?'

'No part of my body is up to anything much these days. Call me when you've spoken to him.'

'Will do.'

'And stop beating yourself up about Harry. Up until this morning you did everything by the book. People don't get struck off for a moment of poor judgement.'

'I'm so grateful, Steve.'

'Now are you sure I can't get you anything for the pain?'

Evi shook her head. 'It's not that bad, really. I'll have something as soon as I get home.'

'OK.' Steve stood up, then seemed to think of something and bent down to the window again. 'There's something about Joe that's bothering me, Evi. He doesn't fit. The detective's right about that at least. He's needed for something else.'

73

TOM WAS SHIVERING. THE GLASS WAS COLD AND THE WALL was cold and everything was cold but he couldn't move. Not until he'd seen the thin beam of light travel up the church-yard path. He started counting. Ten, eleven, twelve. By thirty, his dad would be home.

He heard the sound of a key turning downstairs and the front door opening. His dad was coming back from his look around the graveyard and he would have Joe in his arms, cold, tired, annoying as hell, but Joe all the same. His dad had found him, he just knew it. Tom was running across the carpet, opening his bedroom door, reaching the top of the stairs. Gareth stood in the hall below, still wearing his heavy outdoor coat. He glanced up. He was alone.

Tom watched as his dad took off his coat and slung it over a chair in the hallway before climbing the stairs. He reached the top, put both hands on his eldest son's shoulders and turned him round. The two of them walked back into Tom's bedroom. Tom climbed into Joe's bed; his dad didn't comment. He knelt on the carpet and stroked his son's head.

'Dad, I'm sorry.' Tom had been waiting all evening for the chance to say it, but this was the first time he and his father had been alone.

His dad looked puzzled. 'What for, matey?'

'For not watching him. I know I'm supposed to look after him.'

His father took a deep breath and seemed to shudder. Suddenly his eyes were wet. Tom had never seen his father cry before. 'Tom, it wasn't your fault,' he said, his cold hand taking hold of Tom's. 'It wasn't your job to watch him. There were teachers there. Never, ever think it was your fault.'

Tom had never heard his father lie before.

'We'll find him, won't we, Dad? Promise me we'll find him.'

Gareth's mouth twisted and he pulled it straight again with an effort. 'I'll spend the rest of my life looking, Tom,' he said. 'I promise you that.'

Gareth wrapped one arm round his son and leaned his head against the pillow. Tom, determined to stay awake until Joe came back, found his eyes starting to feel heavy. His dad hadn't promised that Joe would be found, only that he wouldn't stop looking for him. Just the one lie, then. That's all he was going to get.

74

THE BLUE AND SILVER CAR WASN'T IN THE STREET OUTSIDE Harry's house. It was almost eleven. Evi pulled out her mobile and checked the screen. He'd left six messages, all before eight o'clock, but she simply hadn't wanted to speak to anyone until she'd had a chance to think, to talk to someone who wasn't emotionally involved.

She dialled his number and was invited to leave a message.

Her leg was screaming at her and her spine felt as if she'd been stretched backwards over a rock for hours. She needed medication, she needed to eat and she had to rest. She started the car engine.

When she parked, she tried his number again. No response. She was on her own.

75

'I TAKE MY HAT OFF TO BURKE AND HARE,' MUTTERED HARRY, inserting the crowbar beneath the stone lid of the sarcophagus before leaning on it with his entire weight. The heavy slab moved a fraction of an inch. With the skill developed over nearly an hour of practice, he moved the lid just enough to be able to shine his torch inside.

Nothing. Which was precisely what he'd found in the eight stone coffins he'd managed to open. No bones, no mummified flesh, no shrivelled grave clothes, and definitely no Joe. He'd probably never know when the remains of the long-since-dead clergy had been taken away from St Barnabas's crypt, but gone they were.

His nervousness had long since evaporated. There really was nothing like building up a sweat for chasing away the willies.

Only one alcove remained a mystery. The very last in line, closest to the rear of the crypt. None of the keys he'd retrieved from his desk drawer had opened the iron grille. When the police had searched it previously they must have used one of Sinclair's keys. Harry had tapped out rhythms on the ironwork, he'd stuck a wrench through the bars and banged on the two sarcophagi that he could reach, he'd called Joe's name and had spent at least ten minutes just listening quietly. At last he'd been compelled to give up. Joe wasn't in the church. He wasn't in it and he wasn't below it.

At least now he knew.

Harry crossed the first chamber of the crypt and found the

doorway to the second with his torch beam. He was now under his own church, and even close to midnight, some light from the street outside was making its way down.

Harry walked forward. Impressed by his own daring, he switched off his torch. Gradually, vague shapes emerged from the darkness. The streetlights outside were shining through the windows of the church and a fraction of that light was seeping through into the cellar.

How exactly?

He walked over to where the light seemed strongest. Yes, definitely light, a square beam. He reached it and looked upwards. There was a grille of some sort directly above his head. He reached up and tugged. It held firm. He tried pushing and it shot upwards.

Sliding it to one side, Harry heard it scrape along the tiled floor. He reached up and grasped the edges of the hole he'd opened up. His fingers closed around the stone tiles he knew covered the uncarpeted part of the chancel floor. Time to find out how strong his arm muscles were.

Strong enough. One massive push and he was up, looking round. He was directly behind the organ, in the cramped, dust-filled void that often existed behind old instruments. Through gaps in the pipes he could see the pulpit, not four feet away from him.

Time to kill.

'So this is where you were,' muttered Harry. 'Our little friend with the voices.' Harry lowered himself back down, replaced the grille and made his way out of the crypt. The Fletcher children's strange friend, Ebba, knew her way around this church, that was clear enough. It had probably been she who'd led him such a dance the day he'd arrived.

Harry locked the crypt, then checked that the main doors of the church were locked and bolted. He used the lavatory at the rear of the building and then entered the nave. Thanks to Jenny Pickup, he and the Fletchers had eaten a couple of hours earlier. He had a travel rug from his car, which he'd parked half a mile down the hill in a quiet cul de sac. He was all set.

When he reached the altar, he lifted the drapes that surrounded the old oak table. The altar had been spread with a creamy damask linen and the rich purple brocade of the Advent cloth. He pushed a couple of prayer kneelers underneath, then crawled in himself. Pulling the altar cloths back into place and the car rug around him, he lay down.

He was in the killing ground. If someone brought Joe here tonight, he'd be ready.

76

EVI CHECKED HER WATCH. IT WAS ALMOST TEN O'CLOCK, but she could see lights in the first-floor window. She crossed the street and rang the bell. The pain in her leg and back had got much worse during the last hour. She'd been stupid not to take some medication from Steve.

After several minutes, light flooded the landing at the top of the stairs. A dark figure could be seen descending. Evi's chest started to feel tight. The figure reached the bottom of the stairs. The door opened and for a second the two women just stared at each other.

'Hello, Gillian,' said Evi.

Gillian seemed to sway backwards; her eyes couldn't quite focus on Evi's. 'Dragged yourself away from him, have you?' she said. She'd been drinking.

Evi's ribcage seemed to have shrunk. She almost had to gulp in air. 'After you saw me in the church, I came straight down here to find you,' she said, knowing that Gillian would only listen to conversation that was focused on herself. 'When I couldn't, I went to see another psychiatrist,' she went on. 'We spent a lot of the evening talking about you. I'm worried about you, Gillian. Can I come in?'

'No!' Gillian's hands shot to the doorframe, blocking the way in, as if words alone might not be enough to keep Evi out.

'Gillian, there is no intimate relationship between me and Harry,' said Evi, hearing her voice shake but forcing herself to look the other woman in the eye. 'We don't go out together, we don't spend time at each other's houses and we certainly don't sleep together. But he's been under a great deal of strain recently. So have I. What you saw this afternoon was a mistake.'

Evi stepped forward, tried to smile and failed. 'I'm not his girlfriend,' she said. 'But Gillian, I'm afraid you have to accept that neither are you.'

'Lying bitch!'

The fury on the woman's face, more than her words, made Evi step backwards and almost stumble.

'You're the reason he changed,' spat Gillian. 'He liked me. We were close. He kissed me. Then suddenly he started avoiding me. You were spinning him lies about me, weren't you? Telling him I'm nuts. You poisoned him because you wanted him for yourself.'

'I don't discuss you with . . .' Evi stopped. She couldn't even say that any more. She *had* talked to Harry about Gillian.

'You're pathetic, you know that?' Gillian stepped out of the doorway, forcing Evi back towards the road. 'I thought I was bad, but you're just delusional. Well, listen to some plain speaking for once. He might fuck you if he gets really desperate, but that's all he's ever going to want from a cripple.'

'Gillian, stop.' She couldn't deal with this, not now.

'And he'll only ever do it in the dark.'

Dancing in the . . . She was going to be sick. 'I'll come and see you in the morning,' she managed.

'Don't bother.'

'We'll find you another doctor. I know our relationship has broken down and that's my fault . . .'

Evi was talking to herself. Gillian had slammed the door.

77

19 December

WHEN TOM WOKE UP, THE ROOM WAS DARK. THE CLOCK on his desk told him it was nearly three in the morning. He was alone in Joe's bed.

He closed his eyes again. He remembered seeing a television programme about people having a sort of connection in their heads. Identical twins often had it, the programme had said, they could tell what the other was thinking without speaking out loud. He and Joe weren't so very far apart in age. Quite often, he knew exactly what his brother was thinking. Maybe he and Joe had this connection. Maybe if he concentrated really hard, Joe could tell him where he was.

Softly, the church clock began to strike the hour. Bong, bong, bong.

The linen of the altar cloth was brushing against Harry's face. He woke with an effort. He raised his hand to his face and pressed the luminous button on his watch. Ten past three. There was a cold breeze on his face. Someone had opened a door.

As quietly as he could, Harry rolled out from under the altar, got to his feet and crossed to the organ. The church looked empty. The square grille beneath his feet was still in place. No one had come up from the crypt.

He stood still, listening hard. The wind had fallen; the weather forecast earlier that evening had mentioned the possibility of snow.

After five minutes he made his way slowly down the aisle, checking the pews on each side as he went. At the back of the church he tried the door to the crypt. It was still locked and bolted. Upstairs, the gallery was empty. He crossed to the small wooden door that led to the bell tower. It was locked but not bolted. Had he drawn that bolt earlier? He couldn't have done. But he was sure he had.

Nothing. If Joe was sending messages, Tom wasn't receiving them. And it was suddenly impossible to lie still. Tom pushed back the duvet and climbed out of bed. He crossed the landing and opened the door to Millie's room. She was fast asleep, her hair damp with sweat, her little arms clutching Simba to her chest.

What if Joe were outside right now? What if he'd come home and just couldn't get in? He might be huddled on the doorstep, freezing cold. Tom ran lightly down the stairs and peered out through the glass of the front door. No tiny, cold boy on the doorstep.

He was just about to go back upstairs when a sound in the living room made him stop. Hardly daring to hope, he pushed open the door. His mum, still in the clothes she'd been wearing all day, lay on one of the sofas, a blanket around her hips. On the other sofa sat his dad. His head had fallen back and his eyes were shut. He was breathing heavily.

Tom crept into the room. On the third sofa there were cushions and a brightly coloured throw. He lay down and pulled the throw over himself.

Harry unlocked the door to the bell tower. Bloody hell, it was cold. The tower was empty, the bell hanging upside-down just as he'd left it hours earlier. There was no point going up there. No one could climb out through the tower.

No adult male could. A slim woman might manage it. And Ebba was the size of a child. Harry pushed himself up until he could see out properly. The tiled roof sloped away from him. At the opposite corner, at the front of the church, he could see one of the three fake bell towers. Unlike the one he was standing in, they were empty, built only to provide aesthetic balance to the church. He could see the night sky through the stone columns. There was no one on the roof – he couldn't have drawn the bolt earlier. He climbed back down and left the gallery. Crossing the nave, he looked at his watch again. Twenty to four. Might as well go back to bed.

78

A HARSH, GRATING SOUND. THEN A LOW-PITCHED CLANG AS something heavy was dropped on to stone. Harry rolled from his hiding place just in time to see a dark shape disappear into the floor.

'Wait!' he yelled instinctively. He heard the sound of something thudding to the ground beneath him. He reached under the altar, grabbed his torch and sped across the chancel floor. No point in stealth.

Harry dropped to the floor of the crypt and turned on the torch, allowing its beam to pick out every corner, to find any shadows that didn't belong, any movement other than his. The first chamber seemed empty. He was just about to make his way to the second when he heard another sound. Iron clanging against iron, in the second chamber.

Harry ran towards the opening and stopped. No point rushing into darkness. Still in the doorway, he began to sweep the torch beam around, finding the scallop shell, the first of the alcoves, the second, the — the gate on the sixth and last one was open. The one he hadn't been able to search earlier — someone was inside it now.

'Ebba,' he called. 'Is that your name? Ebba, I only want to talk. I need you to help me find Joe.'

No answer. He was passing the third alcove, drawing closer.

'All I want is Joe, Ebba. Can you tell me where he is?'

351

Past the fourth alcove, approaching the fifth. The gate was still open on the sixth.

He slowed his pace as he drew closer. He remembered four sarcophagi in the sixth alcove, a narrow passageway and a small wooden door in the far wall.

Bracing himself for a sudden attack, he stepped inside the gate. The alcove was empty. Ebba must have left through the door at the rear. Harry stepped towards it. It was hardly more than eighteen inches wide and it opened outwards.

The room beyond was a narrow, tall chamber with an arched brick ceiling. Brick-built shelving lay on either side, each shelf carrying stone coffins. The air was dry and earthy, and a cold breeze was coming through another door at the far end. Ebba had left in a hurry, and through the smallest of gaps he could see the night sky.

He glanced at his watch as he strode past the coffins. Six forty a.m. He pushed the door and stepped out into a tiny courtyard, surrounded by high iron railings. He recognized them at once, although he'd never been on this side of them before. He'd left the church through the Renshaw family mausoleum.

Well, now he knew how Ebba was getting in and out of the church without being seen. But where was she? He crossed the courtyard, his feet crunching on gravel, and pushed the iron gate.

It might be six forty and the world might be waking up, but the sky above him was as black as it had been the entire night. He waited, his heart pounding in his chest. No sound, not even wind.

Then the grasses were being rustled and the bushes shaken. Someone was coming towards him. Harry stepped into the shadow of a tall laurel bush. He could see her, a slight figure, creeping towards him, looking all around, as if scared that something would spring out. Harry stepped forward, grabbed the figure by the shoulders and spun it round to face him.

'Tom!' he said, as all the breath went out of his body. 'What on earth are you doing out here?'

Tom looked back at him, wide-eyed and slightly sullen, the way kids did when they didn't want to answer a question. Especially a stupid one. He was looking for his brother, of course, what else would he be doing?

'Do your mum and dad know you're here?' Harry asked.

Tom shook his head. 'They were both asleep. I didn't want to wake them up.'

'OK, but we need to get back.' He put a hand on Tom's shoulder and urged him up the hill. If Alice and Gareth woke to find another child missing they might just lose any remaining sanity they were clinging to.

They found the path and Harry finally felt relaxed enough to speak. 'Tom,' he said, 'I think I just saw that girl you talk about. The one Millie calls Ebba.'

Tom stopped walking and looked up at him. 'You saw her?'

'Yes. Don't stop moving.' Harry pushed Tom gently and they both carried on up the hill. 'She was in the church just now.'

'She's scary, isn't she?' said Tom in a low voice.

'Well, I didn't get a proper look.' They were close to the church-yard wall now. 'Tom, do you have any idea who she is, where she lives?' Harry asked. 'She can't live out in the hills, she must belong somewhere.' She had a key to the Renshaw tomb. Could she possibly . . . ?

'She usually runs away when I see her,' said Tom. 'I'm pretty certain she talks to Joe, though.'

'Do you think Joe's with her now? Do you think she took him?'

Tom gave a small nod. 'I said that to the police,' he said, 'but they said anyone who looks as strange as she does would have been spotted in Blackburn, especially in King George's Hall. They think Joe was taken by a grown-up.'

'All the same, I wish we could find her. Tom, did you ever—'

'Tom! Tom!'

Tom started to trot forward. Harry took a deep breath. 'He's here!' he yelled at the top of his voice. 'He's with me!'

A second later Gareth's head and shoulders appeared over the boundary wall. Pushing himself up, he strode towards his son.

'Do you have any bloody idea . . . ?' he began.

Harry stepped forward. 'Tom couldn't sleep,' he said quickly. 'He came out to look for Joe. He met me just down the hill.'

'Your mother nearly had heart failure. Now get inside.'

'Take it easy, buddy,' said Harry.

Gareth lifted his hands to his face and breathed heavily. 'I know,' he said. 'Come on, matey.' He reached out and pulled his son to him. Tom wrapped an arm round his father's waist and they walked together to the churchyard entrance. Harry followed behind, spotting Alice at their front door, watching them. Her thin body seemed to be jerking; he wondered if she were struggling not to cry – or scream. Across the street, lights were being switched on, curtains drawn back. He and Gareth had woken half Heptonclough with their yelling.

Harry fell back as Gareth and Tom left the church grounds and headed back to their house. It was almost seven. He reached the churchyard entrance and stopped. He should go home and change, eat breakfast. In another hour it would be completely light and Rushton and his team would arrive. They'd have eight, maybe nine hours of daylight.

Someone was watching him. He turned to face uphill. The silver Audi was tucked up tightly against the church wall. Evi had just climbed out, using a stick to steady herself. She waited for him to go to her.

79

'WHERE THE BLOODY HELL HAVE YOU BEEN? DO YOU have any idea how worried I was about you?'

He was holding her by the upper arms; it was too angry to be a hug, too intimate to be anything else. He smelled of sweat and dust and candle smoke. His eyes were bloodshot. She reached up, stroked the stubble on his chin.

'Where did you spend the night?' she asked, feeling her jaw trembling and thinking that if he didn't let her go soon, she'd start to cry and that really would be the end of her ability to function.

Harry took one hand off her arm to rub it across his face. 'You really don't want to know,' he replied, releasing her and pushing his hands into his pockets. 'Come and get some breakfast with me.'

There was nothing she'd like more. Have breakfast at his house, run a bath for him, watch him shave. She shook her head. 'I haven't time,' she said. 'I have to put calls out to all the local hospitals and talk to the district GP when Saturday-morning surgery opens. If a child was born with congenital hypothyroidism in the last thirty years, there must be a record somewhere. And I said I'd go to the press conference with the family.'

'What happened to you yesterday?' Harry asked her.

Evi sighed. 'I went to see my supervisor,' she said. 'He's had some forensic experience so I thought his take on things would be useful. I can fill you in later. Finding Ebba is the key thing.'

'Did you see Gillian?' asked Harry, not quite meeting her eyes.

355

'Late last night. It didn't go well.' Over his shoulder she could see people heading for the church. 'The other thing I need to do is find another doctor to take over her case,' she went on. 'I'm going to try and get her seen today. I'm really quite worried.'

Two elderly women were waiting just a few yards away, obviously wanting to speak to him. She looked at her watch. 'I have to go,' she said. 'I'll be as quick as I can.' She turned to her car and stopped. 'Could use some of that faith of yours right now,' she said. 'Any going spare?'

If he replied, she didn't hear him.

80

HARRY TURNED FROM EVI TO SEE MINNIE HAWTHORN AND one of her friends at the entrance to the churchyard. Their eyes seemed to peel him like a vegetable as he walked towards them, taking in his creased clothes, his unshaven face.

'Good morning, ladies,' he said, wondering where he was going to find the energy to be polite to small-minded, nosy old crones, who were probably only here because they were enjoying the drama unfolding on their doorstep.

'Vigil, was it, Vicar?' asked Minnie, her eyes travelling to his feet and then up again.

'Something like that,' agreed Harry.

'Church open?' asked her friend.

Behind him, Harry heard Evi's car engine start. He nodded.

'We'll help ourselves then,' said Minnie. 'Sort you out with break-fast in a minute, Vicar.'

Harry turned just as Evi drove past without even glancing his way. Stanley Hargreaves, another of his parishioners, was walking down towards them with two other men. Then a Land Rover appeared from the moor road and pulled up outside the butcher's shop. Jenny and Mike Pickup sat in the front. Lights flickered on inside the shop. Dick Grimes and his son appeared from a rear door and came out into the street.

'They won't wait for the police,' said Minnie's companion. 'They'll start just as soon as you've finished prayers.'

'Prayers?' said Harry.

'Prayers for the little lad,' said Minnie, taking his arm and leading him towards the church. 'For his safe return. Come on, Vicar, you seem a bit dopey, if you don't mind me saying so. I think you need a cup o' summat hot inside you.'

Evi wiped her eyes as she drove round the corner and could no longer see the church in her rear-view mirror. They filled again in seconds. Gillian was standing outside the front door of her flat. As their eyes met, Evi took her foot off the accelerator and the car slowed down. But she couldn't stop – what on earth would she say? She put her foot down again and the car shot forward.

Was Gillian planning to join the search? *I've spent years walking over the moors, I know all the best hiding places.* She certainly wasn't dressed for it, in a thin denim jacket and high-heeled boots.

A sudden vision filled her mind of a small boy's body, lying under a hedge. The collies would sniff it out, probably even before the police dogs arrived, and it would all be over.

Stop it. Stop it. It's not over.

She looked at the clock. Saturday-morning surgery ran from ten a.m. to twelve noon. John Warrington was the GP on duty today. The press conference started at ten and would probably run for around forty minutes. It would be tight, but do-able. There was time. It wasn't over.

So why couldn't she bloody well stop crying?

The church hadn't been empty since before dawn. Within half an hour of Evi's departure, Harry had been fed bacon sandwiches and strong coffee and was holding an impromptu service for the search party. Someone had cleared away his makeshift bed of the night before. Someone else had told him not to bother with robes; in the circumstances, jeans and a sweater would do just fine.

Five minutes after he started, the building was nearly full. Most people had just remained standing at the back and down the sides, as though they could spare the time to pray, but not the time it would take them to sit down. After eight minutes, the police arrived, filing in silently at the back.

Sinclair and Christiana Renshaw entered through the vestry door and took their usual pew. Gillian slipped in behind the police and stood, shivering, at the back. He could see people starting to get fidgety. A movement in the gallery caught his eye. Gareth and Tom Fletcher were standing there. A second later, Alice joined them, with Millie in a rucksack on her back. The family was due to make a television appeal for Joe's safe return later in the morning. Until then, they weren't wasting any time. Harry closed his book.

'Let's go and find Joe,' he said. He was the first to leave the building.

81

A GRIM DETERMINATION SEEMED TO HAVE GRIPPED THE people of the moor. 'We'll find him,' Harry had heard muttered more than once. 'We're not losing another one.'

He certainly couldn't fault the efficiency of the police. DC Andy Jeffries had taken thirty of the more able-bodied men and older boys to the highest point above the town. Once on the top road, they'd spread out and begun making their way down the moor. They were looking for anything unusual, they'd been told: clothes, toys, a shoe, anything that might suggest Joe Fletcher had passed this way. When they reached the bottom of the field they turned west and did the same thing again, heading upwards this time.

The sky had been thick with cloud. Harry didn't want to think it could be holding snow, but every time he looked up the lump in his chest seemed to harden. Just before eight o'clock a yellow glow in the east told him the sun was trying to make an impact on the day. He couldn't even give it points for effort. The wind, mercifully, was light, but the day seemed to be getting colder with every half-hour that passed.

So far the search had been fruitless. Thirty heartbeats had gone into overdrive when one of the Pickup collies had started barking at a clump of rocks. The decomposing hind-quarters of a sheep had been pulled out.

*

When they'd been on the moor for nearly two hours and the cold was creeping in through even the thickest coat, they heard the steady, insistent humming of a helicopter. None of the searchers could see it above the cloud, but the rise and fall of the engine volume told them when it was coming close, when it was circling away again. After five minutes, Harry wasn't sure how long he'd be able to cope with the steady assault on his ears. After ten, it felt as if he'd always had the noise in his head. Fifteen minutes after the helicopter arrived, DC Jeffries blew his whistle.

'The boss is calling us all down.' He had to shout to be heard above the drone of the chopper. 'There's too many people on the moor.' He pointed upwards to demonstrate his point. 'The thermal-imaging equipment hasn't got a hope,' he went on. 'We have to evacuate.'

The party turned and headed down to the town.

'I don't know what to say,' Alice was saying. 'I can't think of a single thing to say.'

'Just say whatever's on your mind,' said the press officer, a woman in civilian clothing who had been looking after the family since they'd arrived at the constabulary's headquarters. 'People will know what you're going through. This is about letting as many people as possible know that Joe is missing. We want everyone out there look-ing for him. How are you doing, Tom?'

Tom looked back at her. 'Fine,' he said automatically.

She was bending down to him. She smelled of oranges and toothpaste and her green suit was too tight. 'If anything occurs to you, Tom, feel free to say it,' she went on. 'If you have a message for Joe, for example. He may be watching.'

'Will he?' Tom turned to his mother. 'Will he, Mum?'

His mother nodded and Tom felt his throat start to ache.

'Is it time yet?' asked Gareth as Tom began taking deep breaths. He couldn't cry, not on television, not when Jake Knowles might be watching. Except Jake was on the moor, wasn't he, with his dad and his brothers? Tom had seen them in the church, he'd watched them set off up the road. Jake Knowles was out there right now, looking for his brother.

'There's Evi,' said Alice.

Tom turned round to see Evi wheeling her chair towards them. Funny, he'd always thought of Evi as being pretty. Nearly as pretty as his mum. She didn't look pretty any more.

'Vee vee,' said Millie, from her father's arms.

'Evi, thank you for coming,' said Alice. 'Do you think you could have Millie? She'll probably stay with you.'

Evi held up her arms and Gareth put his daughter down gently on to Evi's lap. Millie grabbed Evi's hair and started bouncing.

'It's time,' said Detective Chief Superintendent Rushton. Where had he come from? He'd been on the moor with the other police. Tom watched him put a hand on Alice's shoulder. 'Are you ready, lass?'

Tom's parents followed the detective through a door and into a large room. There were lots of people sitting on chairs, facing a long table at the front. Lights began to flash as the family took their seats.

The vestry had become a cafeteria. Minnie Hawthorn and her gang of cron— – sweet, good ladies who were desperate to do anything they could to help – had transformed it. Half a dozen kettles were permanently on the boil. Sandwiches were being made and consumed constantly. They were too old to trawl the moors, the women had told him, as though embarrassed by their own frailty, but they could feed those who did; and they could pray for the little lad.

If Harry stayed near them any longer, he'd scream.

In front of the altar, DI Neasden was explaining why they'd had to temporarily abandon the search. When Neasden finished speaking, he'd be expected to lead more prayers. Harry knew he couldn't stay in the building.

Outside, the helicopter was still circling. Towards the front of the church, standing a little apart, DCS Rushton was talking to Sinclair and Tobias Renshaw. Since Rushton was back, the press conference must have finished. Spotting Harry, Rushton left the Renshaws and made his way over. Suddenly exhausted, Harry sank on to the stone-table grave behind him. Rushton approached and sat beside him. He had a lit cigarette in one hand.

Harry turned to look at Rushton properly. The police officer wore a thick overcoat over his suit, heavy gloves and a green wool scarf. He'd possibly had even less sleep than Harry.

'Anything?' asked Harry, knowing what the answer would be but unable to stop himself asking.

Rushton inhaled deeply on his cigarette. 'Not so far,' he said, as smoke billowed around his face. 'Press conference went well. Young Tom was a bit of a star, had the whole room in tears telling his brother he'd tidied his box of soldiers for him.'

Harry dropped his head into his hands.

'It was exactly what we needed,' said Rushton. 'We've got the whole of Lancashire talking about Joe Fletcher.'

'Sorry to keep you waiting,' said Dr Warrington. 'Saturday-morning surgery's always busy.'

Evi forced her lips into a half-smile. She'd raced to get here after the press conference and had sat in the waiting room, watching squirrels run up and down trees in the garden outside, getting angrier as each patient with a cough or an in-growing toenail, not one of them a genuine emergency, was shown through before her.

'I'll have to rush you.' He glanced at his watch. 'We tee off at noon.' There was a book open on his desk. He closed it and reached to put it on the windowsill behind him. He hadn't looked her in the eyes for more than a couple of seconds.

'There is a woman in this area who suffers from congenital hypothyroidism,' said Evi. 'I need to find her. I think it could be relevant to Joe Fletcher's abduction.'

Dr Warrington reached over and switched off his computer. 'Sorry, Dr Oliver,' he said. 'You know the rules.'

'What about up here?' asked Harry, feeling the smoke of Rushton's cigarette fill his lungs.

'Well, the dog handlers went through the church like a dose of salts,' replied Rushton. 'Twice. They've done the cellars and the churchyard. A couple of times we thought they might have picked something up, but it didn't lead anywhere.'

'The boys come into the church quite often,' said Harry. 'They were here last Sunday for the service.'

'Yes, well, that could explain it. We had a bit more luck with the CCTV footage in Blackburn. I've just had a call through.'

'Really?'

'Aye. I haven't had chance to tell his parents yet, so keep it to yourself, but the couple we picked up at King George's were spotted again, getting on a bus in the direction of Witton Park. We spoke to the driver just over an hour ago.'

'Does he remember them?'

'Vaguely. He thinks they must have got off somewhere along King Street because they definitely weren't on board when he approached the park. The bus was just about empty by then.'

'Any trace of them after that?'

'Nope. And not likely to be. They could have had a car parked anywhere along that road. The important thing is, this couple haven't come forward. In spite of their picture being on the news last night and this morning and in today's *Telegraph*, nothing.'

'So you haven't been able to rule them out?'

'Quite the contrary. We managed to enhance the image until we could see some sort of sticker on the heel of the child's shoe. Tom tells us Joe had Spiderman stickers on his trainers. We've also been able to pin down the clothes the two of them were wearing. Remember, both were in baseball caps, both wearing oversized coats?'

'I remember,' said Harry.

'Clothes exactly like them can be found in British Home Stores, not half a mile from King George's. We've been through the till receipts and found a transaction of just those four items, almost exactly an hour before Joe was last seen.'

'Clothes bought specially for the abduction,' said Harry.

'It was a cash transaction, sadly, so we've no hope of tracing the credit card, but we're pretty certain now that the couple on camera are Joe and his abductor,' said Rushton. 'We've got people working on the image, to see if it can be enhanced any more, but we're not hopeful. Small man, tall woman, could be either.'

'The footprint you found in the Fletchers' house on the night of Millie's abduction could have come from a small man or a tall woman,' said Harry.

'Aye, it could. And given that the film footage showed no sign of Joe struggling, it's likely he went with someone he knew.'

'So he could be here after all?'

'Aye, he could. And I'm happy to be proved wrong as long as we find him in time. I've got a team doing a house-to-house search. We're asking people for permission to take the dogs round their homes. We can't force anyone, obviously, but so far everyone we've asked is cooperating.'

'How long will it take to get round every house in Heptonclough?'

Rushton sighed. He stubbed out his cigarette on the gravestone and then dropped it on the grass. 'We won't manage it today,' he said. 'But I've put a couple of cars on both roads out of town. Everyone leaving is being stopped and questioned. We're asking permission to search the boots.'

'Are people agreeing to that?'

'If they don't, we want to know why.'

No, it was not going to end like this. 'Yes, I know the rules,' Evi said, trying not to snap. 'I've read them three times in the last twenty-four hours, Dr Warrington, so don't try quoting them at me. It seems to me that in situations where serious harm may occur to a third party, the doctor isn't just able to pass on information, he's obliged to.'

Warrington leaned towards her, locking his fingers together in front of his chin. 'That refers to passing information to the police,' he said. 'Get the officer in charge of the case to come and see me and I'll see what I can do.' He was bending down, picking up his bag.

'There isn't time for that,' said Evi. 'Look, I know I've sprung this on you and I'm sorry, but I've been up half the night working on this.'

He opened his mouth. She wasn't giving him a chance.

'I have neither the time nor the energy to be polite, so here's the bottom line,' she hurried on. 'If you don't help me and Joe Fletcher dies, I will make certain everyone – the police, the General Medical Council, the media, absolutely everyone – knows about this conversation and that you put rules, not to mention golf, before a little boy's life.'

Silence in the room. Evi was trembling. For a second, she thought it wasn't going to work, that he would order her out of the room and make an official complaint to the GMC even before twelve noon tee-off. Then he reached out and switched the computer back on.

'Right,' he said, not meeting her eyes. 'What exactly are we looking for?'

'Thank you,' she said. 'I need to find a patient, most likely under thirty years old, suffering from congenital hypothyroidism.'

Rushton's phone was ringing. He'd stood up, walking quickly away from Harry, his phone pressed against his right ear. Then he turned back, switching it off as he came back. 'We've had a sighting in Great Harwood,' he said. 'Walk with me to the car, Harry.'

They set off, drawing curious glances as they made their way along the churchyard path. 'A lad answering Joe's description has been seen going into a house,' continued Rushton. 'No children are known to live there and the owner is someone we've had our eye on for a while. We're sure he's a nonce but we can't prove it. He's clever.'

'And you think he's got Joe?' asked Harry, in dismay.

'I hope so, lad. I bloody well hope so. Because this call came within the hour. If it's Joe, he's still alive.'

'Will you tell Gareth and Alice?'

'Not till we know anything for certain. We should have a car there in ten minutes. They won't wait for me.'

They'd reached Rushton's car. The waiting journalists, spotting the detective chief superintendent and sensing the urgency in his manner, came striding towards them. Rushton jumped into his car before turning back to Harry. 'If I were you, lad,' he said, 'I'd get back into that church and do what you do best.' The car set off, disappearing from sight as it turned the corner.

Knowing he couldn't cope with journalists, Harry turned and walked quickly back up the hill. People were starting to leave the church and he realized he hadn't heard the helicopter for several minutes.

Sinclair and Tobias Renshaw, both dressed for the outdoors, had followed Harry and Rushton out of the church grounds. Standing a little behind them, her eyes flicking up to Harry and then back down again, was Gillian.

'Any news, Vicar?' asked Sinclair, as Harry drew close.

Harry shook his head. 'Nothing yet,' he said. Had Joe spent the night with a known paedophile? What state would he be in, even if he was alive? No, he simply couldn't start thinking like that.

Alice and Millie had appeared directly in front of him. Hovering at their side was Jenny Pickup.

'How are you holding up, Alice?' asked Sinclair, in a voice that surprised Harry with its gentleness. Alice looked up at the tall man as though he'd spoken to her in a foreign language.

'Has anyone seen Gareth and Tom?' she asked.

'They were on Lower Bank Road about half an hour ago,' said Gillian, stepping closer. 'They went on to the old railway line with me and a few others. We wanted to check the Collingway tunnel.'

'They would have come back when the helicopter began its search, though,' said Tobias. 'Alice, I wish you'd come back to our house and rest. It's too cold for the little one to be out.'

'You should, Alice,' said Jenny, taking a step closer to her grandfather. 'Or at least leave Millie there. Dad's housekeeper will keep an eye on her. You can't carry her round on your back all day.'

Alice's eyes were drifting. 'Thank you,' she said, to the nearby lamppost. 'I need to keep her with me. I have to find Gareth now.'

She turned away. More and more people were coming out of the church now. The search was back on.

'I'm sorry, I'm afraid there's nothing else to try.'

Wondering how she was going to find the energy to get out of her chair, Evi nodded her head. 'I know,' she admitted.

An hour after John Warrington had agreed to help her search for the mysterious Ebba, they'd been forced to give up. They'd run every search through patient records that they'd been able to think of. Only the records of the last thirty years had been computerized, but Warrington had gone into the practice basement and found several boxes of older records. They'd gone back forty years, knowing the chances of Ebba being older than that were almost non-existent, but although they'd found several people suffering from the condition, all had died. In thirty-four years, no one with congenital hypothyroidism, not even anyone with a goitre, had been registered as a patient. They'd racked their brains trying to think of similar conditions and had run several other searches. At last, they'd been compelled to give up.

'How sure are you that she lives in this area?' asked Warrington.

'She must do,' said Evi. 'Someone with that condition couldn't drive.'

'I wouldn't have thought so,' agreed the GP.

'How can someone like that slip so completely off the grid?' asked Evi, almost trembling with frustration. 'Why wasn't she diagnosed as a baby? Why wasn't she treated? And why, given all her medical needs, do the local doctors know nothing about her?'

Warrington didn't reply and Evi pushed herself to her feet. 'I've taken up enough of your time,' she said. 'I'm sorry you missed your game.'

'I'll phone our receptionists at home,' the doctor offered. 'And a couple who've since retired. It's possible they can remember something, think of something. If anything comes up, I'll let you know.'

'I'm sinking, Harry,' said Alice. They'd got as far as the corner of the churchyard and then Alice stumbled. He'd had to reach out to catch her, to stop her and Millie from tumbling to the ground.

'You're doing incredibly well,' said Harry. He put an arm round her shoulders and led her to the wall. Her breathing was too fast. 'You're calm, you're functioning and you're taking care of your other two children,' he went on. 'I can't imagine what strength that takes.'

'It's the worst feeling in the world,' said Alice. 'Not knowing where your child is. Nobody can feel like this and stay sane.'

'You can,' said Harry, although the truth was he wasn't sure. He really didn't like the way Alice seemed unable to focus on anything.

'I'll tell you what it's like,' she went on, leaning so close to him it felt uncomfortable. 'It's like Joe never really existed, that I just imagined him. And now, I really need to see Tom and Gareth because I've got this feeling that they've gone too. Then I'll look round and Millie will have disappeared. It's like someone's rubbing us out, bit by bit.'

'Millie is asleep on your shoulder,' Harry said quickly, realizing that if he stopped talking he might start sobbing. 'Tom and Gareth are close by, looking for Joe. Alice, look at me.'

She raised her head. He thought perhaps he could have fallen in love with those pale turquoise eyes, had he not already . . . 'We will find Joe,' he said. 'Some time very soon, we'll find him. I wish I could promise you we'll find him safe and well, but you know I can't do that. But one way or another, we will find him. You'll be able to see clearly again, you'll be able to grieve, if you have to, and you'll be able to move on. You'll never be alone.'

'Harry, I . . .' Turquoise eyes filling with tears. A second pair was staring at him. Millie had woken and was looking at Harry as though she understood every word.

'You have incredible strength,' he said. 'Your family will survive because they have you. You're its heart. You're its soul.'

'I can see why you became a priest,' said Alice, reaching out to touch his arm. 'But it isn't real, is it?'

He thought perhaps the tears were in his eyes, after all. 'What do you mean?' he asked, although he knew.

'There's no faith shoring you up right now,' said Alice. 'No direct line to the man upstairs. It's just you, isn't it?'

'Come on,' said Harry. 'Let's get you both inside.'

82

EVI WAS IN HEPTONCLOUGH. THE STREETS WERE QUIET again. She pulled her car up to the kerb and got out. If she'd ever been more tired in her life before, she really couldn't remember. She crossed the pavement and walked up the short path to the terraced house. As she stood on the doorstep waiting, something white floated down and settled on her coat sleeve. The snow that had been predicted all day had arrived.

'I can't get an answer from Gillian's flat,' she said, when the door opened. 'I'm worried about her.'

Gwen Bannister sighed. 'Come in, love,' she said. 'You look fit to drop.'

Evi followed Gwen along the floral-patterned hall carpet and into a small living room. The carpet was worn in places, the room hadn't been decorated in a long time. A television in the corner of the room was switched on.

'Have you seen her today?' asked Evi, glancing at the television, wondering if Gwen would turn it off.

'Sit down, love. I'll put the kettle on.'

The last thing Evi wanted to do was drink tea, but she sank gratefully on to the sofa. 'I'm not sure we should hang around,' she said. 'I'm really quite worried. When did you last see her?'

'About two hours ago,' replied Gwen, after a moment. 'She's been helping with the search all day. Then, about five o'clock, when it was just too dark to go on, I saw her chatting to the vicar.'

The television was too loud. Evi flinched as the TV audience started applauding. 'And did she seem OK?' she asked.

Gwen shrugged. 'Well, I think he might have said something she didn't much like, because she spun on her heels the way she does and flounced off down the hill. Is she definitely not at home?'

'There are lights on but she won't answer the phone or the door.' Evi had waited outside Gillian's house for fifteen minutes, getting colder and stiffer. In the end, she'd had to try something else.

'I'll walk down and check on her,' Gwen was saying. 'Will it wait till I've had my tea?'

'Probably,' said Evi, although she really would have preferred Gwen to go immediately. 'If you're at all concerned about her, especially if she isn't there, I need you to phone me,' she went on. 'If she seems basically OK, could you tell her that someone will call her in the morning? A colleague of mine from the hospital. She's going to be taking over Gillian's case.'

Gwen frowned. 'I thought you and she were doing quite well.'

'We were. I'm sorry, I can't really go into it. Thank you for your help and please phone me if you need to.' Evi pushed herself to her feet.

'I will,' said Gwen, as she did the same. 'There's been no more news on the little lad, then?'

Evi shook her head.

'His poor mother. Makes you wonder what's going on up here, doesn't it? And in church too. I hear they've left a constable in the vestry overnight, just in case . . . well, it doesn't bear thinking about, does it?'

Evi moved towards the door. Gwen was standing in her path but there really was no time for chatting. Evi made a show of looking at her watch and Gwen stepped aside.

'I should be more sympathetic to Gillian, I know,' Gwen began, as she followed Evi down the hall. 'She lost her daughter and two other little girls she was fond of. Course, nobody thought it was anything other than coincidence, what with all the time in between each one. Four years in between Lucy and Megan, then another three before we lost Hayley. And what happened was so different. One fell, one disappeared, one died in a fire. How could we have known they were all linked?'

'You couldn't,' said Evi. 'Nobody should feel to blame.' She stopped, three feet from the front door. *All linked?* 'Gillian was fond of Lucy and Megan?' she asked.

'Oh aye. She did some nannying for Lucy when she was alive. Can you manage that door, love?'

'I think she told me that,' said Evi. 'I didn't realize she knew Megan as well.'

'Used to babysit for her. Sweet little lass, she was. The family moved away. You don't get over something like that, do you? I should have more sympathy with Gillian, I know that. Look, let me.'

Evi watched Gwen reach past her to open the door. She made herself step forward and over the threshold. 'Thanks, Gwen,' she said. 'Keep me posted.'

Outside, Evi leaned against her car. Already a fine dusting of snow was covering the windscreen. She couldn't lose her head now. Find the link, Steve had said: the victims were not selected at random, there is a link between them. Had she found it? Did she have enough to go to the police?

She drove down the hill, noticing Harry's car outside the Fletchers' house. A few seconds later she parked. Ignoring Gillian's flat, she went to the door of the newsagent's beneath it. The shop was in darkness. She banged on the door. Was there a bell? Yes, up there in the top left corner. She pressed it for five seconds, waited a second, then pressed it again. At the back of the shop, a door opened. Lights flickered on and someone was coming towards her. Let it be – yes, it was the woman she'd spoken to yesterday.

'We're closed.'

'I need to ask you something,' said Evi. 'I was here yesterday, do you remember? I was trying to find Gillian?'

'I'm not her keeper, you know.' The woman was in her sixties, plump, short, with straight grey hair.

'You told me you'd seen her catching a bus,' said Evi. 'Do you remember?'

'I may have done,' the woman said, folding her arms across her chest.

'Did you see which bus she caught? Where it was going to?'

'What is this, *Crimewatch*?' The woman's face fell. 'It's nothing to do with that lad, is it?'

'It might be.' Evi was desperate. 'Please, if you can remember, it's really important.'

'It wasn't one of those Witch Way buses,' the woman said, her bolshie attitude gone. 'They're black and red, aren't they?'

'I think so,' said Evi, although she never travelled by bus.

'Green, that was it. I remember now, because I saw Elsie Miller getting on it and realized she must be going for her monthly hospital check.'

'And the green buses go to . . . ?'

'Past the hospital, dropping off in the town centre.'

'Which town centre?'

'Blackburn, of course.'

83

'DEAD TO THE WORLD,' SAID JENNY, WALKING INTO THE kitchen. She stopped in her tracks, one hand on her mouth. 'I'm sorry, that was an incredibly stupid thing to say.'

Gareth glanced at his wife. Alice didn't seem to have heard. 'We know what you mean,' he said. 'They're both exhausted. Tom walked as far as I did today. And I don't think Millie's ever had as much fresh air. Do I need to check the oven, Jenny?'

'Oh, let me.' Jenny squeezed her way behind Harry and bent down in front of the Fletchers' range oven. She opened the door an inch and steam poured out into the kitchen. The smell of cooking meat filled the air and Harry realized he was hungry.

Alice stood up. 'I think I'm going to be sick,' she announced, before turning and disappearing through the back door.

Wondering if he were quite so hungry after all, Harry watched as Gareth turned his back on the room and stared outside. The darkness was complete. Harry looked at his watch, more out of habit than anything. He'd long since given up expecting Evi. When he raised his head again, Gareth had turned back to face the room.

'Jenny, Mike will be forgetting what you look like,' he said. 'Are you sure you don't need to . . . ?' He left the question hanging. Harry wondered if Gareth wanted Jenny to leave, if he wanted them both to leave. Friends were no use to the Fletchers right now. They couldn't help, they could only get in the way.

'I will just nip back,' said Jenny. 'We're staying with Dad tonight so we can get an early start in the morning.' She looked from Harry to Gareth. 'They'll all be back,' she said. 'Mike and all the men. Everyone. We won't give up.'

'Thanks, Jenny,' said Gareth. 'But I think we know by now he isn't here.'

Harry stood up to see Jenny out. 'I'll try and pop back later,' she said in a soft voice as they stood in the doorway. 'Just to check. Dinner'll be five minutes. Make sure they eat.'

He closed the front door and leaned against it. He should go too, he was useless here. At least Jenny had provided food. Nobody would eat it, but she was doing something. Then he heard a noise outside. A car had drawn up, followed closely by a second. Two figures climbed out of the vehicles and approached the front door. He got ready to open it, expecting journalists. What was he supposed to say again? The family are holding up well. They're grateful for everyone's support. Please continue to pray for . . .

Brian Rushton stood on the doorstep, the shoulders of his coat damp with snowflakes. At his side, paler than he'd ever seen her, was Evi.

'No!'

All heads turned to see Alice in the kitchen doorway. 'No,' she said again. Realizing what she was thinking, what the visit from Rushton and Evi probably meant, Harry felt his skin glowing hot.

'Alice, don't . . .' said Evi.

Rushton was inside the house, shaking the snow off his shoes, steering Harry out of the way, striding towards Alice. 'Steady down, lass,' he was saying. 'We're not here to give you bad news. News, yes, but not bad news, so just take it easy. Come on, come and sit down.'

'What?' Harry mouthed the single word at Evi. Giving him a look he couldn't interpret, she banged her heels against the door-frame to get rid of the snow and then set off after Rushton and Alice. Harry closed the door and followed them.

'Let's all sit down,' said Rushton. Harry was about to take the last seat next to Evi when he caught her eye. She looked ill. He turned to the sink and ran a glass of water, handing it over without comment. She drank half of it down.

'Dr Oliver phoned me just over an hour ago,' said Rushton. 'We may have made a breakthrough.'

'You found Ebba?' asked Harry, who hadn't taken his eyes off Evi.

She shook her head. 'That's not what this is about.' She looked at Rushton. 'Do you want to . . . ?' she asked.

'No, you go ahead, lass. You explained it very well to me just now.'

Evi's hands were trembling, she seemed to be making a huge effort. 'Last night I went to see a colleague,' she said. 'He's had some forensic experience so I wanted to know what he made of everything.' She paused and took another sip of water. She swallowed and a grimace of pain shot across her face, as though she had something in her throat.

'Steve made me see that we're looking for two people,' she continued. 'First, this Ebba person, who we think has some idea what's been going on and who, in her own way, has been trying to warn you. But because she can only really relate to the children and because she frightens Tom, she hasn't had much success.' She turned to look at Harry. 'You already know she hangs around the church. I think she's responsible for the blood in the chalice that day and for the effigy of Millie that you found. I think she's been trying to tell you what happens in the church. About the very real risk to Millie.'

Harry sensed Gareth and Alice share a look. He couldn't remember how much they knew about the weird events in church. He saw Gareth opening his mouth to speak and his wife hushing him.

'Most importantly,' said Evi, 'we're looking for the person who's been abducting and killing the little girls. Now, Steve made me see that it's all linked. The church is important, but so is the town itself. It's not coincidence that all the victims come from this town. Whoever the abductor is, he or she has a connection with all of them. They were chosen for a reason. I didn't find Ebba today, but I may have found the link.'

'And what's that?' asked Gareth.

'Not what,' said Evi. 'Who. I think the link is Gillian.'

Tom was awake. Had he been asleep? He thought perhaps he had but he wasn't sure. Whose bed was he in? Joe's. The canopy of his own bunk was several feet above his head. There was light in the corridor, and he could hear voices in the kitchen downstairs. Not that late then. Better go back to sleep. Sleep was a world in which Joe was still OK.

A sudden rattling sound. He sat up. That was what had woken him. A series of sharp, clear taps. Someone was throwing stones at the window.

Joe! Joe was back and trying to get in. Tom sprang out of bed and ran across the room. The curtains were drawn. The fabric was rough against his face and he could feel the draught from outside. 'Joe,' he whispered.

He could still hear voices downstairs. Harry's was the loudest, the most distinct. He could hear a woman's voice too, much softer and quieter. Not his mum though, someone with an English accent. It could be Jenny, she'd been here earlier. Should he call for his parents, tell them he thought Joe was outside, throwing stones up at the window?

But could he do that to his mum? Make her hope Joe was back when really it was just tree branches scraping against the window?

There were no trees anywhere near Tom's bedroom window.

He put both hands on the curtains and got ready to pull them an inch or two apart. Just far enough to see what was out there. An inch. Nothing but blackness. Two inches. Three.

The girl was in the garden behind the house, staring up at him.

In the kitchen silence fell. Then Gareth pushed himself to his feet. Rushton held up one hand. 'Mrs Royle should be on her way to headquarters by now,' he said, looking at his watch. 'I'm just waiting for a call from DI Neasden to tell me she's safely in custody. We won't be able to interview her until the duty psychiatrist is in attendance, but at least we know she won't be able to harm the lad.'

'Gillian?' said Alice. 'Hayley was her daughter.'

'She wouldn't be the first mother to kill her own child,' answered Rushton. 'Not by a long shot. To be honest, I was sceptical myself when Dr Oliver called. I'm still not 100 per cent convinced, but there are enough questions that need answering.' He nodded at Evi. 'Go on, lass,' he said, 'you'll tell it better than I will.

Evi dropped her eyes to the table, then looked up again. 'I've been worried about Gillian for a while,' she said, and the words seemed to come out of her reluctantly, as though, even now, she found it hard to break a patient's confidence. 'I knew there was a lot she wasn't telling me, and I also knew there was more going on in her head than grief. I've suspected childhood abuse from a number of things she's said and the behaviour she exhibits, but the first really worrying sign for me was finding out she'd lied about the manner of Hayley's death. She told me and others that Hayley's body wasn't found, that it just disappeared in the fire. That wasn't true. The firemen found remains.'

'Which weren't Hayley's,' Harry reminded her. 'Hayley was taken out before the fire was started.'

'Yes,' said Evi. 'But how could she have known that unless she was involved in Hayley's removal from the cottage? I think Gillian's refusal to accept that the remains were Hayley's was her way of dealing with guilt.'

'OK, but that's not enough by itself,' said Harry, looking up at Rushton, trying to read the older man's face.

Evi sipped from her glass again. 'No, it isn't,' she said. 'But I've been talking to her mother as well, over the last week or so. Gillian's father was killed in a car accident when she was three. She was in the car with him. She wasn't hurt, but when the police pulled her out she was covered in her father's blood.'

'Christ,' muttered Gareth.

'Well, yes. Enough to have a damaging effect on any child. Gillian's mother married again and – I have no proof of this, but I think Gillian was abused by her stepfather when she was still quite young. Her early medical history shows textbook examples of symptoms of abuse and she talks about him in a way that is very disparaging and full of sexual references. I've had to be very careful when I've been talking to Gwen. Obviously, I couldn't ask her outright if Gillian had been abused, but I could hint around the subject. There was something there, I'm sure of it. Gwen knows more than she's saying. Then when Gillian was twelve her eighteen-month-old sister was killed. She fell from the top of the stairs at her home and landed on the stone floor. Sound familiar to anyone?'

Harry saw Alice reach back and take hold of her husband's hand. Neither seemed capable of speaking.

'It's worrying,' said Harry, looking at Rushton again. 'But isn't it what you call circumstantial?'

'Her stepfather found the child, but Gillian was in the house too,' said Evi, before Rushton could respond. 'She would have seen the blood, heard the man she hated howling in agony. That could make a disturbed teenager feel pretty powerful.'

'It's still speculative, Evi,' said Harry.

'That's what I was saying at this point,' said Rushton, nodding his head.

'Gillian's husband was cheating on her,' said Evi. 'I think she killed Hayley to punish him, the way she punished her stepfather by killing his daughter. She kills because it makes her feel powerful. Gillian and her mother were at the Renshaws the day Lucy was killed.'

'Gwen told you that?' asked Harry. He thought for a second. 'Actually, I think I knew that. I think Jenny mentioned it herself.'

'Gillian helped to look after Lucy sometimes, she was a sort of unofficial nanny,' said Rushton. 'And she used to babysit for Megan. Of course, we can't guess why she would want to kill those two, but as I say, questions need to be asked.'

For a moment no one spoke.

'Gillian was seen catching a bus to Blackburn early yesterday afternoon,' said Evi.

Still silence.

'She knew about the pantomime,' said Alice. 'She was round here yesterday morning with Jenny. I told her where the boys would be.'

Treading softly with bare feet, Tom made his way down the stairs. The kitchen door was closed. He could hear several voices behind it. He stepped into the living room and crossed to the window that overlooked the garden. It wasn't easy, pulling back the curtain, she would be so much closer now, but somehow he managed it.

Two eyes. Large and brown, with crepey, wrinkled skin around them, wrinkles that made her look old and not old at the same time. Two eyes staring in at him, with an expression he'd never seen before. He'd seen her full of mischief. He'd seen her threaten him and Millie. He'd never seen her scared.

'Ebba.' No sound came out, his lips were forming the words.

'Tommy,' she mouthed back.

He stepped away, allowing the curtains to fall back into place. She rapped softly on the window.

What should he do?

If he yelled for his dad, she'd go. And he wanted her to go. It was bad enough without Joe, he couldn't deal with monsters too.

Tap, tap, tap. Louder this time. He had to make a decision before she broke the glass.

Silence. He reached out and moved the curtain. She was still there. When she saw him she pointed at the window lock, her hand jabbing up and down. She wanted him to open the window. She wanted to come in.

Not in a million years. He opened his mouth to yell.

She might have Joe.

He didn't care, he wasn't that brave, she wasn't coming in. He shook his head and took a step back into the room. The curtains fell back but didn't quite meet. He could still see her. He saw her reach down into the neck of her dress and pull something out. He saw her press it against the glass.

She did have his brother. How else could she have got hold of Joe's trainer?

Tom couldn't stop himself taking a step closer to the glass. When he and Joe had got their new trainers they'd customized them. They'd put stickers on the heels and swapped laces, so that Tom's mainly black trainers had red laces and Joe's mainly red trainers had black laces. A red trainer with a black lace was being pressed against the glass and the remains of a Spiderman sticker were visible on the back of the heel.

She had Joe. That's what she'd wanted all along, one of the Fletcher children. She'd tried to get Millie and when she'd failed she'd gone for Joe instead.

She was pointing at the window lock again. She really, really wanted to come in. His dad and Harry were just along the hall. If he let her in he could grab her, then yell for the others, he could hold her until they arrived. Once his dad got hold of her, she'd have to tell them where Joe was. Let her in, yell blue murder and hold tight. He could do that, couldn't he? He could be that brave?

Without giving himself time to think, he nodded at Ebba and

held up one finger. 'Give me one minute,' he was saying to her, without any idea whether she would understand or not. He ran from the room to where the keys were kept in the hallway. One of them unlocked the windows.

Seconds later, he half expected Ebba not to be there any more, but she was. He put the key in the lock and turned it. As soon as the handle was pulled up, she was tugging at the window, opening it and clambering through, as though she'd done it many times before. He stepped back immediately, because he really didn't want to go anywhere near that horrible lump on her neck. Before he'd had time to think, she'd dropped to the carpet and was dashing across the room.

He cried out and ran after her, but she stopped at the door and closed it. She was between him and the grown-ups now, but he could still yell and grab hold of her.

Could he?

'Tommy,' she said. 'Tommy, please come.'

The window was open and the cold from outside was flooding into the room. Tom knew, though, it wasn't the cold making him shake; cold didn't get you like this, not deep down inside. Ordinary cold made by wind and rain didn't turn the most secret part of you to ice.

It took the sound of his brother's voice to do that; Joe's voice, coming out of this girl's mouth like a message, like a cry from a place he could never go to, like a . . .

'Tommy, please come.'

. . . like a plea for help.

'What I don't get,' said Gareth, 'if you're right, is why she switched from girls to Joe. She's breaking her pattern.'

'She is,' agreed Evi. 'And I don't think she was ever really interested in Joe. It was Millie she wanted. I think she took Millie out of the party in September and up to the church gallery, and it was just sheer good luck that Harry and the boys arrived when they did.' She turned to Harry. 'But do you remember, she was there? When you and the children came out of the church, she was waiting for you.'

Harry nodded. 'She carried Millie home. None of us were in any fit state. You think she'd been hanging round just to see . . .'

'I think she realized someone was coming and fled,' said Evi. 'She just didn't go far. There was still a chance it would work, that you wouldn't get to Millie in time. Then I think she tried to take her again, back in November, when Tom and Joe stopped her. Since then, I think she's been biding her time. Until yesterday.'

'What happened yesterday?' asked Alice.

Evi could feel Harry's eyes on her. 'Gillian is seriously infatuated with Harry,' she said. 'And yesterday—'

'She saw me kissing Evi,' interrupted Harry.

Alice looked at her husband, then back at Evi. 'But what's that got to do with—' she began.

'Harry and I don't have children,' said Evi, forcing herself to look Alice in the eye. 'But Gillian knows we're fond of yours. I'm really sorry, but I think taking Joe is about punishing us.'

'She and I had words earlier today,' said Harry. 'I really wasn't in the mood to be patient, I'm afraid. She didn't take it well. Oh shit.' He dropped his head into his hands.

'If Dr Oliver is right, Gillian took Joe from somewhere miles away from here so that we wouldn't connect it with what happened to the girls,' said Rushton. 'Joe knows Gillian. If she'd told him she'd been sent by his mother, there's a good chance he'd believe her.' He looked at his watch again. 'Where is Jove?' he muttered. At that moment, his mobile phone rang. He excused himself and left the room.

Silence fell in the kitchen as everyone strained to catch any part of Rushton's conversation. They didn't have long to wait. After less than three minutes, they could hear his footsteps coming back along the hall. The door opened. His sallow skin seemed to have grown paler.

'Not the best news,' he said, without entering the room. 'Jove and his lads found what they thought was a crime scene in Gillian's flat. Blood everywhere. Turns out she made an attempt on her own life this evening.'

Evi half stood up and didn't have the strength to make it further. She sank back down again. At her side, Harry had gone very still.

Rushton shook his head, as though trying to wake himself up. 'Her mother found her and called an ambulance,' he said. 'She's in

Burnley General now. Slashed both wrists. In a bad way, by all accounts.'

Evi's hand was covering her mouth. 'Oh my God,' she whispered.

'Is she going to live?' said Alice. 'If she dies . . .'

'Take it easy,' said Rushton. 'I'm going over now. They haven't been able to talk to her yet, but I'll see what pressure I can bring to bear on the doctor in charge. And Jove hasn't been idle. He's talking to her mother about any connections she and Gillian have in Blackburn – old friends, relatives, places they used to live.'

'I need to come with you,' said Evi, forcing herself to her feet.

'Evi, I don't—' Harry began.

'I'm her doctor.'

'No disrespect, Dr Oliver, but I doubt you're top of the list of people she wants to see right now,' said Rushton, zipping up his coat. 'If we think a bit of persuasion is needed, we might call upon the vicar. Excuse me now, folks.'

Rushton was leaving. He was wrong, Gillian was her responsibility, she had to go to the hospital. Evi stood up and set off across the kitchen as the front door slammed behind him. She'd made it halfway along the hallway before Harry caught her.

'You're not going anywhere,' he said.

She shrugged his hand off her arm. 'This is all my fault,' she said in a low voice, not wanting to wake the children, not wanting Alice and Gareth to hear how seriously she'd messed up. 'I'm responsible for her welfare and I betrayed her.'

'You did nothing of the kind.' Harry, it seemed, wasn't capable of speaking quietly. 'Since we met, you've gone out of your way to do the right thing. I'm the one who wouldn't leave you alone, and if anyone's to blame it's me. I'm going to the hospital.'

'Neither of you are going anywhere.' As Harry turned from her, Evi could see Gareth in the kitchen doorway. 'And I've heard quite enough self-indulgent crap for one night,' he continued. 'Now get back in here, both of you, and help us work out where she put Joe.'

Tom stood in the dark living room, listening to the sounds in the hallway, hoping that someone would open the door and see him and Ebba but not quite able to bring himself to call out. Then the front door slammed shut. He could hear Harry and Evi arguing in the

383

hall and then his dad saying something. Then the adults all went back into the kitchen.

'I have to get my dad,' Tom said.

The girl's whole body trembled. She shook her head and looked at the door, then back at him, then at the window. She took a step towards it.

'He won't hurt you,' said Tom, although the truth was he couldn't say for certain what his dad would do to someone who'd hurt Joe. She took another step towards the window. She was going, they'd never catch her, an entire team of police officers had been searching the town all day and they hadn't found her. She'd go and his last chance to find Joe would disappear.

Was it seeing her terror that was lessening his? Because although this was one of the strangest experiences of his life – and he'd had a few lately – Tom was discovering that he wasn't quite as scared as he'd thought he would be. Pretty scared, admittedly, just not . . . Joe had never been scared of Ebba.

'Wait,' Tom heard himself say. 'I won't tell him.' What was he talking about? That had been the plan, hadn't it? Hold on to her and call for his dad.

But Millie hadn't been scared either. When Millie had seen Joe's drawing of Ebba, her little face had lit up, as if she was looking at the picture of an old friend.

'Tommy come,' said Ebba, holding out her hand. She was moving towards the window, in a second she would be gone.

He nodded his head. Was he insane? 'OK,' he said.

Alice, Evi and Harry were back at the kitchen table. Only Gareth remained standing. He looked at Evi. 'What's your take on where she'd put him?' he said.

Evi shook her head. 'Forensics really isn't my thing,' she said. 'I've never done any criminal work.'

'No, but you seem to know Gillian better than anyone else. Would she keep him here or somewhere else?'

Evi gave herself a moment to think. 'We shouldn't rule this town out,' she said at last. 'This is where she feels at home. If she's planning to take him to the church when all the fuss has died down, she'll want to keep him somewhere she can get to him easily. If she wants to keep him alive, she'll have to feed him. And she knows this moor better than anyone. I can't tell you how many times she's boasted to me about it. "I know all the best hiding places," she says.'

'That's what I think,' said Gareth. 'She's been here all day. I've seen her loads of times. And she doesn't have a car. She can't nip in and out of town quickly.'

'What if she won't tell them where he is?' said Alice. 'If she refuses, we might never find him. If he's outdoors, he won't last much longer in this weather. We have to get the police back here. We have to keep looking.'

'But the whole moor has been crawling with dogs,' said Harry. 'They used thermal-imaging equipment. He can't be on the moor.'

'The moor is where Gillian feels at home,' said Evi. 'It's the natural place she'd think of hiding him.'

'If he is still here,' said Harry, 'he's somewhere the dogs and the heat-seekers couldn't find him.'

Silence.

'What do you mean?' said Alice, after a few seconds.

'Somewhere out of range,' said Harry. 'Of the dogs and the equipment.'

'Water?' said Gareth. 'Tonsworth reservoir, that's less than three miles away. There are buildings near it, where they keep the pumping equipment.'

'We searched that,' said Harry. 'United Utilities opened it up for us. The dogs went in.'

'Somewhere in the air?' suggested Evi. 'I don't know – in a tree, a tree-house. The dogs wouldn't find him.'

'The helicopter would. A big source of heat like a child, even a child's body – sorry, Alice – would have been picked up by the equipment.'

'What about underground?' said Alice. 'Are there any mines on the moor? Or caves? You know, like in Derbyshire, where they have the Blue John mines.'

'I don't think so,' said Gareth. 'Harry and I were looking at water-resource maps yesterday, I'm sure they'd have indicated any— Oh, Jesus.'

'What?' asked Evi. The two men were staring at each other. Then Gareth ran from the room.

'What is it?' said Alice. 'What have you thought of?'

'Give him a sec,' said Harry.

They waited, listening to the sound of Gareth fumbling with papers in the other room. Then he was back. He leaned across the table, spreading out a large black and white map. His hand hovered over it for a second.

'There,' he said, pointing with one finger. The two women leaned in. Harry stayed where he was. 'The bore hole.'

'What's a bore hole?' asked Alice.

'A deep hole in the ground,' said Gareth. 'Right down to the water table.'

'You mean a well?'

Her husband nodded. 'That's usually what bore holes are dug for.'

'Hang on, mate,' said Harry. 'I can't believe that place wasn't searched. It's less than half a mile out of town.'

'But where is it, exactly?' said Alice. 'Is it that little stone hut just below Morrell Tor? The one the kids call Little Red Riding Hood's house? But we've seen Gillian there.'

'I've seen her there too,' admitted Harry. 'And if she's been coming and going in the Renshaw house over the years she'd have had plenty of time to steal the key. But it must have been searched.'

'There can't be a bore hole in that hut,' said Alice. 'Sinclair told me that Jenny and Christiana played in it when they were children.'

'Bore holes and old wells are usually covered over,' said Gareth. 'It's bloody unsafe to do anything else. But she could have found a way to access it again.'

'I'm sure it must have been searched,' said Harry.

'What's the range of sniffer dogs?' said Evi. 'How deep down a pit would a small child have to be dangling to be out of reach?'

Nobody answered her. Nobody knew. And judging by the looks on their faces, everyone had the same picture in their heads.

'If he's far enough underground, maybe the thermal-imaging equipment couldn't spot him,' she went on.

'I need to get up there,' said Gareth, making for the door.

'I'm coming too.' Alice was already on her feet, following him.

Harry jumped up and caught her. 'You should stay with Tom and Millie,' he said. 'I'll go up. There's rope in my car. And a harness. We can drive most of the way if we take Gareth's truck.' He stopped, a frown furrowing his forehead. 'The door will be locked,' he called to Gareth. 'We're going to need your tools.'

They heard Gareth cross the hallway and open the front door. Harry turned to Evi. 'Do you have Rushton's numbers?' he asked.

She nodded.

'Get on the phone to him. Tell him where we've gone and ask if he can send someone up. Don't take no for an answer. We'll need fire and rescue too.' He turned, found his coat on the back of a chair and shrugged it on to his shoulders. Seconds later, he and Gareth had left the house.

84

TOM HAD FOUND HIS TRAINERS BY THE FRONT DOOR AND A yellow hooded sweatshirt behind one of the sofas in the living room. Even so, seconds after he climbed out of the window he was freezing. The stone of the window ledge felt like ice through his pyjamas. Snowflakes began to land on his head and face. He pulled the window almost closed again.

Ebba had taken hold of his hand and was hurrying him across the dark garden. They reached the gap in the wall and she went through first. He followed and they were in the churchyard.

Harry jumped into the truck, the climbing rope on his lap. Before the door was closed the truck was moving, its tyres making fresh tracks in the snow. Gareth swung out of the driveway and started to turn downhill towards Wite Lane.

'Carry on up,' said Harry. 'Up the hill, out of town.'

Gareth was still looking down the lane. 'Alice and the kids go along Wite Lane to get up the moor,' he said.

'Aye, but that way's steep. I don't know how far you'll be able to take the truck.'

Gareth took a deep breath. 'So what are you suggesting?' he said.

'Three-quarters of a mile outside town there's a farm gate on your right,' said Harry. 'I think Mike Pickup uses it to get feedstuff to his animals. We can drive through and approach the cottage from above. The ground's pretty solid, we should be able to get most of the way there.'

Gareth pressed his foot on the accelerator and the truck moved forwards up the hill. They picked up speed and the flakes whirling in front of them grew larger as they left the town behind.

'Slow down,' said Harry. 'Slower. There it is.'

The truck stopped and Harry jumped down. He ran round the front of the vehicle as it went into reverse. A second later the truck's headlights flooded the metal farm gate.

Harry pushed the gate open and Gareth drove through. The hut was less than a mile away.

A wave of pure weariness swept through Evi as the vehicle's rear lights disappeared up the moor. She wanted nothing more than to lie down, close her eyes, let others handle it from here. 'Right,' she said. 'I need the phone.'

'It's right behind you,' said Alice. 'I'm going to check on Tom and Millie.' Alice ran up the stairs as Evi turned to the phone. It wasn't there. As Evi headed into the hallway, Alice emerged from Millie's room and crossed the landing. Evi lifted her hand for attention but Alice didn't look down.

And then a strangled scream sounded from above. Evi stopped, her heart pounding but her brain refusing to take in the possibility that something else had happened. Something that really wasn't good, judging by the face of the woman at the top of the stairs.

Tom and Ebba were making their way through the white graveyard. *Tommy, please come.* Tom knew he'd be hearing his brother's voice in his head for the rest of his life if he ignored it now.

As they passed Lucy Pickup's new grave, they seemed to be heading for the church, which was pointless, because the church had been thoroughly searched with dogs and everything, and even if it hadn't been, they'd have no chance of getting in now. Tom had heard the grown-ups talking earlier. The front door and the door to the roof had been locked and bolted, and the three sets of keys to the vestry door were now with Harry and the police. Plus, a police constable was spending the night in the vestry – just in case.

Either the snow was deadening sound or it was later than Tom had thought because the night was almost completely silent. He thought he heard a car engine starting up, and then the same car speeding away up the moor, but then silence fell again. They'd reached the mausoleum where all the dead Renshaws were put – except Lucy, because Jenny, Lucy's mother, hated it. The police had searched it today, had opened up all the stone coffins to make sure Joe wasn't tucked away in any of them. They'd searched it and locked it again and Sinclair Renshaw had put a massive great padlock on the door, so why did Ebba have a key to it? They weren't going to go inside it, were they? He couldn't go in a tomb at night, not even for . . .

Tommy, please come.

Ebba had unlocked first the padlock and then the iron gate. It swung open and she stepped inside, as though she wandered into old tombs all the time. Tom stood in the entrance and then took a tentative step forward. They were only in the small, railed courtyard, it wasn't as though Ebba could get inside the building itse—

Ebba was opening the door that led inside the large stone box. She was beckoning to him, her face screwed up with impatience. She was serious, she really was taking him inside. But the church had been full of people all day. Joe could not be in the church. This was some sort of trap.

Tommy, please come.

Hold on, Joe, I'm coming.

The truck wasn't moving. Gareth had been trying for five minutes to reverse it away from the small stream that had swallowed up its front wheel, and the two men couldn't waste any more time. Harry had his climbing rope slung around his neck and a torch in his hand. Gareth had a box of tools in one hand and a sledgehammer in the other. The two men began striding over the snow.

Time to kill. Had Ebba known what Gillian was up to, about the murders of the three little girls, about Gillian's interest in Millie? Had she been trying to warn them?

'Sorry, mate,' gasped Harry as they reached the edge of the ruined mill buildings. 'We should have tried your way.'

Gareth didn't turn his head. 'Wouldn't have made any difference,' he said. 'Driving across the moor's close to impossible on a good day. The snow's covering everything.'

The two men hurried on through the mill ruins.

If Ebba had been trying to warn them, had her torture of Gillian been a sort of punishment? *Mummy, find me.* Why would Ebba say that?

Gareth was pointing to his left, where they could just about make out a small building. 'Is that it?' he said.

'That's it,' said Harry. 'Take it easy. There are all sorts of loose stones round here.'

Gareth slowed his pace as they made their way across the remaining stretch of ground to the hut. Already, snow had settled on its roof, making it look even more like a cottage from a fairy tale.

Gillian had broken into the Fletchers' house on the night of the bonfire? Had tried to abduct Millie? The intruder had worn wellington boots. Had he ever seen Gillian wearing such things?

They reached the door and Harry took a second to get his breath. They couldn't just go charging in. If there were a bore hole in this hut it would be incredibly dangerous to be there at night. He wondered how long it would take the police to get here. They'd have to come on foot. He looked down hopefully. No lights could be seen making their way up towards them.

He put out his hand and tried the door. As expected, it was locked.

'Stand back,' ordered Gareth.

Harry did what he was told. Gareth raised the massive sledgehammer above his head and swung it forward.

Faster than she'd moved for years, Evi made it halfway up the stairs. She took hold of the banister and braced herself. If Alice fell now, she could easily knock them both to the bottom. She watched as the other woman swayed, then reached out to grab the wall.

'Alice, take it easy,' she called. 'Deep breaths. Sit down. Put your head down.'

Alice sank to the floor, staring straight ahead as Evi struggled up the last steps. 'What is it?' she gasped, sinking down beside Alice. Christ, she hadn't known such pain was possible. She was going to faint any minute now.

Alice was already trying to get up again. 'I have to go,' she said. 'I have to get Gareth, go outside, I have to—'

'Alice!' Evi took hold of the other woman's arm.

'Tom's gone,' Alice went on. 'Tom's gone too now. I'm losing them all, one by one, she's taking them all away from me.'

'Alice, look at me.'

Alice tried to make eye contact with Evi and failed. She was struggling to stand up.

'Tom can't be gone,' said Evi. 'We've been here all this time, the doors were locked. Have you checked the bathroom?'

Alice looked as if she had no idea what a bathroom was. She was in shock. The stress of holding it together for the past twenty-four hours had proved too much and Tom's unexpected trip to the loo had sent her over the edge.

'Tom!' Evi called out. 'Tom!' she called again, a little louder, when there was no response. Anxiety growing, Evi struggled to her feet. Her stick was at the bottom of the stairs and the pain in her leg was beyond anything she normally had to cope with.

Alice was moving again, running down the stairs. She pulled open the front door. 'Phone Gareth, please,' she begged, turning back to Evi. 'Tell him to get back here. I'm going to look outside.'

The front door blew wide open as Alice disappeared, and flakes of snow flurried into the hall, melting instantly on the slate tiles. Phone Gareth? Evi hadn't phoned the police yet. She hadn't even found the phone. Holding on to the wall, she made for the nearest room. It was Millie's. The toddler slept on, oblivious to the drama unfolding around her. Evi turned. Tom would be in the house, he had to be.

'Tom!' she called, then decided she wasn't going to try that again. It was just too unnerving to call for a child and hear nothing in response.

'Tom!' That was Alice, yelling outside.

Tom could not have gone outside, the doors had been locked.

She turned and made her way to Joe's room in case Tom was sleeping in his brother's bed for comfort. She pushed open the door and stood, panting, in the doorway. The room was empty.

Shutting her mind to the pain, Evi walked to Tom's room and flicked on the light switch. 'Tom!' she heard from outside. Alice was behind the house now, calling in the garden.

Evi crossed the room and then clung to the window ledge to get her breath back. She could just about make out Alice, tearing about the garden. Right, she had to look in the bathroom and in Gareth and Alice's room. Damn Alice, if she hadn't lost her head, she would have been able to search the upper floor in seconds. It would take Evi precious minutes, when she needed to be talking to the police.

'Tom,' she called out, realizing she was crying. 'Tom, please. It really isn't funny.'

Tom didn't answer her, and she carried on along the landing.

Tom was running, terrified he'd lose sight of Ebba and be left alone in the clawing, creeping darkness. He had no idea how big an underground chamber he was racing through, he couldn't see the walls – not that he was looking; his eyes were fixed on the girl ahead of him.

Every time Tom was tempted to turn back, he made himself think of his brother. Joe, who he sometimes thought had been sent to earth to make his life miserable, who had been a complete pain from the day he was born, who was always getting his own way and who he fantasized about killing at least once a week. Joe, who he really didn't think he could live the rest of his life without.

A wall loomed in front of them and Ebba shot through an archway. Tom went too, before he had chance to ask himself whether this was a good idea or not. None of this was a good idea, it was probably the worst idea he'd ever had in his life, but the strange creature ahead of him had his brother's shoe.

She was balancing on an upturned crate and reaching for something in the ceiling. Then Tom saw light shining through. A minute later he and Ebba were both in the church. There was no sign of the police constable, the door to the vestry was firmly closed. Then Ebba was on her feet again and running up the aisle towards the back of the church.

Tom wasn't in the house. Alice had been right and Evi had wasted precious time. She hadn't even seen a phone. Nor had she heard anything of Alice for several minutes now. She had to get back downstairs and call the police. They could be here in minutes. She would use her mobile – it was just outside, in her car.

As she approached the front door, it slammed shut, startling her. She took a second to catch her breath. There was still a cold wind blowing through the house. Then the door of the living room blew shut.

She crossed the hall and pushed it open again. The window at the far end of the room was wide open. As quickly as she could, Evi walked across the room and leaned out. There was no sign of Alice in the garden any more.

'Tom!' Evi called.

Tom didn't reply, nor had Evi expected him to. Tom had gone. A clear set of footprints leading across the garden to the churchyard wall, far too small to have been made by an adult, was indisputable proof of that.

Evi leaned out further and looked at the ground more closely. A second pair of prints lay in the snow just to one side of the boy's. Knowing how much it would hurt, Evi sat on the window ledge, swung her legs up and twisted round until she could lower herself into the garden.

Already the snow was beginning to cover the prints; in less than an hour they might hardly be visible at all. Now, though, they were clear enough. Not very long ago, someone had crossed the garden from the wall and had then turned and retraced their steps, taking Tom along too. Tom's footsteps were clean and regular, with no indication that he'd been dragged or forced along. Evi peered at the second set of prints. They were adult sized, although not huge, and quite different to the swirled and ridged pattern made by the soles of Tom's trainers. Evi could see the outline of a large big toe, the curve of an instep. These were the prints of someone who didn't wear shoes.

Tom had gone with Ebba.

The door gave way on the fourth blow and Harry caught hold of Gareth by the shoulder to stop him racing in. 'Bore hole,' he reminded him.

Pushing himself in front, Harry shone his torch all around the small stone hut. It had just one room, about four metres long by three wide. Looking up, he could almost touch the beams of the roof. A large metal ring had been screwed into the central beam. Under their feet was pitch-pine flooring.

Gareth moved in, banging the floorboards with the heel of his boot.

'Sounds pretty solid,' said Harry.

Gareth shook his head. 'This is different,' he said.

Harry listened as Gareth moved from one spot to the other, banging his foot down hard on each. The difference was minimal.

Harry began moving slowly round the hut, shining his torch downwards, looking for any discrepancies in the boarding that might indicate that the floor could be raised. There was nothing that he could see. Except, eighteen inches in from the door, there was a small round hole in one of the boards. He bent down.

'What is it?' asked Gareth.

Harry's little finger was circling round in the hole. 'Screw hole,' he said after a second. 'I can feel the thread. Something is supposed to screw into here.' He looked up, shining the torch around, as though whatever was supposed to be screwed into the hole might be lying conveniently by on a hook. 'Something like that,' he said, shining the torch directly at the ring in the roof beam.

Gareth glanced up and then moved to the back of the hut. 'Like this,' he said, pointing at a similar ring that had been fastened into the rear wall. Several feet below the wall ring was a twisted piece of metal. 'This is a lifting mechanism. Give me that rope.'

Harry tossed the rope over and watched the other man thread the end through first the wall ring and then the roof-beam ring. Then he brought it over to where Harry was kneeling.

'This ring's missing,' said Harry.

'Of course it is,' said Gareth. 'With the ring here, it would be too easy to access the bore hole. It was probably removed for safety. Or Gillian could have it.' He dropped flat on the boards. 'Joe!' he yelled. 'Joe!'

Harry couldn't stop himself shuddering. Gareth was pushing himself to his feet again, reaching out for his tool-box, taking out a sharp chisel and hammer. He pushed the sharp end into the gap between two boards and slammed the hammer down hard. The wood splintered. Gareth banged again and again. Then he stopped, found another chisel and hammer and threw them to Harry. 'Other side,' he ordered.

Harry found the tiny, narrow gap and started copying. The wood was old and crumbled easily enough. After hammering through just over an inch of wood, the chisel almost slipped from his hand.

'I'm through,' he said. 'It's hollow underneath.' Gareth was already threading the end of the rope through the hole he'd made and aiming it towards Harry. Harry stuck his fingers into the gap, fumbling around until he felt the rope. He tugged and it came.

Taking it from him, Gareth tied the end together and then jumped up and strode to the other side of the hut. He looked at Harry. 'Stand back,' he said. 'Next to the wall.'

Shuddering with every step, Evi was back in the house, intent on getting her mobile phone from her car. As she opened the front door, she had to clutch at the frame – she was going to fall any second now. A dark shape appeared from around the side of the house.

'Alice?' Evi called, uncertain. Too tall to be Alice.

'It's me.' A woman's voice. The figure stepped into the light. Jenny Pickup, Alice's friend. She'd been here earlier, helping with the children. Thank God.

'Jenny, Tom's missing too.' Evi found herself ridiculously short of breath, every word an effort. 'We have to get help,' she managed. 'He's gone with that girl he's been talking about, the one with the hormone deficiency. The one who's been hanging around the house.'

Jenny frowned for a split second and looked back over her shoulder. Then she stepped forward. 'Evi, you look dreadful,' she said. 'Come back inside. Let me get you something.'

'We have to call the police. Tom's missing. I have no idea where Alice is.'

Jenny put a hand on the door, the other on Evi's arm. 'Take it easy,' she said. 'Get your breath back. The police are on their way.'

'They are?'

'Yes, absolutely,' replied Jenny. 'I called Brian myself. He said ten minutes. Now, Alice asked me to check on Millie. And you really need to sit down.'

'You've seen Alice?' said Evi, stepping back because the other woman was so close it seemed impossible not to. 'Look, Tom is missing, we have to get people looking.'

'Evi, calm down, they are. Listen to me.'

Evi made herself look at Jenny, at her calm hazel eyes. Something about the other woman's composure seemed catching. Evi's breathing began to feel more under control.

'A group of us bumped into Alice in the lane just now,' said Jenny, speaking slowly, as though she were the psychiatrist and Evi the hysterical patient. 'Me, Dad, Mike, one of Mike's men. They've all gone to help her look. Tom can't have gone far.' She stopped speaking and ran a hand through her long, blonde hair. It was loose, sprinkled with snowflakes, damp around the crown. 'Especially if he's gone with Heather,' she went on. 'She hasn't the energy to go any distance. And the police will be here any second.'

Thank God. What did she have to do now? Check on Millie. Evi turned to the stairs, took two steps forwards and grasped hold of the banister. Behind her, Jenny pushed the front door shut.

'Heather?' repeated Evi, turning back as Jenny's words finally sank in. Heather – pronounced by a two-year-old – Ebba. 'The girl who took Tom,' she went on. 'Her name is Heather? You know who she is?'

Harry pressed himself against the door of the hut and watched as Gareth began pulling on the rope. At first nothing happened, then the length of board the two men had been hammering through started to judder. Another tug from Gareth and then the entire floor, apart from a twelve-inch strip around the edge, started to lift up. It was a huge square trapdoor, hinged near the far wall. Once it started moving it came up easily and within seconds Gareth had raised it until it fell with a dull thud against the rear wall.

Harry stepped forward on to the rough stone of the original hut floor. Out of the corner of his eye, he could see Gareth tying the rope and then moving round to join him. Suddenly nervous of the chasm at his feet, Harry dropped to his knees and moved forward on all fours.

A smell that made him think of churches long since abandoned rose up from beneath the ground. He'd expected the bore hole – if indeed they found one – to be perfectly circular. This one had been crudely dug and looked unfinished, the stones around its edge roughly cut and angular. He could see two, maybe three feet down into the hole. After that lay a blackness so solid he could almost have stepped out on to it. By this time, Gareth was kneeling at his side.

'Pass me the light,' said Harry, still not taking his eyes off the well. Gareth didn't move. 'I need the light, mate,' Harry tried again. 'I can't reach it.' He prodded the other man on the arm and pointed to where the torch lay on the ground. Like a man moving in his sleep, Gareth turned, reached out and then handed the light to Harry.

Despite the cold, Harry's hands were damp with sweat. He gripped the torch and moved forwards until he could lean over the edge. The beam seemed to fall like a rock, plummeting away from him into the depths of the earth. Harry saw stonework, roughly held together with crumbling mortar, and could just about make out the clinging slime of some form of vegetation that could exist without light. He thought he might even be able to see water, many feet below. But the only thing he could be sure about was the one thing he couldn't take his eyes off: the rusting chain, hammered into the wall nearly two feet below the edge and disappearing further than the torch beam could reach.

He glanced round and knew that Gareth had seen it too. Speaking seemed like a ridiculous waste of time and energy. Harry made his way round the well until he could lie down flat and reach the chain.

Jenny was standing just inside the front door. The street lamp outside shone through the coloured hall window, turning her hair a strange shade of purple. Her face, though, was as white as the snow outside. 'Of course I know who she is,' she said sadly. 'We lived in the same house for nearly ten years. She's my niece.'

For a second Evi thought she might have misheard. 'Your niece?' she repeated.

Jenny nodded and seemed to pull herself together. 'Christiana's daughter,' she said. 'Shall we go up? Alice did make a point of saying we should check on Millie.'

Evi could only stare. She and Harry had talked about isolated farmhouses, cottages way up high on the moor, yet the girl had been living round the corner all this time, right in the heart of the town.

'Her condition, it's congenital hypothyroidism, isn't it?' she said.

Jenny took a step closer. 'A direct result of the soil up here,' she said. 'It's been the plague of our family for donkey's years. If we'd just buy some of our food at Asda it wouldn't happen.' She'd reached Evi at the foot of the stairs.

'But the condition can be treated now,' said Evi, taking a small step to the side and planting herself firmly in the other woman's path. 'It's picked up on antenatal scans and the baby can be given medication. It's practically been eradicated.'

Jenny sighed. 'And yet we have a fine specimen right on our doorstep. I really should check on Millie, you know. Can I get past?'

'How did it happen?' asked Evi, not sure why finding out as much as she could about the girl was important, only knowing that it was. 'Did Christiana refuse treatment?'

'Christiana was never offered treatment,' said Jenny. 'She spent her entire pregnancy shut up in the house and she gave birth with a local midwife who was paid a lot of money to keep her mouth shut. The birth was never registered.' Her eyes moved upwards to a spot on the landing. Evi resisted the temptation to turn round.

'How many people know about her?' asked Evi, hardly able to believe that no one had mentioned the existence of Heather to the Fletchers, especially after Tom had started seeing his strange little girl.

'Relatively few, I think,' replied Jenny. 'Even Mike has no idea she exists, not that he's the sharpest knife in the box.'

Somehow, Evi had taken a step backwards. She was on the bottom step and was shaking her head. 'How can that be possible?' she said.

'Oh, Evi, you'd be amazed what you can do if you own a town,' said Jenny, her hand reaching out to the banister. She put it down, inches away from Evi's. 'She's not allowed to leave the house, of course. Christiana spends most of the day with her, reading to her, playing simple games. Christy has endless patience, but if she needs a break, Heather watches CBeebies.'

'She's kept in the house all day?'

Jenny nodded. 'None of the staff ever go upstairs,' she said. 'Christiana looks after the upper floors. When everyone has gone home, Heather gets to play in the garden,' she went on. 'To be honest, I think one or two people do know about her – as she got older, she got pretty good at sneaking out at night, even in the day sometimes. She's clearly taken a fancy to Alice and Gareth's children. But people keep quiet, they don't want to get on the wrong side of Dad.'

Something was tightening inside Evi's chest, something that went beyond concern for the Fletcher children. A young girl had been kept a prisoner her whole life – a prisoner inside an unnecessarily damaged body, as well as in her own home. 'Why?' she said. 'Why on earth would your family break the law in that way?'

Jenny blinked her clear hazel eyes twice. 'You're the psychiatrist, Evi,' she said. 'Have a guess.'

Ebba unlocked the door at the back of the gallery and began to climb the short, spiral staircase. The wind caught at her hair, spinning it up and around her head like a flag. Tom stopped. It would be madness to go up.

Tommy, please come.

Before he had time to think what to do, Ebba had grasped hold of his hand and was pulling him on to the roof. She dropped to her hands and knees and he did the same. Snow squeaked beneath him as the wind rushed inside his sweatshirt. Ebba was crawling along the edge of the roof, in a sort of lead-lined guttering. To her left, the roof sloped gently upwards; to her right was a four-inch stone edging that wasn't nearly high enough to offer any sort of barrier if she slipped. Was he expected to go too? He was, because she was looking back, waiting for him. Oh shit.

Tom set off, keeping his eyes firmly on the snow-covered trench he was crawling through. This was insane. There was nowhere on the roof Joe could be hiding. The other three bell towers were empty, you could see that from the ground. You could see the sky right through them. They were heading for the one on the north-eastern corner, the one that always seemed to be in shadow because the sun couldn't reach it. He could see it over Ebba's shoulder, empty as a selection-box on Boxing Day. He could see stars shining through the gaps between the columns, he could see the movement of clouds, he could see the silver ball of the full moon.

But the moon was behind him.

Evi didn't have to guess for long. 'Who's her father?' she asked. 'Is it your father? Is it Sinclair?'

Jenny's face twisted. 'Keep going,' she said.

Evi thought quickly. She knew so little about the Renshaws, only what Harry and the Fletchers had told her. She wasn't aware of any brothers, just the father: a tall, white-haired, very distinguished-looking man, and the . . .

'Not your grandfather?' she said in a low voice, terrified she might have got it wrong, knowing, from the look on the other woman's face, that she hadn't. 'But he's . . .' How old was Tobias Renshaw? He had to be in his eighties.

'He was in his late sixties when Heather was born. Well into his stride by then.'

'Your poor sister. What do you mean, well into his stride?'

Jenny's eyes remained fixed on Evi's. She said nothing.

'He abused you too, didn't he?' said Evi.

Nothing, just a blank stare.

'I'm so sorry,' said Evi.

Nothing.

'How old were you? When it started?'

Jenny gave a deep sigh and then stepped backwards until she came up against the dining-room door. Evi felt as if she could breathe again. 'Three. Maybe four. I can't really remember,' Jenny was saying. 'There was no time in my childhood when I didn't know what it was like to be poked and prodded and fiddled with by big, rough hands.' She turned to look directly at Evi. 'He used to stand in my bedroom doorway and watch me get dressed,' she said. 'He'd come in while I was having a bath and wash me. I've never been in charge of my own body, never. Can you imagine what that's like?'

'No,' said Evi truthfully. 'I'm so sorry. Did he rape you?'

'At that age? No, he was too clever for that. You rape a four-year-old, someone will spot it. He used to masturbate over me, touching me with one hand, pulling on his, you know, with the other. When I got a bit bigger he made me suck him. I was ten when the rape started. In a way I was surprised it took him so long. I heard him, you see, with Christiana. I knew what was coming.'

Evi's hands were at her mouth. She was going to fall. She reached out and grabbed hold of the banister again. 'I'm so sorry,' she said. 'Why didn't you tell someone? Your parents, your mother, surely she wouldn't . . .' She stopped. Jenny didn't need to answer. Children didn't tell. They were told not to and they didn't. Children did what adults told them to do.

'Did he threaten you?' she asked.

Jenny was coming towards her again. She'd been drinking, Evi noticed now. 'He did more than threaten us,' she said. 'He locked us in the mausoleum, with all the stone coffins. Even after my mother was laid to rest there, he'd lock us in. Or he'd carry us up to the top of the stairs, to the gallery in the church, even up to the Tor, and dangle us off the edge. By one ankle sometimes. We had to be good, he'd say, or he'd let go. I know he used to do it to Christiana too; she's petrified of heights.'

Evi tried to blink away the picture in her head. 'You must have been terrified,' she said.

'I never screamed, Evi, there was no point. I'd just close my eyes and wonder if this was the time, this was the day when he'd let go and I'd feel that rush of air and know it was over.'

She'd been wrong. Evi had accused Gillian and she'd been wrong. She'd sent Harry and Gareth off on a wild-goose chase and now Gillian could be dying, Joe and Tom were missing and Alice – where was Alice?

'Jenny,' said Evi, 'has your grandfather been killing the children? Does he have Joe?'

Pull up the chain. No need to think about anything else. Pull up the chain and pray to the God who'd abandoned him that there was nothing on the other end of it. Don't look at Gareth, who was close to losing it, could have lost it already. The only really sensible thing was to get the two of them out of there, before one of them got killed, except Harry knew he'd never do it. So pull up the chain, because they'd come this far and now they had to know.

The chain was moving, coming up with each heaving armful, but there was something heavy on the other end. Pull with his right arm, ease it over the edge with the left, don't think, just keep going. Something was scraping against the side of the walls, something was catching, making it harder to pull up, something was getting closer.

The muscles in Harry's arms were screaming at him and still he had no idea how much more of the chain there was to come up. Twenty more tugs and he'd have to rest. Wasn't sure he'd make it to twenty. Ten more, seven more . . . no more needed. Clipped on to the end of the chain was a large canvas bag with a heavy, old-fashioned zip. Without stopping to think or rest, Harry pulled it up on to the stone floor of the hut, reached out and pulled open the zip.

Eye sockets – empty – were the first things he saw.

Tom blinked. Snow was blowing in his eyes and he really couldn't see that well. He was definitely looking at the moon, shining through the stonework of the north-east bell tower. He risked turning his head around. The moon was over his shoulder. Two moons? Ebba was nearing the tower now. She scampered up to one side of it and looked back, waiting for him. What was she thinking of? The helicopter had passed overhead several times that day. The small roofs on the top of the bell towers would have stopped the helicopter crew seeing inside the towers themselves, but the choppers had heat-seeking equipment, they would have spotted a warm body. Ebba was beckoning him forward.

The church had been full of people. When the helicopter started its search, the police had brought everyone off the moors and they'd all gone into the church. Nearly two hundred people had been inside when the helicopter was searching. Two hundred warm bodies. Where do you hide a needle? In a haystack. Tom was close enough now to touch the bell tower, to put his hand through the stone pillars that sat at each corner. He reached out and saw the reflection of his hand coming towards him, saw his own face in the mirror-tiles that sat between the stone pillars of the tower, to create a small box on the roof of the church, just large enough to take . . .

'Shall I tell you the worst thing, Evi? The worst thing he did to us?'

'What?' said Evi, thinking that she really, really didn't want to know. When was the last time she'd heard Alice calling? Shouldn't the police be here by now?

'We have an old well up on the moor. There used to be a water mill there and some cottages for the workers. The buildings are all gone, but the well was never filled in for some reason. We built a stone hut around it to keep it safe. Safe from sheep and stray children. Not safe for us though, not Christiana and me, because he rigged up a harness and a rope, and if we were difficult, if we dared to say no or if we didn't suck quite as hard as he wanted us to, he'd put us down the well. He'd fasten us in the harness and lower us down. Leave us there, in the dark, for hours. He did it to other children too. Until he left one down there too long and that little game had to come to an end.'

Jenny was too close, Evi had no choice but to step backwards, up the stairs. The minute she did so, Jenny followed her.

'Jenny, you need help,' she said. 'You know that, don't you? None of it was your fault, but you need help to come to terms with it. He's damaged you. Christiana, too. I can find you someone who'll work with you. It will take time, of course it will, but—'

Jenny leaned towards her. 'Do you really think that sort of damage can be mended, Evi?' she said. 'By talking?'

She had a point. Evi just wished she wouldn't insist on standing so close. 'Not entirely, no,' she answered. 'Nothing can take away those memories. But the right therapist can help you come to terms with it. The important thing now, though, is that we find Joe. Harry and Gareth have gone up to that well. Is that where Joe is?'

Something shimmered across Jenny's face. 'They've gone to the cottage?' she said. 'Nobody's been up there in fifteen years. We shut it up after . . .'

'After what? What's up there?'

'Listen to me. Just listen to me.'

Gareth Fletcher wasn't listening, he was screaming, banging his head against the stone wall of the hut, pounding it with both fists. Already, the skin on his forehead was scraped away, blood running down the side of his nose. Harry grabbed hold of one arm and tried to swing him round. Gareth's loose fist came hurtling in Harry's direction. Harry stepped back, dangerously close to the well.

'It's not Joe!' he yelled at the top of his voice. 'It's not Joe!'

Was he getting through? Gareth had stopped howling, was leaning against the wall of the hut, his head hidden in his hands.

'Gareth, you have to listen to me,' said Harry. 'This child has been

dead for years. Look at it. No, you have to look at it. It can't be Joe,
I promise you, just look.'

Gareth raised his head. His eyes looked unnaturally bright as he
took a step towards Harry. Harry braced himself. He was the taller
of the two, but the other man was probably stronger. He really
didn't want to get into any sort of physical struggle this close to the
edge of a well. He took hold of Gareth by his shoulders and forced
him down until both of them were kneeling on cold stone once
more.

'Look,' he said, opening the sides of the canvas bag. His hands
were shaking as he picked up the torch and shone it inside. 'This
child has been dead for years,' he repeated. 'Look, you have to
look. The flesh has nearly all gone. It can't be Joe, it just isn't
possible.'

Gareth looked as though he were struggling to breathe. Each
breath he took was a great, gasping sob, but he was looking at the
bag, at the child inside the bag.

'Not Joe,' said Harry again, wondering how many times he'd have
to say it before the other man believed him. Whether it really was
Gareth he was trying to convince by this time.

Gareth ran a hand over his face. 'Jesus, Harry,' he said. 'What are
we dealing with?'

'Joe!'

Tom blinked the snow from his eyes. He was looking at his
brother, curled like a snail in the north-eastern bell tower, trussed
like a Christmas turkey with ropes around his wrists and his ankles.
Joe, pale as a mushroom, cold as an icicle, but still alive. Joe, shaking
like a jelly and staring up at him with eyes that had lost all their
colour but were still the eyes he remembered. Joe – here – less than
a hundred yards from their house, after all.

Ebba was leaning into the bell tower, tucking a filthy patchwork
quilt higher up around his brother's shoulders, trying to keep him
warm.

'Joe, it's OK,' whispered Tom. 'It's all right now. I'll get you
down.'

Joe didn't respond, just stared up at Tom with his translucent
eyes. His head was juddering, his limbs twitching. He wasn't well,

Tom could see that. Somehow Joe had survived a night and a day on the church roof; he wouldn't last much longer. They had to get him down. Tom leaned into the tower, trying to get his hands under his brother's shoulders. He could reach him, touch skin that felt too cold to be covering living flesh, but when he pulled, Joe stayed where he was.

Tom turned to look at Ebba. She was still crouched on the other side of the box, her over-large hands gripping the edge of the mirror-tiles, staring at him.

'How do we get him out?' Tom asked.

'A child died, Evi,' Jenny was saying. 'A little gypsy girl Tobias found wandering around on her own when he'd gone to look at a horse near Halifax. He just left her there, up on the moor, hanging in the well.'

Where the hell were the police?

'You're nice to talk to, Evi. You listen. You don't judge. I'm going to get Millie now.' Jenny was actually pushing her way past Evi, gently but firmly, manoeuvring herself on to a higher step. Evi turned, kept a tight hold on the banister to stop herself falling.

'No one would judge you, Jenny,' she said. 'You were a child. Did you never think that perhaps you could tell your father what was going on?'

Something glinted in Jenny's eyes. 'You think he didn't know?' she said.

'Surely not?'

'Why do you think he was so opposed to the Fletchers buying this land? He knew they had a daughter. He knows this town isn't safe for little girls.'

Evi was struggling to take it in. 'But his own daughters?'

'He sent me away to school when I was thirteen, just after Heather was born. He couldn't turn a blind eye after that. It was too late for Christiana, of course, she was too old for school.'

Evi reached out her hand, touched the other woman on the arm. 'Jenny, we need to tell the police all this,' she said. 'They have to stop him before another child gets killed. I should phone them again. Get them here sooner.' She took a step down.

'Wait, please.' Now Evi's arm was caught in a tight grip. 'I haven't told you everything.'

Christ, what more could there be? Evi glanced at the window that overlooked the street, hoping to see the flickering of police lights. 'What do you need to tell me?' she asked.

Jenny dropped her head. 'It's so difficult,' she said. 'I never thought I'd tell anyone this.'

'How do we get him out?' repeated Tom. Ebba's expression didn't change, or give any hint she'd understood him. Tom turned back to his brother and tried again to pull at least part of him up. Joe wasn't moving and Tom realized why. The ropes that bound his brother were also securing him to the tower itself.

'Joe, I have to go and get help,' he said. 'There's a policeman downstairs. I'll be five minutes, Joe, I promise.'

Joe's eyes had closed. Leaving his brother in the tower was the hardest thing Tom had ever done, but somehow he made himself turn and crawl back along the roof guttering. He couldn't hear Ebba behind him and hoped that perhaps she'd stayed to comfort Joe.

He was back at the real bell tower that led down into the church. His foot found the top step and a hand closed around his bare ankle.

The two women were sitting on the stairs. Jenny had sunk down, taking Evi with her. They were both shaking.

'When did it all stop?' asked Evi. 'When you went to school?'

Jenny shook her head. 'Things got a bit better before that. He'd found someone else to pique his interest, you see. Our housekeeper's daughter. She was blonde and pretty and very young, just what he liked.'

'Gillian?' said Evi. 'He abused Gillian too?' Was there something at least she'd been right about?

Jenny shrugged, then nodded. 'I think Gwen Bannister guessed what was going on,' she said. 'She'd never have challenged my grandfather, but she got her daughter out of harm's reach. More than anyone did for me.'

'Did he start on you again, after Gillian left?'

'When I was home from school, yes. And then when I was

nineteen, his luck ran out. I got pregnant too. By the time I plucked up the courage to tell Dad, it was too late to get rid of the baby so he talked Mike into taking me on. And he persuaded Tobias to sign over control of the estate to him.'

'I can't believe your father colluded with all this. You must have felt so betrayed.'

Jenny dropped Evi's hands. 'Evi, men have been selling their daughters for wealth and power for thousands of years,' she said. 'You think it all stopped when we got to the twentieth century? But it was good for me too. I got out. And I got Lucy.'

Tobias's daughter. Lucy had been the incestuous child of her great-grandfather.

'What happened to Lucy?' asked Evi in a small voice. 'How did she really die?'

'I loved her so much, Evi.'

'I'm sure you did. Did he do it? Did Tobias kill her?'

'She was only two when he started to look at her, Evi. She was blonde and gorgeous, just like Christiana and me when we were tiny. I'd watch his eyes going over her body. He could still drive back then, he'd come up to the house all the time. I would never change her or bathe her anywhere near him, but he always seemed to be hanging around her. I knew I couldn't let it happen again, not to Lucy.'

'But Lucy was different. She had you to protect her. And Mike.'

'But I knew how clever he was. I knew he'd get to her in the end. So I started planning ways to kill him. It seemed like the only way. Does that shock you?'

Evi thought she was way beyond being shocked. 'I think it's very understandable that you should be so angry,' she said.

'I thought about smothering him in his sleep, putting something in his food, pushing him down the stairs, tricking him to come up to the Tor with me and shoving him off. But then, one day, I realized. I didn't have to kill him to stop him getting what he wanted.'

'You didn't?'

'No. I could kill her instead.'

Tom was being tugged downwards, his back jarring painfully on the stone steps.

'What the fuck are you doin'?' said a voice he knew. Two large hands grasped his waist and pulled him down more steps. 'Back off, let us get down,' the same voice instructed. Tom heard several pairs of footsteps retreating behind them and then he was in the church gallery once more.

'Joe's on the roof,' he managed. 'In the other bell tower, the one that everyone thinks is empty, but it's not. He's in there and he's freezing and we have to get him down now.'

The four boys stared back at him, as if they'd captured an alien that had suddenly started giving them orders.

'Your brother?' Jake Knowles was the first to speak. 'The one we've been looking for all day?'

'On the roof?' repeated Jake's older brother, whose name Tom couldn't remember.

Tom looked back at the four faces and felt like his heart had stopped beating. 'You did it,' he said. 'You put him there.'

The older boy's face twisted. 'What the fuck do you think we are?' he said. 'Fuckin' psychos?'

'He's actually up there?' said Billy Aspin. 'Alive?'

Tom nodded. 'He's tied up,' he said. 'I couldn't get him out. I need to get my dad. What are you doing here? If you didn't put him there, why are you here?'

'We followed you in,' said Jake. 'We saw you and that Renshaw cretin running through the graveyard and we followed. Got fuckin' lost in that cellar. Where'd she go?'

'We have to get help. There's a police . . .' said Tom, realizing he had no idea what had happened to Ebba.

'Come on,' interrupted the eldest Knowles boy. 'Let's see what he's on about.'

Evi felt like she was burning up. Funny, she'd heard patients talk about feeling terror many times. None of them had ever told her how hot it was. Or how it seemed to throw your brain into slow motion. Jenny? Jenny was the one who'd been after Millie the whole time. No, that couldn't be right. She'd misunderstood something. She was overtired.

'And the really ironic thing was, Tobias did love her.' Jenny was clutching Evi again, making it impossible for her to move. Her face was flushed, her eyes unnaturally bright. Evi had to get up somehow. Then what? Upstairs, to Millie's room, or outside to the phone?

'He was absolutely devastated,' Jenny went on. 'I made him watch, you see. I knew he was going to the church – he was churchwarden for years – and I followed him there with Lucy in my arms. I climbed up to the gallery and then I shouted for him.'

Sweat was trickling down between Evi's shoulder blades. The police weren't coming. Jenny hadn't called them. And why did she have to be so close?

'I'll never forget it,' she was saying. 'He came out of the vestry and I was dangling her from her ankles, the way he used to do to me, and she was screaming and screaming and I could see him shouting at me, yelling at me to stop. He started running forward and I let her go, just like that.'

The smell of the woman was almost worse than the heat: alcohol and perspiration and exotic flowers. Evi knew it was going to make her retch if she didn't move. Hands down, push hard, ignore the pain; she had strong arms, it would work.

'It took so long for her to fall,' Jenny went on. 'I had so much time to think, to realize it was always meant to be this way, that I would destroy him in the end, because of what he did to me.'

Do it now. Evi rose up, was caught and dragged back down.

'He almost made it.' Jenny was whispering into her face now. 'Almost caught her. But she slammed down hard on those flagstones and the blood, the blood just went everywhere, it was like I'd dropped a bubble of it. I thought some of it was going to reach me up in the gallery.'

Evi swallowed hard and fought the temptation to hold her breath. She had to keep breathing. If she held her breath, she'd faint.

'I've never had any pleasure from sex, Evi, not once – how could I?' Jenny was saying. 'This orgasm business people get so worked up about, I have no idea what they're talking about. But that day, seeing all that blood and watching him start to scream, I can't tell you the pleasure I felt. I almost fainted away, right there and then, it was so intense. And the sound of the thud when she hit the tiles, like a ripe fruit bursting open, I could hear that over and over again in my head, and all the time the blood was spreading out from around her.

I could see it oozing out in waves, while her heart struggled to keep going.'

Evi knew she couldn't scream. No one but Millie would hear her.

The two men were running down the moor, their torch beams aimed at the white ground below their feet. Through the beech wood, past the abandoned water mill, over the stream. Once Gareth had seemed himself again, a sense of panic had swept through Harry. They had to get back. It was all he could think of – getting back.

It had been forty minutes or more since they'd left the house. The police should have joined them by now. There were police cars on the roads into Heptonclough, they weren't more than five minutes from the Fletchers' house. If Evi had phoned them when he and Gareth had set out, they would have arrived by now. They hadn't, which meant she hadn't phoned. Something else had happened. It was worse now, worse than just Joe, the mayhem that Gillian had unleashed. They had to get back.

His mobile was in the pocket of his jeans. He could stop, call the police himself, phone the house. But to do that he'd have to stop running.

They'd reached a stile. Harry climbed up, jumped down and set off again, hearing Gareth doing the same thing behind him. They were in the harvest field, just above the town. Another hundred yards and they'd be passing the site of the All Souls' Day bonfire. They reached the fence and Harry vaulted over. Past Gillian's old cottage, the cobbles slippery with snow, buildings rising up on either side now. Gareth was breathing heavily by his side. They came to the end of the lane, had just turned into the main road when the church bell began to ring.

'He dragged me away, of course,' said Jenny. 'Back to the house. We both changed our clothes and then we started the search for her. He wouldn't go back to the church, though, he couldn't face her again. I had to do that.'

Think now, stay calm. The police weren't coming, but Harry and Gareth would be back. They'd have made it to the cottage by now, found whatever they had to find, they'd be making their way home. Evi just had to stay calm. Stop this woman from doing any more

411

harm. She had to keep her away from Millie. If only it weren't so hot.

'And then,' said Evi, forcing herself to relax back on the stair, to breathe deeply. 'Was it over then? When you'd punished him? Did you find . . .' Jesus, what the hell was she supposed to say? 'Did you find peace?' she tried.

Jenny nodded. 'For a while, yes,' she said. 'It was as though I'd taken back control over my life, can you understand that?'

'Of course,' said Evi, telling herself to speak slowly, the way she always did with an overexcited patient. 'Control is very important,' she said. 'We all need that.'

'I missed her desperately, of course. I still do. I never really got over it.'

'No,' said Evi, fighting a temptation to look at her watch, and an even stronger one to throw back her head and howl. 'I don't think parents ever get over the loss of a child.'

'But I felt as though a chapter was closed, that I could move on again.' Jenny's eyes narrowed. She looked down at her watch, but the gesture was too quick for Evi to see the time. 'It's getting on,' she said. 'Come on, I'll help you up the stairs.' She stood and bent down, taking hold of Evi under the arms. Evi braced herself, but the other woman was strong. She was hoisted up and then Jenny's arm was around her waist.

'Come on,' said Jenny. 'I'm sure I heard her crying just now.'

'Millie's fine,' said Evi. 'But Jenny, this is really important.'

Jenny paused but kept a tight hold around Evi's waist. 'What?' she said, and her voice had hardened. She was losing patience.

'It's just . . . the other girls,' said Evi. 'Megan, Hayley. Why did they have to die?'

Jenny tilted her head to one side. 'After Lucy died, I was the one in charge,' she said, after a moment. 'Whenever Tobias stepped out of line, if he started paying inappropriate attention to young girls, I could stop him. Come on now, one more step, and another.'

'I'm sorry,' said Evi. 'I find stairs so difficult. Can we rest for a second? So he started to abuse Megan? Even after what happened to Lucy?'

Jenny's hold on Evi relaxed a fraction. 'Oh, I'm not sure it ever got that far,' she said. 'I could just see him looking at her, going out of his way to be nice to her mother. I wasn't having it, not after losing Lucy. I wasn't having him forgetting her and just taking a fancy to another one.'

'So you killed Megan?' asked Evi. 'And Hayley? You tried to kill Millie too?'

Jenny looked at Evi as though she were simple. 'I'd already killed my own child,' she said. 'Do you think it's difficult, after that, to kill someone else's?'

'Then why Joe?' asked Evi, when Jenny seemed about to turn away and head back up the stairs again. 'Your grandfather wouldn't be interested in him. Why did you take him? You did take him, didn't you?'

'Evi, he was starting to taunt me.'

'Joe?'

'My grandfather. You have no idea what an evil old devil he is. He kept cracking jokes about how the Fletchers had more security than the crown jewels, that Millie was never out of her mother's sight, and he was coming here just about every day, sitting for that stupid portrait, and I knew he'd be playing with Millie, getting her to sit on his lap, stroking her legs, his fingers getting higher and higher, and forgetting all about Lucy. I couldn't let that happen.'

'But Joe? What has—'

'I knew the only way Alice would take her eye off the ball was if one of her other kids went missing.'

Evi felt like she'd been slapped. 'Joe was a decoy?'

Jenny shrugged. 'Sweet lad,' she said. 'He came with me without arguing. I told him his sister had had an accident and his mum wanted me to take him to visit her in hospital. Couldn't half fight though, once the penny dropped. I had to knock him out to get him—'

'Where? Where is he?'

'Somewhere they'll never find him. They didn't find Megan, they won't find Joe. Evi, can you manage another step?'

Jake Knowles' oldest brother stepped past Tom and started to climb the staircase again. 'He's tied up,' insisted Tom. 'You can't get him out.'

The boy reached his hand into his jeans pocket and brought out a thin strip of metal about five inches long. His thumb twitched and a long, silver blade shot out. 'No sweat,' he said, as he disappeared into the tower. One by one the other three followed. Jake was the last. His foot on the bottom step, he turned back to Tom. 'Come on,' he said, before disappearing.

Tom followed, not sure if this were better or worse. Joe needed a grown-up, not these four idiots. Even if they managed to get him out, they'd be as likely to fall off the roof with him as bring him down. Ahead, Jake was climbing out on to the roof. Tom scrambled up the last few steps and peered out.

'Dan's almost there,' said Jake. Tom looked across the roof. Jake's brother, Dan, was just a few paces away from the north-eastern tower. The middle brother was just behind him. There was no sign of Ebba.

'He's here!' shouted Dan, who had reached the opposite tower and was bending inside it. 'I've got him.' The second brother had arrived at the tower too now. Tom could see two denim-clad bottoms sticking up towards the night sky as both boys leaned inside. Then first one and then the other began to straighten up.

'Will's got him,' said Jake. 'He's pulling him out, look.'

Jake's other brother had both arms around Joe's middle and was tugging him out of the tower. The patchwork quilt got left behind and Joe's pale naked body gleamed like a shell in the moonlight as he and Will Knowles tumbled on to the roof. Then Dan Knowles bent and lifted Joe. Carrying the small boy in his arms like a baby, he began to walk back along the guttering towards Tom, Jake and Billy. As he neared, they could hear him shouting something that sounded like, 'Well, mell, ding-dong bell, ring the ruddy bell, you wazzocks.' Jake understood a second before Tom did and then both boys were tumbling down the staircase, fighting each other in their effort to be the first to unleash the bell rope and give the first tug.

Clang. The old bell shuddered in protest at being roused from sleep so late at night. Clang. Louder now, getting its confidence back. Clang. Tom half wanted to let go of the rope and put his hands over his ears, but he didn't because tugging on that rope and ringing that bell felt so good. Clang. Get out here, everyone, get out and see Joe being carried across the rooftop. Joe, OK after all, Joe, coming home. He couldn't wait to see his mum's face.

'Jenny, you can't go in that room.'

'And I'm going to be stopped by a cripple? I don't think so.' Jenny stretched up on tiptoe, looking over Evi's shoulder. 'Stone floors in the hall,' she said. 'Do you know what it sounds like, when a child's skull breaks on stone? A bit like an eggshell cracking, only amplified a thousand times. You'll hear it – maybe.'

'Where is Joe?' demanded Evi.

Jenny was walking backwards along the landing, her hand reaching out for the handle on Millie's door.

'Does Heather know where he is?' asked Evi.

For the first time, Jenny looked uncertain. 'No,' she said.

'Are you sure?' said Evi. 'Because I think she knows all about you. I think she's been trying to warn people, in her own way. She's been trying to make friends with Joe, Tom and Millie, to talk to Harry. She's even been trying to tell Gillian what happened to her daughter.'

'She's a brainless idiot.' The handle was turned, the door pushed two inches open.

'She came for Tom tonight,' said Evi. 'Why would she do that, so late in the evening, unless she knew where you'd put Joe?'

Jenny thought for a moment, then she shrugged. 'It makes no difference,' she said. 'He'll be dead by now.'

Evi took a step forward. 'You know what really pisses me off, Jenny?' she said. 'You're a complete fake. You're pretending you're doing all this because Millie is your grandfather's next victim. Well, bullshit. He's probably barely been near her. He almost certainly didn't touch Hayley either, or Megan. You said yourself he was never allowed near Lucy. You're killing these girls because you like it.'

'Shut up.'

'I saw the look on your face when you told me about Lucy's death. You enjoyed it.'

'I don't have to listen to this.' Jenny was turning away.

She had to stop her, had to give her something to focus on other than Millie. 'Your grandfather, everything that happened to you in the past, it's just the excuse now. You're doing it for fun.'

'You have no idea.' Jenny was in the bedroom, making her way across the carpet.

'I'm a psychiatrist,' called Evi. 'I've been dealing with twisted bitches like you for years. Now get away from that cot.'

Jenny was coming towards her. She was out of the room in moments; a second more and her hands were around Evi's throat and the two were staggering backwards, past the stairs.

'Ever wondered what it would be like to fly, Evi?' Jenny hissed in her ear. 'You're about to find out. They'll think you slipped with little Millie in your arms and fell down the stairs. Only old Tobias will know the truth.'

Evi's windpipe was being crushed. The pathologist would know she'd been strangled. Small comfort. The banister was digging into her back, it hurt like hell but it was supporting her weight. She brought her good leg up and kneed the other woman hard in the crotch. Jenny grunted and her hold slackened, but she was a woman after all and it hadn't done too much damage. Evi twisted round and tried to get a grip on the banister but found herself being lifted off her feet, forced over the top of it.

Before she could brace herself, her hips had gone over the edge and she was close to falling. She grabbed out, one hand caught hold of the banister but her legs were lifted high, she was being pushed and something was banging at her hand, stamping on it, and she had no choice but to let go.

It seemed to take a long time to reach the slate floor.

They'd stopped ringing the bell. The three boys climbed inside the tower. Did they still have Joe? Yes, there he was, wrapped up in the patchwork quilt again, his face pressed against Dan Knowles's chest, still bound tight with thin, nylon rope, still shaking, still alive.

Dan Knowles, who seemed to have grown during his brief time on the roof, looking more like the young man he'd be in a year or so than a teenage bully, was at the bottom of the steps, climbing into the gallery. His brother Will followed, then Billy, just as the sound of a heavy door being opened echoed around the church.

'Hello!' shouted a loud Geordie voice.

'He's up here! We've got him!' called back Dan Knowles.

'Joe!' yelled Tom's dad.

'Dad!' screamed Tom.

'Police! Everybody keep still!'

The two groups met on the balcony stairs, Gareth Fletcher and Dan Knowles almost colliding. The small, shivering parcel was passed from one to the other and Joe gave a quiet moan as his father's arms closed around him. Higher on the steps, over his father's head, Tom's eyes met Harry's. Then the vicar turned, pushed his way past the bewildered-looking police constable, and ran from the church.

Evi was barely conscious. She was very cold. An icy wind was blowing all around her. Snow was falling softly on her face and the world was growing dark. Was she back on the mountain? No, in the Fletchers' house. That was Millie she could hear, howling like a banshee. The front door was open and a man was standing not three feet away from her. Brown leather shoes, damp patches around them on the stone. Something in his left hand, long and thin, fashioned from metal, something she thought she recognized, but it seemed so out of place that she really couldn't be certain.

'Put her down,' said a voice. Too late, thought Evi, I already fell.

'Oh, I will,' replied a woman's voice from high above them.

'Don't take another step,' said the man. 'And put that child down.'

'You're not serious,' replied the woman.

The thing the man was carrying was lifted up until Evi could no longer see it.

'It's over,' he said. 'Put her down.'

A silence, when the world seemed to pause; then a footstep and an explosion of sound. Evi didn't hear the second gunshot, but she felt its vibration flutter through her body and she saw the blinding flash of light. Then nothing more.

Harry heard the first shot as he jumped over the wall and dodged his way around Alice's car. He caught a glimpse of Alice herself, racing towards the church, but there was no time to stop. He saw the open front door and the tall form of Tobias Renshaw standing in the doorway, pointing a rifle at himself. A second later the old man's head exploded in a mass of bone and blood. Harry leaped over the corpse before it had completely settled on the ground.

A sharp cry caught his attention. Millie, awash with blood and tiny pieces of grey matter, was standing at the top of the stairs. The prone body of a woman lay across the upstairs landing. At the sight of someone she knew, the toddler stepped forward, dangerously close to the edge of the top stair. Harry ran up the stairs and picked her up. Then he turned. At the foot of the stairs, not three feet from the body of Tobias, lay a young woman in a violet sweater. As he watched, a snowflake settled on her black lashes. Her eyes were as blue as he remembered.

Epilogue

EBRUARY HAD BROUGHT EVEN MORE SNOW TO THE MOORS and men had been out since early morning, clearing the path from the church to the graveside. Even so, the mourners walked gingerly as they made their way down.

Following the low-pitched instructions of the funeral director, the six pall-bearers lifted the coffin from their shoulders and lowered it. The roses on its lid shivered as it came to rest on the thick, flat tapes suspended over the open grave. Harry straightened up and rubbed his hands together. They felt like ice.

The elderly priest who had taken his place in the benefice, who would serve until a permanent replacement could be found, began to speak.

'For as much as it has pleased Almighty God to take from this world the soul of our sister here departed . . .'

The young woman in the coffin hadn't died on the night of the winter solstice, the evening Joe Fletcher had been returned to his family. Her injuries had been serious, but for a few weeks there had been confident hopes of her recovery. Early in the new year, though, she'd caught an infection that had quickly turned into pneumonia. Her badly damaged body hadn't had the strength to fight it and she'd died ten days ago. When he heard the news, something in Harry died too.

As he and the other pall-bearers began to lower the casket into the ground, Harry realized that Alice was standing directly opposite. It might be the last time he saw her. The family was leaving Heptonclough in a matter of weeks. Sinclair Renshaw, who still faced the possibility of a police investigation and charges, was nevertheless determined to maintain his hold over the town. He'd made the Fletchers a generous offer for their house and they'd accepted.

The boys were doing well, Alice seemed to be constantly reassuring everyone who asked. Their new counsellor kept telling them to keep talking, admit when they were scared, be honest when they were angry. Above all, not to expect miracles, it would take time.

Of all the Fletchers, only Millie seemed the same as ever. If anything, she seemed to be growing noisier and cheekier and happier by the day, as though the energy missing from the rest of her family had found a way to channel itself into her. Harry sometimes thought the family wouldn't have survived the last few weeks without Millie.

Standing beside Alice, her oversized hand clutching Alice's tiny one, stood her new goddaughter: Heather Christine Renshaw. Early in the new year, in his last official duty as minister of the benefice, Harry had baptized Heather. The service had been short, attended only by the remaining members of the Renshaw family: Christiana, Sinclair and Mike, and also, at their own insistence, Alice, Joe and Tom. Heather – or Ebba, as he would always think of her – was getting medical treatment now. It was too late for the damage caused by years of neglect to be entirely reversed, but the medication would help. More importantly, her days as a prisoner were over.

Out of the corner of his eye Harry saw movement further down the hill. Mike Pickup, who'd been in church earlier, hadn't followed the mourners. He was standing instead by the grave that was Lucy's new resting place and that now held her mother as well. Tobias lay like a fallen king in one of the stone coffins of the family mausoleum.

The priest had finished speaking. He glanced over at Harry, who forced his lips into a smile. The funeral director was handing round a casket of earth. People were gathering up handfuls, throwing the earth on to the coffin and stepping away. One by one, the mourners turned and made their way back up the hill until Harry was almost alone. A tall, heavily built man he didn't know muttered something and then walked away a few paces. He glanced back once at the two people left at the graveside and then turned to stare across the valley.

'When do you leave?' asked the pale young woman in the wheelchair. Her eyes looked too large in her face and had grown dull since he'd last seen her. They didn't look like violet pansies any more.

'Today,' said Harry. Then he looked up the hill to where his loaded car was parked. 'Now,' he added. He'd said his goodbyes over the previous few days. This one would be the last.

'Are you OK?' she asked.

'Not really. You?' He hadn't meant to sound angry – she had problems of her own, he knew that. He just hadn't been able to help it.

'Harry, you should talk to someone. You need to—'

He couldn't look at her again. If he looked at her he'd never be able to leave. 'Evi,' he managed, 'I can't talk to God any more, and you won't let me talk to you. There really isn't anyone else. Look after yourself.'

He turned from the grave and found the path. The other mourners had all disappeared. It was far too cold to be outside for long. As he strode up the hill, he heard the sexton begin to shovel earth on to the coffin. Thud, thud.

He thought perhaps he heard the squeak of Evi's wheelchair, but he wasn't looking back.

Thud, thud. Harry quickened his pace and the sound of earth falling on to wood seemed to follow him up the hill. The sexton was working fast. Before the hour was done the new grave would be complete, a soft mound of soil covered with flowers. They'd fade and die, of course, flowers always did, but people would bring others, they'd keep the grave neat. The people who hadn't cared much for Gillian in life would look after her grave.

They honoured their dead in Heptonclough; some of them, at least.

Author's Note

Heptonclough

Heptonclough was inspired by, but not based upon, the village of Heptonstall (from the old English hep – wild rose, and tunstall – farmstead) on the Yorkshire Pennines, not far from the border with Lancashire. Like its fictional counterpart, Heptonstall owed its early wealth to the wool trade and today boasts two churches (one old, one very old), the White Lion pub, the old grammar school and numerous cobbled streets lined with tall stone houses. Visitors should not look for Wite Lane, the Abbot's House or the Fletcher family's shiny new home, but teenage boys can definitely be seen riding their bikes around the old church walls. I've watched them do it.

Congenital Hypothyroidism

'I see a head of unusual form and size, a squat and bloated figure, a stupid look, bleared hollow and heavy eyes, thick projecting eyelids, and a flat nose. His face is of a leaden hue, his skin dirty, flabby, covered with tetters and his thick tongue hangs down over his moist livid lips. His mouth, always open and full of saliva, shows teeth going to decay. His chest is narrow, his back curved, his breath asthmatic, his limbs short, misshapen, without power. The knees are thick and inclined inward, the feet flat. The large head drops

listlessly on the breast; the abdomen is like a bag.'
Beaupre, *Dissertation sur les cretins, c.* 1850

Congenital hypothyroidism, which can be genetic, sporadic or endemic, is a condition of severely stunted physical and mental development, caused by a deficiency of the hormone thyroxine. In the UK around one in every 3,500 to 4,000 children are born with congenital hypothyroidism. Similar rates are reported in the USA and continental Europe. It is more common in girls than in boys, but the reason for this is currently unknown.

Without treatment, adult stature is below average, ranging from 1 to 1.6 metres; bone maturation and puberty are severely delayed and infertility is common. Neurological impairment, of varying degrees of severity, is to be expected. Cognitive development, thought and reflexes are slower. Other signs of the condition may include thickened skin, enlarged tongue or a protruding abdomen.

Fortunately, genetic and sporadic congenital hypothyroidism, caused by abnormal development of the thyroid gland before birth, has been almost completely eliminated in developed countries by newborn-screening schemes and lifelong treatment.

The endemic condition arises from a diet deficient in iodine: the essential trace element that the body needs to produce thyroid hormones. The soils of many inland areas on all continents are iodine deficient and food produced there is correspondingly deficient. Iodine deficiency causes gradual enlargement of the thyroid gland, and the resulting growth is referred to as a goitre. The endemic form of the condition continues to be a major public-health problem in many undeveloped countries.

'Cretin', from an Alpine-French dialect spoken in a region where sufferers were especially common, became a medical term in the eighteenth century. It saw considerable medical use in the nineteenth and early twentieth centuries, and then spread more widely in popular English as a derogatory term for someone who behaves stupidly. Because of its pejorative connotations in popular speech, health-care workers have mostly now ceased use of the term.

Acknowledgements

One of the most rewarding aspects of writing is the opportunity to learn, and the following taught me a lot: *A History of Psychiatry* by Edward Shorter; *Basic Child Psychiatry* by Philip Barker; *Crime Scene to Court: the Essentials of Forensic Science* edited by P. C. White; *Postmortem: Establishing the Cause of Death* by Dr Steven A. Koehler and Dr Cyril H. Wecht; and *Practical Church Management* by James Behrens.

Avril Neal, Jacqui and Nick Socrates, Denise Stott and Adrian Summons continue to do sterling work, not only reading and correcting my early manuscripts but also patiently providing advice and information throughout the writing process. Dr Miraldine Rosser joined 'the team' this year, and her help in making Evi a credible psychiatrist was invaluable. Thank you, all of you, and as always, any remaining mistakes are mine.

The folk at Transworld continue to be supportive, encouraging, hardworking and wise. I'm particularly grateful to Sarah Turner, Laura Sherlock, Lynsey Dalladay, Nick Robinson and Kate Samano. In the US, my thanks as ever to Kelley Ragland and Matthew Martz of Minotaur Books.

As for Anne-Marie, Rosie, Jessica and Peter: it simply would not be the same without you.

S. J. Bolton was born in Lancashire. She is the author of two previous critically acclaimed novels, *Sacrifice* and *Awakening*, out now in paperback. *Sacrifice* was nominated for the International Thriller Writers Award for Best First novel and, in France, for the prestigious Prix Polar SNCF Award. *The Blood Harvest* is her third novel. She lives near Oxford with her husband and young son.

For more information about the author and her books, visit her website at www.sjbolton.com